Books by James Brady

Superchic

Paris One

PARIS ONE

A NOVEL BY

JAMES BRADY

DELACORTE PRESS/NEW YORK

Manufactured in the United States of America

First printing

Designed by Leo McRee

Library of Congress Cataloging in Publication Data

Brady, James, 1928–
  Paris One.

   I. Title.
PZ4.B81213 Par   [PS3552.R243]   813'.5'4   76–51800
ISBN 0–440–06815–0

For my mother, for my father,
and for my brother, Tom

PROLOGUE

Quite naturally there was pain. But only at first, when his great weight smashed against the courtyard's tiled floor. He lay there, unable to move. But as the pain diminished and the numbness came, it was not all that unpleasant. He could still taste the red wine and the cous-cous, hear the crickets and the sounds of the African night, feel the tile warm and wet against his cheek. He did not realize the wetness was blood and so he was not disturbed. The shortness of breath as he fell had eased. Vaguely, in the distance, he could hear footsteps receding fast. Was it the boy? he wondered. Obviously he must have run off for assistance, realizing that unaided he could not possibly get the man back to his feet. That was it! Soon the boy would be back with a doctor to solve all this nonsense of weakness and shortness of breath. The big man inhaled deeply. He remembered the sound of his weight smashing into the tile and the footsteps of the boy. He remembered vaguely an exquisite ballerina, the war, a priest, applause; oh, yes, he remembered Maggy. And, very clearly, a child, a small girl running to him, leaping into his ample lap and kissing his mouth. Beyond these pleasant memories he could smell the African foliage and the flowers. How lovely they are, he thought. As distinct and lovely as the flower gardens of Grasse. He tried to raise his great head to discern which flowers these might be, but

1

he could not. He tried again, but it was beyond him. And then, quite peaceably, he died.

The inspector of police was, for a North African, tolerably methodical. Having been trained by the French, he relished system. Paperwork was a bore, the bane of a policeman's life, but essential to the system and one accepted it. But for a foreigner to die like this during one's tour of duty, during the quiet, ominous early hours of morning, was really merde. Especially a foreigner with something of a name. Merde and merde again, the inspector thought. Why couldn't this fat old man have died in Paris where he belonged? Where someone else would have been burdened with the paperwork. Why did he have to come to Marrakesh to gorge himself on cous-cous and to swill the wine and to purchase Arab boys and then die? The inspector indulged his self-pity, and then he took up his Bic and began to fill in the forms.

The Shah's man in Paris was called Zader Nafredi. He lived in a lovely house that gave on the Parc Monceau and he held no formal portfolio. But everyone knew he was the Shah's man and so, within reason, he could get to see the people who mattered and could afford to ignore those who didn't. There had been dancing Thursday evening and an exquisite girl who worked for Dior, and he had been asleep for only an hour or two when the phone rang. Nafredi was irritable until he realized the call was from Teheran, where it was already midmorning of a working day; and then he sat up smartly amid the tousled bed-linens by Porthault and listened very attentively. Yes, Nafredi told his caller, it was quite likely this unfortunate death could complicate matters. Yes, he would begin to probe the situation. Yes, he would keep Teheran informed. Nafredi put down the telephone, carefully removed his hairnet, and rang for the valet.

Every morning some twenty copies of *The New York Times*, eight *Wall Street Journals*, and a half-dozen *Women's Wear Dailys* arrived at the headquarters of the Delaware Chemical

Corporation. Although the local Wilmington paper had nothing about the death, the others did. At ten o'clock a brief meeting was held on the ninth floor, the executive level, and it was agreed the situation had now become delicate. It was decided that a senior vice-president should go up to New York on the noon train for a chat with Henry Rousselot.

Marianna Troy was in bed when she heard the news. The clock-radio had clicked on automatically at eight o'clock and the death was the lead item, right after the Paris weather report. "Shit," Marianna said aloud, thinking of the six pages planned for the June issue. She'd worked hard on those pages; they represented one of the first important assignments *Vogue* had permitted her to handle, and they meant a lot. She fluffed the pillows and sat up in bed, a beautiful young woman with long hair, wearing a man's T-shirt as a nightgown. The T-shirt's legend, "University of Denver," sloped gracefully over her small, high breasts. She reached for her first cigarette of the day and tried to remember what the fashion copy said. Maybe, just maybe, the spread could be salvaged. She couldn't remember, but she thought they hadn't really referred to the man but only talked about the clothes themselves. Once she worked out that problem in her head she permitted herself to think about him and how he had always been très gentil with her. Always. Even when she had first come to Paris, lanky and untutored, speaking only the book variety of French they'd taught her in boarding school and at Yale. A gentleman, literally un gentil homme with her. She sniffled then, and her eyes began to water. She shook her head angrily. She wasn't crying. Not really. It was probably just the first cigarette of the morning. It frequently did that to her. Even when no one had died.

Maggy Moal did not learn about it until lunch. She never rose from her bed in the Ritz before noon and she refused to have a radio squawking in her ear at any time of day. The death was the talk of the Espadon Grill, and it was the headwaiter who gave her the news.

"Ah, well," she said at first, resisting the quite natural impulse to show surprise, "it's to be expected. A man of that age. And gross, as well. An old fool who dissipated and carried on. I fully expected it," she declared.

The headwaiter nodded, took the order for her solitary lunch, and she sipped a bit of Perrier water. Old, she thought, he was old. And then, without wanting to, she thought of how he had been years before, when he was not old, not fat either, nor an enemy, but tall and massive and rich with wicked delight. The smoked salmon arrived with the chilled vodka and she put memory aside. The man was *old!* she told herself firmly, old and at a time to die. She consciously blocked out the undeniable fact that the dead man had been twenty years younger than she.

Anthony Winslow did not know the man who had died. He did not know he was dead. And if he had known, he would not have cared. It was Friday noon and he had cleared his desk of paper and, skipping lunch, he got the old Mercedes out of the basement of his building and drove through the Queens-Midtown Tunnel toward East Hampton and a weekend of tennis and walking on the beach. April was a treacherous month for weather, but he looked forward to the break. Working for Rousselot & Partners was a young banker's dream, but it was also mind-bending labor under tension. The last twelve months had been a kaleidoscope of boardrooms, jet planes, and hotel suites. He ran out of fresh linen, lost weight, his social life went to hell. He relished a rare long weekend like this away from the job. As the old car moved smoothly onto the Long Island Expressway and picked up speed, he wondered about the girl. He remembered what she looked like in her United Airlines uniform and he hoped she would look as good out of it. Winslow was delighted to have no place to go but the beach and no challenge more weighty than an attractive young woman in an empty beach-town on an April weekend.

In his apartment the phone would ring all through Saturday and Sunday as Henry Rousselot tried vainly to reach him on certain matters relating to the death of a Frenchman in Morocco.

REQUIEM

One by one the Paris fashion giants had gone. Dashing young Fath, prematurely, a quarter century ago; Dior in '57; Coco Chanel in '71; Balenciaga soon after. And now Jacques Fayol. Dead, in, of all places, Marrakesh. Among those who hated the man, envied his success, or were simply appalled by him, there were snide, knowing smiles. He died of overeating, it was whispered; of syphilis; strangled! Who could be certain? Fayol: controversial, creative, passionate; the last of the great egomaniacs who made Paris the capital of world fashion; the irritating, charming, scandalous, generous, impossibly sacred monster who devoured newspaper galleys and magazine covers with the same hunger that he (reportedly) consumed beautiful women and teenaged boys. Left to mourn, his troupe of "little monks," those slim young persons of dubious gender who slaved in peonage for the honor of apprenticing in the House of Fayol, who capered about the master in white butchers' coats, waving their soft hands. Also left, perhaps to mourn (one could not be sure), the slender girls of clearly female persuasion who modeled his clothes, who would stand motionless for hour after exhausting hour while the genius Fayol built a coat or a suit or a new dress shape on their lithe bodies, raging and cursing at them to arch their buttocks, to tilt their heads, to suck in already-flat bellies, to suffer without flinching when a basting pin skewered flesh instead

5

of cloth. Another left—but not to mourn—Madame Jacques
Fayol, once the prima ballerina of the Ballet Russe, now a
wealthy, aging, still-handsome woman flirting with the lunatic
fringe of Roman Catholic evangelism in France. Also left, unsure
whether to mourn or simply to sniff a little more cocaine and bed
a new lover, Fayol's only child, Anne.

The funeral mass was at the Madeleine, that big echoing barn
of a church at the head of the rue Royale, a few hundred meters
from the Ritz. The requiem was to begin at ten o'clock. The
morning was warm, with a spatter of rain, when people started to
arrive. Television cameras and gaudy floral arrangements
crowded each other on the top step, and the journalists and the
curious had to stand to the sides as mourners arrived or fresh
busloads of Belgian tourists debarked to be shown through "the
attraction." In France, in the spring, one does not inhibit tour-
ism, not even for the dead. Fashion designers, movie stars, ex-
pensively dressed women, arrived, and the TV cameras rolled.
When Dali came up the steps, preceded by his cane and his
waxed mustache, the television journalists pushed microphones
into his face. Dali's eyes darted. Models struck poses and rival
designers issued statements. It would have been tasteless had
anyone really been sad. One pretty girl in dark glasses came up
the steps and she, at least, might be grieving. But it was impossible to tell with the glasses. An elegant middle-aged couple recoiled as a television technician fell over an especially vulgar
floral tribute, and the man said, "How Jacques would have de-
spised all of this." The woman, giving a short, horsey laugh,
declared, "My love, he would have *gloried* in it."

At ten precisely, the hearse drew up and the last of the crowd
hurried inside to find pews. It was cool and dark, with that pecu-
liar smell of old churches, the smell of incense and piety and dog-
eared missals. There was a nice touch when the current mannequins from Fayol's cabine arrived ensemble—not in black, but
wearing the latest bright tweed suits from the collection. The
eight girls, soignées and dutifully solemn, sat together where the
family should have been. Only Madame Fayol, tall, poised, dis-

creet, shared the front pews with them. Fayol's young men had
the good taste to sit a few rows back. One of the boys sniffled
into a handkerchief. It had been decided that at least *one* of them
ought to cry, and they'd drawn lots. The one who wept had gone
especially to Hermès to choose a suitable handkerchief.

The couturiers were there. Easily recognized. Cardin with his
head perched birdlike on one shoulder; ancient Maggy Moal rapping her cane loudly against the pew to protest an altar boy who
was scratching his bottom during the first blessing; tall, elegant
Givenchy towering above his seatmates; polite, shy little Crahay;
flamboyant Antonio del Castillo; bespectacled, blond Saint Laurent with his mother; elfin Gérard Pipart; Robert Ricci, as always,
gray-gloved, somber; Ungaro, neat, dark-suited; Madame Grès,
in the inevitable turban under which she was said to be bald as an
egg. The Rothschilds were there, a pride of Rothschilds. How
could they not be? The president of I. Magnin had flown in from
California, one of the Marcuses from Dallas, someone distinguished from Saks Fifth Avenue. There were other familiar
faces: the publisher of *Vogue*; the couture buyer of Ohrbach's; a
vice-president of du Pont; the managing director of Harrods;
Zumsteg, the Swiss fabric designer; and women whose names one
might confuse but whose faces were to be seen any lunchtime on
the banquettes of La Grenouille or the Relais Plaza.

The mass was suitably lengthy. The plump little priest
mounted heavily to the pulpit, after considerable music and fling-
ing of holy water, to launch into an enthusiastic eulogy. He re-
counted virtues even Fayol himself would not have claimed.
Those in the back found themselves drifting off. They tried, some
of them, to keep awake by recalling what they knew of the fabu-
lous Fayol as he really was, and not this phony plaster saint the
good father was attempting to canonize.

There was no shortage of material about Jacques Fayol in
print, of course, with some of the best stuff a *Time* magazine
cover story in 1968. Being a *Time* magazine cover story, it was
well written, pithy, quotable, and not necessarily accurate. But
then, neither was the priest, and *Time*'s style was more amusing.

Fayol had been born in the Auvergne, a region of France whose inhabitants were noted chiefly for their shrewdness. During the French Revolution, any number of plagues, and as recently as 1940 when Parisians fled south to escape the Blitzkrieg, Auvergnats had turned a profit by selling drinking water to the desperate refugees, their fellow countrymen. Fayol had demonstrated an ability to sketch and a nice color sense that led to an apprentice tour in the fashion house of Captain Molyneux, and then, in 1938, he had launched his own couture establishment on the rue Cambon in the first arrondissement of Paris. The house was an instant success, and only the war prevented Fayol's becoming a world class fashion innovator before the decade was out. He was quoted in *Time* as having later referred to the war and the German Occupation as "damned inconvenient and not at all helpful to business." Unlike Chanel and a few others who closed their doors, Fayol continued to make and sell clothes under the Nazis. "Would it have freed France one day sooner for me to have starved?" he demanded of an antagonistic court of inquiry in 1945. In 1947 Christian Dior created the "New Look," but eighteen months later Fayol narrowed shoulders and raised the waist and was hailed in *L'Officiel* as "a young Worth."

In the early fifties he marketed a perfume, signed a number of lucrative licensing deals with du Pont and Courtaulds, and by age forty-five was a millionaire. In 1954 he shocked the shadow world of fashion homosexuals by marrying the brilliant ballet dancer Hélène Serrat. After several years they had a child, a daughter, and three weeks later separated. It was said that Madame Fayol had come from the lying-in hospital to find her loving husband in bed with one of his mannequins. And a young man.

Hélène refused an offer to return to the Ballet Russe and instead buried herself in a private house on the Avenue Foch to raise the child and dabble in religious fanaticism. She informed Fayol she would never grant a divorce, but this hadn't seemed to upset him. Twice a year he turned out fashion collections that succeeded both artistically and commercially, and the French government, turning a conveniently opaque eye to his wartime activities, enrolled him in the Legion of Honor in recognition of his contributions to the French balance of payments. Always a large man with an enormous appetite for haute cuisine and fine wines, Fayol now grew huge. He affected a cape at opening nights, hosted sit-down dinners for sixty people, wrote reasonable poetry, and feuded with his competitors. Chanel once accused him of trying to burn down her couture house, and only the arrival of a squad of police had prevented his fighting a duel with another rival in the Bois one summer morning. It was said that Fayol himself had called the police, timing his call to ensure that the duel would never come off. The right-wing press hailed him as a great creative force, *L'Humanité* called him a Fascist, and when he was nominated to the Académie Française in the mid-sixties, three of the "immortals" threatened to resign if he was elected, while two others quit when he wasn't.

Unlike most fashion designers, Fayol seemed to tread an erratic line between men and women friends. His bisexuality was rather clearly established when one of the paparazzi for a scandal weekly bribed his way inside Fayol's country house at Montfort L'Amoury and came away with two sets of pictures: one showing Fayol making love to an exquisite girl from the chorus line of the Lido; the other showing him being made love to by a rising male star of French television. Money changed hands and the photographs were never published, but enough people had seen them informally so that the story was taken as truth.

Fayol owned racehorses, briefly managed a welterweight boxer, bought a demipalace in Marrakesh, laid down one of the three greatest private wine cellars in France, and subsidized a number of young painters, writers, and composers. Of both sexes. He publicly denounced de Gaulle, and was denounced in turn by that unforgiving titan; backed right-wing candidates; wrote letters to *Le Figaro* supporting unpopular causes; barred the press from his fashion collections for five consecutive seasons on a whim; sold exclusive rights to his fur label to Marshall Field, and then turned right around and mischievously sold the same exclusive rights, for a higher price, to Neiman Marcus. He was driven about town in a prewar Bentley decorated with gold leaf; once petitioned the Pope to have his estranged wife installed as abbess of a chic convent near Nantes (he thought it would embarrass Hélène); declared loudly that no one, and certainly not the Americans, had ever walked on the moon ("C'est un truc de télévision!"); and wrecked a Japanese geisha house during a business trip to Tokyo when one of the geishas complained of having been underpaid.

The priest was winding up. The obituaries in *The New York Times, Le Monde,* and *Women's Wear Daily* had all agreed on the major points: overweight, suffering from high blood pressure, and more irascible than usual, Fayol had left on holiday in Marrakesh ten days earlier. With him, Max, chief of his "little monks." Five days ago, after eating a heavy dinner laced with several bottles of cheap red wine in a well-known Marrakesh café, Fayol dismissed Max and said he would stroll home alone. He was found, dying, some hours later on the tile of the inner courtyard of his Moorish house. Verdict: death by natural causes. According to Max, who transported the body to the hospital, Fayol left no final message.

Outside, on the broad steps, the Widow Fayol shook a hand or two and quickly descended to her car, escorted by some variety of private priest and by two women in long gray robes. She was not noticeably weeping. That was left to Max, who held court in the church vestibule and who broke into sobs whenever the television cameras turned his way. Several of the lesser "little monks" tried, without success, to console him. One of the boys giggled, and Max had to speak to him, sternly. Reporters took notes as the mourners emerged: a member of Giscard-d'Estaing's cabinet and the leading nude dancer of the Folies-Bergère and a writer who had won that year's Prix Goncourt. When a beautiful girl in dark glasses emerged, one reporter nudged another and the second mumbled in irritation, not knowing: "Il faut travailler, tu sais." Then, as the last mourners came out, there was a commotion at the church door, a woman screamed, reporters ran, and people shouted and wheeled to see.

Maggy Moal had set herself afire, not in tribute to the late Fayol, of whom she did not approve, but in her haste to light a cigarette. An hour's abstinence (even Maggy would not sneak a smoke during the mass) had caused her to rush. Lighting up with the same trembling hand that clutched her purse, precariously balanced on her cane with the other, the old woman had let the cigarette fall. Unfortunately it had dropped into her bodice, and now she hopped about furiously on a bad leg, losing the cane, cursing and spitting, while others of the mourners beat at her thin chest with the flats of their hands to extinguish the blaze. When they had it out, the cane recovered, her wig straightened on her head, the straw hat still awry, Maggy Moal glared about her indignantly.

"Merde, alors!" she shouted to no one and to everyone. "That's what comes of allowing requiem masses for pansies!"

She hobbled off, still swearing under her breath, and the other mourners departed, leaving on the steps the last reporters finishing the last of their notes. Paul Delane, a fashion designer himself and an agnostic uncomfortable with churches, realized he was alone on the threshold of the Madeleine. He shivered and went down the steps and crossed the Grands Boulevards into the rue Cambon, where he ordered a stiff drink in the small bar of the Ritz. He felt he deserved it. He was not much for funerals and he had never seen anything like that business of Maggy Moal. He sipped his vodka and marveled that so many people would bother to attend a Roman Catholic mass for a bisexual fashion designer who had alienated most of them in life and then died, of overeating or of buggery, in a tiled courtyard in North Africa. Paul Delane's own motives for attending the funeral were quite clear. He had long wanted to *be* Jacques Fayol.

He fingered the cable in his pocket and resolved to remember everything. It would make a pleasant story to tell Winslow over dinner tomorrow night.

CONCORDE

The Concorde dipped its grotesque aluminum beak and began to roll. It was precisely 1 P.M. of the day after Jacques Fayol's funeral. The great airplane gathered speed until, almost unexpectedly, it lifted its tilted nose and sprang off runway three into the hazy April sky vaulting over John F. Kennedy International Airport. As it climbed, the shock of sound rolled and echoed across the field to a sawhorsed patch of sidewalk in front of the Air France departure gates, where a half-dozen housewives pulled the cotton wadding from their ears, listlessly folded signs and banners, and prepared to go home. The professional agitators and the politicians who saw Concorde as a popular issue had quit their protests months ago. But next day, when the daily New York to Paris SST lifted off again, the housewives would be there.

Anthony Winslow loosened the seat belt, pushed the seat into a reclining position, and stretched his long legs comfortably before him. He'd seen the housewives when the bank's limousine delivered him to the airport and he was sympathetic. It must be ghastly living near JFK and having to listen to the damn thing as it came and went on its transatlantic rounds. He was sympathetic, but how did you halt progress? Personally, and because he did not live next door to the airport, Winslow liked the Concorde. It trimmed three hours from the flight and there was plenty of leg

room. He knew he should feel guilty flying the Concorde, knowing the plane was a loser, economically doomed while still in
blueprint, a status symbol the bankrupt British couldn't afford
and the proud French couldn't not afford, but he didn't. He flew
the Concorde because he was a man who spent too much time in
airplanes, because it was comfortable, and because (only a bit
guiltily) these things meant more to him than the picketing
housewives.

He leaned down and tugged out from the seat in front of him
the battered old Louis Vuitton case. Since Winslow was a man
with no need for status symbols, he felt comfortable with the old
piece of Vuitton. He carried it not because it was chic, but because it was efficient, a good bag into which he could jam all his
papers.

"Champagne, sir?"

He looked up at the standard pretty girl in her French blue
uniform and shook his head.

"No, but I'll have some coffee. Black."

He would also turn down earphones and last evening's *Le
Monde* and this week's *Paris Match* and the movie and everything but that morning's *New York Times* and the fresh apple off
the lunch. It was under four hours to Paris and Winslow had a lot
to read. The big jet slipped smoothly through the sound barrier a
hundred miles east of Montauk, climbed to 51,000 feet, and
settled into its flight plan. By then Winslow was as paper-strewn
as the Collyer brothers, memoranda and correspondence and
manila folders and computer printouts across his lap and the tray
table and piled messily on the next seat. He'd shed his suit jacket,
opened his vest, and pulled his tie away from his throat. Around
him music played, people talked, stewardesses showed their
teeth, and the sky rushed past. Winslow saw none of it; heard
none of it. He read. And read. And read. Very much your ordinary commercial traveler boning up for a tough sales call.

Except that Anthony Winslow, thirty-four years old, unmar-
ried, an elegantly rumpled six feet four inches tall, was not your
ordinary commercial traveler.

Henry Rousselot had called him in on Monday. At Rousselot
& Partners, 18 Pine Street, Henry Rousselot did not call in junior
partners to exchange pleasantries or to discuss the prime. In the
wood-paneled, embossed-leather world of merchant banking,
months went by between summonses from Mr. Rousselot. If too
many months went by, the junior partner might find himself in a
branch office. In Cleveland, perhaps. Or to crueler exile at another, *lesser* merchant bank. Or, dread fate, to a commercial
bank. Winslow knew men at Rousselot who would, literally, have
committed suicide before going to work at Chase Manhattan.
There was little danger Tony Winslow would end up in Cleveland, or at Chase.

There was "a problem," Henry Rousselot explained. Somewhat complex, and requiring, well, the usual tact, the usual tal-
ents, the usual . . .

"You speak French, I believe," Henry Rousselot said.

Winslow nodded. He knew that Rousselot knew that his
mother had been French and that Winslow had lived in France.
Henry Rousselot accepted the nod and went on, precisely, as he
always did. Making certain, as he always did.

"The Delaware Chemical Corporation has a problem. In
France. I think we'll have to ask you to go over."

"Yes?"

There was a property Delaware wanted to buy. Delaware
thought it had an . . . understanding with the owner. A few
sentences on paper, you understand, nothing binding, nothing but
the man's word. And now suddenly Delaware was . . . concerned.

"The man renege?" Winslow asked.

Henry Rousselot looked at him across the desk.

"No," he said mildly. "He died."

They expend very little energy mourning the dead at merchant
banks. You don't leverage your money by mourning. And in this
instance, what was it? an aging Frenchman? Rousselot explained
the problem, rather more sketchily than Winslow would have
expected, and promised that a file would be in the car when it
came by Winslow's apartment to pick him up.

"I don't have all the pieces," Henry Rousselot said. "You'll find some of it in the file; more of it in Paris, I'd assume. This is a deal Delaware badly wants, it seems. What more can I say?"

He put the rhetorical question and stood up. Winslow stood too.

"Oh," said Rousselot, as if remembering a thing forgotten. "There's some sort of deadline on this business. May tenth." He paused. "The French elections are that day." He stopped again. "They hold French elections on Sunday, you know."

Winslow said he knew.

"I don't like deadlines," Rousselot said. "They don't make for good banking practice."

"No," Winslow agreed.

Rousselot looked narrowly at him.

"But in this instance I suppose you might keep the deadline in mind. Delaware Corp. seems to place weight on it."

Rousselot fixed him with those pale eyes. "Place weight." That meant the deadline was important as hell.

Winslow had never been shy about asking questions. "But isn't this a legal problem? Shouldn't the lawyers be handling it?"

Rousselot nodded. "Correct. Absolutely. But there's a ripple of anti-Americanism in France right now, and Delaware doesn't want this business getting into a French courtroom until we at the bank can tie up some very loose ends for them. That's your job ... the loose ends."

Since Winslow loved Paris and the stewardess of the weekend had turned out to be banal and since he had a touch of tennis elbow, he stifled further objections and listened as Henry Rousselot talked.

"We're the merchant bank in this. The commercial banks will put up the money once the deal is set. It's up to us—to you—to firm up the deal. Nail it tight and then turn it over to the lawyers and our French correspondent bank to tidy up. The man died of natural causes so there seems no threat his papers will be sealed. There's a will, everything left to the family. You'll have to interview the heirs, I expect, get their agreement to carry out negotia-

tions Fayol began with Delaware before he died. Delaware's
agreement with the man is on paper but it's tenuous. Wouldn't
stand up for a minute in the courts. You've got to convince the
family this deal is in their best interest, keep it away from the
damned lawyers, and go through the man's papers. There are
references to deeds and rights but Delaware hasn't ever seen
them. You know the French. Very sloppy paperwork. The documents are there, Delaware says. You've got to find them, find
anything that will corroborate Delaware Corp.'s claim." He
paused. "Oh, yes, there's a complication."

Winslow waited. "A complication." Wasn't there always?

"There could be a rival claimant. Don't know who, don't know
how serious. The Arabs? Perhaps. Or maybe the late Monsieur
Fayol thought a bit of competition would inflate his payout.
Delaware's vague on it. Just watch out," Rousselot warned, "just
watch out for the competition. Whenever there's a hundred million involved, otherwise respectable business rivals have a way of
becoming . . . difficult."

The younger man nodded.

"You'll represent the firm. Competently, I know." Rousselot
extended his hand. Winslow shook it and went out.

Henry Rousselot expected Winslow to represent the firm. But
not merely with "competence." This was one of the coming stars,
a junior from whom Henry Rousselot expected, *demanded*, more
than "competence." The Delaware Chemical Corporation, known
through Wall Street and in the worlds of commercial and merchant banking as "Delaware Corp.," was one of Rousselot's
biggies—for that matter, one of the world's "biggies." With that
delightfully iconoclastic wit that always surprised his associates,
Henry Rousselot had once remarked, over cocktails at Christ-
mas, that Delaware Corp. was *more* than just another client.
Delaware Corp. was a force of nature. "You don't," Rousselot
had said in that dry, quiet way, "you don't fuck around with
Delaware Corp."

Winslow was not likely to. He was a man who understood the
priorities, who exercised cool judgment, and who seemed to

know instinctively a good move from a bad. He took no credit for these qualities. He knew whereof they derived.

Anthony Winslow was the product of a marriage only marginally successful except in the conception of a child who inherited the best of each of two remarkable, but flawed, parents. His father was stern, righteous, unyielding; his mother, artistic, warm, impulsive; the one frosty New England, the other emotional France. Even as a boy Winslow was aware of the conflicting stresses. Now, as a man, he recognized them in himself, the alternating chill of a calculating father, all pragmatism and logic; the warmth and instinctive openness of the Gallic mother. Something of a headliner at Princeton, he graduated with honors in literature and had played reasonable Ivy League basketball for two years before being forced to the bench by a gangling genius of a sophomore called Bill Bradley. On graduation, there being a war, Winslow had taken a commission in the Marine Corps, as much to spite his father as to serve a flag, and had come home healthy and with a sense of professional competence, though without medals (the war had become unfashionable). Not yet quite sure what he wanted to do with his life, he deferred a decision by going on to Harvard's graduate business school. At the "B" school, as it is known, he did well. Not top of the class, but well. There followed a year in a big brokerage house, another three at Marine Midland, and then, in 1974, New York City began to fall apart.

Like old Joe Kennedy, Tony Winslow's father had once served on the Securities & Exchange Commission. And like Kennedy père, old man Winslow had used the experience, ever afterward, to screw the government. Tony had a theory that Joe Kennedy, not saintly Mother Rose, was the reason the boys went into public service. They owed a debt, and they wanted to pay it off. So when New York trembled on the brink of default, when the pitiful call for help went out, Winslow decided to answer it. In a minor way, he too owed a debt. And it was, as with the Marine Corps, an opportunity to ignore his father's advice ("Let the bastards go broke.").

Felix Rohatyn of Lazard Frères put together the team, a score of the brightest, toughest, iron-assed bankers, lawyers, accountants, and labor negotiators ever assembled. They were young, they thrived on work, they slept a few hours at a time, they got drunk on rare days off, they chain-smoked and grew mustaches, and under the pressure of time and the distraction of the work, they were virtually celibate. Winslow remembered Hagen's exhausted confession to him one night after a bargaining session with the teachers: "Tony, if we ever get out of this thing, someone's going to have to teach me all over again how to screw."

They got out of "this thing," but none of those who went through those months with Rohatyn would ever be the same. One man killed himself, another died when he fell asleep at the wheel of his car; there were breakdowns and broken marriages. But the survivors came out of it leaner and shrewder than when they went in. And they came out of it with reputations.

Rousselot & Partners hired Winslow. He was down to 165 pounds, thirty under his usual weight, he'd developed an annoying tic in his right eyelid that no one could see but he could feel, he was smoking eighty cigarettes a day, and his suits all bore scorch marks. Henry Rousselot put him on the payroll, immediately sent him to rest at his own house at Lyford Cay for a week, and within a year had named him a junior partner. The new job was challenging, but there were times Winslow found himself missing the tension, the fear, and the camaraderie of the Crisis months. It was like having been in the war: you were pleased it was over but glad you had been there. A bit embarrassed at feeling this way, he mentioned it to Rohatyn, who nodded and said, yes, he knew the feeling. But one didn't really want to go through it again.

Winslow finished reading the files. He had taken notes mentally. There were three key elements, two of which he understood, the third of which puzzled him. First, Delaware Corp. was eager to purchase controlling interest in the Maison Fayol but lacked a firm agreement on paper. Second, the deal, if it be made at all, had to be nailed down within the next three weeks before

the French general elections. And third—and this was what mysti-
fied Winslow—Delaware's opening bid to purchase Fayol was
$85 million. "Will go higher to close," a memo noted. Winslow
shook his head. By any standard accounting practice, no matter
how high you valued the inventory, how low the bad debts, there
was no way the Maison Fayol was worth $85 million. Or any-
thing close to that. Winslow looked again at the brief document
signed by Jacques Fayol in which he said he was "interested" in
talking sale. "Interested." No wonder Rousselot didn't want the
lawyers in the act as yet, not with legal language as flimsy as that!
And that exasperating reference to "certain real property and
property rights." Now what the hell did that mean? Real estate,
obviously, but what? And where? Buildings in Paris, off-shore oil,
mineral rights, tracts of land? If a Paris couture house wasn't
worth anything like $85 million, and the books indicated clearly
it wasn't, then it must be this "real property" that was. "Valid
deeds are held in my name" to this real property, Fayol had
written. Winslow shook his head. He supposed he would get the
answers when he went through Fayol's accounts. There *must* be
better documentation than this for Fayol's holdings to attract an
offer of $85 million. Delaware Corp. was not, he reminded him-
self, noted for its philanthropy.

There was a lengthy report on Fayol's funeral in *The Times*.
And a photo of mourners leaving the church. He scanned the
picture to see if there was anyone he knew. Walking toward the
lens was an extraordinarily pretty girl wearing dark glasses. She
did not look particularly sad. Winslow wondered if she was a
member of the family. Perhaps a journalist. He did not know her,
and when a girl looked like that, he was sure he would have
remembered. Thinking of the girl, he had begun to daydream of
Paris when the Concorde shuddered, dipped its nose, and began
to slow.

"This is your captain. We are now approaching the French
coast, just south of Deauville. We have begun to decelerate and
will be landing in Paris in approximately twenty minutes."

Winslow looked out of the window. It was still afternoon. He

began to push the computer printouts and the *Time* cover story
and the other papers back into his case. There hadn't been much
there. Not nearly the sort of briefing he was used to getting from
Rousselot. Was the old man losing his touch? Or, the thought
occurred to him, was it that Rousselot simply didn't know? Perhaps Delaware Corp. was playing this one close to the vest, not
even giving their merchant bankers all the numbers. Winslow
smiled, remembering the shocked silence, followed by the nervous laugh. "You don't fuck around with Delaware Corp.,"
Henry Rousselot had said.

For some traffic control reason the plane came down at Orly.
Winslow, who hated the Buck Rogers surrealism of the newer
Charles de Gaulle airport, thought it was a good omen. There
was a Peugeot cab at the curb, roomier than the Simcas, and
Winslow dumped his bags and got in. The cabbie half turned to
remind monsieur that during the rush hour, "l'heure d'affluence,"
there would be a slight additional charge. "Don't shit me," Winslow advised cheerfully, in his colloquial French. The cabbie was
pleased. "Ah," he said, "Monsieur est parisien." The tourist
season was just starting and you couldn't blame a man for trying.

At the hotel on rue Jean Goujon the manager descended from
the little gallery above the front desk and greeted Winslow. His
usual room was reserved. (Yes, business was good. Plenty of
fashion buyers in town for the prêt-à-porter showings. As for the
elections, who knew? Giscard was an intelligent man. It was folly
to write him off yet.) The bellman dropped the bags and Winslow opened the French windows. It was dusk and the rooftops
looked fine. The room was on the top floor, with a tiny balcony,
and it looked out over the Radio-Télévision-Luxembourg building and on toward the Arc de Triomphe, just now being lighted
in the dusk.

The April evening was warm and Winslow cranked open the
wooden shutter and tied back the doors. He undressed and drank
some Évian and smoked a cigarillo. It was eight o'clock and the
lights of the city flicked on. Across the street on the top floor of
one of those modern "grand-standing" apartments they advertise

in *France-Soir,* he could look into a lighted bedroom. A young woman came into the room and began to take off her clothes. Even at this distance Winslow could see that she was quite fit. He watched her for a few minutes, then turned away and washed and dressed. It was wonderful to be back in Paris in the springtime, especially on what promised to be an interesting job.

Winslow was still savoring the look of the young woman in the window when the concierge rang to say Monsieur Delane was waiting downstairs in his car.

PARIS

It was a new car, a Porsche, and Paul Delane wanted to show it off, so they did a roundabout tour along the Seine to get to the Left Bank and dinner at La Coupole. Delane was one of the more promising of the young fashion designers and he was also a madman behind the wheel. The American found himself pressing his feet against the floorboards as if applying brake pressure to slow Delane's manic speed through the narrow streets and along the quais and during the controlled skids at the turns. They found a parking space along the Boulevard Montparnasse and Delane bounced up over the curb and brought the Porsche to a halt just short of a chestnut tree. Winslow grinned, but his hands were sweaty. It was still early for a Paris dinner and there were empty tables in the huge room. Winslow looked around the place, remembering the pleasant past. Not for the first time he found it difficult to imagine the Gestapo had used the second floor to "question" French men and women during the Occupation. He shuddered involuntarily. No wonder the management sealed it off after the war. A dramatic Gallic gesture, surely, but who the hell would want to eat up there? The waiter brought a bottle of the young Moulin-à-Vent even before they ordered, and Winslow listened while Paul Delane gossiped about the latest scandals, about business, and about what the national elections might bring.

"You Americans aren't terribly popular right now, you know," Delane said, speaking in French.

"Oh?"

There was a gaffe the Secretary of State had committed, Delane said, and some business about floating the franc versus the dollar, and worst of all, what seemed to the French another round of American economic imperialism. General Electric had been buying up shares in one of the few computer companies still in French hands, American wheat was depressing the local farm prices, and "your Monsieur Tom Hoving," had just bought another Postimpressionist masterpiece to hang on the walls of the Metropolitan Museum of Art. "With an election coming up," Delane said, "the government is very sensitive. The Communists accuse them of turning France into a colony of the United States, of letting Wall Street dictate our future, of surrendering French sovereignty to a lot of ruthless American bankers. Like you," he smiled pleasantly.

"Who's going to win the election?" Winslow asked.

"It's going to be a close one," Delane said. "The balance of payments looks terrible right now and it's probably even worse than it looks. A lot of people are getting their money out, and you know Frenchmen; they aren't necessarily telling the currency control people about it. If the Left wins, and tries to put in a popular front government, the army is honor-bound to commit unspeakable acts."

"A coup?"

Delane shrugged. "It would be in the classic tradition. We French have never had much respect for a colonel who isn't ready to overthrow the government on any given morning. Some of the old OAS boys de Gaulle didn't purge are still around. And there are the 'paras.' They don't much care which side they're on as long as there's someone for them to shoot."

They ordered rare steaks and pommes frites and a second bottle of the red wine. Delane asked, politely, what brought Winslow to Paris.

"Dull stuff, really," Winslow replied with the typical banker's caution. "Rousselot and Partners are merchant bankers for a couple of American firms that manufacture under license from the Maison Fayol. They're a bit uneasy about what's going to happen now." He paused, and then casually began to probe. Delane must have known old man Fayol.

"But of course. How could I not? An admirable figure. Huge, perhaps three hundred of your pounds. A man who tasted life to the fullest. Ate himself to death, they say. Never missed an opening night at the theater or a masked ball or an evening in the discotheques. Always an entourage—beautiful girls, handsome young men. Bisexual of course and voracious both routes. And naturally some sort of fashion genius. They damned near elected him to the Académie Française one year. The Left blackballed him. Some nasty little business about collaboration in the war, turning over Jews to the Gestapo or some such. All very vague, very Henri Montherlant. He had a wife, a daughter as well, but he didn't seem to work at being père de famille. Anything else you need to know about him?"

As much as he liked Delane, Winslow had decided, while still in the air, to keep Henry Rousselot's instructions to himself. Talk about a deal and the price went up. It was inevitable. So now, even with a friend, Winslow played the hand close.

"Oh, don't sweat over it. There's some talk Fayol was thinking about selling the business. We don't know how that might affect the licensees."

Delane shrugged. "Difficult to say. In the couture, everyone's secretive about stuff like that."

Still probing, Winslow laughed. "And I thought you all got together once a year in a smoke-filled room and dropped hemlines."

Delane was indignant. "That's what everyone thinks. That's all merde. The truth is the designers all hate one another. Dior can't stand Saint Laurent. Saint Laurent sued Dior. A young designer threw a brick through Lanvin's window. Cardin fights with everybody. Ungaro and Givenchy don't speak. Maggy Moal slanders all of us. The reason clothes get to look alike every year is because we all buy from the same handful of fabric houses, we're all sensitive to the same fashion cycles, subject to the same cultural influences, the same films, the same galleries, whatever new actress is all the rage."

"And there's no collusion?"

Delane assumed a hurt innocence.

"I'm shocked, Tony, that you would even suggest such a thing. We may occasionally *steal* from one another. But we never, absolutely *never*, cooperate."

Winslow grinned. He liked Delane, liked him very much, but the man could be an elusive quantity. For a fashion designer, Paul Delane certainly didn't fit the mold. He and Winslow had met at Harvard. Delane was the only member of their graduate school class who had never even been to college, and he was certainly their only couturier. He'd stayed only a year, didn't bother taking any of the exams, failed to turn in a thesis, and had run up the most cuts of any candidate the "B" school had ever had. In the few classes Delane bothered to attend, he'd been brilliant, understanding instinctively the school's case method, often challenging the professors and the more conventional students with questions and answers that went outside the "method" but which, under examination, proved correct.

During one of a number of drunken nights that began at the Copley bar and spilled over into raucous pursuit of liberated Radcliffe girls, Delane had told Winslow something of himself. Already a figure of relative importance in the French fashion business, Delane said he'd realized quite early there were any number of more talented fashion designers in Paris. "But not one of them knows a fucking thing about modern business practice." Since Delane was inordinately ambitious ("I really want to *be* Jacques Fayol or Dior or Saint Laurent"), he had decided to educate himself about business. He had dropped out of fashion for a year to "do" Harvard. "I only attend the classes that will help me turn a profit," he said. "Exams? Marks? Hell, I'll get them when I go back to work. On the profit and loss sheet." A student of capitalism, Delane was a voting socialist; a designer,

he was a former rugby international; one of the few raging het-
erosexuals at his level of haute couture, and surely the only designer in Paris with a Harvard pennant on his bathroom wall.

They finished dinner with some good Brie and the last of the
wine and got up to leave. By now there was a lineup of people
waiting for tables over in the bar on the left. The pretty girls had
begun to arrive and their voices and laughter filled the room.
"Doesn't sound much like a crisis, does it?" Delane remarked.
The wine had not helped Delane's driving. After narrowly missing a truck, they pulled up at the rue Princesse and got out. Here,
on the Left Bank, the walls of the buildings were covered with
the usual political slogans and posters. Just outside Castel's
someone had scrawled a line Winslow liked: "Merde à tout le
monde . . . shit on everybody." Delane laughed. "An anarchist,
évidemment." He threw a kiss to the girl at the peephole and
they went into the dark of the discotheque.

Jean Castel was sitting at the "table de concierge" on the right,
drinking with a couple of old rugby players. He got up and shook
hands. "A long time," he told Winslow. They sat down and took
a whisky with Castel and his pals, and then, as the place began to
fill, Delane and Winslow went downstairs to watch the dancing.
Betty Shreiber came over. She was a tall, attractive woman in her
thirties with a marvelous body. She was also lesbian. The two
men asked her to join them.

"But just for a moment, darlings," Betty told them. "There's
some wonderful talent here tonight and I don't want to miss
out."

They had some scotch. Shifting into English, Delane asked
Betty to tell them about the animals. She laughed. Winslow, who
knew he was missing something, asked, "What animals?"

"Oh, it's delicious, what happened," she said. "You know
Marie-Hélène who married that Arab, the one with the money
who died in the plane crash? Well, anyway, Marie-Hélène and I
were, well, we were close. Except for those damn animals she
kept taking in, I guess I was her closest friend. Then, last year—I
don't know, I suppose the pound sterling was in difficulty or she

thought she might have to have a bust-lift—there was some crisis, and poor Marie-Hélène killed herself. I don't think the dear girl meant to; it just happened, and there I was, executor of the will. As if I knew anything about wills! But the court confirmed it, and all of a sudden there were these millions in Swiss francs and she'd left it all to the goddamn animals. Well, naturally, as executor, I had a solemn responsibility to see that the money didn't go to waste, so I've actually set up three or four of the brutes in kennels . . . charming places, really . . . and of course I live on the rest. After all, isn't it an executor's duty to preserve her own health and happiness so I can conscientiously fulfill dear Marie-Hélène's final wish?"

"Your solemn duty," Delane agreed. They drank some more scotch, and then Betty saw a girl and boy dancing and she rather liked the look of the girl and she got up to dance with them. Ten minutes later, when Winslow looked again, the boy was gone and Betty and the girl, who was perhaps eighteen, were sitting together. Talking.

Winslow nodded toward her.

"Betty—she's not American, is she? She talks like an American."

"Mexican," Delane said. "But she married a German and they lived in America."

"Not Argentina?"

"Tony, you're a bad one."

"Why does she bother getting married? It doesn't really interest her."

Delane made a Gallic gesture. "I think it was the German liked to be whipped. And if a wife can't supply small pleasures, well . . ."

Winslow and Delane drank and listened to the music and watched the girls. Then Winslow remembered why he was in Paris and that May 10 was not that far off. He decided to take a chance on Delane. He recalled once having argued politics with the Frenchman and being completely disarmed when Delane declared, righteously, "I see nothing wrong with being a loyal Socialist and still wanting to maximize my profit! Isn't that what free enterprise is all about?"

Winslow had laughed. Now he looked at Delane and asked: "Suppose someone told you the Maison Fayol was worth a hundred million. In dollars. What would you say?"

"I'd laugh."

"No, seriously."

Delane looked at his American friend. He nodded; stuck out his lower lip. "Well, then, I'd say the fucking Arabs were buying into the couture."

"That crazy, huh?"

"It's not crazy if you're an oil Arab and you have three Rolls-Royces and a Boeing already and there are no more German girls you want to purchase. No, then it's not crazy. Otherwise, it's . . . it's crazy."

Winslow considered.

"Paul, is there anything you can think of, something that isn't public knowledge, that would *make* the House of Fayol worth that kind of money? Not to Arabs. To pragmatic businessmen?"

"You *are* serious."

Winslow nodded.

"Well, if Fayol didn't discover oil beneath the rue Cambon, or if he hadn't found a way to do business without the unions, then it has to do with perfume."

"Perfume?"

"Bien sûr, Tony. Believe me, I don't know what Fayol might have come up with. But it *has* to be perfume. You just don't make big profit margins on clothes."

"A new license deal? In the States?"

Delane shook his head. "I have twelve license deals. What do they bring me? Maybe two million a year in dollars? So, Fayol is five times as big. Make it ten million. No, it's not women's wear or licenses. Only perfume gives you the big profits." He paused. "But even then, I just don't understand it. Fayol has a fine perfume. Very profitable. But nothing to generate an offer of what . . . ? A hundred million?"

"Approximately."

"Maybe I shouldn't have cut so many classes at Harvard," Delane said regretfully.

"Leverage," Winslow mused.

Delane threw up his hands.

"That's the word I always forgot. Leverage. No wonder I flopped out."

"Flunked out."

Delane laughed. Then, more seriously, "Look, Tony, you know all the perfume, the good stuff, the fifty-dollar-an-ounce perfume that bought Fayol all those horses and pretty boys, that buys me my Porsche and my girls—well, where does it come from? It comes from one place. From Grasse. All the great perfume in the world comes from Grasse. So, maybe . . ."

"Maybe I ought to take a look at Grasse?"

Delane shrugged. "Why not? There's always something going on down there. Those fucking peasants, they're always after . . . 'leverage.' Maybe Fayol knew something. I dunno. Ask Maggy."

"Maggy Maol?"

"Sure. That old bitch, she's forgotten more about perfume than Fayol or I ever knew. Talk to her. She hates everybody so much she'll tell you the dirt. I'll call her tomorrow. Make an introduction for you." He paused. "But be careful. She's eighty years old and she'll grab your leg. Get you in bed, you know."

Winslow looked skeptical.

"I don't kid," Delane said. "At Fayol's funeral yesterday, right there at the church, she set herself on fire."

Delane told the story, and Winslow was still laughing when a very lovely girl in dark glasses came by, holding the arm of a smooth, dark man in dinner clothes. Winslow looked at her. He wondered if he knew her.

"Paul, that girl. Do you . . . ?"

"Who?"

Winslow pointed her out. "There was a picture in the New York paper today of Fayol's funeral. That girl . . ."

Delane looked. "I know the guy she's with. An Iranian guy.

Works for the Shah, I think. Nafredi. Zader Nafredi. Lots of money, lots of girls."

"And the girl?" Winslow persisted.

Delane focused. "With the shades?"

Winslow nodded.

Delane laughed. "One of Madame Claude's girls. Very high-priced hooker. Expensive but worth the money. Very classy stuff."

"Ask her over," Winslow said.

"You're kidding, Tony. I can't do that. The girl's working. She's on the job. That guy's paying for her time, not for her to have drinks with you and me."

They watched the couple disappear into the other room. "You say she was at the funeral?" Delane asked.

"It looked like her in the photo."

Delane pursed his lips.

"It must be part of the religious revival. Throughout the world, hookers and sinners like me are going to church. Myself, I find the trend very uplifting. But mystifying."

"Oh?"

"Sure. The Shah's bag man, Nafredi. He was there too."

HÉLÈNE

In the morning, despite jet lag and a minor hangover, the hard, dull, gritty work began. Every great merchant bank has correspondent banks in other countries. Rousselot's was a small but prestigious house in the Place Vendôme. Winslow had presented himself and a letter from Henry Rousselot. One of the senior men gave him an hour and he had another three hours on his own in the files. Much of what was there he knew already. Fayol had run a tidy little business. Winslow assumed there were two sets of books. What French entrepreneur didn't keep two? How else to evade taxes? But even making that assumption, it was clear the Maison Fayol functioned profitably with a rather impressive sales growth, and if the old rascal had bought racehorses and playwrights and wine cellars and young women, well, he did so out of income. For a fashion house, the Maison Fayol was a paragon. Still, on the basis of these papers and those Rousselot had supplied, the company was worth, say, $20 million. Which brought Winslow back to the nagging question: Why were those sons of bitches at Delaware Corp. opening the bidding at four times that figure? He remembered Delane's declaration of the night before: "Dior is the richest couture house there's ever been, and not even Dior is worth $100 million." The bank's senior man made some telephone calls for Winslow and gave him a letter of introduction, and Winslow thanked him and went out to hail a cab.

* * *

Hélène Fayol lived halfway down the Avenue Foch on the right side. A wall, a hedge, a secret garden. It was hard to imagine it was the middle of the city. "The Widow Fayol." Winslow had a giddy instant when he imagined addressing her that way: "Veuve Fayol . . . Veuve Clicquot." He sobered when she came into the formal drawing room—tall, straight, still very much a dancer's body. She was in navy. On her it looked very chic, not mournful at all. From somewhere out of the past he remembered one of those silly fashion editor lines: "Navy blue is this year's black." Madame Fayol gestured for him to sit. He said the usual things. As they talked, Winslow thought he could hear a radio or a record player somewhere far off. It sounded like religious music, Gregorian chant perhaps.

"I took no interest in my husband's work," Hélène Fayol was saying. "For some years we led . . . rather separate lives. And even earlier, I had the ballet, and he had . . . clothes."

"Had he ever mentioned *selling* the Maison Fayol?"

They never discussed business. Never.

"Had he ever talked of the Delaware Corp., some deal that might have . . . ?"

They did not discuss business. Ever.

The chanting was louder now—it might be actual voices, not just a tape or the radio. He hitched his chair forward. This wasn't getting him anywhere.

"Your daughter. She would now be . . ."

"My daughter does not live here."

"Oh?"

No reaction. No elaboration. Her tongue was as disciplined as her dancer's body.

"The people running the business, for you, have they reported to you on the state of affairs since . . . ?"

"Since my husband died?"

Leaping at straws, "Yes."

Hélène Fayol looked at him, the eyes very clear.

"No," she said.

Jesus, Winslow thought, this isn't going well at all. Not at all. He patted his pockets.

"May I have your permission to smoke?"

Anything for a break in this cold non-dialogue.

"But of course."

There was a knock on the door of the sitting room. Madame Fayol said something and a woman came in. She was very oddly dressed, in what looked like gray flannel, but cut very full, very long, the sort of thing nuns used to wear before John XXIII.

"The service," the woman said. "It's time."

"Oh, yes," Hélène Fayol said. For the first time, her face came alive, the icy control thawed. She was smiling now.

"I'm sorry, Monsieur Winslow. We are punctual in this house. A prayer service. Several of my friends and I . . ." She gestured vaguely toward the back of the house where the chanting was coming from. Winslow jumped at the opening.

"I *thought* I heard chant," he said enthusiastically. "Reminded me of when I was a child. My mother . . . church . . . candles . . . kind of thing you never forget . . ." He babbled on.

Hélène Fayol smiled. She was still very beautiful.

"One tries to keep the tradition alive," she said. "And it *is* haunting."

The other woman still hovered, half servant, half companion.

Given this acolyte as worshipful audience, Hélène Fayol turned charming.

"I'm sorry not to be of more assistance," she said, "but you see, my husband long ago made a settlement with me. It is my daughter, Anne, who inherits the Maison, whatever else there is. And she . . ." The widow waved a graceful hand.

Winslow nodded. ". . . does not live here. Yes, I understand."

Hélène Fayol rose. "I must go now."

Winslow jumped up, desperately searching for the last question that might elicit some information, when Madame Fayol said:

"It might be of some help to your bank to see my husband's huissier. His name is Grumbach. His office is in the rue des Petits Champs." She held out her hand to be kissed. Winslow took it, trying to stifle the very strong suspicion he was being manipulated. As a servant let him out, Winslow could hear the chanting very clearly. It was in Latin, a dead language the Pope had ordered French Catholics were no longer to use.

Winslow walked up to the Étoile to Le Drugstore to look up Grumbach's number in the phone book. He had a sandwich and a glass of beer and watched tourists buying picture postcards. He thought for a moment of buying a card and then he realized there was no one he wanted to send it to. Damn, he thought, I'm getting as dour as the old man. A pretty girl at the lunch counter smiled, which made him feel better about things, and he went off to see Jacques Fayol's huissier.

Grumbach was a dusty man in a dusty office up three flights of dusty stairs. A huissier is a kind of accountant, a notary public who does sums. The office was full of files, brick-red manila folders with raveled strings. There were fountain pens on the desk, the old Watermans. Not a sign of an adding machine, to say nothing of a computer readout. Discovering a man who still kept handwritten ledgers cheered Winslow immensely. He glanced around at the files. None of them seemed to have labels. He wondered how old Grumbach could tell them apart. Maybe they each had a distinctive smell.

Winslow gave old Grumbach some story about having been sent over by Mme. Fayol ("call her, then") and mentioned someone's name Grumbach recognized from the correspondent bank, and the old fellow got on a chair (Winslow nervously wanted to get up to support him, the legs trembled so) and pulled down a folder that looked just like every other folder. Then a second, and a third. Dust hung on the sunbeams that came through scrubbed patches in the window grime. Winslow took off his jacket, opened his tie, and sat down. He lighted a cigarillo, but this time without asking permission. After all, Grumbach wasn't the goddamned widow.

After two hours Winslow stood up to straighten his back. He hadn't found much. But he liked these files. They were messy, a CPA's nightmare, but Winslow liked them. You found things in messy files no one knew were there. Orderly files told you what people wanted you to know. He sat down again. The ashtray was half full of butts. He lighted another cigarillo. Grumbach had no Xerox machine, which in itself was wonderful. Winslow was a modern man who clung to few outmoded notions, but one of them was that there was too much paper in the world and that if it all still had to be copied out by hand, by monks, the result would be less villainy, more forests, and considerably less eyestrain.

"What about the will?" he asked Grumbach, knowing the answer but wanting to try the old man.

Grumbach told him. Dust came out of the huissier when he spoke, as if he were a heavy smoker and the smoke hung in his clothes and hair and mustache only to puff out when he moved.

The will was no secret, Grumbach said. Not yet probated, of course, but no secret. Fayol had spoken openly about it for years. Everything went to the girl, Anne, the daughter. Except for 250,000 a year to the wife. He corrected himself, "the widow." New francs, naturally; one doesn't speak of dollars in France, monsieur, we are not *yet* a colony.

Winslow had been taking notes. There seemed to be some files missing. The huissier nodded. Of course, he'd been working on the files himself, ever since the shocking news had come from Marrakesh. In a few days—a week, perhaps—he'd have everything in good order, ready for the probate. But right now, well, he had to admit it, things were a bit confused. The old man gestured toward his own rolltop desk. "More of Monsieur Fayol's papers. Not yet collated. I'm going through them, page by page. It is not easy being huissier to such an active man."

Winslow agreed. He consulted his notes. "There are several file references here that seem to be missing." He read them off. The huissier listened. He exhaled loudly and some more dust floated across the room. If they ever cast a wide-screen remake of *Bleak House*, Winslow thought, they've got to get this fellow.

"But what about this file marked 'Grasse'? I don't see it."

The huissier nodded. That was one of the bulky files, contracts

with local farmers, labor negotiations, all dealing with purchases
of essential oils for Monsieur Fayol's perfume business. Dull
stuff, really, but important. He was going through that himself.
Could Winslow take a look at it now? But no, it simply wasn't
organized. Perhaps in another week or two.

Winslow looked at his notes again. He asked about this file
and that. The huissier explained one or two of them away as dead
files, negotiations planned but never executed. Stuff that matured
ten or fifteen years ago and no longer had relevance. Another file.
No, the old man said, that had been a planned takeover of a
hosiery mill. The deal had been canceled in 1965. Another file.
Winslow again looked at his notes.

"There's a file marked 'Paris Une.' There's nothing in it. What
was that?"

Huissier Grumbach seemed to stiffen. Then he smiled. It was
the first time he had smiled in more than two hours, and Winslow
noted it. The old man took out a handkerchief and blew his nose.
More dust. He smiled again.

"I'm sure it will turn up in that stack over there," he said.
"Who knows? Monsieur Fayol had two perfumes on the market:
'Paris Sept' and 'Paris Quinze.' Perhaps this was a new scent he
was thinking of marketing. Or"—and he paused mischievously—
"perhaps was that Monsieur Fayol was growing old, and forget-
ful? Like all old men?"

Winslow said he didn't understand. The huissier smiled:

"Paris Une. Paris One, in English. It is the arrondissement of
his couture house. 'The Maison Fayol, rue Cambon, Paris
Première,' or one might say, 'Paris One.' Maybe he made a little
note so he wouldn't forget where he worked."

Two hours later, Winslow, his back sore, his eyes grainy, got
up and put on his coat. He had a pocketful of notes but nothing
very promising. The huissier showed him to the door. He was still
chuckling over his witticism. Winslow was sure he had been
shown only what he was supposed to see. Still, there were these
notes in his pocket referring to the empty files. Maybe they held
meaning. If he could ever get to see them. The Grasse folder, for

example. And then the "Paris One" file. He hadn't seen that. And it had been the only one to bring a smile to the wrinkled face of the old notary public. A new perfume? Bullshit.

Winslow went down the dusty stairs and out into the street. It was late afternoon and the traffic was starting to build, and he decided to walk back to the hotel and clear his goddamn head.

The single piece of paper Delaware Corp. had in hand referred to "real property," to deeds, to certain rights. Where the hell were they? Not among the documents held by the correspondent bank. Not among Grumbach's mummified folders. Where was the material on Grasse? What was "Paris One"? He wasn't sure whether he preferred Mme. Fayol's stonewalling or the old huissier's evasions. Either way, he wasn't getting very far very fast. Another few days like this and Henry Rousselot would be sending telexes. Delaware Corp. considered there was "urgency" in this matter, and he'd already wasted two working days.

As Winslow's long legs carried him west on the rue des Petits Champs a gray Cadillac with diplomatic plates drew up in front of Monsieur le Huissier Grumbach's building and Zader Nafredi got out of the back seat and went inside.

SOIRÉE

At the hotel there were messages. One from Paul Delane. Winslow stripped down to his shorts, lighted up, and propped himself up on the bed with the phone cradled. Delane's slangy English sounded cheerful.

"Hey, you got a 'smoking'?" he asked.

"What banker would ever think of traveling without a dinner jacket?" Winslow demanded. "Why?"

"I got you invited to a party tonight. Very fashionable. You gotta wear a smoking. I was gonna lend you one, do the alterations myself, charge you a bloody fortune. Maggy Moal will be there. Good chance for you to pluck her brains. About perfume, that stuff."

"*Pick* her brains," Winslow said. "What time, where?"

He jotted down the details and hung up. He went to the closet. The dinner jacket looked fine. Most of the wrinkles had come out. After he'd showered it was dark, and he switched on the lights in the bedroom, glancing across the street. The girl wasn't there, the one in the window. Well, perhaps later. It was too far to see her features, what she looked like, but you could tell the body was fine. Just fine. He laughed. If he were *really* dirty-minded he could buy a telescope, some cheap glasses. He laughed again and began to get into his evening clothes.

"I'm so glad you were able to come," Willis Blatter told him without a great deal of sincerity. "I'm a great pal of Henry Rousselot's."

Winslow said the usual about Rousselot and he asked Blatter how business was, and then as soon as he could politely do so, he left his host to greet other guests and slipped away to the bar. He got a whisky-Perrier and sipped it, watching Willis Blatter organize the evening.

Blatter was the biggest man in American cosmetics, a hard man in a hard business, about sixty now, as polished and awkward as an orthopedic shoe. He reminded Tony of Nixon, the same lack of grace, of small talk; the same intensity of purpose. It was typical of Blatter to have picked a place like this for his party: one of those sprawling restaurants in the Bois de Boulogne, once a rich man's house, now the sort of place you went on Sunday afternoons and ate too much, badly. The gardens were alight with Japanese lanterns, liveried waiters pushed trays of drink, and a rock group and some very corny Hungarian strings alternated on the bandstand. The crowd was as motley: American retailers here for the prêt-à-porter showings; a smatter of French fashion names; dozens of pretty girls hired for the evening; the usual freeloaders from the press; Japanese buyers; synthetic fiber salesmen from du Pont, Monsanto and Celanese; a couple of minor French officials encouraging the export trade.

Blatter worked the room. In the cosmetic business *everyone* was a potential customer. He shook a lot of hands, smiled, but seemed really happy only when one of his flunkies whispered to him that, yes, another "important" guest had just arrived and had thereby paid him homage. One such was Maggy Moal.

Winslow recognized her from photographs. Delane was there by now, splendid in a velvet smoking ("I'm gonna do a menswear line next season, Tony, but keep it to yourself"), and he and Winslow watched as Maggy made her way into the main salon, swinging her cane like a blindman, clearing the dance floor and the drinkers before her. Blatter hustled over and a waiter was summoned. Various drinks were offered. Maggy shook her head firmly. "Bière," she said in a loud voice, and when the waiter hesitated, Blatter, who could not speak French, repeated the order even louder. The waiter went off to fetch the beer, which Blatter mistakenly assumed was some sort of exotic aperitif, and Maggy Moal planted herself firmly in a corner of the room. Winslow could see Blatter pantomime a chair, but Maggy shook her head and chain-lit a fresh cigarette from the damp butt she wore à la Jean Gabin in the corner of her crimsoned mouth.

"She hates to sit down," Delane whispered. "She's forever setting her lap on fire with the ashes."

A few of the younger fashion designers, fags, went up to her and paid their respects. She seemed to take little notice.

"I want to meet her," Winslow said.

Delane nodded. "*Later*," he said, "when she's finished with her stage business. She always spends the first thirty minutes establishing herself as an eccentric. After that you can talk to her and she'll make sense. But not yet."

Delane went off to talk with somebody and Winslow danced with a girl who worked for Saint Laurent and who wore chiffon that moved smoothly over her body the way it does when there is nothing under it to impede the movement. The girl chattered on about who was there while Winslow steered her around. Did she know him, that good-looking boy with the patent-leather hair? The girl peered around Winslow's broad shoulder. She shrugged.

"Zut, it's just Max. He runs the Maison Fayol. He's very smart. Nobody likes him. But smart. He was a whore in St. Germain and then Fayol took him up. They say he was wonderful at the funeral, cried real tears and rattled his beads. The Comédie Française ought to audition the bastard."

"What happens now to the Maison Fayol? Will they close down?" The girl tossed her head. With fashion houses, you never knew.

Dior died twenty years ago and the house was better than ever. Balenciaga died and they shut the doors. Maybe it was because he was a Spaniard. The Spanish, they had an obsession about death. With the Maison Fayol, it was hard to predict. They said he left everything to his kid, a girl. But you could be sure Max would have something to say, however the will read. The music stopped and Winslow thanked the girl. She seemed surprised that he was leaving her. She liked that he was so tall and she would have liked to know him better. And for an American, he spoke good French, not like most of them. She was considering his lack of an accent when a vice-president from Bloomingdale's asked her to dance, and she turned on her vendeuse's smile and moved into his arms. Winslow made his way through the dancers and the waiters and the watchers to Max.

"I read about Monsieur Fayol in New York," he said. "It was very sad, the death of such a man."

Max was cool. He nodded.

"I do some banking for the Maison Fayol's licensees in the States. There everyone says it was you who made the important decisions. That you were the real 'patron.' "

Max smiled. A winning smile. He was less cool now. He asked Winslow's name. Which bank? Ah, yes, he said, a great bank. He had never heard of it but it must be a great bank. He did not admit he had never heard of it. So long as it knew of him, that signified its greatness. Max snapped his fingers and a waiter came with fresh drinks. Max, too, took whisky-Perrier. It was the only civilized drink, was it not? And all these buyers swilling champagne. What did they know?

Winslow agreed. Max must know New York.

Ah, but of course he did. Besides Paris, the *only* city. Max knew it very well. Had he not taken the Fayol collection to New York three times now? To show at Lincoln Center for some charity or other? Of course he knew New York. Elaine's, the Anvil, P. J. Clarke's, the Twenty One Club. They knew him at all those places. Winslow was impressed. There were many Americans, many New Yorkers even, who didn't get into those places. Max smiled. It was the best smile Winslow had seen since Jimmy Carter. He thought to himself, this boy must have done very well selling himself. Winslow admired professionalism of any sort, and despite the fact that this boy was a total shit, he found himself complimenting him. Could he perhaps pass by the

Maison Fayol one day and see the operation? He'd never seen a couture house function. It must be fascinating, especially with Max directing it. Max smiled again. Winslow realized he was wrong. This was better even than Jimmy Carter. Max gave him the number to call and said that he, *personally*, would show him the house. Winslow could barely restrain his joy. They shook hands. Max had a good grip. He must work out. Every morning, Max said. Winslow smiled. "Mens sana in corpore sano." Max looked slightly fuddled. "I'm sorry," he said in French, "my Italian is very . . ." He waved his hands. Winslow smiled this time. He promised to call for that tour. As Max went off, Winslow thought, Bill Bradley would have eaten this kid alive.

Delane grabbed his arm.

"There's our pal from Castel's. Nafredi. The Iranian who attends Catholic mass."

Winslow watched Nafredi handshake his way through the room. He was even better at it than their host, Mr. Blatter. With him was the same girl, the hooker from Mme. Claude's, the one he thought had been at the funeral, in the dark glasses. She was not wearing glasses now, and he was more sober than at Castel's so he could see her more clearly. She had brown hair, very clean and shiny, and green eyes. She was tall for a French girl, perhaps five eight. She moved nicely. No wonder Mme. Claude had her in the stable. She must do very well for the firm.

Willis Blatter had come over to greet Nafredi. Compliments were exchanged, and then, lacking the social graces, Blatter looked about desperately for someone to come and chat with the Iranian and his girl. Expecting this, Winslow was at hand. Blatter made the introductions, getting his name wrong.

"Winslow, not Wilson," Tony said. They shook hands. The girl looked at him briefly, then her eyes drifted. He had not caught her name. Nafredi made up for her disinterest. He was very charming. But of course he knew Henry Rousselot. Who did not in the world of finance? And had not Winslow himself been one of that remarkable team Rohatyn put together, the team that saved New York?

The girl standing by, looking fine but saying nothing, Nafredi and Winslow talked. No, Nafredi said, he did not expect that OPEC would do anything naughty about petroleum prices. Certainly not until the fall, "when it turns cold in Boston and Brussels," he said, making the requisite small jest. He and Winslow, as men of substance will, chatted meaninglessly about great matters, and then, when someone asked to meet Nafredi, Winslow found himself alone with the girl.

"I didn't get your name," he said, knowing what a stale line it was.

She restrained her enthusiasm.

"Anouk," she said.

"Oh? Is that short for something?"

The girl looked bored.

"No," she said. "It is short for nothing."

Pushing her, wanting to know who she was, why she was with Nafredi, why she'd been at the funeral, why a girl like this worked the cribs at Mme. Claude's, and knowing he was sounding very much the mental defective, Winslow asked:

"Your last name?"

The girl laughed. It was not a funny laugh.

"Last names are a bore," she said. She looked toward Nafredi. He was finishing the requisite politesse.

"Please excuse me," Anouk said. "I see Zader wants me."

She left Winslow standing there. He felt as thoroughly put down as he had not been since those dreadful freshmen mixers at Princeton when he was too tall, too skinny, and very much aware of it among all those smooth young women from Goucher and Bryn Mawr in cashmere and kilts.

Desperately, he scanned the room for Delane. The Frenchman was in a group of six or seven women, talking loudly, enjoying himself. Winslow tried to catch his eye. No luck. He saw the vendeuse from Saint Laurent across the room, dancing with a Japanese buyer. He started for her, wanting to talk to anyone and not simply stand there awkwardly, when he heard a woman's voice order him sternly, "Young man. The tall one. Come here."

He turned. Maggy Moal was there, leaning against a handy wall, her cane tapping imperiously against the floor. A cigarette dangled from her mouth and she had a glass of beer in her hand.

"You're too tall to be French," she said. It was a statement. There was little interrogatory in Maggy's vocabulary.

Winslow grinned. He may have been a flop with Nafredi's green-eyed girl but he knew how to handle old women. Not too deferentially. They didn't like being patronized, old women didn't. It reminded them of their years. They preferred the flirtatious give-and-take.

"Givenchy's as tall as I am. And he's French."

The old woman laughed, roughly.

"But you're not a fashion designer. If you were, I'd know you."

"Oh?" he said. "Do you catalogue them?"

"They catalogue themselves."

Winslow grunted. He liked that.

"You're right," he said. "I'm not French. I'm a Japanese buyer."

She tossed her cigarette aside; dove into her purse for another. Winslow lighted it.

"You know, cigarettes are bad for your health," he said.

Maggy Moal laughed, a dry, raucous laugh.

"I know. I may never see ninety," she said.

He decided it was time to ask questions. Therefore, he began with a statement.

"You were at Fayol's funeral."

She narrowed her eyes, narrow already under the brim of her flat, uncompromising straw sailor.

"But of course. We are . . . were . . . members of the same club. It was my duty to be there. To mourn."

"And did you?"

She smiled. "No, I failed in my duty. They may give me ten demerits. But you, why are you in Paris, a 'Japanese buyer'?"

It was time to learn something. "I'm educating myself. We Japanese may go into the perfume business."

She looked at him shrewdly as the ash on her cigarette grew to impressive length.

"Even alive, Fayol couldn't have told you much."

"Oh?"

"Patou, Lanvin, old Chanel before she died. *They knew.*" She paused. "*I* know."

Winslow nodded.

"I know you do. Paul Delane told me you were the one to see."

The ash fell straight down, skimming her flat chest.

"Get me another beer and then you can go off and rub against those young girls or whatever it is men do these days. Then come see me tomorrow, if you really want to ask questions. I lunch on clear days in the garden of the Plaza Athénée. One o'clock."

A waiter went by and Winslow sent him for the beer. As they waited, Winslow said, "You didn't think much of Fayol."

"A pansy. And like all of them a man of immense vulnerability. But he had taste, at least. An aging pansy. And during the war, ah, a dubious quantity at best." The beer came and she swallowed half of it.

"Light another cigarette, will you. Well, Fayol, what does one say of the dead? Even pederasts like that? And a competitor as well? Though he had a style. But that wife of his . . ."

"I met her," Winslow said.

"Hah!" Maggy Moal exploded. "That one. No wonder he chased boys. That one. Burning incense and telling her beads and carrying on. She's got that house of hers full of pilgrims and necromancers and fakirs whose hands bleed on Fridays. She's got everything there but a Rasputin. And can you imagine, on the Avenue Foch? It used to be the best address in Paris."

Just then the Iranian, Nafredi, danced past with Anouk. On a hunch, Winslow asked Maggy who the girl was. The old lady squinted myopically and said no, she didn't recognize her.

"Do you . . . ah, wear glasses?"

"What piggishness is this?" the old lady demanded. "Young men putting questions of a personal nature to their elders! No wonder the Americans are in decline. No wonder . . ."

Winslow interrupted her. "I'm sorry," he said. "It's simply, I was told you sat in the middle of the cobweb. That you knew everyone in Paris and what they were. . . ."

"Assez," she ordered, obviously pleased. "Stand in front of me."

Winslow moved and Maggy dove into her purse, spilling a couple of packs of cigarettes and a lipstick. She found her glasses and furtively slipped them on.

"Which girl?"

Winslow pointed Anouk out. The old lady looked and nodded. She removed the glasses.

"Well? What do you want to know about her?"

"Her name. Who she is. She was at the funeral too, I understand."

Maggy Moal laughed, dryly.

"I should hope so," she said. "She's Fayol's naughty little girl, Anne."

Maggy Moal cackled on, but Winslow only half listened. His eyes were on the girl, on Fayol's daughter, a tall green-eyed beauty who was now worth $85 million, perhaps more, and who sold her body by the night, by the hour, for a few hundred francs. He watched the way she moved, holding tight to Nafredi, looking up at him with that lovely, desirable face. Suddenly Winslow's instincts stiffened. Henry Rousselot had warned of a rival claimant to the Fayol empire. Could it be the Iranians? Could this unlikely pairing of Fayol's daughter and the Shah's agent in Paris be business instead of sex? He was chewing away on that bone of an idea when Nafredi and the girl broke off in the middle of a dance and started for the door.

"This fellow Blatter," Maggy Moal was saying, "a vulgarian who breaks wind in the salon and then waves a checkbook to sweeten the air. No style, no class, a man who . . ."

"Excuse me," Winslow said abruptly, "but if we could continue this at lunch."

Maggy, instead of being offended, snorted her gravelly laugh. "Alors, you must have caught an eye. Ah, well, if anyone understands men, I do. A demain, à une heure."

He kissed her bony hand, impatient as she gripped his arm, and then finally was set free. He paced up and down the driveway as a boy was sent to fetch his rented car. There was no sign of Nafredi and Anouk Fayol. Damn, he thought, the girl was the *one* person he had to talk to, and now she was slipping away. As the car came up someone behind him said:

"Can you give me a lift back into town?"

Winslow wheeled. It was a girl he'd seen at the party.

"Sure," he said brusquely. "But get in. I'm in a hurry."

The girl got in without waiting to be helped, and Winslow drove off, the wheels spinning in the gravel. Damn, he thought, he didn't even know what kind of car the Iranian was driving. He pulled into one of the Bois' winding roads and headed toward town. There was very little traffic. He looked vainly for taillights ahead.

"Shit," he said, half aloud, realizing Maggy's fond farewell and now his passenger had caused him to lose Nafredi.

"Whatever you say," the girl said.

Winslow grunted. "Sorry. I was trying to catch up with someone."

He glanced to his right. The girl had put her head back and her long hair streamed over the back of the seat. She had nice legs.

"You in the fashion business?" he said, once again scanning the road ahead.

"Sort of," she said in American. "I work for *Vogue*."

"My name is Winslow, Anthony . . ."

"I know," she said. "I'm Marianna Troy."

"How did you know who I am?"

She laughed. "Listen, a party like that one. I'm *supposed* to know everybody. And I usually do. When I don't, I ask. Nafredi told me. I'd seen you two talking."

"Smooth type," Winslow said. "Friend of yours?"

She shrugged. "I haven't really been fond of any Persian since Cyrus the Great. And the Greeks beat the shit out of him."

Winslow laughed and started to say something when a car roared up on them from behind and he had to twist the wheel violently to the right. The right front wheel hit the shoulder and bounced, and the girl cursed and he fought to bring the car back onto the road. He had it under control now and he pulled over and got out. It had been close. His hands were wet. There didn't seem to be any damage, just some mud on the tire and the right front fender, a few stalks of weed stuck in the bumper. The Bois was very quiet, except for a few birds. There was no other traffic.

"Jesus," he said. "Their driving doesn't improve, does it?"

The girl looked at him.

"You did fine, Winslow. Now, if you're not too shook, could we get on to Passy? I've got to work tomorrow."

He got in and they drove through the Bois and out into Auteuil and across the Avenue Mozart to the rue de Boulainvilliers, where she lived. She shook his hand briskly, pressed the door release, and ran inside. He watched her go.

MAGGY MOAL

Zader Nafredi was sweating. Being an Oxford man, he considered it quite good form to sweat when playing squash, skiing in the spring, or making love. What was *not* good form was sweating under tension. As he was doing on the telephone.

"We had the impression, Nafredi," his caller was saying, "that you had an understanding with Fayol. Even after his unfortunate death you assured us the agreement would stand up. Now I am informed Rousselot & Partners have a man in Paris asking questions and poking into files and promising all variety of nastiness."

Nafredi nodded into the phone, unconsciously, as he did whenever his chief in Teheran chivied him in this manner.

"So if we have a binding agreement, why does Mr. Henry Rousselot waste his money and the time of one of his bright young men to fish among the late Fayol's undoubtedly messy files? I shall answer my own question, Nafredi. He does so, does Monsieur Rousselot, because he suspects, as I myself am beginning to suspect, that our agreement with the tragically departed Fayol is *not* as ironclad as once you indicated."

Nafredi nodded again, and patted his glistening forehead with a gorgeous square of silk.

"May I suggest, my dear Nafredi, that it would be measurably in your interest to determine a) Do we or do we not have a

49

binding agreement with the deceased? and b) Whom does this Rousselot fellow represent and do *they* have a valid claim?"

There was more of this. Nafredi disliked being abused at any hour. This early in the morning (it was just nine) such abuse was nearly intolerable. But he took it because he had no choice. Being permitted at last to comment, Nafredi said (lied) that he was already well advanced in his investigation of Rousselot's man, that he had cleverly arranged to put himself alongside the American just last evening (what a stroke of luck, he admitted to himself). In addition, he had an agent in his employ within the Maison Fayol. And, of course, he was "very close" to the heiress herself and was making great progress. As for just how binding Teheran's claim might be, well, the French were a smarmy lot but he was confident the deal would hold.

"It had better, Nafredi. We want the Maison Fayol and we want it without spending ten years in courts of law to get it."

As the perspiring Nafredi gratefully put down the telephone, the French government man assigned to wiretap his line punched a button on the tape machine, ejected a cassette, and whistled for a boy to run it into the Economic Intelligence Section of the Ministry. Who the devil cared whether the Iranians and the Americans were squabbling over some couture house? But the government man was to record all substantive conversations and to forward them to the department with jurisdiction. Being a government man, he did what he was told. "Smarmy." That was a word he'd not heard before. He must look it up in his dictionary.

Anthony Winslow slept late. At ten he called down for orange juice and café complet. The boy picked up the papers at the door to the room and brought them inside, and Winslow got back into bed to read and breakfast. He had a slight ache over his left eye which could be sinus or too many drinks the night before. Probably it was the drinks. They would also explain—at least in fairness he thought they might—the near miss on the road through the Bois. With that girl, the American from *Vogue*.

Marianna. He was damned if he could remember her last name. It was something short, like "Ford," but it wasn't Ford. He sipped his orange juice, marveling that it was the real stuff, pits and pulp and all, when he came fully awake. He'd let the Fayol girl slip away last night and without a clue of how to contact her again. He snatched up the phone and asked the hotel operator to try to get a number for Anouk Fayol or Anne Fayol. No listing, sorry. Damn! He phoned the Maison Fayol. Monsieur Max wasn't in yet and only he might have such information. There was the one o'clock lunch date with Maggy Moal. He jotted down some questions to ask her. About Fayol, about perfume, about Grasse. About "Paris One." Then he phoned Paul Delane.

"I am still asleep, barbarian, and not alone." It wasn't even noon, for God's sake, Delane reminded Winslow. "This isn't Boston, you know." He promised to call back after lunch.

It was again warm, and Winslow swung the French doors open wide while he finished the croissant and coffee and lighted the first cigar of the morning. Across the rue François Premier the windows were also open, the curtains moving languidly in the breeze, but he couldn't see his neighbor. He got up and wandered around the bedroom, already piled with newspapers, and drifted into the shower. As the water hit his head he remembered, "Troy!"

Marianna Troy got to the office at ten. But it had been a struggle. Laurence was a sweet boy and he had that wonderful body and she was sure he was in love with her . . . but, dammit, she had got to stop him from hanging around that way. Like last night, after Winslow had dropped her, and all she really wanted to do was wash her hair and get some sleep, there was Laurence waiting, practically on the damn doorstep; and it was three o'clock before she could get him to get up and go home and let her sleep. She resolved, not for the first time, to stop seeing him and begin to do something about her career, to say nothing of her energy levels.

Marianna Troy was twenty-three years old, and two years

earlier had won the same *Vogue* essay contest Jacqueline Bouvier
had won in 1951. The prize was six months' employment in the
Paris office of *Vogue* magazine in the Place du Palais Bourbon.
She did the six months, running for coffee, sobering up the models, toting gear for the photographers, chain-smoking Gitanes,
brushing off any number of American college boys on the loose
in Paris, and sleeping with several Frenchmen, one Italian with a
minor title, and the sweetest English boy from Cambridge. When
the six months were up she went home to Connecticut, spent
three weeks assuring her mother and father that Paris was *the*
most incredibly prim and decorous place imaginable, and talked
the editor of *Vogue* into hiring her on a full-time basis as the
junior girl in the Paris office. Now it was seventeen months later
and she considered herself the *senior* junior girl in the Paris
bureau.

The phone rang.

"Miss Troy, please."

"This is she."

"Tony Winslow. I didn't think you'd answer your own phone."

"Both my secretaries are running errands. May I help you?"

"Yes," Winslow said.

"Good."

"Dinner tonight?"

Tonight was the one night she was absolutely going to sleep.

"Sure," she said.

Just before one o'clock Winslow strolled into the lobby of the
Hôtel Plaza Athénée and through and into the garden. He started
to ask the headwaiter and then he saw Maggy Moal. He went
over to the table. Sitting with her under the beach umbrella was a
distinguished-looking man in his middle years.

"You know the 'King'?" Maggy said.

"No. A pleasure."

"I am so pleased," the "King" said.

Winslow shook hands and sat down.

"He's not really a 'king,'" Maggy explained. "Only a pre-
tender. But if certain regimes are overthrown, and certain war-

ring factions combine, and if the Russians don't march in and
shoot everybody, well, he could once again have a throne."

"It's not very likely, Monsieur Winslow," the "King" said.

"One can always hope," said Maggy. "In the meantime he
does public relations. I'm one of his—what d'you call it?—
accounts."

"Oh?" said Winslow, hoping to sound as if he were a man who
deeply respected both kings and PR men.

"I give parties for her," the "King" said matter-of-factly.

"Damn good parties," Maggy interjected. "Not like that visiting trade-delegation affair Blatter imposed on us last night. None
of that trash."

The "King" got up. He kissed Maggy's hand and made a court-
ier's bow toward Winslow.

"Have to be off," he said. It was well done. He gave the effect
of announcing he'd summoned a session of the privy council.

When royalty had departed they ordered drinks. Maggy
wanted vodka, "the good Polish mark you keep in the cellar and
not that swill you peddle the tourists," she ordered.

"No beer this time?" Winslow asked, smiling.

"Ah, well, you know, mon vieux, one is expected to create a
scandal at parties. I play my role. Even for fools like Blatter."
She looked at Winslow. "You were gracious with the 'King.'
Showed good manners. The poor fellow. Hopeless."

"I suppose he's grateful to have a job."

"Of course. He's penniless. *France* should have a king. The
country hasn't been the same since the monarchy. Those Socialists before the fourteen-eighteen war, then the Jews during the
thirties, then that brigand de Gaulle. Pompidou was a banker.
An employee of the Rothschilds'. But he had taste. This fellow,
Giscard . . . ah, well, let's not talk about it. I become easily
depressed."

The drinks came and they ordered lunch.

"What's to happen to the Maison Fayol now?" he asked.

"Oh, they'll hire some young genius of a pederast and he'll
work from the patterns Fayol left behind for a few seasons and

gradually it will all fade away. Sooner, if the daughter takes a hand. Or the widow. That one! A nun without a wimple."

"There's talk Fayol was thinking of selling out."

Maggy's face tightened. "Ah? Is there? And to whom?"

Winslow decided to start pressing his inquiries. All this charming chat was pleasant, it was polite, and it was getting him nowhere.

"Perhaps the Iranians. That fellow Nafredi . . ."

Her eyes widened.

"France has become so decadent, it would be a good thing if the Persians bought the whole place. But what do I know? The Shah, he has some style. Not that basketball player he married. Perhaps he'll buy Fayol as a trinket for the girl. Every woman, even a schoolgirl like that one, wants to own a couture house."

"But he wouldn't buy it as an investment? A serious purchase?"

"No, no, of course not. No one makes money on couture. Not even me."

"The perfume? There's money in that."

Maggy smiled, shrewdly. "Last night you wanted to know about perfume as well. You Americans, very single-minded."

The ash from her cigarette fell into her lap and she brushed it away, knocking over her cane at the same time. "Merde," she said. Winslow picked up the cane and then lighted her fresh cigarette. He said nothing. Maggy laughed, a guttural laugh from deep inside her.

"Well, then, what do you want to know?"

"How much would the House of Fayol, including its perfume interests, be worth?"

She shrugged. "I don't know. Eighty million francs, a hundred. Not more."

"Did Fayol plan to launch a new scent? A label called 'Paris One'?"

She shook her head. "You can't keep a marketing secret like that. My man in Grasse would have heard. I would have heard. Monsieur Barbas at Jean Patou would have heard. No, it's impossible."

"What *do* you hear from Grasse?"

She smiled, coyly. "That the roses of May (les roses de mai) are nearly in bloom."

Winslow leaned forward.

"Tell me about the roses," he said.

Two hours later Maggy Moal was still talking, the lunch plates had been cleared, and Winslow, who recognized a good security analyst's briefing when he heard one, had a sheaf of notes and a crudely effective understanding of how a Paris couture house made its money. The couture collections, shown twice a year, in January and July, were losing propositions. *Always*, they lost money! Maggy explained. But they generated publicity (How else could you get your merchandise on the cover of *Vogue*?) in the magazines, in the newspapers, on television. American stores and Seventh Avenue manufacturers, the cutters, bought these originals at prices as high as eight thousand dollars for a single dress, buying them not to resell but to copy in cheaper fabric, with machine techniques, by the thousands, the hundreds of thousands. Oh, surely, there was still a handful of rich, idle women who would buy couture originals and were willing to stand for hours being fitted. But that was marginal income, and dying off fast as the handworkers of the ateliers demanded higher wages or went off to work in the electronics trade, putting transistors into radios ("or whatever unfathomable nonsense they're up to").

No, the couture made no money. In fact, Maggy admitted, her couture collection last January showed a net loss of a million francs. Two hundred thousand dollars! But one might think of money spent on the couture line as the cost of running a fashion laboratory. For out of the couture collection came the very profitable ready-to-wear line, the prêt-à-porter group of assembly-line clothes adapted from the look of the couture but designed and manufactured for mass sale in boutiques and the great department stores. It was there, in ready-to-wear, that a couturier began to make money. Then there were the licenses.

"Take Monsieur Cardin," Maggy said, snarling her disapproval. "Cardin has sold the rights to his brand name to an

American firm that makes sheets and pillowcases, to a company that makes fancy chocolates, to a cutter of hundred-franc neckties. Monsieur Givenchy put his name on the interior design of an American automobile. Monsieur Saint Laurent's name is on bath towels, and Dior, well, Dior puts its brand on virtually everything. Stockings, infants' wear, shoes, jewelry, raincoats. There's no end to it." In some instances, Maggy explained, the couturier actually supplied design ideas, functioned as a creative consultant. In others, well, he simply peddled his name to the highest bidder.

"And the perfume?" Winslow prodded.

"Voilà," Maggy announced, *there* was the big money.

Saks Fifth Avenue or Julius Garfinckel or whoever would sell it at thirty-five to sixty dollars an ounce or more. The retail price the American consumer paid was twice or slightly more than the store had paid the perfume maker, in other words, a markup of 100 percent. So Maggy Moal would get at least twenty-five dollars on every one-ounce bottle of perfume her company sold to a retail store. Her costs? Modest, to say the least: just over two fifty for the fancy bottle and the elegant pearl-gray box, neatly embossed; eighty cents for shipping; six fifty for overhead; another three dollars for advertising; and as for the perfume itself, the stuff in the bottles, "counting everything, the flowers, the extraction of the essential oils, the fixatives and other ingredients, even the purity tests, and accounting for spillage and evaporation, four seventy-five!" Under eighteen dollars for the whole business, and she cleared seven or eight on every ounce. There was generous profit margin in the trade, Maggy admitted, before sourly pointing out that some of her competitors spent more than she on advertising, hiring to plug their wares "actresses and the like, such as Madame Deneuve, who is on the payroll of Chanel, and Miss (Mees) Hutton for Revlon."

Going over his notes later, Winslow wondered whether he might not be in the wrong business.

MARIANNA

Marianna Troy had told Winslow she'd meet him for dinner, but he told her no, he'd come by her apartment. It was just before nine and he was in a taxi, having turned in the rented car, which was more trouble than it was worth. He felt the same way about the afternoon. He'd gone to see Max, the director of the Maison Fayol; and except for a tour of the establishment and a good deal of charm, he'd gotten very little. Maggy Moal had given him a good start over lunch, a "tour d'horizon" of the perfume business, and a letter to her man at Grasse ("a stupid fellow but loyal, and very knowledgeable on the trade"). And she'd told some marvelously scandalous stories about Fayol and Max.

"Le pauvre Max was drafted into the army when it was time for him to serve, and so Fayol carried on terribly. His right arm, his key assistant, his fragile 'little monk' . . . the usual thing. But when Max finally had to go, they shipped him to North Africa and Fayol cut and sewed a uniform for him. Surely Max was the only private soldier in the armée française wearing a couture uniform. Quel scandale. Then another time Max caught Fayol sneaking off with some young girl, a painter I think she was, an exquisite creature. Fayol had this weakness. He could never say 'no' to anybody, whatever the sex, and certainly never to himself. So off he went, and Max stamped his little foot and wept and had to be restrained physically from going over to Avenue Foch, to

57

Hélène, the wife, to complain about her husband's unfaithful-
ness."

With Winslow, Max had been smooth.

The couture house of Jacques Fayol, like so many couture
houses in Paris, looks more like an apartment house than a fashion laboratory. It stands catty-cornered to an old church on the
rue Cambon near the rue de Rivoli in the first arrondissement, the
city's central district, an area pleasantly mélangée between great
hotels, luxury apartments, office buildings, shops, and restaurants. Winslow walked up from the Plaza Athénée along the
Champs Élysées and then across the Place de la Concorde, dodg-
ing the traffic and enjoying the warm April sun. There was no
doorman at the Maison Fayol, no display windows, only a polished brass plaque with the single word FAYOL. He went in
through a dark archway and into a marble stairwell where a tiny,
glass-fronted elevator perched within the coils of the winding
stairs. No receptionist, no signs. Inside the elevator the floors
were indicated, again in brass. The quatrième étage, the fourth
floor, was marked "Direction." Winslow pushed four.

"Let me show you through the place," Max said. Merchant
bankers are always being "shown through the place" just before
someone asks for a secured loan or a longer line of credit. Winslow tolerated the cutting rooms, the ateliers, the fur workroom,
the beading and appliqué department, the fabric room, the sample workroom, the design studio, and the rest. He drew the line at
the employee cafeteria and the press office. Only at the mannequins' cabine did he perk up. There were six or seven girls dressing for the daily midafternoon show for private clients. They
were all tall, all quite pretty, all in their underwear. Max made
several offhand introductions to a couple of French girls, the
exotic black and the usual broad-shouldered Swede. Then he
came to a girl with black hair and a face that suggested the
crossbreeding of an Italian madonna and a Mongol raider.

"This is Soroya," Max said. "She's our first Iranian. No rela-
tion to the former empress, of course, but regard those eyes, the
cheekbones." He spoke as if the girl weren't there. She smiled

vacantly. "Mr. Winslow is from New York. He is a banker." The girl's smile became less vacant.

"I know several bankers in Teheran," she said. She mentioned two names.

"I know the firm," Winslow said. "But I've not had the pleasure."

They chatted and then they went back to Max's office. A portrait of Jacques Fayol smiled down on them from the wall. A liveried page, perhaps twelve, with a beautiful face and blond bangs, brought them cups of impressive coffee. Winslow said some complimentary things. Max smiled, with those smashing teeth.

"I keep an apartment here—nothing to speak of, just a bedroom and bath. I love the feel of this great old house at night. All this beauty, these riches, about me, and only the garde-porte and myself to savor them." He was very pleased with himself. Winslow decided to break the spell.

"I'm sorry I never met Monsieur Fayol," Winslow began.

Max dabbed at his eye with a bit of linen.

"A genius. The couture suffered a loss. Irreplaceable. And I, I lost a friend, a guide, a counselor, an inspiration." He looked up at the portrait of the late Fayol, with respect.

"And his death, it was totally unexpected?"

Max was less reverent.

"The man ate too much, of course. And wine. Oh, the wine. And never to bed before dawn. Parties, girls." He paused. "The occasional young man. Enormous appetites. A titan among the pygmies."

"Maggy Moal said his wartime experiences were, well, dubious."

Max slammed a hand delicately on the escritoire.

"That old bitch! Jealousy. Totally passés, her clothes. The perfumes, well, they sell."

"And your perfumes? What are they, numbers what? 'One,' for example, is there a 'Paris One'?"

Max did not seem to react. No, he said, there was no "number one." He ran down the others in the stable, gave Winslow a brief appreciation of their market position. The reference to a "Paris One" had elicited no discernible pause. Having entertained the small talk, he got to the point: What precisely did Rousselot & Partners want to know?

Winslow double-talked for ten minutes about certain unnamed American retail stores and manufacturers-under-license who were concerned about the future of the house of Fayol following the founder's regrettable death. Naturally, they wanted to be assured that Fayol would continue in business and they were curious as to what directions, if any, the dead man had left behind. New products, new pricing structure, that sort of thing. Would Max run the show? Or would the heirs come in?

Max made a good show of being assured. Of course the policies of the house would remain the same, new projects were always being explored, he valued highly the various commercial arrangements with America, and surely he would remain as the "patron." The heirs would want it that way, he was certain. Winslow didn't think he sounded all that certain. They agreed to dine one evening. Max would delight in playing host, organizing a small party, perhaps, at some pleasant spot on the Ile. Winslow said that would be very nice.

"Where are you planning to go this evening?" Max asked. Winslow said he had a dinner date but hadn't yet decided. "You must try L'Orangerie," Max said. "You'll need a reservation. I'll have my secretary call." Winslow told him the time and the men shook hands. "Jacques Fayol was my patron saint," Max said piously. "It shall be my solemn task to keep his great house number one."

As if in afterthought, Winslow asked how he could get in touch with Fayol's daughter. There was some business the bank wanted to discuss. Max shook his head. The girl was a bit, you know, flighty. He had no idea where she lived. "You might ask the mother," he suggested. Winslow, playing the rustic, said that was a splendid idea. Knowing it was not.

Marianna Troy lived on the second floor of a hundred-year-old apartment building two thirds of the way up the hill of the rue de Boulainvilliers. There was a fine-looking meat shop, a seedy hardware store, a splendid bakery, and a chocolatier on the ground floor. She showed Winslow through the apartment; huge rooms, high ceilings, and marble fireplaces. "It's grand right now," she said, "but it was hell staying warm last winter. If I didn't have a date I'd get right into bed with my coat on when I came home and eat dinner off a tray and worry about falling asleep. I'd read somewhere that was how you froze to death."

While she finished her hair, Winslow roamed around the big living room. Marianna had a desk covered with papers and old copies of *Vogue* and the French fashion magazines. There was something in the old upright Underwood. It was the Sunday crossword puzzle from the Paris *Herald-Tribune,* the same one that runs in *The New York Times.* Winslow was impressed. He had never seen anyone do a crossword in a typewriter before. There seemed to be no x-ing out, and what he could see of the puzzle was completed. He had an idea this girl, a journalist in and out of couture houses all day, partying with designers and their hangers-on at night, might be useful. She came out of the depths of the apartment, looking very good, smiling but cool, and he was glad he had called her. She might turn out *damned* useful. And not only on l'affaire Fayol.

At L'Orangerie, Max's call had gotten them one of the good tables, along the wall on the left. There were people waiting, but he and Marianna got their table right away. Her French was very good; slangy, well accented, suggesting the aristocratic 16th arrondissement drawl. He asked her about it.

"Well, I just always studied it. All through school, then at Yale, and I had my junior year here with a French family just up the street at La Muette. Then *Vogue* sent me over as a go-for after I won some sort of essay prize. And I've been here almost two years now. What about you?"

Winslow talked about himself, something he usually avoided. "My mother was French, a minor actress in Paris in the thirties when my old man met her. She died a couple of years ago. My father hibernates up in Rhode Island, clipping coupons and reading *The Wall Street Journal* and grumbling about the Democrats and me. Marrying my mother was about the only instinctive thing he ever did. He fell in love, and he was kind of shocked to realize it. He's been trying to live it down for thirty years."

"My mother and father are terrific. I'd hate to have a parent I didn't like."

"Oh, I guess I like him," Winslow admitted. "It's that sometimes I find some of him in me, characteristics I don't especially admire: coldness; a calculating way of looking at people. I suppose I'm reacting against things I don't like about myself when I criticize him."

The girl was listening carefully, so Winslow sheered away from self-analysis and turned flippant.

"We get along in a formal sort of way: he calls me 'Anthony' and I call him 'sir.' We just don't agree on much. When my mother was alive she maintained a sort of uneasy truce. She'd listen to us nattering for just so long and then she'd explode in wonderful backstage French idiom. I went in the Marines to devil my father and then got into banking just to keep the peace. But I realized I really *liked* it, which surprised hell out of me. I *liked* working with money, liked the leverage, and I had the right instincts. Psychiatrists and clergymen and doctors are always coping with infinities. There are no precise answers. But banking is a finite world. No matter how enormous the problems, the dreams, the plans, no matter how complex, there are *always* solutions. When my mother died, New York was going into the hole, so I dropped out and went to work with a guy called Rohatyn who was trying to keep it functioning. My father thought I was a fool." He paused. "All I got out of it were two of the best, toughest years of my life and a tremendous offer from a fine old merchant bank. So, once again, I think my old man was wrong. And he's still absolutely certain I was."

He paused, "Isn't this boring you?"

"Not at all," she said.

The food came and they got into it. The place was crowded, noisy; but pleasantly, the clientele attractive.

"You come here much?"

She shook her head. "It's a bit pricey for the men I usually see. Sometimes. A visiting American or some dirty old Frenchman with the usual motives. It's, I don't know, a bit staged."

"Max suggested it."

"He would."

"Oh?"

"Jacques Fayol was one of the big gourmets. 'Gourmands' may have been more like it. Max usually tagged along. A place like this, they'd make a fuss over Fayol. He'd spend a couple of thousand francs here in an evening. You know, a Latour '61 out of the cellar, the oldest brandy, gobbets of caviar to start. I had dinner with them once, a whole bunch of us from *Vogue*. Fayol stood us a meal and then was outraged two months later when we put a Saint Laurent dress on the cover instead."

"You like fashion?"

She shrugged. "I don't like or dislike it. I'm not a fanatic. I'm easy to fit, I like nice things, but I could never get caught up in that hysteria." She mimicked nicely, "Oh, darling, it's divine. Glorious. Perfection." Marianna shook her head. "I'm a reporter, really. I look at the clothes and take notes and I ask questions. Surprising how much you can learn simply by asking a designer how he achieved a certain effect and why."

Winslow decided he had an opening.

"I've been asking questions too. Trouble is, I don't understand all the answers."

"Maybe you ask the wrong questions."

The waiter cleared the plates and they ordered the Brie and soda crackers to finish off the last of the wine.

"How do I learn the right ones?" he asked.

She laughed. "You take bright young junior editors from *Vogue* to dinner in expensive restaurants and ply us with wine and cheese and soufflés and we tell you everything you want to know. Even if it isn't true."

"Miss Troy," he said, "you are on the payroll as of now. Three soufflés a week and all the Brie you can eat."

There were some people at the next table who seemed to be

half listening to their conversation, and so over the coffee Winslow suggested they go somewhere else to talk. "How about Régine's?"

"You have an exotic notion of where people go to talk in Paris. At Régine's you can't hear anything but the music. Come on, I'll take you to a place. We can have a brandy and it'll be quiet."

The place was Les Nuages, in an alleyway just around the corner from St.-Germain. It was smoky and nice. They got a table. Young men in turtlenecks and pretty girls in jeans or suede skirts sat talking, drinking, laughing. There was no music. "This is a great hangout for young journalists from *L'Express*. Some of the left-wing writers. The young ones. Not Sartre or that crowd. They're much too grand for a dive like this." They ordered brandy, and Winslow gave the girl an edited version of his assignment.

". . . so, naturally, as bankers for several American companies that do business with Fayol, we want to know what the hell's going to happen. Can a guy like Max really keep the house operating?"

"Don't underestimate Max," she said seriously. "Fayol surrounded himself with good-looking boys like Max. Called them his 'little monks.' They were all talented, some of them very bright. And it was competitive as hell. For Max to emerge on top, he had to be pretty good, pretty tough."

"Then it wasn't just sex?"

"Oh, sure," she said, "that must have been part of it. A big part. Old Fayol wasn't your usual fashion pederast. He'd go through periods, just girls. He'd devour them by the score. I suppose it was like that when he married Hélène. I've seen pictures of her. Incredibly beautiful in those days. Then, he'd go into one of his 'boy' periods. Max was recruited during one of those times. He'd been a male hooker; did some modeling; tried to get into the movies. A tough guy for all he's gay."

"How old are you?"

"Twenty-three. Why?"

"They teach you all this at Yale?"

She laughed. "At boarding school. New Haven was really very conventional."

"I never doubted it." He smiled. "Do you know his daughter, Anne?"

"Sure, Anouk. Her pet name. She was at that silly party Blatter gave. Tall girl, dark hair. Supposed to look a bit like me. She sleeps around, sniffs coke, hates her mother. The usual happy, well-adjusted young Parisienne."

"You're not cynical?"

"Me? A cynic at twenty-three? Just say I'm a bit skeptical. I question people's motives."

"Mine?"

She looked at his face. "Yes," she said slowly, "but I'm not terribly anxious about it."

They got a cab and went back to her apartment and she poured another brandy for him. "Not for me. Not while I'm still questioning motives. And as long as I have to work tomorrow."

"It's Saturday."

She knew, but there was a photo session. During the prêt-à-porter showings they couldn't get the clothes out of the couture houses to shoot during the week. The buyers were trying them on. You had to take the pictures over the weekend, she said. Winslow finished his drink. She'd put some music on, Leo Ferre songs. They sounded good. He took her arms with his hands. She raised her head and kissed him. He could feel her breasts through the man's shirt she wore. He reached the top button and opened it. He felt her breast. She leaned against him.

"Is this part of the employment contract?" she asked in a whisper.

"Oh, yes," he said. "Standard part of the deal."

Her shirt was open to her waist. Winslow stepped back and looked at her. She was very lean. She pulled the shirt out of her skirt and let it drop to the floor. She had very nice breasts, not large, but firm. Her nipples were erect. She ran a slender hand through her long hair.

"I don't know why," she said, "but I'm embarrassed. I'm not usually embarrassed."

"I'm sorry."

"No," she said. "Don't be. I'm not sorry. I do this sort of thing occasionally. Well, maybe more than occasionally. But it's just part of being an American girl on the loose in Paris. It doesn't really mean anything. With you, I don't know. I feel uptight."

He smiled. Then he bent down and picked up her shirt and draped it around her shoulders.

"Of course you feel uptight. You're still questioning my motives. Maybe tomorrow you can question them again. And maybe you won't be uptight."

She frowned.

"Look, you can stay. I mean, we can . . ."

He shook his head.

"Kiss me good-night. I don't want to hustle you."

"No," she said. "Don't hustle me." She said it quietly.

Winslow hailed a cruising cab at the corner of Avenue Mozart and told him the hotel. It was funny, he thought, the way they'd gone to the verge and then backed away. The girl wasn't a tease, he was sure of that. But she'd pulled back. And in a way, he was glad she had. Not that he wouldn't have enjoyed making love to her. He could see her body, bare to the waist. He wondered what her legs were like. You couldn't tell with the mid-calf skirt she wore. Hell, he told himself, she's got *great* legs. He remembered them from the car. Everything else was right, why shouldn't they be?

There was a message: "Telephonez à M. Delane."

He called. The designer was asleep. He sounded groggy but intent.

"I found out something. Maybe it's nothing. Tomorrow, we go to the Stade Colombes, watch the rugby international. It'll be a good match. And we can talk." They agreed to meet for lunch at a restaurant on the rue de Longchamp. Delane would have his car. "I was afraid of that," Winslow said, but Paul was too sleepy to riposte.

Winslow turned out the light and undressed. It was another warm night, and he opened the shutters. The apartment across the street was dark. He stood there for a moment smoking a last cigarillo and thinking how fortunate it was Marianna Troy knew Anouk Fayol. If he couldn't track down Anouk any other way, he could use Marianna. Then, annoyed with himself for this tendency to "use" people, especially someone like this Marianna that he liked, he switched back to thinking about how she looked and about things they might be doing together. He stared out into the night. He did not see the black Citroën parked in the alley between the hotel and the RTL building. And if he had, he would have assumed it was simply parked there for the night.

THE STADIUM

With the possible exception of polo, international rugby is the most exclusive of all the great team games. Only five European countries play world class rugby, and except for France, they are all from the British Isles. And when one of these "foreign" teams comes to Paris, university-educated Frenchmen flock to the Stade Colombes as cripples to Lourdes.

Delane parked his Porsche about a mile from the stadium, paying an enterprising householder a few francs to let him park on the lawn, and he and Winslow walked through the stucco town of Colombes with its dozens of cafés. The afternoon was warm and the café doors open and they could hear accordions playing. Outside the stadium, men lined up for a last piss against the concrete wall. French sports arenas are not noted for their sanitary facilities.

The two men had eaten at Jamin, the horse-players' restaurant, drinking Bordeaux and eating the eggs and truffles and talking only of the match and not of Fayol or of their telephone conversation of the night before. The English were in town. Delane said it would be a good match. Whichever team won today would win the Tournoi des Cinq Nations. It was always good when the French played the English. "We've never really forgotten Agincourt, you know," Delane said.

They had pretty good seats, halfway up in the grandstand.

Some Englishmen ran out on the field before the match, waving signs and shouting "For England and Saint George!" The French whistled derisively and then gave a roar when some French kids ran around the green turf carrying cardboard roosters. The English players wore white shirts with little roses embroidered on the chest. They were big, blond boys with powerful legs. The French, in blue, were darker, faster. When they moved the ball the crowd swayed, singing "Allez la France, Allez." The French passing, even among the more ponderous forwards, was intricate. The English dug in and held. One boy came out of a scrum with blood running down his face. The referee whistled a halt and the English trainer ran a sponge over the cut and the match went on.

"I may have something for you," Delane said in a normal conversational tone under the noise of the crowd. "About perfume." Winslow nodded and leaned slightly closer to Delane, his eyes still on the field.

"Yesterday was the weekly meeting of the Chambre Syndicale de la couture," Delane explained. "All the couture houses get together to discuss matters of common interest: labor difficulties, taxes, foreign duties, that sort of thing. Nothing about fashion itself, you understand, just the commercial aspects. Anyway, at yesterday's meeting there was a bit of talk about Grasse, where the essential oils come from."

"What sort of talk?" Winslow asked, his cigar bobbing in his mouth.

Delane lifted his hands. "Well, it began innocently enough. The usual complaints about price, some talk of labor unrest, rising costs. The usual chat. Cardin and Givenchy were represented. Their managers did most of the talking. But since they are always complaining, I took no notice. Perhaps it was nothing. But since all of us lose money on clothes and make it on the perfumes, we listened. Who knows? Maybe there really is trouble.

"Then someone, it may have been Courrèges, said this was old ground, that he was more alarmed about something else, some vague talk about a cabal among the landowners. I can tell you, my dear Tony, my ears perked up at that."

Winslow puffed out slowly. "Why?" he asked, still watching the match.

"Ah," Delane said, gesturing dramatically even though he was speaking English, "that is what I asked myself. Because such a thing is patently absurd. Those farmers of Grasse, they hate everybody. Superstitious peasants. They could never be organized. Never."

"Then why did your ears perk up?"

"My dear . . ." Delane began.

"You know, that sounds better in French," Winslow protested politely, with a glance at the macho rugby fans all around them.

"Okay, *mon cher*," Delane continued, "but fashion designers are like women. We are *worse* than women. Every month a small crisis. Every month the end of the world. It is like California (he pronounced it *Cal-ee-fornia*) where your San Andreas Fault is always going to put Hollywood among the fishes. So when I hear ridiculous rumors of cabals in Grasse, I report them faithfully to you. Even when I believe such talk is groundless; impossible, hysterical ravings."

Delane was satisfied he had made the point and he stared out at the field, puffing at his cigar and poking Winslow to call attention to a marvelous passing maneuver by the French halfbacks.

Winslow's face was still turned toward the field but his eyes glazed over and he missed a game-saving tackle on the touchline by one of the English.

"Why," he asked Delane, "is Grasse so fucking important? They grow roses everywhere."

Delane turned to him. Patiently, almost patronizingly, he began.

"My dear, it is in Grasse that we distill the natural oils from the flowers. Not only the roses. In fact the Bulgarians grow better roses for perfume. We have *les roses de mai*, but more important we have the lavender, the lilac, a little violet, the narcissus, the jasmine, some mimosa, some oak moss that looks like the moss on your trees in Georgia and Florida but which is different. Grasse is the heart of the floral end of the perfume trade. The flowers are grown, the petals are picked, and wholesalers buy by the pound, by the burlap bag. The petals go into vats ... into steam distillation, into ether baths, into hot wax. I don't understand all the mechanics, but what happens is, when you put the petals into one of these solvents the oil floats to the top and you draw it off.

"And that oil (he emphasized the words) *is essential to* the manufacture of quality perfume. Other things go into it, but without those oils, nothing happens but some cheap cologne the whores of Les Halles douche themselves with during menstruation. Nothing."

Winslow nodded. When Delane started to elaborate, Winslow cut him off. He wanted to absorb that much and chew it a bit.

"Back up a bit. What I don't understand is the Grasse angle. Roses grow in America. You say the Bulgarians grow roses. Then why ...?"

Delane was patient. "For one thing, Bulgaria is in another sphere of political influence. They sell their attar to the Warsaw Pact market. For another, why American roses or English roses or the 'rose of Tralee' just won't do, well, consider the analogy of our vineyards. Everyone grows grapes, and yet it is French grapes, and then only grapes from certain precisely defined regions of France, that produce great wine. The soil, the annual rainfall, the angle at which the sun strikes the slope of the hill, the temperature at harvest time, all these variables combine to create a drinkable grape. So it is with the flowers of Grasse. God knows why, I don't, but there it is."

He grinned, sure he had satisfied Winslow's curiosity. But the American, trained to ask questions and then more questions, was already thinking about Maggy Moal's promise to put him in touch with her manager at Grasse. As helpful as Delane was trying to be, it was apparent he wasn't the expert. Perhaps Maggy's man would be. Perhaps the riddle could be solved in Grasse. Perhaps ...

"Regard, Tony," Delane broke in, "there *was* a move!"

After the match, a draw that satisfied no one, drunken Englishmen and sulky Frenchmen pushed their way slowly out of the stadium. Winslow and Delane let most of the crowd dissipate before they started down out of the grandstand toward the exit tunnel. Delane was blaming the result on the referee.

"You get a Welshman in a situation like that and what do you expect? To the French, he's a coal miner who should be singing in chapel. To the English he's one of their goddamn provincials, fit for drawing water and making bricks. The poor fellow didn't make a decent call all afternoon, he was so awed." He looked toward heaven. "God save us from Third World domination."

Winslow laughed. "I'd never considered Wales part of the Third World."

"Ah, but what does an American know? I once . . ."

He stopped in mid-sentence. Then, very calmly, he said:

"Antoine, do not look up or around but anywhere except at your feet and the step ahead. We are not alone."

A thrill ran through Winslow. He wanted to look up, to look around. Instead, he concentrated on the concrete steps that led to the exit. They were at the 11th row now, then the 10th, then the 9th . . .

"Two men," Delane said, still speaking quietly and without any great sense of drama. But there was an edge to his voice, as if he was rather pleased to be involved in something after such a bêtise of a match. "Watching us. Watching *you*, I suppose. Who the hell wants to see me?"

"They French?" Winslow asked. He was at the third step now.

"I suppose. Their suits are tacky enough. Hey, you haven't been fucking around with some married woman? Could be her husband and the brother, you know."

They were at the tunnel now.

"Do we go through?"

"Sure." Delane said. "Can't stay in the stands."

There were a few men ahead of them in the tunnel but they were fans, moving toward the gate. Winslow felt a damp feeling at his back, but in a moment they were through the dim tunnel and out in the sunlight. He touched Delane's arm, thinking to suggest that they wait and see just what the hell this was all about; and then, as Delane looked up, he shook his head.

"Nothing. Let's get the car."

There was no point to having an argument here—or worse, a brawl. Junior partners at Rousselot did not brawl in public; they did not get into slanging matches with Frenchmen who, for all he knew, were just a couple of rugger fans. They passed out through the gate, past the last spectators pissing against the stadium wall, and down the street and into the town.

"Okay, we're clear," Delane said from the corner of his mouth.

"How do you know they were watching us?"

Delane shrugged. "In the Occupation, when I was ten years old, I ran messages for six months for the maquis. I *always* know when someone is watching me."

They went through the town and got the car. There was no indication they were followed. The two men in their tacky suits were gone. Delane went up and down Colombes streets for a few minutes, getting himself thoroughly confused and nearly hitting a 2 CV at an intersection. He shook his head.

"Gone," he said.

"If they were ever there," Winslow said dryly. Delane gave him a pained look and they headed for the autoroute and Paris.

Delane successfully got the Porsche halted in front of Winslow's hotel without, for once, ricocheting off the curb or another car. Winslow started to get out, then stopped.

"Paul, what's Madame Claude's phone number?"

Delane gave it to him from memory, without even a wisecrack. Why not? he thought, even Americans need it once in a while. Winslow scribbled the number on his program from the rugby match and asked, "Do you think those guys were really watching us?"

Delane frowned. He hated being doubted.

"Okay," Winslow said. "Have a good weekend. I'll be in touch."

He went in, picked up his messages, and opened the door to his room. The laundry was on the dresser, neatly boxed. He opened the box to be sure the shirts were unstarched. He got out of his clothes and took a shower. Clouds were building up in the west, coming off the Channel and across Flanders and northern France, promising rain, but it was still warm. He wrapped a towel around his middle and sat up on the bed with the phone in his hand.

"ETOile 56-73, s'il vous plaît."

The phone rang a couple of times.

"Allo?"

He asked for Mme. Claude. The woman said this was she. Winslow spoke English.

"I'm a banker from New York. My name is Winslow. Paul Delane gave me your number. I'm at the Hôtel ——. There is a young lady I met the other evening. I believe she is a . . . friend of yours. Her name is Anouk . . ."

The woman who said she was Mme. Claude promised to call back. She would have to track down this Anouk. These girls, so young, so beautiful, all with their little sports cars and their friends in the country, it was impossible to keep track. But she would do what she could. When she hung up he understood very well this meant his hotel would be called, Delane would be queried, and Winslow's credentials as a visiting businessman with money to spend would be carefully checked. Mme. Claude had paid protection money for too long to too many high officials to do anything reckless. Winslow looked at his watch. He thought about phoning Henry Rousselot. It would be early afternoon in Connecticut. Rousselot would surely be on the course at New Canaan. Besides, what did he have to report? Not that much, and Rousselot was a man who wanted final reports, not interim meanderings and hunches.

Marianna Troy was still working. He'd phoned her apartment and then the *Vogue* office and someone told him she was at a shooting at the Place du Trocadéro. Winslow got up from the bed and pulled on his shorts and some flannel trousers and tugged a turtleneck over his head. He got the Burberry out of the closet and shoved some cigars into his pockets. He told the cab driver to drop him at the opposite side of the Place, near the café. Taking photographs, getting everything in focus, and not cutting off the heads or the feet was a profound mystery to Anthony Winslow, and he did not want to drive up to where they were doing their pictures and screw things up and get Marianna into difficulty. He could have spared himself the worry.

It was eight o'clock, the sun nearly down, and the clouds cutting the last of the light as he walked diagonally across the Place toward the Palais de Chaillot. The Tour Eiffel directly across the river had just been illuminated and against its light he could see the team of photographers and models working on the broad, polished, almost-marble flagstones on which the French kids love to roller-skate. As he got closer he could pick out the photographer himself, an elfin little man entirely in black, with what looked like a woman's stocking over his head, keeping his hair tidy in the damp wind. One assistant was holding a bit of aluminum reflector sheet, another had a sort of silvery umbrella. The models—there were two of them—struck poses and the photographer capered, shooting all the time with a flash and jabbering at them nonstop. Staying always behind him, moving easily on her long legs in the well-cut dark-blue velvet jeans, was Marianna. She wore a khaki shirt with big patch pockets over her breasts and a quilted down ski anorak that flopped open as she moved. She saw Winslow coming and smiled over the head of the photographer at him. She had a clipboard in her hand.

Winslow stood there, a few yards away. They changed models now, and Marianna wrote down something on the clipboard. After another few moments the photographer looked up at the darkening sky and groaned.

"Alors, c'est fini."

The assistants began to pack up the equipment and the two models huddled together, talking about whatever it is models talk of endlessly, and Marianna came over to Winslow.

"Well, and now you see how glamorous it is."
He laughed.
"I'm nothing but a bloody script girl."
"With no dialogue," he said.
"Oh, you get dialogue. Those models. My god, they say nothing but they talk constantly."
"Drink?"
She nodded. "Maybe something hot. It's windy out there." She took his arm and they strode back across the Place to the café, both of them tall and moving neatly through the traffic. They got a table and sat down. A waiter took the order. Marianna threw her down jacket over the extra chair. Winslow noticed she had blue eyes under the long, dark hair. It was funny, he hadn't noticed that the night before. He had a beer and she sipped hot chocolate.

"Tell me about the fashion business," he said.

"Well, if you want the big picture, you subscribe to *Vogue* and you read *Women's Wear* every day and you go to lunch at grand restaurants and give intimate little dinner parties for Valentino and Bill Blass and Madame Grès. If you want the small picture, you buy yourself a clipboard and get sore feet standing around for five or six hours telling the girls not to chew gum and fetching coffee for the photographer and trying to make sure the dresses get back to the couture house without being stolen or having too many cigarette holes burned in them."

"But you don't have to do that tonight."

"No, Scavullo is a jewel. He's the one with the stocking cap. He has to go by Rykiel and he said he'd drop off the clothes. Thank God, I'm really flaked out."

"Ever been to Grasse?"

"No, isn't that where the attar comes from?"

"Yeah. I might go down there for a day or two. Sounds like an interesting place."

"I don't know much about it," Marianna said. "But every night before he climbs into bed with his lover, every couturier says his prayers for Grasse. They make their big money from perfume."

"That's what Delane told me. We went to the rugby today. England versus France."

"Quels sports! Well, Delane would know more about it. But what happens is, the couture is sort of like a lab—all experiments and punctured dreams and tantrums and back to the drawing board in the morning. They lose money on it, all of them."

"Even at a thousand dollars a dress?"

"Even at fifteen hundred—two thousand. Because everything is made by hand, the fabric is forty or fifty dollars a yard, everything is constructed: the interlinings and so on. No automation at all. But the couture clothes, if they're any good, are what get the headlines. They show up on the cover of *Elle* or *Vogue* or *WWD*, and Eugenia Sheppard goes ape in her column and *The Times* runs a sketch and voilà, Delane or Chanel or Fayol or whoever is suddenly a genius. So everyone rushes in to buy the copies of the couture clothes, the machine-made mass-produced ready-to-wear, the accessories, the handbags, the furs, the pantyhose—anything with his label on it. And, the most profitable of all, the perfume."

"The clothes get the publicity and the smelly stuff makes the money."

She shook her head. "Only a banker could put it so neatly."

"And where does a famous fashion editor like you buy her clothes?"

"Oh, me. Well, I got this anorak last winter at Val d'Isère and the shirt from an army-navy store at home and the pants at New Man."

" 'New Man'?"

"Sure, I always wear men's jeans. They fit better. Don't you think?" She seemed quite serious.

"I think they're the most beautiful pants I've ever seen."

Two hours later, after a steak and pommes frites and two bottles of Brouilly, the beautiful pants were tossed carelessly over the back of a chair in her bedroom and Marianna Troy of Yale and *Vogue* magazine was kneeling astride Anthony Winslow of New York and Rousselot & Partners, thrusting herself up and down, as her small, high breasts bobbed and she panted with pleasure.

When she had rolled off and now lay cradled in his arm, her head against his shoulder, she said in a low, happy voice, "I've never screwed a banker before."

"You're my first *Vogue* editor," he said.

"And?"

"I'll send in my subscription first thing tomorrow."

GRASSE

On Monday morning Anthony Winslow flew to Nice, rented a car, and drove north from the sea over the coastal hills to the town of Grasse. Wherever he turned in Paris, someone—Maggy Moal, Delane, Marianna—was talking about Grasse. Maybe there would now be some answers. He stopped once for directions at a gas station and to phone ahead, and when he got to Maggy's factory her man, large, hearty, and competent-looking, came out to greet him.

"An honor, monsieur. To think, all the way from America. From New York."

Only from Paris this time, Winslow said. It was good of the manager to receive him.

"When there is a message from Madame Moal," the man demanded, "could I do otherwise?"

There was more politesse and then the ritual tour of the factory, the storerooms half full of petals ("the season is still young"), the great vats brimming with hot liquid, distilling off the essential oils, then a brisk walk through the town ("to clear the head, monsieur. The flowers can intoxicate") followed by lunch.

"Now," Maggy's manager said, "what can I tell you?" He wielded a toothpick rather daintily behind his napkin and sat back, waiting for Winslow's questions.

* * *

79

While Winslow was doing his homework in the town of Grasse that Monday, other things were happening. In other places.

The bureaucracy of Teheran is like all bureaucracies everywhere. Except, in these times of rich oil, more so. On this particular Monday morning Zader Nafredi's chief, a stooped, angry little man who might have reminded you of Mohammed Mossadegh, issued certain instructions. Oh, of course he had faith in Nafredi's competence. The man was too frightened *not* to succeed. But it was well to hedge one's bets when playing at the heavy tables. He dialed a certain number and issued instructions. The American, representing the competition in this affair, should be bribed, if possible. If not, he was to be muscled. His listener asked what if bribing and muscling failed.

Nafredi's chief made a small moue. "Then, of course, you must do what must be done."

He hung up, buzzed for fresh coffee and those sweet biscuits he had flown in from Fortnum & Mason, and meditated upon Nafredi. It was unfortunate they had to rely on such men, to employ dancing masters to turn the heads of young women. Nafredi's record in such matters was impressive indeed. His chief wondered what young women saw in him. And then, remembering a pleasant interlude the previous evening, he wondered what Nafredi saw in these young women he was assigned to seduce, when there were so many young boys there for the asking.

The chief considered informing Nafredi of the new "arrangements." No, he concluded. The fig and the date prosper in the same oasis without necessarily having been informed of the other's existence.

In New York there was a call for Henry Rousselot. From Wilmington, an expression of . . . disquietude at the Delaware Corp. There had been no reports, no indication of progress from Rousselot's man in Paris.

"Interim reports are discouraged," Rousselot said coldly. "A good man has been assigned to the problem, and if there is a solution you can be reasonably assured he will find it."

But of course, Wilmington appreciated that, without question. *But*, and the "but" had an edge, acquisition of the House of Fayol was of considerable importance. Certain other deals hinged on its satisfactory conclusion. More than a measly $85 million was involved. Rousselot's ears perked. He's been uncomfortable with this assignment from the start. Deadlines . . . interim reports . . . offering $85 million for a company worth $20 or $25 million. Not at all the sort of tidy banking he understood. Instead of clarification, Rousselot got more questions.

"We understand the key to the whole business is this young woman, Anne Fayol. Only she can sign over. Once the necessary deeds and leases are procured, Miss Fayol must say yes. Or no." There was a pause. Then: "Is this fellow Winslow the sort who . . . ?"

Henry Rousselot cut off the question. Angrily he snapped, "Rousselot & Partners employ bankers. Not gigolos. We are not . . . an . . . escort . . . service."

The caller apologized; smoothly sought to calm the ruffled banker. Delaware knew it was in good hands, "the best hands." The Delaware Corp. would be patient.

Unmollified, Rousselot coughed into the telephone and hung up.

In Wilmington, the Delaware Corp. executive put down his telephone. Rousselot was a fine banker, none better, but the executive was concerned. This Fayol business wasn't all as cut-and-dried as they'd intimated to Rousselot. Perhaps the banker, celebrated as a hard man but punctilious, was beginning to sniff out Delaware's plans, and did not like the smell. Well, if there were any doubts about the reliability of Rousselot and of his man in France, Delaware Corp. might have to get into the act itself. The executive picked up an internal line. "Carl," he asked, "do we have anyone who knows his way around the French couture?"

In his apartment over the couture establishment of the late

Jacques Fayol, Max was dressing for the office. He was not content.

It was not fashion that was worrying him. It was this nagging silence on the part of the heirs. You'd think Hélène Fayol or that junkie daughter of hers would have called on him already; would have begged him to keep the house of Fayol together, maintain the business, ensure that the collection was made. But there wasn't a word, just this unsettling silence. By every right Max knew he should already have been confirmed as permanent director of the establishment with a tasty new contract and a share of the profits.

Fashion was not the immediate concern. The July couture collection would be fine. Fayol had done the sketches before leaving for Marrakesh, the fabric had been ordered, some of the patterns had been cut, even a few of the canvas toiles had been basted up. The May ready-to-wear collection was virtually complete. The cutters and tailors of the Maison were certainly up to turning out a "representative" ready-to-wear collection in two weeks' time and the couture collection in July for the press, the buyers, and the rich private clients. Thinking of the press cheered Max slightly. He knew how they loved an angle, and here was one ready-made for them: Jacques Fayol's *Last* Collection!

But *after* July, what about the ready-to-wear collection in November, and then next January's couture collection?

Suddenly, Max felt less than secure. Of course he could hire a top-notch outside designer to come in and do the job if none of the "little monks" in the design studio seemed up to it. But giving that sort of power to one man would create a monster. What would the Maison then need of Max himself? No, better to keep the thing a team effort. Perhaps he could "discover" some "lost" drawings by the old man, keep the legend going until he'd gotten Hélène and the girl, Anouk, to give him the long-term contract that would ratify his authority.

He would think about it.

Somewhat brighter, he slipped on the silk-lined vest of his narrow-bodied Renoma suit, very "English gent-luh-man," and began to select a tie. Memories of last night crowded in. He really must stop picking up boys on the street. They were usually so unsatisfactory. He must look over the "little monks" again today. Perhaps, with the old man out of the way, he would bestow his blessing on one of them. A more-or-less permanent arrangement of that sort was really much more suitable to his new position than the casual liaisons of the Boul Mich.

Now if only this American fellow Winslow weren't complicating the picture . . .

On that same Monday morning Paul Delane was still in bed. He regarded himself in the mirror of the armoire across the room. But without pleasure. His hair was tousled, obviously he had not shaved, the eyes were heavy, and he was fatigued. Truthfully fatigued. Time was, Delane told himself, when he had either the good sense to go to bed, early and alone, on Sunday nights, or the youthful resilience to indulge in idiocies and survive them. Last night he had lacked both good sense and resilience.

The trouble had been an Australian girl, tall and blond and with the most delightfully funny speech mannerisms. Although he did not tell the Australian girl this, Delane was convinced his English was better than hers. He wondered if they all spoke that way in her country. He also wondered if they were all as voracious. He had met her at Castel's, dancing with someone left over from the rugby match, one of the larger Englishmen. The boy had had the decency to go outside into the rue Princesse and be ill in the street, and that had given Delane his opening. More drinks, more music (the girl was a sublime dancer), the hailing of a taxicab when the Englishman staggered back inside, the giving of instructions and the paying of bribes to assure that the Englishman got back to his hotel safely, and then more drinks.

He had gone to the girl's hotel. She had taken off her clothes right away (no need for diplomatic niceties with this one) and they had made love. They had made love again. They had made love a third time. At that point it was three o'clock in the morning and Paul Delane was void in trumps. When he notified the

Australian girl of this she became annoyed. She sat up in bed,
the long blond hair flowing, those incredible breasts standing
erect, and her eyes flashing. "And I was told you Frenchies *had*
something."

She got out of bed, and despite his fatigue, Delane had
watched her buttocks and her long legs and the narrow waist as
she stalked into the bathroom. He half expected tears, perhaps a
brisk comb-and-brush-up, and a renewed and more meaningful
relationship. Instead, she emerged as indignant as before, with a
short, translucent robe wrapped around her. "You get some
sleep, luv," she declared, "I'll be down the hall." Oh? Delane
said, down the hall? Yes, the girl said. "That bloody Englishman
must be recovered by now." Sadly, Delane had watched her go.
More sadly, he got up, dressed, and went home.

Now it was morning and he felt, approximately, like death. He
wondered absently how Tony Winslow was doing down in Grasse.
He hoped he wouldn't get into trouble. He hadn't liked the look
of those gorillas at the Stade Colombes. Then, feeling his own
pain, he consoled himself in the knowledge that banking was a
sober and dignified trade and that bankers rarely were roughed
up or knocked about in the normal course of business. Except,
and he smiled despite the hangover, by Bonnie and Clyde and
that lot.

Zader Nafredi had passed a delightful weekend, and now, on
the Monday, he had just completed his usual gallop in the Bois.
He walked the horse back slowly to the stables, chatting with the
pretty girl on the roan, cooling out the horse and realizing just
how well riding clothes suited him. The girl had noticed as well.
How could she not? The English hacking jacket, the putty-
colored britches, the polished boots . . . no wonder she had fallen
in next to him on the path and had ridden along, stride for stride,
chatting amiably about "chère maman" and next weekend's
revels at Deauville. Ah, Nafredi told himself, not for the first
time, this was indeed Paname. There was nothing in Teheran to
match it. He hoped this American would not cause trouble.

Trouble was something Nafredi did not need right now. He was glad he had taken certain steps to ensure that Mr. Winslow would not disturb his tranquility.

"Handbags, Marianna, handbags, that's your assignment. Creamy, luxurious leathers, horse brass fittings, erogenous tones, startling colors." Marianna listened and took notes. The editors of *Vogue* always spoke this way. Hyperbole was the language of fashion and no one spoke it more fluently than *Vogue*'s editors. "Marianna, I want to see handbags that will cause me to laugh, to weep, to shudder with intensity. Bring me handbags that sing, that dance, that dominate a room. Handbags that carouse, that whisper, that titillate my every appetite. Fetch them, dear girl, fetch them in the hundreds. I shall reproduce them in full color on our pages and millions of American women will thank you."

"Yes, ma'am," Marianna said, and prepared to go out into the handbag market and pick out the bags to be photographed. It had been like this all morning. No time to think about Winslow. Well he probably wasn't thinking of her. It had probably been a mistake to go to bed with him so soon. Probably now he wouldn't even call again. Well, tant pis. The voice of the editor broke in, addressing another of her lackeys.

"Now, you, tell me about lingerie. I want to be aroused, amused, shocked, delighted, frightened, sent wailing and weeping from rooms, driven to desperate limits, elevated and forced to my knees, canonized and rendered mute. Tell me, girl, tell me."

Marianna smothered a giggle, grabbed her notebook and tote bag, and went out into the market. She wondered whether Tony would call.

Winslow flew back to Paris on the 6 P.M. out of Nice. Maggy Moal's man in Grasse had been helpful, but not all that much. He was a technician, a "modernist," and full of contempt for the locals, the farmers who produced the attar.

"These small holders, monsieur, they are not men of the world, like you and me. They are a difficult breed, suspicious, shrewd, wed to the land. These little farms, many of them in the same family for generations. Even during the war, when the Germans were here and the regime tried to get them to increase production, there was no reaction. Just a mulish indifference to outside forces, a shrug of the shoulder, and nothing more."

Winslow asked why the Germans, of all people, had wanted flower production increased during their desperate war for survival.

"Speer was to blame. Albert Speer. Someone at I. G. Farben or one of those big German chemical complexes had an insane notion they could put our essential oils to industrial use. All nonsense, of course, and it never came to anything. From what I've read of Speer, he was the only scientist Hitler really trusted and he was always coming up with schemes, some of them sensible, others, like this, crack-brained." Maggy's manager paused. "But of course the poor fellow was an architect and not a chemist, though perhaps Hitler didn't distinguish. But, as I say, nothing ever happened, and these farmers of Grasse plodded doltishly on their way despite the threats and warnings and brave speeches. These fellows"—he shook his head—"these fellows are mules."

Winslow absorbed what he was told. Then, just before he got into his car to drive back to Nice, he tried once again.

"Have you ever heard the phrase 'Paris One'?"

The man thought, ponderously. "Isn't that the central district of Paris?"

The clouds had blown out and Orly was in the clear as the plane came in. Winslow picked up a cab. There was very little traffic on the autoroute. The driver asked his expectations of the elections. Winslow said he thought it would be close. "Next week, then we shall see," the driver predicted.

"Next week?"

"The first of May. The workers will be out. Marching. The city will be truly fucked that day."

"The traffic."

"Sure," the driver said, "the traffic is always shit when there is a parade. But besides that, the politicians will be out. Both sides. And then, there is the army. Who knows?"

Winslow said he did not understand. The driver was patient.

"Look, monsieur, next week, May Day, if there seems to be a big shift toward the Left, with the unions and the workers demonstrating, well, then, will the colonels sit sipping their citron pressé or will they call out the 'paras'?"

"A coup?"

"Monsieur," the cab driver said solemnly, "it has occurred before, you know."

When he had gotten into the hotel elevator, the concierge picked up a telephone. "Monsieur Winslow est revenu," he said, and hung up. The concierge smiled. This was earning fifty francs the easy way.

Tony Winslow sat in the bathtub, his knees high and dry, the rest of his long body soaking comfortably. He was reading the Paris *Herald-Trib*, specifically Red Smith. The Paris *Herald-Trib* was Winslow's favorite paper in the whole world. It had the look of the old dead New York *Herald-Trib*, it had the good features of *The Times* and the *Washington Post*, and it was only 16 pages long. Red Smith was writing about some drinkers he had known in the early days of the pro football leagues. Winslow was very happy sitting there in the tub reading Smith and thinking perhaps he should have made himself a drink to go with his cigar and the newspaper and the tub when the phone rang. Goddammit, Winslow thought, as soon as a man gets comfortable . . .

The call was from Mme. Claude. She had been able to contact Anouk. The young woman was free that evening. She would phone Winslow within the hour to arrange the rendezvous. Did Monsieur Winslow wish to open an account? His friends recommended him very highly, and if convenient, he might pay by check or by cash. After he hung up, Winslow stood naked, dripping on the hotel-room rug, a bath towel hanging uselessly over his shoulder.

Anouk Fayol! Now, perhaps the deaf would hear and the dumb speak and he would *finally* learn something. He ran his fingertips over his chin and decided to do that rare thing, to shave a second time in the same day. He remembered the girl vividly.

Thirty minutes later she called and they arranged for her to pick him up at the hotel at ten.

"I'm really looking forward to meeting you," Anouk said in near-perfect English. Her voice had a throaty quality. She sounded very much as if she meant it. Winslow stuffed a wad of hundred-dollar American Express traveler's checks into a suit jacket hanging in the closet and began to dress.

ANOUK

Anouk Fayol had a little Lancia and she drove it beautifully. Much better than Paul Delane, Winslow concluded. Even though she drove fast, his feet remained relaxed, not reaching for brake pedals that weren't there. Here and there they passed roving packs of students testing the nerves of the riot police, testing themselves, engaging in dress rehearsals for the obligatory riots of May Day. Winslow noticed something he had not seen the previous week: the riot cops, the C.R.S., had tommy guns slung over their shoulders on leather belts. And there seemed to be more of the big blue buses with mesh over the windows parked in alleys and on quiet corners, full of men in uniform who smoked or slept or talked quietly through the night. Anouk turned to him.

"Do you prefer that we speak English or French? Madame Claude told me your French is very good."

"Ca m'est egal," Winslow said.

"Okay, then, we'll talk English. I don't get all that much opportunity."

It was too early to go dancing and Winslow had not eaten, and on Anouk's suggestion they drove into Les Halles and got a table in the back room of L'Escargot. The girl pulled the little car halfway up onto the sidewalk and they went inside. The place was full of middle-aged men, some with their wives, some with

ladies who were obviously not their wives. There was a good
smell to the place, the hum of conversation, and the serious
sounds of glasses tinkling, of corks being pulled, of knives and
forks on the dinnerware. Winslow noticed, as the girl walked
ahead of him, that every man in the restaurant saw her. Not
every man acknowledged he had seen her. But he had. Winslow
understood why.

Anouk Fayol was a very physical girl. As tall as Marianna
Troy, and with the same long, dark, heavy hair, the same articulate, graceful movement, the girl turned crossing a room into a
minor performance. Winslow wished he could be farther back, to
enjoy it better, without the foreshortening of proximity. She wore
a long patchwork skirt with a white silk shirt opened one button
too low and then knotted at the waist, and a heavy peasant shawl
carelessly tossed around her shoulders. Under the skirt was the
hint of highly-polished heeled boots. She wore gold chains around
her neck and on her wrists. They had no reservation, but that
seemed to pose no difficulty. How could any maître d'hôtel say
no to this tall young man and this woman? They sat side by side
on a banquette and Winslow ordered drinks, a vodka martini
with olive on the rocks for both of them. "Whatever you drink, I
shall drink," Anouk had told him. "That's part of the adventure."

When the drinks came they toasted one another and Winslow
said, quite casually, "You know, we have met before."

"Oh?"

"At that party in the Bois, last week. You were with Nafredi.
I . . ."

"Please," she said coolly, "I never discuss one client with another."

It was almost as if she were establishing ground rules, reminding the American she was a whore, perhaps reminding herself of
the fact at the same time. Winslow let it pass.

"But you don't remember me," he said.

"I remember meeting someone very tall. It must have been
you. But I never look at the faces."

Winslow said he found that rather sad, that the faces were
often the best of people, the most interesting. Anouk looked at

him, through him, and without being obvious, at his body. "I'm
sure you're mistaken about that," she said. Her voice had a
sensual hunger in it.

Winslow found her not at all what he'd expected. What had he
expected? A spoiled, middle-class brat in rebellion against family
and class; more vaguely, perhaps, against society, convention,
religion, whatever. Instead, or maybe for those very reasons, she
was being very much the professional; the tough, sexy hooker—
no fencing, no false modesty, no wanting to be talked into it, and
claiming all the while that circumstance was to blame, that she
was really pure at heart. He examined her while they drank. The
shirt and the peasant skirt exposing a midriff that was lean and
brown. He asked her about the tan, this early in the season.
Someone had taken her south last month, to the islands. She had
done a lot of swimming. Strangely annoyed, Winslow thought of
the sleek Iranian and was jealous.

"How did you learn your English?" he asked.

"On the job," she said, again being tough. Then, for the first
time, she unbent fractionally. "No, in England. At a boarding
school. And your French?"

Winslow told her about his mother. They ordered, had another
martini, the dinner came (disappointed), and Winslow made a
note to check the *Guide Michelin* to see whether they were still
giving L'Escargot a decent rating. The girl didn't seem to notice
the food; she pushed it around the plate but didn't eat much. He
got the check and they went out and she said she preferred
Régine's, and she drove and Albert took the car at the curb of the
rue Ponthieu, and when they went inside, Luciano found them a
good table. They were on scotch now, and when they danced
Winslow could feel the booze in his knees. If he was to get
anything out of this girl, he'd better slow down. She danced well,
using her body against his. God, she felt good. That was another
thing he'd better slow down on. Back at the table she sat very
close, curling in against him and taking a drag on his cigarillo. It
was all very sexy. She was being pliant, suggestive, ripe. Everything you wanted in a call girl. Then he dropped the bomb.

"I know who you are, you know."

She tensed, then laughed. "Of course you do. I'm one of Madame Claude's young women. My name is Anouk. And in another hour or so I will be fucking you."

Nice bluff. He ignored it.

"I know who your father was. I've been to see your mother. I . . ."

She told him, in French, to do something foul to himself. She kept her voice low: Madame Claude's girls never made scenes, but there was no masking the intensity of her anger.

"What are you, some goddamn tabloid journalist after the dirt?" she demanded.

"No, I really am a banker. We have some dealings with the House of Fayol. I'm over here looking at papers, trying to track down some deals your father was . . ."

"Don't call him 'my father.' Call him 'Fayol,' whatever. He's not my father."

Winslow let that pass. "There was a negotiation your . . . Fayol was working on with one of my clients, a big American company. They thought they had an agreement. Then, he died. Now they're not so sure. They need something more on paper. You understand, don't you? You and your mother . . ."

"The nun," she interrupted bitterly. He ignored it.

" . . . are the heirs. I've been to see the huissier, seen the files at the bank, talked to Max, but there are loose ends. No one seems to . . ."

She pulled the shawl around her lean shoulders. "I don't think you want my services, Mr. Winslow. My specialties are of a rather different sort. I think you need an accountant, or a barrister, perhaps. I suck cocks and wear leather underclothes and occasionally permit people to whip me. I used to think these were shameful things. But now I think I'm in a decent trade. Decent, compared to yours."

It was a hell of a good speech, Winslow admitted that to himself, and a grudging admiration for the girl wormed into his awareness. But now she started to get up. He grabbed her arm, firmly.

"No, you don't," he said.

She stared at him angrily. "Don't worry," she said, "there'll be no charge. Obviously I haven't been satisfactory."

"Sit down," he ordered. When she hesitated he pulled her down onto the seat. "I paid for the night with you, we made a bargain, and you're damn well going to carry out your share of it."

There was hatred in her face. Then, unexpectedly, she took a deep breath and said, quite calmly and in French, "Might I have another drink?"

He started to order two more scotches but she interrupted and said she wanted a "fine" this time. Oh, he thought, so it's going to be like that. The whore's tricks were put aside. He ordered and then he began to ask questions. All around them people laughed and danced and flirted and the discs played and he asked questions which she did not answer. Or, rather, she answered, but without telling him anything.

Finally he said, "There are several files that seem to be missing. One of them is called the 'Paris One' file. Do you know anything about that?" She shook her head.

"I never discussed business with my . . . with Fayol. Nor did his wife. And besides, I haven't spent much time in France recently. I don't know anybody, and I thought nobody knew me." Her curiosity made her ask how he had known.

"Maggy Moal pointed you out. The night you were with Nafredi. I mean, one of your clients."

She nearly smiled for the first time since he had told her he knew who she was. "Maggy. I should have known. My father and she were lovers once, I suspect. When he was very young and she reigned over the couture."

Winslow noticed the slip. "My father." Maybe the hate didn't go all that deep.

He took advantage of the opening to dig in. "Hasn't any of your father's fashion sense rubbed off on you? Don't you care about the couture house? It's yours now."

She made a face. "Since I was twelve they've shunted me from one boarding school to another. Always in England. To keep me out of the way. There was a year in London, the College of Design. Poof! Fashion. What do I care for it? I know enough to wear the clothes that suit me. Women obsessed with fashion I find pitiful. Ridiculous! As for the rest, the money, Max runs the house. He's capable. I take no interest in it. And"—she looked down at herself, provocatively—"I am quite obviously able to earn money in my own line of work."

I'll just bet you are, Winslow thought. Aloud, trying to get her back on the track, knowing he sounded ponderous, he said:

"The files seem incomplete. There are leases, property rights, my client needs to see, there may be a rival claim. There's so much I don't know."

She shrugged. "Couldn't old Grumbach tell you? He kept all the Fayol secrets."

"He didn't seem to know, himself. There was a mountain of paper. He wasn't half through it when I saw him. I suppose I'll go back again this week. Maybe it'll turn up."

The girl said in a dreamy voice, "Poor old Grumbach. When I was a little girl I'd see him at the office or he'd come to the house. Even then he was bent and old and trembling and always with a thousand papers under his arm. He was a good old man. He wrote me when my . . . when Fayol died."

"You mean, condolences, not about the estate?"

"No, just a sweet letter. Some advice my father had once given him for me. Some shit about seeking spiritual guidance, I don't know. A romantic notion, I suppose, born of guilt."

"How old are you?" Winslow asked, without knowing why.

Now she was again the whore.

"How old do you want me to be? Some men like me to be seventeen, others, well, they like twenty-five." When he looked stern she said, "I'll be twenty in May."

She was only nineteen, Winslow thought. My God, a girl like this.

"Is it possible your mother might have some information that could . . . ?"

"My mother! That wax saint! A foolish woman without the heart or the mind to understand that a genius like my father will always have flaws, that no man can create the way he did without some wild drive twisting him this way and that, forcing him, torturing him. No! I despise my father for what he was. But I hate my mother for what she wasn't."

Anouk ordered another "fine" and then another and then she excused herself. Winslow let her go, wondering if she would try to slip out. He watched the dancing and sipped at his scotch, and then she came back, very bright now, her eyes shining, and, if possible, even more desirable. He asked if she wanted to dance but she said no, that she wanted to go somewhere else. He got the check and gave Luciano fifty francs and they went outside, the men turning to watch her go, and he gave old Albert ten francs and he limped off at a sprint to get the car.

"Should I drive?" Winslow asked. He noticed she was high.

"You can do anything you want," she said. She was back to the tone of earlier that evening, the pliant whore tone that promised so much.

She gave him the directions, and when she told him where to turn on the Avenue Georges Cinq he asked where they were headed and she told him.

"The Crazy Horse. Maybe all those Teutonic tits will inspire you."

Winslow bit back the retort. He couldn't blame her for turning nasty, but it was odd how quickly she slid from one mood to another. Watching her face, the lovely green eyes so bright, despite the drink and the smoke and the hour, he wondered if she was on something.

Inside, she quickly whispered to him, "Don't get a table. They rob you. They rob you at the bar too but not so badly."

They wedged into a space at the bar and Winslow looked around. The place was jammed. Up on the stage an absolutely lovely young blonde was dancing. She was naked except for some silly plastic boots. He ordered drinks and they leaned against the bar watching the show. Anouk maneuvered her buttocks back against his thighs and moved them slightly. He felt himself hardening. The blonde went off to applause and then two girls came on, and the crowd, most of them foreigners, cheered. Apparently they knew the drill. The two girls undressed to music and then faked a lesbian act. It was very well done. Anouk turned and looked up into his face.

"I could phone another girl if you want. If you enjoy that sort of thing. We could . . ."

"Shut up," he said.

Then Anouk laughed. But it was not a cheerful laugh. "Sleek cows," she said contemptuously. "Stupid Swedes."

Winslow said impatiently, "This was your idea. Not mine."

"Well, so it was a bad idea." Then she said something Winslow couldn't hear against the noise of the room and the beat of the music. He said "What?" and she looked into his face and then away.

"I started to say I'm one of them. A bit slimmer, better educated, more intelligent, perhaps. But just like them."

"I don't think you are."

"Hah! Don't delude yourself. We're all angry at something, we're all striking back at somebody. If I could dance and had bigger tits, I'd be up there too. But because I speak languages and have some chic, I fuck rich foreigners like you and Nafredi. But *really*, I'm just like those peasants up there. Rebellious, guilty, angry, and not knowing what to do about it, except to strip or to take drugs or to fuck."

Winslow didn't want any more of this second-rate drunken moralizing. Any more of this and he'd be handing her his handkerchief and they would both be agreeing that, yes, it was a hard, cruel world and the deck had been stacked against us. He thought of the old Kennedy line, "Life *is* unfair," and decided it was time to get out of there.

"Come on," he said. "I've had enough."

They pushed through the crowd toward the narrow hallway. Anouk was a few paces ahead of him. As Winslow squeezed between the men and a few women queued up at the entrance, someone grabbed his arm.

"Qu'est-ce que tu fais, monsieur?"

Winslow half turned to see a heavyset Frenchman, perhaps a head shorter, holding his arm. Winslow lifted his head and said, "Hein?" and the man pushed a bulky envelope into his hand. "C'est pour toi," he said, and slipped past Winslow into the club. Winslow stood there for a moment and then a tourist behind him said, "For chrissake, pal, let's move it," and he shoved the envelope into his pocket and joined Anouk at the curb. The cab drivers at the hack stand were looking her over. She smiled at one of them and the man licked his lips.

"Come on," she said. "Get in the car."

"Look," Winslow said, "I can get a cab from here. Or walk."

She drove this time. They stopped in front of his hotel. He turned to look at her.

"I'm sorry to have tricked you this way. But I had to ask questions. I hope if you think of something, anything, you'll let me know. It's important to me and it could be damned important to you. Quite a bit of money is involved."

She shrugged. "I prefer to earn my money."

"Sure," he said. He started to get out of the car. She turned the engine off and opened the door on her side.

"Wait a minute," she said.

She came around and joined him on the curb. "We have a contract, remember?"

The night concierge leaned down and unlocked the door and they went inside and got into the elevator. The concierge waited until the door had closed and he picked up the telephone. Inside the elevator Anouk leaned against Winslow and lifted her head to kiss him, her mouth moist and slightly opened.

Inside the room she dropped the shawl and turned to him. "Do you prefer the lights on or off? Do you want to undress me or should I ...?"

"You have to play whore, don't you?"

"Why not?" she said. "I *am* one." She looked around. "Is that the bathroom?"

He nodded.

"I'll be right out," she said.

Winslow was sober now. He threw his suit jacket on the bed
and loosened his tie. Jesus, this is sick. The girl was beautiful,
wanton, and he was certain that in bed she would live up to the
promise. He wanted her and at the same time was repelled. There
was nothing of the well-scrubbed, refreshing sexuality of Marianna Troy about her. With Anouk it would be a dark journey
into pleasure. He heard the water running in the sink, the toilet
flush. He lighted a cigarillo and then remembered the bulky envelope shoved at him in the entrance to the Crazy Horse Saloon.
He ripped it open. There were ten crisp one-thousand-franc
notes, about two thousand dollars. And a bit of good notepaper.
And a photo torn from that morning's *Le Figaro*, a wire service
shot of an auto wreck on one of the suburban roads. "Trois
morts à 160 KPH," the headline said. He looked at the notepaper. The typed message, unsigned, was in English:
"France can be dangerous. Buy yourself a ticket home."
The notepaper had a scent to it. He sniffed, but with the cigar
smoke in his nostrils, it was vague. He wished he knew more
about perfumes. Maggy Moal's man in Grasse had told him
about the specialists, the professional "noses" employed in the
trade. Perhaps he could have one of them sniff the paper and . . .
From inside the bathroom there was the sound of a body
falling. He pushed open the door. Anouk Fayol lay on the floor.
He picked her up and carried her to the bedroom. She was wearing just the shirt and a pair of bikini underpants, curiously childlike with little yellow daisies on a white field. He wet a hand
towel and washed her face with it. She mumbled something he
could not understand. Back in the bathroom was her purse. On
the shelf she had lined up four tiny mounds of white powder. One
of them was diffused, a plastic straw discarded nearby. It must
have been the cocaine and the booze, he thought. He went back
to examine her again. She was breathing normally. Asleep, he
guessed, just asleep. He breathed out, relieved. But he picked up
the phone, just to be sure.
An hour later Delane's physician pal had left, assuring Winslow the girl would be fine once she slept it off. He grinned
mischievously at the American.

"I'm sure she'll have nothing but a hangover and some pleasant memories," he said, looking down at Anouk's long legs and lovely face.

Playing his playboy role, Winslow grinned right back. "Won't we all?" the grin seemed to suggest.

Now he tidied up the place, hanging her skirt in the closet and flushing the drugs down the toilet. It was cooler now, and he pulled a sheet and blanket up to the girl's chin. She slept quietly. He thought about the bikini with the daisies. It was apparent Anouk hadn't thought him the type for leather underwear.

He undressed and got into the other bed. He tried to review the night's bidding. Had she said anything at all, *anything*? that might unravel the tangle of Fayol's deal with Delaware? Just before he drifted into sleep it occurred to him there *had* been something. Something she had said had struck him as false. But he couldn't remember what it was.

In the morning when he awoke, Anouk was gone.

MAX

The morning began badly. Anouk had slipped away and the evening gone by without getting the girl to talk seriously about the sale of her father's business. Worse yet, he still didn't have any direct way of contacting her, just the awkward conduit of Mme. Claude. On top of that, a hangover. And now, a call from the American Embassy.

Charlie Casey had called, now the commercial attaché and once, years earlier, one of Winslow's professors at the Harvard Business School. Casey had heard Winslow was in town, they really must get together for a drink, but first, well, there was something unpleasant Casey had to say.

"Yes?" Winslow asked.

"Don't tell me, Tony, if you don't want to. But we hear you're in Paris to buy a French company, one of their precious 'national treasures.' A year or two ago one of the big American distilleries tried to buy Château Margaux, which is just about the most famous vineyard they have. There was hell to pay, I can tell you. The distillers had to pull in their horns and cancel. And now, with an election right around the corner, Giscard isn't about to allow a prestigious Paris fashion house to be sold to the goddamn Yanks. The Opposition would just murder him if he did, and a hell of a lot of Frenchmen are pissed off already about American muscle. You get me?"

Winslow did, but he decided to be obtuse.

"Charlie, first of all, I may not be buying a damn thing. And secondly, even if the French are unhappy, why should the American Embassy care? You're supposed to be representing us, not them."

"That's the rough part of it, Tony. Washington likes Giscard. They don't want to see the Left win this election. They've got enough trouble with Italy already. They want Giscard to win— unofficially, of course—and Washington doesn't want some smart young banker of Henry Rousselot's coming in here and handing the Socialists and the Communists a tailor-made emotional issue that could lose Giscard some votes."

There was more of this, and then, less businesslike, Casey's assurances of friendship and a promise to help Winslow in any way he could without breaching Embassy policy.

"Thanks, Charlie, I appreciate that," Winslow said, recognizing his old teacher's dilemma.

"One last thing, Tony. Be careful. Assume you're under surveillance. The French are damn serious about this election and they can play rough."

None of this helped Winslow's morning mood. He'd been moved by Anouk, angry with himself for having tricked her, frustrated by his failure to pin her down on the House of Fayol, irritated by her sluttishness and the drugs. And, he had to admit, the thought of sleeping with her had not been all that repugnant. Instead, the night had produced nothing but the crude bribe-threat and the nagging notion Anouk had said something, something quite innocent, that rang false and might possibly be vital. Except that in his stupidity he could not remember what it was.

He walked down to the Place de l'Alma for breakfast and to clear his head, and halfway through his brioche he realized there might be a very simple way to trace the origin of the bribe note. He hurried back to the hotel. The shoe designer who was one of the hotel's permanent residents hopped into the elevator with him just before the door closed. The man was a White Russian. He was very elegant. He tipped his hat. Winslow was cheered.

Any city where men still tipped their hats to one another couldn't be all that perilous.

He phoned Paul Delane.

"Do you have a 'nose' in town? Someone who can . . ."

"I know what a 'nose' does. The good ones are in Grasse. But I can probably find one. Why? You gonna start bottling perfume now? This is a hell of a thing to compete with another Harvard man right here in his own town."

Winslow agreed.

"Oh, another thing. Maggy Moal's secretary called. She's trying to run you down. Wants you to go to dinner there tonight."

Winslow took down the number. He would leave the piece of scented notepaper in an envelope in Delane's name. This business of a "nose" was important, tu sais? Delane complained for a moment and then said he would do what he could.

"That's the old school spirit," Winslow told him, and hung up.

Marianna Troy looked very lovely. "It isn't a real Moal," she said when he remarked on the dress. "But it's the nearest thing to it that I can afford."

"And I thought all you fashion editors got your clothes free in exchange for plugs in the magazine."

Marianna laughed. "For a banker you do have the most astounding notions of morality."

They were in a cab, headed for dinner chez Maggy Moal. Marianna had not been laughing when he called. She was quite cool, his silence of the last few days rankling. He had made no excuses; told her he wanted to see her again and that Madame Moal was giving a small dinner party. He picked her up at eight. She wore a strapless black dress in something Winslow imagined was silk. It clung just ever so. He supposed they designed it that way. She poured a drink, less cool now. By the time they were in the cab she was smiling again. She liked Winslow, she liked him very much, and she realized now how badly she felt when he hadn't called since they'd made love.

Maggy Moal lived in the Ritz Hotel in a small suite that gave on the gardens on the rue Cambon side. But the dinner was in the couture house, just across from the Ritz and perhaps 200 yards from the Maison Fayol. A liveried doorman let them in and directed them to the winding, mirrored staircase. Marianna went up first. Winslow watched the smooth motion of her hips as she climbed the stairs. She looked around at him. "I've been here. For shows. But never at night." She looked happy now.

There were cocktails first in the sitting room with all the chinoiserie. A waiter in white gloves served. Maggy was very good. She said the right things to Marianna, how pretty she was, how young, how American girls had a freshness so many European women lacked. "Confidentially," she said, "we don't wash often enough. It makes a difference." She screwed up her nose and laughed. The other guest was a middle-aged Frenchman, one of the senior editors of *Paris Match*.

Maggie put Winslow on her right and Marianna at her left for dinner. The editor played host. Two servants worked the table. They began with vodka and caviar and progressed from there. Marianna was nervous at the start, having seen Maggy from afar but never this close, but the old couturier relaxed her. "What sort of thing do you do?" she asked, and when Marianna said she worked for *Vogue*, Maggy launched into a history of fashion magazines dating back to some of the later cave drawings.

"Fashion editors are the most pretentious of women," Maggy declared. "They contribute nothing, they know less, they assume airs, they lack taste, they are rude and unlettered, and most of them have bad legs." Having delivered this fusillade, she leaned over and put her hand on Marianna's thigh. "But you, my dear, are exquisite."

The *Paris Match* editor was gloomy.

"This, then, is the scenario for the next fortnight as I see it, chère Maggy. On May Day the workers are choreographed in the thousands. Someone drinks too much cheap wine and throws a brick at a policeman. The mounted police, anxious to prove themselves anything but anachronistic, charge the marchers. A seven-year-old child, all pigtails and blue eyes, will be trampled by a horse, and her mother, a poverty-stricken La Passionaria, will weep for the television cameras. The resulting riot will find a number of policemen being thrown into the Seine and a jittery government will mobilize the reserves. Some colonel in the Camargue, fretting about his pension, will decide this is a marvelous opportunity to reestablish the monarchy and he will march on Paris. Madame Gandhi, who has troubles at home and wishes to divert the world's gaze, will summon the UN Security Council on grounds a Hindu fakir in the 9th arrondissement has been illegally detained. Forces from all the world's great powers, including Cuba, the Malagasy Republic, and Zaire, will occupy France, and Giscard will fly to London, where he establishes a government in exile and rallies the Resistance during a commercial break in a replay of 'Upstairs, Downstairs.'" The editor paused for breath. "It promises to be a splendid season." He sat back.

Winslow knew he was supposed to be amused. But he wasn't. Maggy cackled and said the Communists were to blame. "His Majesty tells me . . ." and she went into a long story. Marianna looked puzzled and Winslow whispered, "Her PR man is an ex-king."

The meal was wonderful. When they were on the tarte au pomme Maggy got up and went to the window. With a trembling hand, her cane and a cigarette balanced precariously, she announced: "They watch me. I suppose I'll be one of the first they shoot."

"Who watches you, ma chère?" the editor asked, continuing to shovel the tarte into his mouth.

"Those bastards out there. What did Peron call them? It was a splendid phrase."

"Los descamisados," Marianna said. "The shirtless ones."

Maggy turned, dropping ash on the carpet. "Ah, you're a treasure. Why you work for a filthy scandal sheet I don't understand. I'm sure you could get a position on *Vogue*."

"I'm sure she could, Maggy," the editor said smoothly, ignoring her lapse, "but who is it that watches? Are they out there now?"

Maggy pushed ineffectually at the curtain. "They're there. In a car. A Citroën. Nobody drives Citroëns anymore but the Left. Suddenly it's the chic car for the radicals."

Winslow got up and went to the window. "May I?" he said, and peered out. There *was* a car, lights off, across the street. He couldn't tell if it was empty or not.

Maggy gibbered on. "Or it might be that baggage I showed the door last week. My directrice, she called herself. A whore with a title. Ever since then she drives past and shouts obscenities at me. There's no sense of decency in France since the first war. The gentlemen all died and the women became whores." She lit another cigarette and blew the smoke up into her brown wig.

While the men drank brandy and smoked Havana cigars, Maggy and Marianna disappeared into the depths of the apartment. Winslow didn't like the editor, but he felt he had to make talk and so he asked him about the elections. Without Maggy as an audience, the man dropped the mocking, sophisticated tone and said, quite seriously, that he was worried.

" 'Alarmed' would be too strong a word. But I worry. We can live with a Front Populaire government. We've done it before. In the thirties. But I'm afraid of the Right, of the army, of the pieds noirs who never really forgave democracy for having surrendered Algeria. These things concern me. Not Giscard. He's an arrogant fellow, intellectually vain, but au fond for the Republic. There are men around him, however, men I fail to trust."

Winslow thought for a moment. "Would sale of a French company to foreigners become a campaign issue?"

"It could. Why? You buying one?"

Winslow laughed. "No, I just wondered."

The editor told the latest oil sheikh story, the one about the Danish girls and the 747, and they were still laughing when Maggy came back, leaning on Marianna's arm.

"It's an offense," she rasped, "that the men save all the really filthy stories for when I'm out of the room. It's the only argument

I share with the feminists, this business of excluding women from the really gamey stuff. I have to settle for old women's twaddle. Not at all the same thing." She cackled then and told a story that was far riper than anything the editor or Tony Winslow had told, and when Marianna's eyes went wide, Maggy put her hand on her thigh once more and patted it fondly.

"My god, she's incredible," Marianna said when they were on the street. "How old is she? Eighty, eighty-five?"

"She liked you," Winslow said.

"Did she not. I thought I'd never escape from that bathroom of hers. Have you seen it? The fixtures are solid gold. And she kept wanting me to try on dresses." Marianna paused. "I think she knew I wasn't wearing anything under this."

"Oh?"

They found a cab at the corner of the rue St.-Honoré and got in. It was agreed, without having to be spoken, that they would make love. The cab turned right and right again into the rue de Rivoli, and Marianna fell lightly against him. He softened his shoulder but did not try to hold her or to kiss in the back of the cab. Once he glanced out of the rear window. There were cars following, but it was impossible to tell one from another. He had directed the cabbie to take them to the hotel. Somehow, it seemed the right thing to do: the first time in her apartment, the second in his bed. There was no mincing, no coquettishness. She leaned against his shoulder and looked happy.

It was still before midnight and they passed some students, not demonstrating but simply hanging around, bunches of them on the street corners, watched warily by the riot cops. Both sides seemed to be marking a truce. The doors of the hotel had not yet been locked and they went inside. The fat concierge said bon soir and dove down into the pigeonholes to come up with a batch of messages. Winslow thanked him and jammed them into his coat pocket. He watched to see if the concierge smirked, but the man sensed his dislike and busied himself with meaningless paper shuffling, not looking at them. In the elevator Marianna kissed him. It was the first time since the night they made love. She tasted clean and fresh. He suspected he tasted of cigars and brandy.

They undressed together, in the same room, neither staring at one another nor looking away. There was none of the teasing of Anouk. But it was infinitely more seductive. Winslow turned off the lights and opened the French windows. A soft light from the streetlamps and the other buildings flowed into the room. He threw down the bed covers. Marianna came over and kissed him. They stood, two tall, lean bodies pressed together. Then they fell into bed.

During the night Winslow woke. Marianna was lying next to him, on her back, looking at the ceiling and smoking a Gitane.

"Can't sleep?" he asked.

"Don't want to," she said. "It's a good night. I want to think about it for a while. I don't want it to drift away while I sleep."

He reached over and put his hand on her breast. She drew smoke into her lungs and then snuffed out the cigarette and they made love again.

In the morning, as with Anouk, she was gone. But printed neatly on the bathroom mirror in lipstick she put this message: "Don't just vanish again. Please? M."

He went back to the correspondent bank during the morning and went through the files again. This time he had more of a sense of what he was looking for, something to do with Grasse, with perfume, with a missing file that might be called 'Paris One.' Or again, and he scratched his head, it might not. He lunched alone in a bistrot, reading the Paris *Herald-Trib* and noting with perverse pleasure that Bill Bradley had scored only eight points in the Knicks' first playoff game. He dropped by Rizzoli, the bookstore, and bought Kaufman's massive book on perfumes. A coffee-table book. In fact, damn near a coffee table itself. He hoped they'd buy it back used, once he was through with it. At three he talked to Delane. The designer was ecstatic.

"Aha, so I have finally conquered the case-method so dear to the hearts of our faculty at Harvard."

"Yes?"

"Yes, and again, yes! My 'nose' has done his work. Ah, what a magnificent thing is the human olfactory system. How subtle. Did you know, cher Antoine, that each of the tiny hairs within the nostril has the capacity to . . . ?"

"Merde. What did you find out?"

Delane sounded injured. "I haven't quite completed my treatise on the nasal mechanism," he said.

What it came down to was, the scent was a new one, not yet marketed, but one that various "noses" had been called in to sniff. It was a pleasant, light scent, lavender-based, with low musk content, and would be priced to reach the market at, oh, say thirty dollars an ounce? Winslow restrained himself.

"And who plans to market this wonder?" he asked quite calmly.

"Oh," Delane said, "the Maison Fayol, of course."

Got you, you sleek bastard! Winslow said to himself. To Delane he said, "Now we can nail it down through the notepaper itself. We can . . ."

"Attends, mon vieux," Delane protested. "I find you a 'nose.' In Paris, for me, that is not so difficult. But now, to find a man who can analyze notepaper . . . ?"

"No," Winslow said, not to analyze, "to compare it with other paper. I'm sure this damnfool note came from Max. Just get hold of a letter from Max, compare it to . . ."

"I know I should be hurt," Delane said, "but Max very rarely writes little notes to me. Almost never."

"That trade association you belong to, the Chambre Syndicale, wouldn't they have a file of letters from members? Max is director of the house. Surely he'd have had occasion to write a note, query something?"

"I hardly think of the Chambre as a, what d'you call it, a 'trade association.' But, yes, you are perhaps right."

"Then get over there and . . ." Winslow said.

"Oui, mon capitaine," Delane said, and hung up. About seven that evening he phoned Winslow at the hotel and said, yes, it was the same paper. There were several letters from Max to the Chambre on the same stationery.

"What do you do now?"

Winslow had been thinking about that. "Better you don't know, Paul, but if the cops call, tell them it was evil companions led me astray."

The couture houses would be closed by now, or nearly so. He would give it another hour, then he would drop in to see M. Max. Without an invitation.

He went up in the same elevator as before. The Maison de Couture was still and empty. He got off a floor below this time. He walked through a door, another. In a large room there were furs stacked and stretched, ready for the cutting. There was the musky smell of animal hair. The bright overhead lights were out, just a shaded work light or two to show the way. He found the back stairs, wooden, worn, no linoleum even. Moving as quietly as he could, he climbed to the next floor. Here everything was deeply, lushly carpeted. He passed several doors until he came to a double door, heavily padded with leather, studded with decorative nailheads. Winslow put his ear to the door. He thought there was some sound from the other side, music perhaps, low and indistinct. Inside that door there was another door, and now the sounds were quite distinct, music playing—something synthesized, very contemporary—and other sounds: a girl's voice and a man's. That surprised him and he stopped. What the hell do you do when you've broken into someone's house and get to his bedroom door and you expect to find him alone or with another fag, which wouldn't count, and instead he's in bed with a girl?

Winslow knocked.

"What the devil!" someone said in French. It didn't sound like Max.

"Who's there?" Definitely Max.

"Winslow. Anthony Winslow. I've got to see you."

There was some low talk inside and a girl's laughter. Then Max said to wait a moment, he would be right out.

Winslow backed away from the bedroom door and sat down in a leather armchair. This was awkward as hell. He hoped Delane's "nose" was right and that there'd been no mistake about the notepaper. In a moment Max came out, tying a navy robe that suggested Sulka, and looking cross. His hair was slicked back. Despite his bedmate.

"I'll have to ask you the meaning of this," Max said.

Winslow considered for a moment being apologetic. Then rejected the notion. It was this son of a bitch who'd sent that fucking corny note and the picture of the auto accident and the lousy ten thousand francs.

"I came to ask about that silly note you sent me. The note and the newspaper clipping and the money."

Max's eyes went huge. His face was pale.

"I don't know what you're saying. I . . ."

Max lied badly. Or, more properly, he lied badly when he'd been caught. Winslow waved the note in front of him.

"Your notepaper. I've checked it with specimens from your office (he didn't hesitate to lie himself, not about this). And the scent all over it, that new fragrance you're testing that isn't yet on the market. I know it all. The bills themselves were traced. Bankers have ways, you know." Winslow was rather enjoying laying it on now.

"I swear to you, Winslow. On my . . ."

"Shit," Winslow said.

He got up out of the chair. He got up simply because he didn't like looking up at the miserable Max. But the Frenchman, thinking Winslow about to attack him, cowered, his hands out in front of him, palms facing Winslow.

"Of course I'll cooperate."

Winslow mimicked him. "Of course you will."

Max shrugged. "D'accord, I sent it. Is that what you want me to say?"

"I want to know why. *Why* you want me to disappear," Winslow said.

"I assure you I . . ."

Winslow erupted. For the first time since he left New York he had become angry. Being tailed by mysterious thugs, adrift in a sea of tantalizing leads that led nowhere, now this perfumed dandy offending him doubly with bribes and threats. He reached out a long, sinewy arm and grabbed the lapels of Max's dressing gown.

"Goddamn you . . ."

Max pulled back and brought up his hands as if to cover his face.

"Please, don't. Don't hit me." He began to whimper.

Winslow pulled him closer.

"Then tell me what this shit is all about."

Max stopped blubbering and the words flowed. He was concerned about his place as director of the house of Fayol. If the house remained in the hands of Anouk Fayol, he was confident she would permit him to run it. If it were sold, his position would be in danger. He was desperate. He thought if he could get Winslow to give up his quest and go home, even temporarily, he could solidify his directorship, negotiate a long-term contract, so that whatever happened he'd be secure.

Winslow nodded. It sounded plausible. Max was too frightened to lie, especially face to face like this. It rang true. Having Max in a talkative mood, he pressed the questioning.

"What about Grasse? What the hell's going on down there? What's this 'Paris One' file Grumbach can't find?"

Max started to whimper again. "I don't know. Fayol had something going on. He didn't tell me. There was something. But I don't know. He . . ."

Winslow cut in. "He was your employer. Your patron. Your lover, for all I know. And you mean he didn't tell you? You were director of his couture house and he kept you in the dark? Don't pull that on me, Max."

Max pulled himself free from Winslow's relaxed grip, straightened his lapels, and tried to regain his composure.

"There were a lot of things he didn't tell me. A lot of nasty work he didn't talk about to anyone. Like what he did during the war. With the Germans." He saw the disgusted look on Winslow's face and said hurriedly, "And don't tie me into that. I was five years old when Paris was liberated."

And you were a bastard even then, Winslow thought.

"Fayol would drop a hint occasionally, something about screwing Maggy Moal and Patou and Dior and everyone else. He'd have them all by the balls one day. He used to laugh over it. 'We're all fashion geniuses,' he'd say, 'but I'm the one who'll make the big score.' "

"He used to say that, did he?"

Max nodded.

"Not very loyal to your old boss, are you?"

Max's whine turned bitter.

"You think he's so great. Everyone thought he was so wonderful, so eccentric, so charming. Well, let me tell you. It wasn't just being in bed with the Germans. It was, well, it was a lot of things. The way he ate, the way he drank. Gorging himself. The fat pig! Leaving the house to the girl without taking care of me. And sex! Men, women, boys, girls. Anything. Everything. You think you know something about sex? Until you knew Jacques Fayol you didn't know anything. Every day a new boy. A new girl. Take that filthy little Arab boy in Marrakesh. Do you think it was pleasant for me to sit there in the café while he . . ."

"What Arab boy? When? Just before he died?"

Max made an effort to calm himself.

"Just don't be too sure, Monsieur Winslow, that Jacques Fayol died of overeating."

"What do you mean by that?"

"Just what I said. I can't prove it. I can't prove anything. But Fayol was playing a nasty game, and there were people who hated his guts. That Arab boy, he could have been sent to lure him away and . . ."

Winslow sat down again.

"Tell me about the Arab boy, Max," he said quietly.

The two men spoke for another fifteen minutes. Winslow took notes. Max was calm now, self-image at least partially restored. He puffed on an exotic cigarette holder. When they were nearly finished the door to his bedroom opened. Winslow looked up. It was Soroya, the Iranian mannequin. She looked as good as she had the first time he'd seen her. Perhaps better. This time she wasn't wearing any clothes. Just a very fine gold chain around her waist.

"Hello," she said.

Winslow said hello.

"Are you going to be much longer?"

"No."

"That's good. Max, we're waiting. We haven't finished, you know." She turned and went back inside. Through the open door Winslow could see a large bed with a red satin headboard. A blond young man was sitting up in bed, smoking a joint.

The girl went back to the bed and climbed in. The young man handed her the joint.

Winslow got up.

"No more notes, Max," he said.

The fashion director laughed, nervously. "Of course not."

Winslow left. Back in the bedroom Max took off his robe. "Soroya, remember his face. I might want you to be nice to him."

The girl smiled. "Yes, Max." Max got into bed next to the young man.

They resumed.

MARRAKESH

The great Paris fashion designers once took their holidays in Deauville. That was before the 1939 war. Deauville was chill and damp, but it was convenient, only a hundred miles from Paris. After the war, with the regular air service to Nice, the Côte d'Azur became the place. In the sixties St.-Tropez enjoyed a brief vogue. Today, with the fast jet buses, the designers and the other fashionable people escape the rain and the cold and the gray skies of Paris in Marrakesh.

Marrakesh is a big, neat, high, desert walled-city in the interior of Morocco. The flying time from Paris, direct, is just under two hours. Anthony Winslow took the eight o'clock plane out of Charles de Gaulle airport Wednesday morning. He had waked Charlie Casey at home the night before. Casey was still feeling guilty about parroting embassy policy. He promised to call a pal, the acting consul, to help smooth Winslow's path in Marrakesh. "Savio's a good man, Tony. Just for God's sake keep everything unofficial."

Winslow promised he would. Casey sounded morose. "Just remember, Tony, I'm just the goddamned commercial attaché. Not E. Howard Hunt."

Savio, the American acting-consul, greeted him at the airport. He was a plump little man, balding, damp even in the dry heat, and he drove an air-conditioned five-year-old Ford station wagon. "We have eight kids. You ever try to get eight kids in a Ferrari?" Winslow liked him. "Charlie told me to keep this strictly unofficial. Tell me what I can do for you. But don't tell me *why*. When the inevitable congressional investigation takes place a year from now I want to *be* as uninformed as I sound." Winslow wanted to interview the police official who handled the investigation of Fayol's death, the doctor, the people at the café where he took his last meal, "and some Arab boy he picked up." Savio roared.

"Some Arab boy?" He shook his head. "Mr. Winslow, there are maybe 200,000 people in Marrakesh and two thirds of them are Arab boys who sell themselves to rich, fat foreign pederasts for fifty cents an hour. How many Arab boys do you want? I can get them wholesale. The local A&P is running a special."

On the highway from the airport to the town, Savio drove at, perhaps, eighty miles an hour. And he was in the slow lane.

"What the hell," Savio said, "you hit a camel, you hit a donkey. Peasants you aren't supposed to hit. It makes a mess on the fenders and corrodes your radiator. Back home, if I drove fifty miles an hour I knew I was drunk."

Winslow had never been to Africa. He stared out of the window at the robed women, the occasional farmer working a field, the palm trees, the snow-covered mountains off in the distance.

"The Atlases," Savio said. "Beautiful. Little villages up there haven't changed since the Third Crusade."

"They come through here?" Winslow asked.

"Hell, everyone comes through here. Once."

The police officer was cooperative. But not very helpful. He told Winslow he had not himself seen the body but had read the medical report and the transcripts of questions put to, among others, le beau Max. "What about this Arab boy?" Winslow asked. The cop threw up his hands. "Monsieur Winslow, there are Arab boys and Arab boys. We questioned those at the café. Some remembered a boy, vaguely, others did not. The quartier is rife with ragamuffins. Did the unfortunate M. Fayol effect a liaison with one of them? Only he, or Allah, might enlighten us.

I've said over and over again, and now most recently to you, we consider this 'death by natural causes.' Had there been something suspicious, we would of course have followed it up."

Winslow thought for a moment. "Over and over again? You mean, someone else has inquired?"

The policeman looked a bit flustered. "Well, the press, of course. The dead man was rather famous, I'm told. And the French consulate. And . . . well, you know, the idly curious."

"Of course."

Savio drove him to the café. En route Winslow asked, "Do you have any graft in the police department here?"

Savio shrugged. "Sometimes."

"See if you can find out who else has been asking questions about Fayol. I don't mean the newspapers or the French authorities. Private parties, commercial interests."

"Okay," said Savio.

He pulled the Ford up in front of a café. "This is supposed to be picturesque, you know, for the tourists. So if a cockroach finds its way into your coffee cup, please understand, this is local color, and unless you mention it, there will be no additional charge."

They went inside. It was just noon and the hot sun beat down. The cool gloom of the café was refreshing.

"So this is the den of iniquity," Winslow said doubtfully.

Savio made an apologetic gesture.

"Look, it's noon. Give it time to develop. At midnight, you know, it's better."

Winslow looked around the room, his eyes now accustomed to the darkness. A half dozen old men were drinking sweet coffee. A fat waiter, wearing a red sash with gravy spots, worked the tables. There wasn't a woman in the place. There wasn't a nubile Arab boy. There were senior citizen homes in New Hampshire, run by nuns, that promised more.

Savio was very embarrassed. Casey had told him Winslow was an important man, that his errand was substantial. He had made Savio swear to watch over young Winslow in this evil garden of delights. And now Winslow was yawning. It reflected badly on Savio, on the consulate, on the entire American presence.

"Listen," Savio said, "there are other cafés. There are districts in this town you wouldn't believe. I know a nightclub that specializes in the abduction and subsequent gang rape of English schoolmarms."

"Ummm," Winslow said. He didn't seem impressed. Savio got the proprietor over and a few coins changed hands. The proprietor waved his hands, stroked his beard, and looked sage. Winslow waited patiently, not understanding the language. Finally the old man shuffled away, muttering runic wisdom.

"What'd he say?"

"He wasn't here that night," Savio said. "That was the night man."

Savio took Winslow to lunch at the Anglo Club. They ate on a marble terrace overlooking a swimming pool. Savio had invited one of the local gentry to join them. "Name of Wa'Hoosh. Means 'The Wolf.' Ferocious character. Knows damn all about everything. Desperado of the worse sort. You'll like him."

"What is he, some bandit?"

"Why, yes, I suppose he is," Savio said. "He sells antiques."

The midday sun beat on them and a waiter brought tall iced drinks in glasses beaded with sweat. Lean tanned kids frolicked in the pool. Savio watched the teenaged girls. "My God," Winslow said, "how hot does it get?" Savio smiled. "In the summer, pretty warm. Right now, oh, in the nineties. But the sun can be a problem." Winslow mopped his face.

Abdul Wa'Hoosh wore a seersucker suit from Brooks Brothers and a rep tie and buttoned-down shirt. They went very nicely with his fez. "Permit me to order," he said. "Foreigners never know what to order." The waiter came over and took notes. Abdul Wa'Hoosh ordered Caesar salads and rare lamb chops. "It's like Athens," he said, "you eat the lamb, the poultry, and the fish but stay away from the beef. It's usually horse. Or camel."

Savio spun some tale that explained Winslow's presence and Winslow took it from there.

"My bank represents people in the travel business: hotels, an airline or two, developers. I'm told Marrakesh is at the same stage now that Acapulco was fifteen years ago. Aren't the fashion designers, people like that, taking it up?"

Wa'Hoosh nodded enthusiastically. "The most chic people in the world are flocking here, Mr. Winslow. I can tell you that, and without being contradicted. Mind you, I have a vested interest. But I also revere objective truth. Some of the smartest people anywhere come to Marrakesh these days. They buy houses. They rent apartments. The climate, the scenery, the cheap labor, the low prices. Ah, if I *didn't* live here I'd live here."

Hadn't one of the chic people died here recently? Winslow inquired innocently.

Abdul Wa'Hoosh threw up his hands.

"Quel tragédie," he said. "Jacques Fayol. One of my closest friends. A loss to mankind. But what is life? A scratch on the blackboard of infinity. Poor Fayol. I loved that man."

"Oh?" said Winslow, "you were close?"

"Like brothers," Abdul Wa'Hoosh declared. Then, with Savio looking at him through skeptical eyes: "Well, I met him a couple of times."

Winslow shook his head sadly. "The poor man."

Savio got into the act. "A genius," he said piously.

Abdul bowed his head.

"He had high blood pressure," Winslow said.

"He ate too much," said Savio.

Abdul Wa'Hoosh, the Wolf, smiled.

"Well, of course, if that's what the family is saying . . ." His voice rose, doubtfully. Winslow took the cue, leaned toward him.

"You mean, that *wasn't* the cause?"

Abdul gave a short laugh, like a bark.

"My dear fellow, among men of substance like ourselves, need one accept as truth every innocent little falsehood?"

Winslow shook his head. He looked toward Savio.

"Absolutely not," Savio said. "Not among men such as we."

Abdul Wa'Hoosh became very cozy. In a confidential tone he said, "I have information that says his death was, well, that it was *not* high blood pressure."

"No!" Winslow said.

"But yes," Abdul said. "There were other people about. A young man from Paris. A young Arab lad. A boy of surpassing beauty, I am told. A boy of the most intricate of tastes. You get my meaning?"

Winslow nodded.

"Mind you," said Abdul the Wolf, "one hesitates to speak ill of the dead."

"Of course," Savio said, "but try."

The salads came and another round of tall drinks. Abdul said he usually avoided alcohol, "for religious reasons," but he would make an exception. The salads were excellent. Winslow complimented Abdul.

"They manure them with human excrement," he said, "which some feel adds to the flavor."

Winslow pushed his plate aside and drank for a while. Wa'-Hoosh explained that his first name, Abdul, was a very common name in Morocco. "As common as 'Joe' in an English-speaking country. So my name is really not all that exotic. 'Joe the Wolf,' as simple as that."

Savio suggested that Joe the Wolf tell them more about Fayol.

"You see that man over there, under the green-and-white striped umbrella?" Abdul asked. They nodded. "That is a very important artist from Paris. Those people with him? Very rich collectors. That man has a house here, lovely house. Fayol had a house. A little jewel box with a courtyard and a small pool. Fountains. Wonderful marble. Well, my point is, this town has been discovered. Painters, sculptors, not the ones starving in garrets but the ones who sell at Galerie Maeght in Paris, at Parke Bernet, at Félix Vercel in New York. What do they find here? Sun, dry heat, servants, spacious rooms with high ceilings, light. What an artist wants. So they come here because it is pleasant." He paused. "To work and to relax."

He held up a finger. "Then, there is another reason. They

come, some of them—and I fear we must include the late Fayol —they come to indulge their weaknesses, if you care to pass judgment, to amuse themselves, to satisfy themselves in ways not as readily available, or as economical, in Paris or London or New York. They come here to purchase boys."

SPIRITUAL GUIDANCE

Joe the Wolf beckoned a waiter with a languid wave. Winslow noticed that there were no wasted motions. In this climate, in this heat, exertion cost you. Another round of drinks was ordered and Wa'Hoosh suggested they try the local cigars, which he claimed had nearly achieved parity with the good Havanas. The three men sat smoking, sipping their drinks, and watching the children and the teenagers splash in the blue pool while the older and the affluent finished their lunches and drank coffee or cool ades under their umbrellas.

"As I say," Abdul Wa'Hoosh continued, "they come here to buy boys. Not literally, of course, not anymore, though there was a time not too many years ago when a flourishing traffic existed. And it is not that our women, our young girls, are any more virtuous than their counterparts in Europe. Or the boys *less* virtuous. It is simply that, as with the fig and the date, we have discovered a plentiful commodity, locally grown, that satisfies a growing demand on the world market. Sex," said Abdul, "may well be our single greatest invisible export." Having pleased himself with the aphorism, he went on. "There is the trade in unnatural sex, of course, between older, usually foreign, men, and our home-grown boys. But it would be a mistake to assume this commerce to be totally homosexual. There are women who come to Tangier, to Fez, to Marrakesh, from all the great cities of the

121

western world, to taste the local pleasures. I know a titled lady from Kensington who spends a month here every winter. She has a charming flat, with a private entrance, over near the market district, where she rarely if ever rises from bed for four weeks. An industrious and tasteful merchant of the quartier keeps her supplied with teenaged boys who mount the stairs to her apartment one after the other, and subsequently mount the titled lady. She pays handsomely, presumably the boys enjoy their work, and the lady returns to London and to her set in Kensington after the month, refreshed, sated, and positively blooming. That"—and he shrugged—"is of course one of more traditional of our visitors. Not everyone who comes here is quite so 'establishment' in his or her sexual activities. While the titled lady is entertained by these young boys 'seriatim,' there is another woman I know, the wife of a big man in international diamonds, who insists on the most intricate of sexual tableaux. *Her* local procurer is under instructions always to provide never less than three, and often as many as six, boys simultaneously. The lady in question may go for a week without indulging herself, but when she does so, it is an extraordinary business. I myself have seen some photographs she has commissioned to be taken during the act, and I can tell you, messieurs, the woman's athleticism is quite wondrous to behold."

Winslow was feeling the drinks and the heat, and he could have sat listening to this born storyteller for hours, but this was getting him no closer to the death of Fayol. He nudged Savio, who was dragging lazily on the cigar and enjoying Abdul.

"This is all most enlightening," Winslow said, "but I am still curious about Jacques Fayol. Did he deal with one of these procurers? Was the boy he was with that night he died sent him by someone? Or did he simply pick up the . . . ?"

Joe the Wolf interrupted. "Ah, we are coming to that. With Fayol, the situation was somewhat different. And more complicated. He had these young men who accompanied him from Paris —I think he referred to them as his 'little monks'—men who worked in the couture house. The last of them, and the most important, was this fellow Max who was here with him on the final trip. It was not a straightforward arrangement, the sort of thing I described with the Englishwoman or the wife of the diamond merchant. For one thing, Fayol owned the house here and maintained a full-time staff of servants, including a number of young Arab boys. For another, there were apparently some rather complex sexual and emotional relationships between the various 'little monks' and Fayol himself. Occasionally outside talent would be recruited, of course, and then, to muddy the waters further, Fayol still enjoyed the occasional girl. They used to come down with him from Paris; very chic tall girls with long blond hair; mannequins with dark hair that framed their faces like the madonnas in pictures by lesser Renaissance Italians; the impulse purchase, so to speak, some strapping American college girl with tennis shoulders and a peeling nose and a yen for experimentation. Drugs entered into the situation, surely—they are always at hand here in Marrakesh—and one assumes the girls who attended his parties quite frequently were there for hash or cocaine and stayed on for the sex. So with Fayol, it is difficult to say."

"This boy, this Arab kid of the last night, would it be possible to find him?"

Abdul Wa'Hoosh looked at Winslow as if he were a retarded child to be humored.

"It is possible, naturally. It is also possible a snow storm will come down out of the Atlas mountains this afternoon. But it is not likely."

Savio apparently had Abdul on a retainer for the day. Leaving the Anglo Club, the three men visited the hospital and by a stroke of luck spoke to the physician who had signed the death certificate. He referred to his charts of that night. Could the death have been "not natural"? Winslow wanted to know.

"When the police bring in a man in the small hours of the morning who has been found dying on his doorstep, you immediately look into the possibility," the physician admitted. "And there were bruises. On the right arm, on both knees, and on the temple. Also his lips were badly split and a tooth broken. But these marks, these injuries, were not at all inconsistent with what would be suffered in a fall. The man was, you are aware, a huge person, weighing some 135 or 140 kilos. Falling onto tile, with that weight, would cause abrasions of this sort."

"And you performed an autopsy?"

"But of course. A foreigner, a well-known person, no witnesses? One must."

"And . . . ?"

"Stroke. Not immediately fatal. The man lived for an hour or less. The classic symptoms, weight, high blood pressure. The liver somewhat damaged. Drink, naturally. Arteries slightly clogged. But the heart, huge, powerful, a faithful pump to the end. It was the brain that killed him."

Winslow had hoped to fly back to Paris that evening. Obviously, that was impossible. He had learned nothing. Savio drove him to a tourist hotel and arranged a room. It was now four o'clock. Winslow would try to nap. Abdul Wa'Hoosh would meet him at ten that evening in the Café de Paris, Fayol's last bistrot. Savio would have to come along later.

"Unfortunately, I'm spoken for in the early evening. Members of the consulate are putting on a performance of *Hello, Dolly.* I play Horace Vandergelder." He looked slightly embarrassed, and Winslow began to understand why, as a senior diplomat, he was still only the "acting" consul.

Winslow showered and tried to sleep. Even in the air-conditioned, darkened room, he imagined he could feel the heat; imagined the afternoon sun still hammering on his head, his shoulders, the back of his neck. After a while he got up, tied a towel around his waist, ordered room service to send up some beer on ice, and he threw open the curtains so he could watch the mountains. He had a copy of the *Saturday Review* in his Vuitton case and he pulled it out. There was a wonderful critique of western movies by an Oxford don who attacked them as both racist and sexist. "There are very few women portrayed as leaders," the don complained, "and you almost never find a Puerto Rican or an Oriental in the famed Seventh Cavalry."

The beer came and he drank one bottle and half of the second, and between the beer and the *Saturday Review* he was sufficiently tranquilized to be able to nap until the desk woke him at nine.

At midday the Café de Paris had been seedy, artificial, and dull. By night it was seedy, artificial, and electric. Joe the Wolf had a table against the wall next to the opening used by the waiters and performers, such as they were. He smiled a greeting to Winslow. The banker wondered what all these smiles were costing Savio. And how he was supposed to get Savio to accept repayment. Maybe it came under the heading "contingency funds" in the State Department appropriations bill.

A zaftig young woman did a dance involving several veils and a tambourine. The various sheikhs and tourists at the tables sipped their coffee and their cognac and restrained their excitement. Then a slender boy, utilizing fewer veils, came out and did the same dance. The place began to move.

"One cannot term it a first-class nightclub," said Abdul Wa'Hoosh, "but among the second-class clubs it certainly is near the top."

Winslow drank scotch with Perrier and Abdul ordered Coca-Colas with Pernod on the side. Just before midnight there was movement between the tables as, apparently on cue, a number of young boys entered the place and began to circulate. Abdul raised his eyebrows as if to say, "You see what I mean?" It reminded Winslow of Elaine's in New York, where the Irish kids with homemade haircuts come in to peddle the bulldog edition of the *Daily News*. Here the kids were selling something else. Abdul shooed away the first two or three who came by until Winslow held his arm. "Let's talk to one of them," he said. The next kid they told to sit down, and the boy ordered a diet cola.

"If they get fat," Abdul explained, "only the specialists will buy."

The boy said his name was Aziz. He had an incredible face. Winslow pictured the face framed with longer, softer hair, and he could see Isabelle Adjani. The boy wore tight, faded jeans and a white tennis shirt with the Lacoste crocodile. His skin was more golden than tan. He spoke slangy French. They chatted for a while and then Winslow asked if he worked the Café de Paris every night. Not every night, Aziz said, sometimes he went off with someone for a few days. He had been to Tangier just last month with a client. They had stayed in a wonderful hotel, very luxe, of very grand standing. But what of mid-April—around the 15th, the 16th—was it possible he had been around during that week?

Aziz calculated. He was a shrewd little bastard. He calculated some more. He would try to recall, he told Winslow, but it was so long ago. Perhaps if monsieur could tell him why those dates were of importance his memory would function better. Winslow passed him a fifty-franc note. Aziz' lovely brown eyes narrowed. He would think hard, he promised. Very hard.

"There was a Frenchman here on several of those nights," Winslow began. "Later he became ill and had gone to the hospital. A young boy had been with him here, with the older man and another. The boy had gone off with the older man. In consequence of the boy's kindness, the friends of the older man wished to find the boy, to reward him."

"Is the older man dead?" Aziz asked.

Winslow was unsure whether the question was knowledgeable or simply a skeptic's quest for detail. "The older man is very sick," he lied. "Perhaps he may die, as men do. Perhaps a large amount of money is involved for the boy who was so kind, so thoughtful." Aziz remained blank. Could the older man be described more precisely? Winslow told him how Fayol looked, how Max looked. The boy screwed up his face. "I rather fancy the second over the first," he said. "Those fat ones, sometimes they injure you."

That at least had the ring of honesty, and Winslow pushed another fifty francs at the boy. Stay with us, he said, and think about it. Perhaps one of the other boys is the one. You can help us by pointing him out. Of course, Aziz said, it would be a pleasure.

There was a phone call for Winslow. He went behind a beaded curtain and picked up. It was Savio.

"The audience loved it," he said. "Three curtain calls for

Dolly, two for me. I can't tell you how fulfilled it makes one feel. All those rehearsals in the heat, all those hours. And now, one understands the pull of the theater." Winslow agreed, it must be a splendid feeling. "Look," Savio said, "there's a small party going on. For the cast. I'll come over if you need me, but I really hate to miss out on this. It's, well, unless you've been on the stage you probably wouldn't . . ." Winslow told him to enjoy the party. "Joe the Wolf and I have the situation well in hand. I'll phone in the morning."

When he went back to the table there was a second boy.

"He isn't the one, but he knows who it was," Abdul said. He seemed excited, as if for the first time caught up in the chase. The boy nodded. "I remember the fat one. He came here sometimes. Sometimes with women (he looked slightly disapproving), sometimes with other men, like the handsome one (Max). The last time I saw him, a fortnight ago, he invited a boy called Hassan to the table. Then they went off. I'm not sure if Hassan went with them. I assume so."

"Have you seen Hassan since?"

No, the boy said, but he himself had been out of town. A German, a very distinguished man in the electronics business, très gentil, had taken him on holiday. If Hassan had been around he would not necessarily know it. Did the boy know where Hassan lived? Of course, he said, but (with a shy smile and lowered eyelids) surely it was not necessary to make a tiring journey across town in the middle of the night to find Hassan when he, and young Aziz, could provide whatever services were . . .

Winslow told Abdul to remain in the café until he heard from him. "Keep asking questions. This may be nothing. If I find the boy, I'll bring him back. If I don't, I'll call you here. We can meet with Savio for breakfast." Joe the Wolf nodded. He was quite comfortable at the table and Aziz had been making sidelong glances. Winslow hoped they'd be very happy. There was a cab rank just outside the Café de Paris, and the boy gave an address and got in first, as if he were the woman. Winslow tried to keep track of the turnings in case he wanted to come back again, alone. They stopped in front of an apartment building and Win-

slow gave the cabbie some money and promised an extra tip if he
would wait. The driver said that would be possible, but if monsieur could pay a small advance on the tip, the thing would
become probable. This seemed reasonable, and Winslow gave
him another ten francs.

The building was one of those hideous modern blocks, institu-
tionalized boredom relieved by little boxed terraces. They went
inside and climbed the stairs to the second floor. The boy
knocked and a woman came to the door. She was sleepy, annoyed. No, Hassan was not there. He didn't live there any longer.
Winslow tried to ask more questions but the woman pushed the
door shut. He knocked again and the woman shouted something
he didn't understand through the door. He lighted a cigar and
wondered what to do next. When he looked around his guide had
disappeared. When he came out onto the sidewalk the taxi was
gone.

Winslow jerked his necktie open in annoyance. A goddamn
false lead. Which was okay. You don't expect everything to be
tidy when you go looking for a teenaged homosexual in the middle of the night in North Africa. But it was a pain in the ass to be
led up the garden path like this and then left to hoof it back to
the fucking hotel. Around him the night was still. A light breeze
had come down off the mountains and the stones of the old town
had begun to cool. Winslow started to walk, glancing over his
shoulder whenever a car went by, watching for a cruising cab. He
could hear his footsteps echoing on the stones. Except for them,
everything was quiet. This surprised Winslow. He would have
expected an African night to be full of sound. Somewhere a
shutter slammed. A car rolled past. He crossed from a narrow
street into a broader. Several blocks ahead he could see a boulevard of some sort, cars passing, a cruising cab. He was not sure
of the direction, either back to the Café de Paris or to his hotel,
but when he reached the boulevard it would be all right, he would
ask directions, stop a cab. The shops he passed were shuttered
with the big steel "volets." The apartment buildings dark, the
streetlamps and a sliver of moon the only light. He crossed an-

other street. His long legs carried him toward the lighted boulevard. He wondered if he should go back to the Café and Joe the
Wolf, or call Savio at home. He laughed to himself. What a
mixed bag they were: a merchant banker, an antique dealer-cum-
scandalmonger, and an acting consul out of a little theater group.
If Delaware Corp. could see them—an $85 million deal in the
balance and this ill-gotten crew blundering around North Africa
handing out tips to fairies and getting lost in the native quarter.
Wilmington would shit. Just then he heard footsteps.

"Monsieur?"

Winslow froze. A man had come out of the building just ahead
of him. An Arab, complete with robes. Winslow started to move
again, edging toward the gutter so as to pass the man at distance.

"Monsieur."

Winslow stepped into the street. He was abreast of the man
now. He glanced to his left. The way was clear. Nobody else
there.

"Monsieur!" This time the word was an order. Winslow
slowed. He was in the street and the man was edging crabwise
across the sidewalk toward him. "Oui?" Winslow said, trying to
keep his voice steady.

"Puis-je vous aider?" He could still hear the footsteps, behind
him, coming on.

"Non, je vais bien."

The Arab's hand moved toward his robe. Winslow decided
then. He leaped at the man, reaching him in two steps. The
Arab's hand was inside the robe now and starting to reappear.
Winslow knew there would be something in that hand. Without
plan, without thinking, Winslow swung one arm horizontally to
catch the Arab across the face. Instantly, he brought up the other
arm, the palm flattened into a knife edge, and slashed down at
the man's shoulder. He heard the crack of bone and a scream
simultaneously. The Arab staggered; reeled toward the building
wall. Winslow started to follow him. Then he heard a door open
nearby and he turned and broke into a trot. Behind him there
were the footsteps and the whimpering of the injured man. In

another hundred yards he had reached the boulevard. He pulled his necktie closed, ran a hand through his hair, and walked briskly until a cab rolled up and he got in.

It was four o'clock in the morning. Winslow sat on his bed, still dressed. His right hand had already begun to purple. It hurt like hell. He must have broken that son of a bitch's collarbone. He looked at the hand. Angry-red and fast going darker along the outer edge, the killing edge. Jesus, he'd never hit a man like that before. He noticed the hand was shaking. He laughed. He was shaking all over. He picked up the phone. The desk clerk, sleepy, answered.

"Oui, monsieur?"

"Please send up a bottle of scotch and some Perrier. Black Label, if it exists."

"Le bar est fermé, monsieur."

"I don't want to enter the bar. Send up the scotch."

"Mais le bar est . . ."

". . . est fermé. Oui, je sais, and now send up the fucking scotch." He slammed down the phone.

He looked down at the hand again. Hitting a man like that, full force, with the leverage of his great height and reach, nearly two hundred pounds behind it, it was a wonder he didn't break the bastard's neck. Suddenly he sat up. Suppose the Arab had been a panhandler? Suppose he'd simply wanted a handout? No, that hand diving swiftly into the folds of his robe. A knife, a gun, a blackjack. But suppose it was just a deck of dirty pictures he wanted to pitch? Winslow shook his head. That way lay madness.

The desk clerk, understandably surly, brought the scotch. Winslow poured a stiff one. When had he last fought, hit anyone? He remembered the instructor at Quantico telling him that a man his height, his weight, an athlete, could turn bare hands into lethal instruments. He'd shrugged and told the instructor he was having enough trouble just learning how to throw a knee to the groin without rupturing himself. His last real fight? At Ithaca, it must have been, the year Bradley was still playing freshman ball and Winslow was starting at forward. That big black kid from Cornell

—he must have been six seven—practically broke his ribs with an elbow, and Winslow, blind with fury because Princeton was losing and this kid was manhandling him, had swung. He could still remember the sound of his fist hitting the big black sweating face, the sound of it and the feel, from his knuckles through his wrist and right up his arm to the shoulder. And that son of a bitch just stood there and grinned, and then had hit Winslow back. And knocked him down. The only thing about the fight worth remembering, the only part that wasn't shameful, was that he got up, and kept getting up, until they stopped it. That night, after the game, he had dressed in a hurry and had gone outside to wait for the big black. Winslow had held out his hand and the black had taken it and they'd talked for a while, awkwardly, but no longer angry; and then the team bus was ready and he'd left. Funny, he should remember the guy's name. But he couldn't.

Remembering that way, now he remembered something else. The footsteps. There'd been someone behind him, not the Arab he hit, but *behind* him. He'd heard steps *before* the Arab stepped out of the doorway, he'd heard them afterward. Alarmed, he thought of the others. Of Savio, of Joe the Wolf.

He got the desk clerk to ring the Café de Paris. After a dozen rings someone answered.

"Le Café est fermé."

"Listen, a friend of mine was there. With a boy. They . . ."

"You want a boy?"

"No, his name is Abdul . . ."

"We don't got boys here. You want, I look up the number for boys."

"Abdul Wa'Hoosh, not the fucking boy. Is he there? Did he leave?"

"Yes, he left. Long time ago."

"Alone? Do you know where he went?"

The man at the café assumed an injured air. "Monsieur, we do not report on the goings and comings of our faithful clientele. This is a respectable house. Most respectable."

He rang Savio. The diplomat answered, grunting his way out of sleep.

"Jesus, I'm glad I got you. Is everything okay?"

"Who the hell is this? Winslow?"

"Yeah. Listen, don't go out tonight. Just take it easy, huh?"

"Tony, it's four thirty. I'm asleep. I'm not going anywhere. You drunk?"

"No. Just, I was worried about you."

"Don't worry," Savio said. "Did I tell you about the show? About the curtain calls?"

Winslow went to sleep after another drink. He was still wondering about the footsteps. In the morning he woke with a hand that hurt like hell, a vague sense of unease about the night before, and a headache. Then, without even trying, he remembered what it was Anouk Fayol had said that made no sense at all. The letter from old Grumbach. The last message from her father:

"Some shit about seeking spiritual guidance."

He slid off the bed and looked at his watch. He might be able to make the morning plane.

SEARCHING

At a fashion show you look at the people first. Then at the clothes. Marianna Troy knew this. Intuitively. Her editor had gone back to New York and *Vogue*'s complement of front row seats was unfilled and Marianna had claimed one. Junior editors traditionally sit in the second row, taking notes, mentally swatching the fabrics, watching everything, and occasionally venturing a whispered comment to one of the grander, senior people allotted a little gold chair in the very front row.

It was the first press showing of Maggy Moal's fall ready-to-wear line. The German buyers and the Japanese press and the Seventh Avenue copyists and whoever was a current enemy would be sent a ticket for the second day. The first day belonged to Maggy and the important press and a scatter of pals and private clients and the usual names from the cinema. Marianna had a seat directly across from Maggy's pearl-gray couch. The old lady smiled when she saw her. Marianna wondered if Maggy remembered her from dinner or simply because she was a pretty girl with good legs and Maggy was in an acquisitive mood. On one side of Maggy was the editor of *Elle* magazine, a dried-out woman in boots and Chanel chains. On the other, a beautiful child who had just starred in her first film and who was, it was said, Maggy's latest protégée.

Most fashion designers remain offstage during the showings of

133

their collections. Givenchy peeks through a pinhole in the door of the mannequins' cabine. Marc Bohan of Dior helps dress the girls while his assistant sneaks looks through the drapes. Saint Laurent never looks, he's too shy. Chanel used to sit at the top of the winding stairs watching through the multiple mirrored images. Captain Molyneux sat smiling in the audience, but then he didn't actually design anything; his "nephew" did. Cardin opens with an endless speech no one can hear and then hides away. Courrèges prances onstage with the models. And Ungaro remains invisible, watching through closed-circuit television. But Maggy Moal? Maggy took the best seat in the house and enjoyed the show.

Even before the first model came out into the pearl-gray room, Maggy was in action: talking, chain-smoking, dropping her cane and retrieving it, brushing ash from her lap, and adjusting her teeth whenever the upper plate slipped.

"It's all a bêtise, tu sais," Maggy rasped, her eyes darting this way and that. "What the Jews don't take from you the government does. Or the unions. I found one of my 'premières mains' proselytizing for the union during working hours last week. I gave her the door. Twenty years with me and then, a dagger in the back. Hand me that ashtray. I won't tolerate treason. They want to sleep around, get a dose, that's their affair. But I won't have them coming to work unwashed or carrying picket signs. (Her cigarette went out.) Who has a light? And the mannequins! Cows, most of them. They all want to be Madame what's-her-name, it starts with a 'B' I think, Bardot, that one, a very pretty little bottom and nice legs, but up here (the chest) it becomes gross. Gross! Ah, here comes the first dress. I don't like it, but tell me what you think."

Maggy dropped her cane again and swore softly. The little actress, who seemed to Marianna beautiful but quite stupid, covered her little cupid's-bow mouth with a tiny pink hand and sobbed with joy. "Madame," she hissed, "it is too lovely to be real."

Maggy cackled. "Ah," she said, loud enough to be heard

throughout the room, "when one has an ass like yours you can wear hopsacking."

Marianna took notes. Not on Maggy's comments, which would have been amusing but valueless, but on the clothes, which were predictable, dull, and of vital interest to *Vogue.* Mick Jagger's wife slipped in late and took a seat saved for her by a vendeuse. She was wearing a bowler. Maggy lit one cigarette from another and spilled the ashtray's contents with a trembling hand. "Ah, regardes ça. What an offense to nature for a woman to support a hat like that. On a man, well, that's another matter entirely. I remember when I lived in London . . ."

Marianna took notes on the first half dozen numbers that came onto the runway and then realized, as inexperienced as she was, that Maggy Moal was simply ringing a few changes on the bell, that the clothes were what they had been six months earlier and what they would be six months from now. Like Balenciaga and Chanel and Madame Grès, Maggy had become a classic. The younger, less established designers had to do it over again every spring and every fall. A Maggy Moal could cheat a little.

Again, the harsh, rasping voice. Maggy was in a state, punching with one arthritic hand at her brown wig, which had somehow come unanchored, and which she kept trying to push back up into her straw hat. The cane was discarded now, lying on the carpet for a careless mannequin to trip over and earn a sound cursing. One cigarette burned in the ashtray, another in the crimson corner of her mouth.

"Now this," Maggy told the editor of *Elle,* "jetez un coup d'oeil at this one. Not bad, though I say it who shouldn't." The fashion editor nodded like a bird and jotted down a number. "The girl is horrible," Maggy announced. "Pregnant surely by that blackamoor she sleeps with. Can't wear clothes. Not in that state. Not at all." She flicked the ash from her cigarette onto the lap of the young actress. The fashion editor nodded again. The actress smiled, and when Maggy wasn't looking, brushed off her ripe lap. Marianna looked around the room. Parkinson, the British photographer, towered in one corner. The Puerto Rican fag in another. The English press ladies huddled together, all bad legs and veiny noses. A Mitteleuropean who called himself "Baron" and who supplied pirated fabric swatches to the reused woolen mills of Prato, took assiduous notes. Two French dancers, male, pressed their knees together. Picasso's natural daughter smiled at the photographers. A pretty blonde from *Glamour* shredded her program and the *Women's Wear Daily* editor nursed a hangover.

"I can't abide this dress," Maggy Moal barked. It was a lovely chiffon number in a sort of apricot tone. "It will sell, of course, taste being what it is. As for me, chiffon is nothing. Rien. The merest breeze blows it right up your crotch."

She lighted another cigarette and inhaled deeply. Some of the smoke went down the wrong way. Maggy leapt to her feet, coughing and gagging. The cane was kicked further out onto the floor and the ashtray went flying. Her straw hat tilted crazily and she dove into her handbag for a huge silk bandanna. The next few moments were occupied by sneezes and blowings of the nose. "Numéro quatre-vingt-huit," the vendeuse announced. "Merde!" said Maggy Moal. "They grind up turds in the tobacco these days."

Tony Winslow was waiting for Marianna on the steps of the house.

"Hello," he said.

"Well, hi."

"Drink? Or do you have to go back to the office?"

She shook her head. "No, I can have one."

They went down the street to the zinc bar on the corner. Marianna ordered a citron pressé and Winslow had a beer. They stood at the bar. It was only four thirty, too early for the workmen to come in, too late for the lunchtime drinkers. A rummy played the pinball.

"Well?" Winslow said, sensing her reserve.

Marianna looked at him.

"Hey, listen, I know all about liberation and stuff. Really I do. And being with you those times was great. And no regrets. But, hey, you don't think you can just come and go this way and never . . ."

"I was in Africa," he said, feeling slightly self-conscious about the sound of how it came out. "On business."

"Africa?"

"Yeah, Marrakesh."

"Oh, hell," she said. "That's just Morocco. I thought you meant *Africa*."

"Listen," he said. "I need some help."

"Yeah?"

"Anouk Fayol. Jacques Fayol's daughter. I've got to find her."

Marianna lifted her hands. "Oh, boy," she said, half to herself.

"She's one of Madame Claude's girls, but when I put in a call from the airport, Claude played dumb. Where does she live? Does anyone have a phone number?"

Marianna looked at him.

"Winslow," she said, "I've got to hand it to you. We go to bed once. You fly off to Grasse. We go to bed again. You fly to Africa. You come back telling me you've got to find some hundred-dollar-a-night hooker and complaining the madame doesn't know and can I help? I mean, Jesus!"

He nodded. "I know it sounds crazy. But it isn't. It's damned important."

Marianna pulled out a cigarette.

"Important?" she asked.

"Yes."

She exhaled deeply.

"Okay. I'll help. I'll *try* to help. But listen . . ."

"Yes?"

"Don't you think you can trust me enough to tell me something? I mean, you're running all over Paris, in and out of the country, desperate straits, kill the lead dog, ride the horses into the ground, but keep the flag flying . . . and I don't know what the hell you're doing or looking for or chasing. Don't you think I *ought* to know? Something?"

"Okay," he said. "Do you have to go back to *Vogue* or can we sit and talk?"

She looked into his face. "We can talk," she said. He reached out to light her cigarette and she saw his hand then, bruised and purpled. "Hey?" she said, instinctively reaching out to touch it. Gently.

"Okay," Winslow said. "Here's what happened."

He did not tell her the whole story. In fairness, there were parts of it still unclear to him, other parts that were not essential. But he gave her most of it and did not hold back on what seemed vital. She listened, occasionally asking an intelligent question, and always watching his face as he talked and never wisecracking or saying a silly thing. Toward the end he said:

"That note from Grumbach, the old huissier. The posthumous advice from her father, that's the part doesn't make sense. That's the part I know is important but I need Anouk to tell me for certain."

"... seeking spiritual guidance ... that part?"

"Yeah."

"I don't understand. A dying man, his only child, it's not an unnatural thing to say."

"For *Fayol* it was. Remember what I told you about his wife. How she hated him for playing around, but just as much for rejecting religion, the church, God?"

"A deathbed confession. It happens."

Winslow shook his head. "Fayol didn't know he was going to die. This was a message he'd left with Grumbach some time before. Something that was to be transmitted to Anouk if and when he died. A message conceived by a man who had no intention of dying. No, it's got to mean something *more* than it says. There has to be *more* to it than that."

That seemed to make sense, she said. All right, then, where did they start looking? Castel's? New Jimmys? Winslow said that was the damnable part of it. Anouk might just have gone off with someone for a day, for a week. She might be at St.-Trop, in Italy, spring skiing at Val d'Isère. Who the hell knew? Did Marianna have any ideas? Any hunches? Where would a beautiful young whore spend the last day of April?

"I think I know whom to ask," Marianna said.

"Who?"

"Zader Nafredi," she said.

There was an argument. They left the café; walked through the streets. It was still daylight but getting darker, clouds on the wind off the Channel. A spatter of rain.

"The government hopes it rains like hell," he said.

"Why? Oh, for May Day."

"Sure," he said. "Just like New York. During the hot summer. The cops always hope for rain on the weekends."

"Do you think there'll be trouble?"

He shrugged. Then he stopped and took her arm. "Look, I don't want you fucking around with Nafredi. We'll find Anouk. We'll drop by all the usual places tonight and . . ."

"Oh, come on, Tony. He's easy. He's always been after me. I can call him, make a little date. Just drinks. I can . . ."

"You don't know whether he's dangerous. I don't either. But I told you about those guys tracking me. Nafredi's men, maybe. He . . ."

"Don't be silly. He's a fop. A sleek ponce. Thinks every girl in Paris is mad for him. I can . . ."

"He's an Arab and I don't want you to . . ."

Marianna shook her head. "Persians are *not* Arabs. They're Moslems but they're not Arabs. They . . ."

"Oh, shit."

They were walking again now, not so much because they wanted to, not because they were going anywhere in particular, but simply to walk. To argue and to walk. Because now it was raining hard and they had no coats. And they didn't really care.

Henry Rousselot had lunched at the Bankers' Club. Not La Grenouille or even the Twenty One Club, not by any stretch, but passable food and good service and a place where the pulse of the Street was never far beneath the surface of the steam tables. Now, shorn of his guest, he sat over a second coffee, toyed with the idea of dessert, and instead bit into a rare cigar.

He knew these Delaware Corp. people. When they sent "A" to see him, it meant information. When they sent "B" it meant litigation. When they sent "C" it meant the bond market. And when they sent ".D" it was trouble.

Henry Rousselot wondered if he should call Winslow home. It was, after all, a banking matter. Not a war. He puffed at the cigar and worried.

He had just bought lunch for "D."

Zader Nafredi hated the Pakistanis. Oh, he knew they were all part of the same Moslem League, that he should be indulging in fraternal bonhommie. But really, what shits they were. What *total* shits!

To play two hours of deadly serious squash, without a single, "très bien joué," without a smile, and . . . uncouth peasants . . . never to concede a single casy point, well, you could keep your Pakistanis. And welcome to them.

He emerged from the shower room of Le Jockey Club and strode into the dressing room. The Pakis had gone. Probably, he thought, they don't even shower after a match. Quelle saleté! He toweled down and drank off two glasses of the iced water the boy had fetched. There was a full-length mirror on the wall opposite. Nafredi looked at himself. His anger began to slip away. He half turned. Not a pound of fat. Not an ounce. Anywhere.

He smoothed back his damp hair and picked up the can of deodorant aerosol. The evening stretched pleasantly ahead. A new girl, that was what he needed. A different face, *not* just another girl from Claude. A foreigner, perhaps. An English girl. Or an American.

He looked at himself again. Yes, he thought. He had begun to stiffen.

SÉDUCTION MANQUÉE

Marianna Troy giggled. It was not like her to giggle. Not standard operating procedure at all for Yale graduates from Connecticut with decent grades and junior editorships at *Vogue* to giggle. Not at all the thing for a twenty-three-year-old woman with a realistic image of herself and of her relationship to the world around her. And to men. Marianna liked men, she enjoyed sex, and without indulging in adolescent ego-tripping she understood quite clearly that to most men she represented a readily negotiable piece of tail. But Marianna was giggling now. It was just before midnight and she was alone with Zader Nafredi in his apartment and she was nervy as hell. Nervy and also stoned.

Tony Winslow had dropped her at her place at six. They were still arguing. She was still being protective about his hand.

"It's okay. Just looks awful."

She stroked it, the part that had gone purple. She said nothing, but shook her head.

"Now don't, dammit, start crying on me," he said.

"Who's crying? I'm not crying. I'm mad." Tears ran down her cheeks.

"Angry," he said.

"Okay, angry. Sore as hell. Here you are, a nice civilized banker in your nice civilized suit and people are beating you up and trying to kill you and I thought this country was at peace."

141

"Just to keep the record straight," Winslow said sensibly, "I half killed that poor son of a bitch getting this." He looked at his hand. Then: "What country's at peace?"

"The U.S. of fucking A.," she said. She was still crying but she was smiling, too.

"All right, let's just keep our goddamn countries straight. Let's not go getting our countries mixed up."

"I never mix up countries. I got straight A's in social studies in boarding school."

"Which used to be called geography."

She reached up and kissed him on the mouth. "Now get the hell out of here and let me go inside and get dressed up sexy and go and seduce Mr. Nafredi and find Anouk Fayol for you."

"I don't like it," he said. "That greasy Arab."

"You sound like a little boy. And he's not an Arab. He's . . ."

"I know," Winslow said. He looked unhappy.

Now it was nearly six hours later. Marianna had phoned Nafredi. "Ah, quel coincidence merveilleux," he enthused. "I said to myself not two hours ago that it was time for me to be seeing some new faces. That Paris was going stale. And now . . . voilà, you call." They met at Lapérouse. Nafredi, lean, dark, the hair going gray just ever so, the English-cut clothes, the long, tapering fingers. Marianna wore a silk shirt, a suede skirt, and boots.

"You should have let me send the car."

"No," she said. "I like the rain."

He had arranged one of the small, private dining rooms. She smiled over that. How corny could you get? Well, all the better to heat you with, my dear. She giggled then, but to herself. Nafredi snapped his fingers and the sommelier brought the first wine. Only the first. For a Moslem Nafredi had an enormous capacity. Marianna did not. When the soufflé de chocolat arrived she was drunk. Nerves, nerves, and the wine and the necessity to play a role had done it. That and the Percodan Nafredi had dumped into her glass.

"Hey," she said. "What's that for?"

Nafredi pointedly sprinkled a bit of powder into his own glass. They were at the Dom Pérignon stage of the dinner by this. "To make you fly, my dear. And to permit me to fly a little bit as well." He smiled.

Oh, my God, she thought, if I really have to fuck this character I won't be able to live with myself. I laughed off better lines than his in junior high in Greenwich. Instead she smiled with what she hoped was half lechery, half mystery, and permitted him to stroke her thigh.

There was a knock on the door of the little room.

"Entrez."

The waiter came in. He was a great diplomat. He was probably a second secretary at one of the lesser embassies when he wasn't moonlighting at Lapérouse. He did not look at Marianna. And with a straight face he suggested, "Monsieur, the Brie is very good. Runny, just as it must be. Also the Port Salut and naturally there is a decent chèvre."

To his credit, Nafredi made an effort to consider the plateau of cheeses before settling on the chocolate soufflé. It was at that point Marianna realized she was drunk.

Thirty minutes later they left the restaurant. The chauffeured car sped them across town in the rain and Nafredi grappled with her in the back seat while she alternated between giggling and wondering how the hell she was going to get Anouk's home phone number out of him and avoid being screwed at the same time.

She was too drunk to notice the lines of buses and trucks rolling into Paris and the CRS riot cops and military policemen who were waving hooded flashlights to direct them to the appropriate assembly areas.

Now she was in his bed. Or, rather, she was still lying atop the bed, fully clothed, the shirt open a bit, but the rest of her very comme il faut. Nafredi smirked. Marianna tried to suppress a giggle. There was something she wanted to ask him, some reason she was here.

"My dear," Nafredi said suavely, "you really must let me

help you take off those wet boots." He brightened. "Or do you prefer wearing them in bed?"

She giggled. How banal could he get? Nafredi smiled, thinking her laughter complaisance. She remembered.

"Zader, that girl you were seeing. Anouk. I liked her. She was sweet."

"Oh, yes, a splendid girl. A bit sullen at times. Not like you, all sunshine and laughter. You Americans, such an optimistic people."

"Hey, Zader, I think Anouk's sexy. Let's call her. Let's see if she's home."

The Iranian's eyes went wide. Mmmm, he thought, what a marvelous idea. Two girls. Both of them tall, dark, beautiful. One French, the other American. Who would have thought this college girl (as he thought of her) could stumble on such a diverting scheme.

"Marianna, you're delicious. I'll phone her." He went to a tall dresser and took a small leather book out of the top drawer. Ah, here it was. Her number. He was sure Anouk would enjoy it. The American, well, he was not so sure. It was the drink talking, that and the Percodan. But once they had begun, what could the American do? Lie back and enjoy it, he smiled to himself. What a vulgar way they had with words. Yet how descriptive. He moved to the phone.

Marianna sat up. She hadn't worn a bra and the shirt was unbuttoned nearly to the waist. Nafredi's eyes were on her. "No," she said, "lemme call. I want to talk to Anouk."

"Whatever you wish, darling."

Marianna took the phone from him.

"ETOILE 67-82," he said.

"Etoile what?"

"ETOILE soixante-sept-quatre-vingt deux."

"Okay," Marianna said. She dialed half the number and then dropped the phone, sat back against the headboard, smiled weakly at Nafredi, and said, "You do it."

He picked up the phone and untangled the cord. Perhaps he

would watch, just watch, the first time. Watch these two beautiful young women make love. Then, when he was fully aroused, first one and then the other. Perhaps later, some photographs. He wondered if there was film in the camera. What a pleasant sight it would be. He began to dial.

"Zader?" Marianna said dreamily.

"Yes, my pet?"

"Zader . . ."

"Yes?"

Marianna Troy leaned over the side of the bed and vomited.

"ETOILE 67-82," Marianna said. "Least, I think so. I'm still kinda stoned."

Winslow wrote down the number.

"You're sure you're okay?"

"I'm home, I'm almost in bed, and I'm alone." She made a face. "And my mouth tastes like sneakers at the end of the season. Look, Tony, lemme go. I'm going to get sick again."

He laughed into the phone. He thought she was being funny. "What did Nafredi say when you bailed out?"

"He called his man to clean up the mess, sent for the chauffeur to get rid of me, and mumbled something impolite about American women."

"The bastard."

"You would have said something impolite too if I upchucked on your best Persian carpet."

Winslow called the ETOile number. He called it over and over. There was no answer. Damn the luck, he thought. Marianna had done her job, tricked Nafredi, spent a miserable evening, and now Anouk was away or coked up or just too damn lazy to answer. He called the phone company. No, there was no way they could give him the address. Finally, at four in the morning, he woke Paul Delane.

"Haven't you got some friends in the police department or at the telephone company?"

"Who is this?"

"Winslow. Wake up."

"Winslow, you're fucking crazy. Do you know what time it is? What time is it?"

"I have this phone number. Anouk Fayol. But she doesn't answer."

"Damn smart she is, I'd say."

"If I give you the phone number, will you . . . ?"

"I shouldn't have answered."

"Paul . . . !"

"Okay, okay, give me the number. But I'm not calling anyone before eight. My reputation in this town is bad enough as it is."

Winslow gave him the number. He thanked Delane and then he called the number a few more times and finally, still dressed, he fell asleep.

He woke just before eight to the sound of drums. Confused, he looked at his watch. Then he threw back the curtains. The rain had stopped. It was a lovely morning. It was May Day.

MAY DAY

The rain *had* stopped. The streets were washed clean, the trees
and the grass were a startling green, and despite the best efforts
of the government's meteorologists, the sun rose, shone brightly,
and the first of May, celebrated throughout Europe and in most
other civilized places as Labor Day, had begun.

Winslow put on a robe and went out onto the balcony. He
could see only a bit of the street. Men and women, some of them
wearing sashes and uniforms, some carrying furled flags, milled
about. From the top floor they seemed a jolly lot. He went back
inside, turned on the radio, and rang for coffee and brioche. The
eight o'clock news told him about the parade. They estimated
200,000 people would demonstrate in favor of the government,
and being a nice, manageable government-regulated radio station,
mentioned only in passing that a workers' parade was also sched-
uled for that morning. They neglected entirely to say nearly half a
million people were expected to march in *opposition* to the government.

Winslow phoned Delane. The Frenchman told him grumpily,
"I'm calling, I'm calling," and hung up. He tried Anouk's number. No answer. He thought of calling Marianna and decided
against it. She needed the sleep and it was a holiday. Across the
street he was pleased to see that his neighbor had come out on
her balcony to see what all the noise was about and that she wore

147

a very pretty short pink robe that looked fine above her tanned legs. By nine thirty Winslow was shaved, showered and dressed, and he decided to go out and see the show.

The day concierge greeted him and then Winslow remembered there had been no papers at the door. "C'est la grève," the concierge said cheerfully. There was a strike. Nothing serious. But certain services might endure a disruption for the day. "Vous savez, monsieur, c'est les syndicats." The unions. It was the unions. Winslow and the concierge exchanged shrugs, as experienced men do, and he stepped out into the morning sunlight where the page bowed and where one of the porters was sweeping. It was a lovely day for a parade, Winslow thought. The sun was warm, nothing like the Marrakesh sun, but pleasant. He walked left and went up to the avenue Franklin Roosevelt. Here the street was already closed off by the cops and a band and several hundred men with arm bands smoked cigarettes and waited impatiently for something to happen. He turned left again and walked up to the Rond Point. There was still vehicular traffic on the Champs but there were a half dozen motorcycle cops in helmets waving the cars on, and it was apparent they would soon shut down the Champs as well. If you want to get anywhere today, Winslow told himself, you'd better plan on walking. That or the Metro. He wondered if the subway was running.

He crossed the Rond Point and ducked into one of the cafés on the other side. He tried Anouk again and then called Delane and told him he'd check in every hour or so. The Frenchman said he was working on it. He sounded less annoyed now. Winslow assumed he had had some coffee. Winslow sat at one of the tables on the sidewalk and ordered a citron pressé. It was getting warm. The waiters were already hustling with most of the tables taken by tourists and a few curious Frenchmen. Away off in the distance he thought he could hear other bands, other loudspeaker trucks. He wondered if it was all part of the government parade or if this was the workers. He hoped to hell the lines of march of the two parades didn't cross. That could be bad. Very bad.

Winslow tried Anouk's number again. Goddammit, where *was* the woman? He knew exactly what he would ask her, it would take only a few minutes, and then he could go on and . . . suddenly, he stopped. Grumbach! The huissier! Why hadn't he *thought* of that? Grumbach could tell him just what was in Fayol's last note. Jesus, why hadn't he thought of that? He hurried away from the café and his long legs carried him toward the Faubourg St.-Honoré. Grumbach might have taken the day off, he might not talk. But if he was on holiday, surely he could bribe his home address out of the concierge. And he was confident he could charm, or bully, the old notary into giving him something. Anything was better than waiting for Anouk. He took off his suit jacket and slung it over his shoulder and strode along. All Paris seemed to be on the march and he had to push his way past the cops and through the crowds.

The rue des Petits Champs was too narrow to be a marshalling area. The street was quiet, shuttered, and except for one or two children playing and a concierge washing down the steps, it was deserted. He rang for the concierge of Grumbach's building. An old woman peeked through the lace curtain and then, recognizing him to be neither an obvious rapist nor a bill collector, she opened her door.

"Fermé," she said. Closed for the day.

"Oui, je sais. Mais Monsieur Grumbach? Il n'est pas là?"

She looked confused.

"Monsieur Grumbach?" he repeated.

The old lady stared at him. "Monsieur Grumbach ici? Evidemment pas."

Did she perhaps have his home address? It was a matter of some importance. He and Grumbach were close friends, practically brothers, and Monsieur Grumbach would be disconcerted indeed if his old friend who had come so far were not to spend a pleasant hour with him.

"You are his friend?"

Winslow assured the old woman this was so. In all the world, perhaps his closest, his dearest, his . . .

"Then I am sorry to have to break the bad news, monsieur."

What bad news? He wasn't out of town? En vacances?

No, the concierge said, "il est mort."

"Dead? But he can't be . . ."

The old woman smiled. She was quite pleased to have such a divertissement on a dull morning. "C'est vrai. Il est mort depuis cinq jours. Six, peut-être."

Dead five or six days? My God, when had Winslow seen the old man? He started to count back. The concierge was pointing.

"Là, right there. Death was instantaneous. The truck, the way they speed these days, it's a wonder any Parisians are still alive and . . ."

"A truck killed him?"

"Ah, mais oui. The poor fellow."

"And he . . . ?"

"You know how he was, since you were such a close friend," the concierge said, eyeing Winslow shrewdly. "So feeble, shaking, and the trouble with his eyes. All that close work. He stepped into the street, never looking this way or that, and voilà . . ."

The detective at the local precinct regarded him bleakly. Grumbach had been the victim of an auto accident. The truck driver might face a technical charge of involuntary manslaughter, nothing beyond that. He had been released, of course. The old gentleman had been buried. Winslow tried to probe. The cop stood up. It was a holiday, a half million people were marching, a general strike had been declared with fortunately only so-so effectiveness, monsieur must understand the police had other things to do than to review a routine traffic accident that had occurred five days earlier. Winslow phoned Delane from the stationhouse. Delane rummaged through his issues of *Le Figaro*.

"Yes, here it is. He was seventy-two. Most unfortunate accident. The Société des Huissiers plan a memorial service. No flowers, please."

Had he found Anouk?

No, but he had the address. Did Winslow want to meet him

there? In an hour? Make it an hour and a half. It was a bitch trying to get around town with parades and the strike.

Winslow was angry as he walked back across Paris toward the Étoile, toward Anouk's apartment.

Old men got run over every day by careless truck drivers. Arab toughs held up tourists who'd been drinking in dubious parts of Marrakesh at three in the morning. Fathers with high blood pressure sent last words regarding spiritual advice to wayward daughters. Rich, sleek men like Nafredi preyed on long-legged American girls with blue eyes and erect nipples. Fags sent anonymous threatening notes and promised bribes. And spoiled 19-year-old French girls took drugs and wore leather underwear and disappeared for days at a time. These things happened. There was nothing bizarre about any of them. Except when they all happened at once. And when they all happened because a merchant banker from New York found himself in Paris trying to track down some dull, dusty files about a modestly profitable fashion house that suddenly seemed to be worth a hundred million dollars.

"I'm *damned* if it's all coincidence," Winslow told himself. "Damned!"

Both parades were in full flower now. The workers, many of them carrying red flags, snaked through the streets heading east, toward the Place de la Bastille. It was a cheerful march. The Left sensed it was coming to power and it wanted to demonstrate its maturity, its cohesiveness, its capacity to rule the nation. This wasn't a day for surly defiance, for the baiting of the police, for window smashing or the overturning of cars. The bands played. The "Marseillaise," the "Internationale," martial music, and popular tunes clashed and blended. Children romped alongside, and occasionally a drunk staggered into the line of march to be shoved gently back to the curbside.

At the other end of Paris, along the Champs Élysées, there were fewer smiles, more martial airs, uniforms, determined faces. There hadn't been a Popular Front government in France since the thirties, and these people didn't mean to have one now. Their march was somber, pugnacious, and slightly nervous. The pro-government forces were decidedly not looking forward to the tenth of May, to the elections, possibly to the end of an era of privilege and the start of a time of social revolution. Especially grim were the officers, the CRS riot police, and the veterans groups. Only among the detachments of "paras," of marines, of air force troops, and among the sailors with their red pompons was there joy. To be in Paris, on a pleasant holiday in the spring, meant pretty girls, cold beer, and a few hours away from the drudgery of garrison tedium.

Winslow was having even more trouble getting through the crowds this time. Anouk's flat was in a good building on the Avenue Marceau, a few steps from the back door of Le Drug-store. When he finally got there, Delane was waiting. He looked very happy. Holidays bored him. He hated parades and loathed politics. The general strike upset the routine of his life and he could not amuse himself by working, since there was no staff. Winslow's summons, the mysterious death of the huissier, the search for a beautiful girl with dubious morals, this pleasantly conspiratorial mission, and the sense of being wanted, being *needed* even, erased the ennui of the day. Paul Delane was at the top of his form.

There was no answer at Anouk Fayol's apartment. Delane was sent to fetch the concierge. The old gentleman performed as advertised: with petulance, fatigue, and irritation—outraged at this proposed invasion of his tenant's privacy.

"You expect me to open the door of an apartment of one of my finest young clients?" he demanded.

"It's important," Winslow said lamely.

The concierge shook his head. He stamped his foot, but he was wearing soft carpet slippers and the gesture was wasted energy. Therefore, he spoke louder:

"I have never heard of such an impudent suggestion! Mademoiselle Fayol pays her rent on time, she is most generous to my staff (the concierge and his wife), she is a young woman alone whose safety and privacy I am sworn to uphold."

"He wants fifty francs," Delane whispered.

Winslow handed over the money.

"But of course," the concierge declared as he inserted his pass-key, "if it is a matter of importance, then surely I would be less than faithful to Mademoiselle Fayol to prevent her friends from entering."

He opened the door, gave a half-bow, and shuffled off.

Except that it was more luxurious, better appointed, the living room was about what would be expected of a nineteen-year-old Paris career girl. There was a good stereo, a well-stocked bar, several rather nice pictures, the usual magazines, a stack of news-papers ranging from *L'Humanité* to *The Sunday Times* of Lon-don. It was in the bedroom that the scene changed.

"Jesus," Delane said.

Winslow nodded. "Frederick's of Hollywood."

"Comment?" Delane asked.

"Never mind," Winslow said.

The room was constructed around the circular waterbed. There was an electric cord. Delane held it up. "Complete with thermostat." There were mirrors everywhere, including, of course, the ceiling. An intricate strobe light setup included several different-colored jellies. A flip of the switch sent them revolving and the room was turned into a nightmare of rapidly moving, constantly changing colored lights.

"I wonder if she has video tape."

Delane shook his head. "When I was her age I was happy to make love in the stairwell. Considered myself damned lucky to get it anywhere."

Winslow nodded. "But you're a romantic, Delane." He opened a closet. There were the usual street clothes and then there were . . . well, costumes. Winslow held one up. It was sheer, black, and apparently composed mostly of open spaces.

"Don't put that away," Delane said. "I need ideas for my next collection."

Winslow's natural distaste for prying capitulated to curiosity. He opened a dresser drawer. Sweaters. Another. Stockings and pantyhose. A third. A collection of dildos. He held one up. "Ah," Delane said, "how can mere man compete with the genius of the rubber specialty trade?" He took the device. "I didn't know they came so large."

On the back of the bathroom door, on a hook under a terry robe, they found the dog whip.

"Well," Winslow said, "she wasn't kidding, I guess."

By the phone on the night table was a small revolving file. Phone numbers. Boy, he thought, what the tabloids wouldn't give for this. Curious, he spun to the "W's." His name hadn't yet been entered. He didn't know whether to be sore or relieved. Under the "N's" there was Nafredi.

"Antoine," said Delane, "don't you think it's about time you gave me some rational reason why you've taken up breaking and entering? Why this morbid interest in Anouk Fayol?"

Winslow thought for a moment.

"Yeah," he said, "yeah, I guess it is time."

They closed the apartment and Winslow gave his phone number and another fifty francs to the concierge. "When Mademoiselle Fayol returns, please call me at the Hôtel. At any hour. It is most important."

The concierge would not fail to do so. For gentlemen such as these there was very little he would fail to do.

Tony and Paul worked their way through the May Day crowds and went into an American bar on the rue de Berri down the street from the *Herald-Tribune* building. They ordered drinks.

"Well?" Delane asked.

Winslow lighted a cigar. "Okay, I'll give you everything I can. I'm getting a bit pissed off trying to play a lone hand anyway. I need help. I've told most of this to Marianna. Now to you. But you've got to keep it quiet."

Delane nodded. "She went to Yale, did she not? The lovely Mademoiselle Troy?" Winslow said yes.

"And you to Princeton, and I am a *Harvard* man. Ah," said Delane, "an Ivy League entente cordiale." He was pleased by the line. Withholding only the name of Rousselot's client, Dela-

ware Corp., Winslow told him the story. They had finished their
second scotch by the time he finished.

"You think the huissier was murdered?" Delane asked, uncharacteristically somber.

Winslow looked at his friend. "What else is there to think?"

As May Day was celebrated with marches and music on the
Right Bank, with student riots and bloody retaliation on the Left,
as Anthony Winslow and Paul Delane picked their way through
Anouk Fayol's underwear, there were other happenings, more or
less significant. In her suite in the Ritz, Maggy Moal, not for the
first time, packed her several passports, a great deal of money,
and several open tickets to Zurich, to Nice, and to London, and
prepared herself for flight. In suburban Montfort L'Amoury,
where there were no riots or marches but only some very decent
polo, the Shah's man, Zader Nafredi, congratulated himself on
having successfully bribed the one person who might deliver into
his hands the great fashion house of Fayol. In New York, where
it was not a holiday, Henry Rousselot puffed at his pipe, fretted
about the rain that threatened to wash out his golf the next day,
and wondered whether he should acquaint young Winslow with
his suspicions about the Delaware Corp. and the *real* reason they
were willing to pay $85 million (or more) for a Paris fashion
house and the "real property" the house presumably owned. And
in her flat on the rue de Boulainvilliers, Marianna Troy once
more threw up and, once more, vowed never again to mix alcohol
and drugs. Or to have anything to do with Persians later than
Cyrus the Great.

As for Anouk Fayol, it would be Sunday night before Winslow
would have news of her.

A RELIGIOUS EXPERIENCE

Winslow phoned Marianna late Friday night. He gave her a reprise of events, excepting the death of the huissier. He saw no point in upsetting her. He would tell her later. Marianna promised to stay home that night, in case of trouble following the parades. "Anyway, I still feel lousy," she said. Delane took Winslow to a bistrot near the Porte des Ternes. Marchers, some of them wearing armbands or carrying furled flags, came in and settled down to the serious business of a French dinner. There were rumors of fighting on the Left Bank, but here, at the western gate of the city, it was quiet, the marchers being more interested in the menu than in politics. By midnight, when they started home, the streets had been cleared and there were plenty of cabs. Delane continued to insist they were being followed, but at no point was he able to isolate the trackers as he had done at Colombes. Back in his hotel room Winslow wearily stripped and got into bed. He made one more call to Anouk's apartment. The phone rang and rang. There was no reply.

"I've got an absolutely brilliant idea," Marianna said.

It was ten o'clock Saturday morning. Wakened by her call, Winslow sat up in bed and reached out a long arm to pull back the drapes. Dazzling sun burst into the room. He flipped a ciga-

rillo out of the pack and lighted it, cradling the phone between
ear and shoulder.

"You are a constant source of brilliant ideas. Give."

"Madame Fayol. We'll go see her."

Winslow drew in the smoke. "Yeah?"

"Sure. She's a religious fanatic. We'll tell her about her husband's last message to Anouk. About 'spiritual guidance.' She'll
know what it means."

"And she'll tell you?"

"Of course. Aren't I a product of the best schools?"

They met at Brasserie Lipp for lunch, took turns calling
Anouk, got no answer, and then took a cab to the Avenue Foch.

A woman in gray admitted them. From somewhere deep in the
house came the same chanting he had heard before. Marianna
stood close to him.

"Monsieur Winslow et Mademoiselle Troy pour Madame
Fayol, s'il vous plaît."

"Veuillez attendre."

The woman disappeared into the depths of the house. Winslow
took Marianna's arm. He could feel her trembling, just slightly.
"If she asks," he said, "try to be enthusiastic about Gregorian
chant."

She smiled, cool now, the trembling over. Hélène Serrat Fayol
came into the anteroom.

"Yes?"

Winslow told her it was vital they contact Anouk.

"You mean Anne," the woman said.

"Yes."

Mme. Fayol led them into a rather formal sitting room off to
the right. She beckoned them to sit. She herself took a straight-
backed chair.

"When you were first here, Monsieur Winslow, I told you I
had very little knowledge of my late husband's business affairs
and I think I also informed you that my daughter and I have had
very little contact for some time. Nothing has altered that situation since last we met."

You're a cold one, Winslow thought.

"I think something has altered it," he said.

"Yes?"

"Monsieur Grumbach, the huissier to whom you kindly sent me, is . . ."

"He is dead. Yes, I know. An unfortunate accident."

Winslow let that one slip by. "Of course," he said smoothly. "But before his death Grumbach had sent a last message from your husband to Anouk . . . Anne."

"Oh? And how do you know this?"

Winslow dove in. "Anne told me."

Hélène Fayol looked pointedly at Marianna. "Your stay in Paris seems to have been full of event. But if Anne told you, then I fail to see what light I can . . ."

"Anne mentioned the message, told me roughly what it said, but not the details. I need those details. And Anne seems to be . . . out of town."

"I cannot help you."

"Madame Fayol," Winslow said, speaking quietly, intensely, with what he hoped was at least a facsimile of religious fervor, "that last message dealt with Anne's spiritual life. It urged her to seek 'spiritual guidance,' to . . ."

Hélène Fayol laughed. It was a bitter sound.

"Forgive me, Monsieur Winslow, mademoiselle, but it is a bad joke to associate my late husband's name with references to higher realms. His very being was so rooted in this earth, in materialism, in pleasure, that it is simply inconceivable that he would have anything to say on the subject of spirituality. The message is clearly fraudulent."

She stood up. Winslow knew it was hopeless. Then Marianna spoke for the first time.

"What a lovely sound that is, Madame. Might we possibly listen for a moment?"

Hélène Fayol smiled. For the first time her face took on life.

"Of course," she said. "Come."

Like most private homes, "hôtels particuliers," along the Avenue Foch, the house seemed to have more depth than width.

Hélène Fayol led the way through several other large rooms and down a hallway into the back of the house, into what had apparently once been a solarium with high vaulted ceilings and walls of glass. But instead of a room flooded with the afternoon sun, everything was dim and dusty. Ivy crept everywhere on the outer surface of the glass, crawling upward over the windows, upward over the glassed ceiling, screening and obscuring the light, throwing the solarium into churchlike gloom, creating a stained-glass effect through clear panes. Madame Fayol halted, just inside the great high room, as if to adjust her vision to the artificial dusk. The chanting was all around them now, strong and beautifully done, but disturbing. Winslow could feel Marianna standing very close.

There were perhaps a dozen people in the room. Five or six wore the same dull-gray stuff of Hélène Fayol's costume. There were several monks, cowled and kneeling at prie-dieux. The women formed a semicircle around a small organ at which was seated a slender young man with tonsured head and white flowing robes. Two younger women, girls really, in the same white robes, flanked the organist, holding tall lighted candles. The young man seemed to be leading the chant. He sang a line in a strong, pure tenor and the women and the monks responded, the young man accompanying them on the keyboard. Winslow wondered if he and Marianna were supposed to join in, to kneel, or simply to listen.

Hélène Fayol motioned them to stand with her. The chanting was solemn, lonely, beautifully done. Even Winslow, who had no ear at all, could tell that. He let his gaze wander around the room. There were a number of candelabra, some religious pictures, a crucifix, what seemed to be an incense burner, some icons that might have been Russian, and a curiously primitive painting of the Virgin. Hélène Fayol joined in the chanting. She had a high, sweet voice.

" . . . . " they chanted.

Winslow's eyes were watering. He blamed it on the incense. Marianna stood close to him.

" . . . . " they chanted.

It was like nothing he had ever heard. It throbbed, it lifted him, carried him. His face felt damp and his eyes continued to run. Beside him Marianna followed the chant with her lips. He reached for her hand and squeezed it.

Goddammit, Winslow swore at himself. He drove the nails of his free hand into the palm. He pulled Marianna closer to him and felt her smooth hip against his. He concentrated on breathing deeply, slowly.

"............" they chanted. And then it was over.

Hélène Fayol led them back through the house. Winslow was shaken by the scene in the solarium, by his own reactions. He had nearly fainted, something he could never remember having done. Ever. Marianna and Hélène were chatting, pleasantly, as if they had just heard a pleasant bit of chamber music in somcone's music room. He could not seem to hear clearly what they were saying. He could smell the incense. Then Hélène Fayol was extending her hand and he was taking it. She was smiling, a controlled smile, but a smile. And saying something. He mumbled something in French in return, ". . . je vous en prie," some meaningless politesse. Marianna shook hands and then, instinctively, reached and kissed Hélène Fayol, lightly, on each cheek. There were more vague words. Then, blessedly, they were in the open air, in front of this ordinary house on the Avenue Foch. Winslow was surprised to see it was still daylight. They went down the path and out through the gate to the footpath.

Winslow sighed. "Another blind alley."

Marianna laughed.

"Yes?" Winslow said.

"You mustn't have been listening," she said.

Winslow looked blank.

"When we were leaving. When Madame Fayol took us to the door. You weren't listening."

"Listening? I was just trying to stay on my feet. That damned incense. I . . . well, what was it I didn't listen to?"

"Nothing much," Marianna said. "Just the name of the priest."

Winslow tensed. "What priest?"

"The one who's going to provide Anouk Fayol with spiritual guidance."

Tony Winslow stayed with Marianna that night. Delane met them for dinner. Having survived May Day without an explosion, Paris was in a Saturday night mood. Delane drove them to the Grand Comptoir and they had steaks and pommes frites and bottles of young Brouilly chilled. Winslow was still shaken by his experience at Hélène Fayol's. Delane told him that was all nonsense, that people reacted in different ways to different stimuli, that not having been inside a church for years, all that chanting and nuns and monks and incense had been too much for him.

"My God, man," Delane said in exasperation, "one minute you're on the Avenue Foch watching the jeunes filles go by, the next you're in the Sistine Chapel among the cherubs and the seraphim and the thrones and dominations ..."

"Paul," Marianna asked, "how do you know so much about religion?"

"I am a man of parts, chérie. Most couturiers spend their lives basting and tucking and swatching and creating lovely nothings. I am a man pursued by two demons, the making of money and the amassing of knowledge." He paused. "And, needless to say, there is money in religion. Right now, at this very moment, I am negotiating for a commission to redesign the Dominican habit. If all goes well—and with God's blessing, why shouldn't it?—the Cistercians, Benedictines, and Trappists will all clamor for my work."

"No Franciscans?" Winslow asked, pleased to know the name of an order.

Delane shook his head. "A poor lot. Their vow of poverty ... it impoverishes them so." He brightened. "I also refuse the Jesuits. Their intellectualism, it leaves no room for a color sense."

At the next table were a family of four: the mother and father, très bourgeois; the son and daughter, radical, yé-yé, anti-establishment. Winslow found himself listening to their talk. The parents had attended the pro-government parade the day before;

their children had marched with the Left. They were discussing the issues now, very politely, very solemnly. It made a nice change from an election in the States, Winslow thought; and then he remembered the dead huissier and the men shadowing him, and it didn't seem all that nice.

"Don't you want to know what Hélène Fayol told me?" Marianna asked, a bit deflated.

Of course, Winslow said, very much so. Delane leaned forward.

"Well," Marianna said, "there was a priest called Masson, during the war. Apparently he and Fayol had some dealings. The old priest was something formidable with the Resistance, blowing up bridges, baptizing children, ambushing Germans, reading his office, all at the same time. Fayol was, well, he was a bit fuzzy. Collaboration one day, flag-waving patriotism the next. Anyway, this priest, Masson, and Fayol became very close during the war and used to have these ferocious theological debates. Fayol clenching his fists and damning heaven, the old priest sprinkling holy water and telling his beads."

"And?" Winslow asked.

"And, simply, that there was something of a bond between them. If Fayol had wanted Anouk to turn to anyone for guidance, it would have been to Masson."

"My God," Winslow said, "what a break. Where is he?"

Marianna's face sort of changed. "Well," she said, "Hélène Fayol says she thinks he's dead."

Paris had a curious style that night as Delane drove them home. The Saturday night theatergoers, the well-fed emerging from the restaurants, the lovers on the Seine bridges, the buses and the taxis and the cars hurrying along—and on the silent street corners, just out of the lamplight, the CRS boys with their machine guns, the big blue buses parked in the shadows, the cruising police cars and motorcycle cops.

When they entered the apartment Marianna turned out the hall light and led the way, her long legs striding, into the bedroom, where she put on a low light and some music on the radio

and matter-of-factly stripped off her sweater and shirt and began
to unzip her jeans before Winslow had even loosened his tie.
When she was naked she turned down the bed clothes and then
looked at him as if to say "Well?" and then she got into bed and
waited.

Later, after they had made love and were lying in the dark
talking and smoking and sipping brandy from one glass, Winslow
thought how comfortable and domesticated he felt, and how,
without having made a judgment, he very much liked the feeling.

On Sunday they bought the English papers and some fresh
croissants, and Marianna ground coffee and brewed it, and they
spent the afternoon in bed. Delane called to say Maggy Moal was
having the vapors over the political crisis, and could they dine
with her?

"The old dame wants some young people around to tell her the
world will not end next Sunday," he said.

"You've got the wrong man," Winslow told him. "I'm convinced it will."

Marianna said she couldn't face one of Maggy's monologues,
the weekend having been emotional enough, and would Delane
mind terribly going along without them?

"Once more into the breach, dear friends," he said, and hung
up.

Marianna creased her brow. "I wonder if he has any idea of
the origin of that line."

Delane came by after dinner to report.

"Well, the old lady's convinced the country is for the shit pile.
She rather hopes for a putsch. But only if the army gets some
decent uniforms and brings back red stripes on the trousers."

"D'you discuss Madame Fayol with her?" Winslow wanted to
know.

Paul threw up his hands.

"But of course. I lied a bit, told her I'd dropped by Avenue
Foch to pay my respects—grieving widow, all that nonsense—
and asked her what she thought of the lady.

" 'Mean, narrow-minded, puritanical, priest-ridden, a spiritualist, necromancer, and assuredly a witch.' Maggy said Hélène dabbles in the occult, has a string of paid lovers, all of whom are renegade seminarians, takes drugs, overpays her servants to ensure their discretion, serves bad wine, always *was* a lousy dancer, and probably had a lesbian affair with Madame Nhu. Beyond that, Maggy says she's quite fond of her."

Delane drove Winslow back to the hotel.

"They're still on you, you know," the Frenchman said.

"Same ones?"

"Dunno. But they were lurking outside Marianna's place when I came by tonight. Hope to hell they don't start leaning on her."

Winslow glowered. "I should have had her come to the hotel," he said.

Delane told him not to worry, and Winslow said he'd try not. In the morning, Monday, they would begin checking out priests.

Winslow was in bed and nearly asleep when the concierge called.

"Mademoiselle Fayol," he said portentously, "has returned."

CANON MASSON

Anouk Fayol opened the door of her apartment. Winslow was there standing in the hall, annoyed, impatient, angry.

"Where the hell have you been?" he demanded.

Anouk looked absolutely marvelous. She was wearing white duck pants and a striped jersey. She was very suntanned, her long hair tied up in a rag of crimson silk. The striped jersey gave it all away and the long legs looked even longer in the tight white pants. Just two hours earlier Winslow had left Marianna Troy, thinking her as exciting a woman as he had ever known. Now he stood facing Anouk Fayol. And had he thought on it, he would have realized he was not thinking about Marianna. Not at all.

"Well?" he asked.

"Fuck you," she said.

Winslow had been waiting for her for so long, it seemed he should be the one aggrieved. Instead, here was this slim young woman standing in the doorway of her own home and he felt the interloper.

"I've been trying to get in touch," he said weakly. "Ever since the other night."

"And?"

"Well, you weren't here."

She put her hands on her slim hips. "That's rather obvious, isn't it?"

Winslow realized this wasn't at all the way he intended it

should be. "Look," he began, "it was important to get to see you. I had a question ..."

"Oh, come on," Anouk said, "the other night was a bit of a flop. I'm sorry for that. If you want to buy me for another evening, très bien, anything you want. But set it up properly. Through Claude. I'm not in the mood right now for all that filthy bargaining."

Anthony Winslow, Princeton, Harvard, and Rousselot & Partners, did not know quite what to say. Here was this nineteen-year-old girl toying with him, putting him down, leaving him on the doorstep like a teenage boy lusting for a good-night kiss. He had the manic notion he should tip his hat and go off alone into the night, his corduroy knickers whistling regret. Instead, he said:

"Shut up. Get inside. I want to talk to you."

His belligerence was just irrational enough to be effective. Anouk stepped back and Winslow walked in.

The girl stood there watching him, her fists clenched, as if she were not sure if she was to defend herself.

"Anouk," Winslow said, more gently, "do you know a priest called Masson?"

"Masson?"

"A friend of your father's. From the war."

"My father's friend ... ?" She seemed dazed by the question.

Winslow thought it the time for tact. "Look, Anouk, where the hell have you been? I've been calling and coming by here since last Friday. You ..."

"How did you know where I lived?"

"A long story. I saw your mother. She told me about Masson. The man I went to see a week ago, Grumbach, your father's huissier, he's dead."

"Dead? He can't be dead."

"Hit by a truck. An accident, the police say."

She was vague now, really vague. She sat down on the nearest chair. Suddenly she looked like a teenager and not the practiced courtesan.

"He isn't dead," she said. "He sent me a letter. A message from Fayol. From my father," she corrected herself.

"I know," Winslow said. "You told me. The other night."

Anouk began to laugh. "I go off for a pleasant weekend with friends and come home to find a strange American telling me my father's notary has been run down by a truck and asking questions about a priest my father knew during the war. You don't find all this a bit odd?"

Winslow sat down without being asked. The damn thing *was* odd: nearly keeling over during some silly prayer service, going to rugby matches just to hold a private conversation, bribing concierges, dawn flights to Marrakesh, priests and notaries, being tailed like some unfaithful husband.

"I'd like a drink," he said.

"All right," she said, sounding very sensible. She brought ice and glasses and Winslow poured stiff scotches for both of them. The girl was lovely, but under the tan she looked tired. There was something about the eyes. He wondered about her "pleasant weekend with friends." Having an active imagination rather handicapped him in talking to her. He kept seeing mustachioed men whipping her in her leather underwear.

"A Greek," she said, apropos of nothing.

"What?"

"It was a Greek this time. His name doesn't matter. Not Niarchos, one of the others. His yacht. It *was* smashing."

She talked like an English girl from one of the home counties. The same adjectives. "Smashing." It must have been the private schools.

"The sex too?" he asked.

She shrugged. "Oh, well, you know, the sex is part of it. It's expected. But the yacht was the terrific part. And several cinema stars. They're gathering for Cannes, for the film festival."

"Oh, you were at Cannes."

"Nice, actually." Once again the Anglicism "actually." He smiled over it.

"Why are you laughing? Is it at me?" Suddenly she was stern, defensive.

"I would never laugh at you, Anouk." He was quite sincere.

"I can't believe my mother would tell you about Canon Mas-

son. About anything. She usually refuses to discuss my father.
She really hates him. Hated him."

"I tricked her, I'm afraid. But she did give me Masson's name.
Said she was sure he was dead."

"Ha!"

"Oh?"

"She knows he's not dead. What a silly thing to do—give you
his name and then, when it's so easy to trace a Catholic priest in
France, to lie about that. How foolish she is. A stupid woman."

"Canon Masson," Winslow said, trying to be nonchalant,
"where would I find him?"

"But don't you know?"

Winslow shook his head.

"In Grasse. He's the pastor in Grasse."

He left her at three o'clock in the morning. They had made
love. He pretended to himself that he did it because he needed
her, that he was using her, that this was the most effective means
of insinuating himself with her, getting Anouk on his side. It
didn't wash. He'd wanted her the first time he'd ever seen her,
and now, after all the twists and turns, he had her.

They had talked, of course, over a second drink. Masson and
her father had been together during the war. She didn't know the
story, but apparently Masson was some sort of great hero in the
Resistance and her father had been, well, equivocal about the
Germans. But there was a bond between the two men, something
that held the hero and the collaborationist together, something
that . . . she broke off. "Look, I don't know the story. Why don't
you go see old Masson? I've never met him, but my father used
to tell me stories. He's quite a numéro, apparently—swills wine
all day and preaches great sermons and raises the dead, that sort
of thing. Might be good for your soul, as well."

"I'm sure of that," Winslow admitted. Then, half to himself:
"But does he have 'Paris One'?"

"What?"

"Nothing. Is there more scotch?"

Anouk got up and went into the kitchen for ice. Winslow knew now that he would go to Grasse to see Father Masson. And that the girl would go with him. Would *have* to go with him. She was the key to Masson. A priest, already practiced in the art of keeping his mouth shut, and a Resistance hero besides, would not likely be terribly chatty, with an American he did not know, about his old friend, lately dead, and the old friend's only daughter. No, it was essential that Anouk and Winslow visit Grasse together. And call on the parish priest. To discuss, well, Anouk's "spiritual guidance."

She came back into the room. She had no ice. She was naked. Winslow got up and she moved into his arms, standing on tiptoes so that her mouth could reach his. She did not taste of scotch or cocaine or of Greeks with yachts. She tasted marvelous.

In bed, after they had made love the first time and now lay together, her arm across his chest, their legs entwined, he asked her, Why?

She looked into his face and said quite simply, "Because I wanted to."

"Can we talk about the Maison Fayol?" he asked. "About the people who sent me here to buy it? About the money they . . ."

"Shut up," she said.

He moved to free his right arm, and with his hand he began to rotate her nipple. She shivered slightly and then, sliding down to where they were still wet, her tongue began to move and he felt the first renewed stirring of erection. He watched the top of her head, the silky, shining hair, and for that moment at least, her answer seemed sufficient.

The concierge woke Winslow. There were two men, from "the Ministry," waiting in the lobby. They wished to see him.

"What ministry?"

Regrettably, the concierge did not have this information.

"Give me five minutes and send them up," Winslow said. He swung his legs out of bed. What the hell was this all about? He thought about showering and then decided just to pull on pants and a shirt. There was a knock. The two men came in and shook hands. One of them handed him a business card. It identified him as from the Ministry. Winslow asked what he could do for the ministry. The one who had handed him the card launched into a complicated review of Franco-American commercial relations dating back to the Treaty of Versailles. Winslow half listened. The men had the smell of policemen, bad haircuts, heavy shoes, cheap raincoats, and those silly flat French fedoras affected by the civil service.

"I think you've got me confused with the commercial department of the American Embassy," Winslow said.

"But you are here to negotiate the purchase of a French company, are you not?"

That, Winslow said flatly, was a confidential matter. If and when any serious negotiations were undertaken, the ministry would of course be notified and the various clearances sought.

The answer was not entirely satisfactory, the lead Frenchman regretted to say. The ministry was aware that negotiations with the Maison Fayol had already reached an advanced state. It was essential that . . .

Winslow stood up, tired of fencing.

"Look," he said, "who is it, precisely, who wants this information?"

The men's eyes bugged. But they thought he knew. How stupid of them to have rambled on this way. Could he possibly forgive them?

"Mais, certainement," Winslow said. But if only they could now inform him as to just who . . . ?

"Monsieur le ministre," the junior partner said reverentially. They were the first words he had spoken.

"And does the minister wish to speak with me?" Winslow asked.

Oh, if only that could be arranged, what a ben?ficence for all concerned, how quickly all these confusions would be cleared up, how their careers would flourish, how Franco-American relations would ripen and deepen . . .

Winslow got the idea.

"D'accord," he said. "Now if you'll retreat to the lobby and let me finish dressing, I'll be with you in ten minutes and we'll go see Monsieur le ministre."

The two flunkies bowed and backed out the door, taking their flat hats and their bad haircuts and the cheap smell of the national police with them. Winslow got dressed.

There was a touch of Mussolini about the cabinet minister. His desk, an ornate Empire affair, rested on a pedestal only slightly more subtle than one of those platforms used by college professors to anchor, and elevate, their desks. The room was long and relatively narrow, and it took a long time to get to the desk. A single straight-backed chair was placed so that a visitor would be somewhat below the minister and would be looking directly into a large window that during certain of the daylight hours provided a sort of halo around the minister's head. Winslow, who didn't like the setting, remained standing.

"Now," the minister said, "we seem to have a small problem, Monsieur Winslow."

"Oh?"

"As you are doubtless aware, our national elections will be held on the tenth of May. The indications are that the government will prevail quite comfortably . . ."

"Oh?" said Winslow again. "I'd heard it would be quite close."

The minister looked at him narrowly. "My sources indicate otherwise," he said coldly. "What concerns us here this morning is l'affaire Fayol."

"And what affair is that?" Winslow asked, at his most obtuse.

The minister realized the interview was not going at all the way he'd planned. Alors, if it's to be an adversary proceeding . . .

"Monsieur Winslow, my government do not intend that on the eve of the national election the Maison Fayol be sold to a foreign group. Nor that any suggestion the house may be sold in future be discussed publicly. Later on, after the election, well, that's another matter. These things can be arranged. But for now, non, absolument non!"

"You have me at a disadvantage, Minister," Winslow said
mildly. "I am not negotiating a purchase of the House of Fayol
or anything else. On behalf of *any* purchaser."

The Frenchman slammed his small fist on the large desk.

"Semantics," he shouted. "Semantics. Rousselot didn't send
you here to sample the new vintages. We know that. . . ."

"How do you know?"

"Our intelligence sources are rather competent."

"So?"

The minister stood up. He was tired of looking up at Winslow.

"Monsieur Winslow, you are a highly respected banker. Rousselot has a considerable reputation. Isn't there some accommodation two gentlemen can reach in this matter?"

"Such as?" Winslow asked.

"Take a fortnight's holiday," he said, speaking quickly as if
sensing a sympathetic opening in Winslow's manner. "After the
elections, complete your negotiations. The Maison Fayol will still
be there. Paris is not going to get out of the fashion business.
Women will still buy perfume. The world will not end in the next
few weeks."

"Suppose the government loses and the Front Populaire comes
in? Maybe they'll nationalize. Where would I be then? Assuming,
of course, your thesis that I'm interested in buying Fayol or
anything?"

The cabinet minister walked around to Winslow's side of the
desk.

"Such a preposterous remark suggests you are not talking seriously," he said quietly.

With something approaching candor for the first time since
he'd entered the room, Winslow said soberly, "Monsieur, I would
always speak seriously with a member of the cabinet of France."

The minister seemed curiously pleased.

"Will you be staying in Paris?" he inquired.

"Yes," Winslow said. "I expect to be here." He wondered if
the question were simply a ranging shot or if he knew something,
about Grasse, about Anouk, about the priest Masson.

"And we cannot come to an accommodation?"

Winslow resumed his earlier pose.

"I'm afraid I don't understand," he said.

The minister stamped his foot. He did, he really did stamp his foot, Winslow thought.

"I won't permit a sale! I won't!" he screamed.

Innocently, Winslow inquired, "Does the Minister advise that I consult my embassy on this matter?"

The Frenchman breathed deeply.

"This interview, monsieur, is over."

That same morning, another "interview," also bearing on the matter of the House of Fayol, took place in another quartier of Paris. It concerned two men who had attended the Graduate School of Business of Harvard University. One of them, the man who had sought the interview, was employed in Europe by a great American corporation. The other was Paul Delane.

THE WATCHERS

For all his ridiculous posturing, the minister had frightened Winslow. It was one thing to have good old Charlie Casey tell you the French government was opposed to your doing something. It was quite another to stand before a minister of France and be threatened. It was a healthy scare, an intelligent fright. Winslow was concentrating completely now, his senses heightened, the tension curiously pleasurable. It was a feeling he had known before. Briefly, in combat; and then, sustained, over a longer period, with Rohatyn during the city crisis. Winslow knew the time had come to move. To move quickly.

Staying away from the hotel and using phone booths, he recruited Paul Delane. Delane would cover his tracks in Paris, leaving messages at the hotel to indicate Winslow was still in town: he was expected here for cocktails, there for dinner—a fragile stratagem but one that might provide a brief confusion. Delane was strangely argumentative.

"Why can't I come with you? I could be of immense help."

"Look," Winslow said patiently, "stay in Paris and cover me. Keep an eye on Nafredi. Keep tabs on Max. I don't need you down south."

"Where will you be staying?"

"Oh, hell, Paul. I dunno."

Delane paused. "You don't even have a gun, I'll bet."

"A *gun?*" Winslow said. "I haven't even held a gun in ten years. What the hell would I do with a gun?"

"You could shoot somebody," Delane suggested.

Winslow sighed. "And you were in the Resistance?"

"Well, yes, but I didn't carry a gun. I was only a kid." He brightened. "Antoine, why can't I go with you? Then, if you don't want to shoot somebody, I could do it on your behalf."

"This is what comes of permitting fashion designers to attend Harvard," Winslow told him.

Delane made Winslow promise to keep in touch. "I should know where you are at all times," he said.

"Sure, sure," Winslow said impatiently. "Do you have any contacts with the minister?"

"That fascist!" Delane spat out. "What would a good socialist like me have in common with a capitalist-roader like that?"

He went up to the *Vogue* studio to see Marianna. Avedon was shooting some pictures. When Winslow started to talk, Marianna hushed him. "For god's sake," she hissed, "not while *Avedon* is shooting." Winslow paced up and down the office for nearly an hour. Marianna came in. She was gorgeous. He had a bad case of the guilts about Anouk. They went across the street for coffee. It was four thirty. Winslow told her about going to Grasse. With Anouk.

"With Anouk? You and that baby assassin alone in the south of France? Ha!"

Winslow talked fast.

"Look, Anouk's essential. Two reasons. First, the old priest has this famous message for her. 'Spiritual guidance.' That's got to be these deeds or whatever that make Fayol so goddamn valuable. 'Paris One,' if my instincts mean anything. And he sure as hell isn't going to turn them over to anyone but Jacques Fayol's daughter. Second, if the paperwork looks legit, Anouk is the inheritor. She's the only one who can talk sale. If she's willing to sell, we can get a written commitment right on the spot, beat the election deadline, wrap up this goddamn mess, and go home."

Marianna was stubborn.

Exasperated, Winslow warned the trip could be dangerous; two could move faster than three, Marianna had to work, a half-dozen other reasons she couldn't go.

Coolly, she dismantled his arguments. "Suppose you lose her. I could impersonate her. I can drive better than you. As for work, I could have my period. *Everyone* always takes off for that. And who says it'll be dangerous? The most dangerous part of this entire madness is that turkey, Anouk."

"Who said I was driving?"

"It's logical. With the French sicking their hounds on you, they'll have the airports and the trains under wraps. You got a cigarette?"

There was more of this. In the end Winslow surrendered.

At six he phoned Anouk. She sounded very friendly.

"I'll come by about nine. That okay?"

"Mmmm," she said. "I think it's more than okay. I think it's sensationelle!"

"Yes," Winslow said, clearing his throat. Anouk's voice was very low, almost sleepy.

"Come as early as you want," she said. "There were one or two things we neglected to do the other evening."

When Winslow hung up he had a vaguely dirty feeling. He'd wanted to tell the girl to stop the shit, to turn off the electricity, and drop the Xaviera Hollander act. He wanted to tell her to be nineteen years old again. Instead, because the girl was unstable, because he needed her cooperation, he had said nothing.

At the hotel there was a letter from Rousselot:

"Why don't you call me at home toward the end of the week. I don't want a progress report. I just want to know your judgment as to whether all this huffing and puffing is constructive."

Well, Winslow thought as he packed his little Vuitton bag, by the end of the week, we ought to know. We surely ought.

He took a cab to the rue de Boulainvilliers and went upstairs to Marianna's apartment. She was excited about the trip. She was in lean suede jeans and a pullover. Her hair was pulled back. She looked very good.

"My car's gassed and ready," she said.

"Well, let's see. Maybe Anouk will want to use hers. It's a Lancia."

Marianna looked at him. "You sound like an account executive I used to know." Winslow ignored the sarcasm. He was looking out the window. He saw the men.

"Those sons of bitches," he said. "Listen, show me the back way out. Then, after a couple of minutes, go in the bedroom and make a big deal about going to bed and turn off the lights. Maybe they'll think we're in the pad."

"Okay," she said. She didn't sound sleepy or petulant or teasing. Nothing like Anouk. She just sounded as if she knew what he was asking and what she had to do. "Drink first?" she asked.

Winslow nodded, still watching the street, "Yeah," he said, "scotch. And let's drink it in the bedroom."

They went down the hallway arm in arm. It felt comfortable. Right. The drapes were only partially pulled in Marianna's bedroom. "Leave them like that," Winslow ordered. He took the girl in his arms and they kissed. When they broke, he loosened his collar. "Okay, now, where's the back door?"

"Through the kitchen. Then down the stairs. You'll come out in the cave. From there, there's an alleyway."

He nodded. "Now kiss me once more and I'll act as if I'm going to the bathroom. I'll call you from Anouk's. For God's sake, don't tie up the phone."

She kissed him and he went out of the bedroom, peeling off his shirt, as if preparing for bed. Marianna waited a moment and then, moving slowly, she went to the wall switch and flipped off the overhead light. The two bed lamps bathed the room in a warm glow. Marianna stretched and then pulled her sweater over her head. In a doorway across the street stood two men. Without being obvious about it, Marianna could not know if they were reacting. Being a woman, she was certain they were.

She heard the kitchen door close. Winslow was out! Now, to keep the watchers amused. And keep them across the street and not snooping around the alley. Marianna walked back across the room to the dresser, making sure the open blind kept her in view. She lighted a cigarette, breathed in deeply, and blew out the smoke. She looked down at her breasts, as if to examine them, and picked up the bottle of Y perfume. She moistened both forefingers and then slowly rubbed the perfume into her nipples. Now, one of the men moved. Then the other. She recoiled for a moment, thinking they were after Winslow. Then she relaxed. They were only moving to where they could watch her better.

The perfume stung. But it felt good. The tension, the playacting, the silent watchers outside, provided a sensual excitement she could nearly taste. She wished Winslow were here now. It was impossible, she knew, but she wanted him. She shuddered slightly. The excitement was tangible now. She knew what she was going to do and the knowledge both frightened her and caused her to shiver with pleasure. Goddammit, Marianna, she thought, you *dig* this act.

Winslow was by now three blocks away. He'd gotten through the alleyway, scaring himself when a cat darted between his legs, and had avoided the brightly lighted Avenue Mozart. He picked up a cab just short of the avenue and gave the driver Anouk's address. He hoped to hell Marianna was putting on a convincing shadow play.

"Jean-Pierre, regarde!"

One of the two watchers poked the other. Marianna had undone the waistband of the suede jeans and unzipped. Slowly she pushed the leather down her legs, her back to the open window. When they were off she stood there for a moment in her bikini pants and then turned to the window, yawning rather theatrically. The watchers were a good audience. They didn't notice the overplaying. They were looking at the rest of her. Marianna picked up a drink, it was Winslow's, and took a long sip. The maneuver lifted one breast. The second watcher groaned with pleasure. "Ah," he said, "quelle poitrine."

Anouk was stoned.

"It's something new," she told Winslow. He stood awkwardly in the middle of the living room wondering how a merchant banker from New York got into these things. Anouk was wearing a T-shirt and jeans. She looked happy but stupid-happy. She had a glass in her hand.

"Have some?" she asked.

"No," Winslow said curtly, not sure whether she meant a drink or the "new" drug. He didn't want either at the moment.

"Won't hurt," the girl said. "They're just pills. You pop them. And they pop you." She laughed.

"Anouk," Winslow said, "I want you to drive down to Grasse with me. To see Canon Masson. About your father's message. It's important."

"Don't want to go anywhere," she said. "Just to bed and fuck. But you've got to try this stuff too. It's sensational."

Winslow nodded. "Yeah, I want to. And we will. But later. In Grasse, or we could stop at a hotel along the way."

She shook her head, the silly smile still on her face.

"Bed," she said. Then she brightened even more. "Or did you want to do it in the bath? We didn't do it there last night." She paused. "Did we?"

"Anouk, this thing about Grasse. It's . . ."

"Oh, merde," she said, angry now, the little girl deprived of a favorite toy. "I'm sick of Grasse. Sick of my father. I don't want to see any old priest. I want . . ."

Winslow blew up.

"Goddammit, you little bitch. This is something we're going to do. And we're going to do it if I have to slug you first."

She licked her lips. "Do you want me to put on my leather underwear?"

When she asked that, momentarily she sounded sober. Then, without saying anything else, she crumbled into a graceful heap on the floor.

Marianna was naked now. The two watchers had moved again, getting a better angle on the bedroom. They were watching her and talking out of the corners of their mouths, exchanging rather specialized commentary on her anatomy and the various attitudes they might like to see her assume.

"Jean-Pierre?" the one said. His voice was huskier than before.

"Oui?"

"What do you think would happen—I mean, what would the boss say if we went up there?"

Jean-Pierre laughed. It was a rough laugh. "He'd have our balls," he offered.

The other man shrugged. "I've had my balls cut off by bosses before, tu sais."

"Alors," Jean-Pierre said, "me, I've got only two. I have to be more prudent than you."

"No, wait a minute," the other one said. "I'm serious. We go up there, beat up the American, take the girl, have some fun."

"And what do we tell the boss?"

"Shit, we tell him they tried to get away. The guy pulled a knife, a gun, whatever; we didn't want to lose them. Meanwhile we take the girl."

Jean-Pierre again demonstrated his prudence. "The American," he said, "he's a big one."

The other made a face. Through the window he could see Marianna drain a glass. Then, moving across the room, she turned off the light.

The watcher was decided then. "We'll give them ten minutes. Let him get the girl warmed up. Then we go in."

Jean-Pierre licked his lips. He didn't like it, he didn't like it at all. The boss had very little patience with this sort of amateur behavior among his professionals. Still, he remembered the girl's flat belly and those long legs and how the breasts rose.

"D'accord," he said. "In ten minutes."

Jean-Pierre's partner looked pleased. His name was Émile and he was quite ugly and he had never had a girl who looked as good as this one.

Winslow had picked up Anouk Fayol and laid her on the couch. He went into the bathroom. Jesus, he thought, it's a goddamn pharmacy. He had no idea what she had taken; what, if anything, he should do to revive her. He picked up bottles of pills, rummaged among the cocaine straws and the powders, opened a charming ceramic jar and found marijuana. He returned to the living room. Anouk was smiling in her sleep, her lips just slightly parted, the way a child sleeps. He felt her face. It was cool. Her breathing was regular, her pulse normal. He went into the kitchen and poured himself another scotch, this one straight. Then he went back into the living room and again examined the girl. Well, he thought, now she can't argue the point. Now she *has* to go to Grasse. He lighted a cigar and picked up the phone to dial Marianna's number.

Jean-Pierre and the other watcher crossed the street. Jean-Pierre pushed the button and the heavy iron door unlatched. There was a small glass elevator on the right. They passed it and walked carefully up the carpeted stairs to the first floor. Marianna's front door was one of those big, heavy double wooden affairs. Émile took out a Swiss army knife and opened the large blade. He wiggled it into the gap between the lock and the door, and then, finding the angle he sought, he leaned his body weight against the knife and there was a sharp, metallic crack. He kept the knife out and turned the doorknob with his free hand. It opened.

Marianna's bedroom was along the hallway on the left. The two men moved silently along the bare hardwood of the hallway, Jean-Pierre in the lead. A floorboard creaked and he looked over his shoulder nervously. Émile, just behind him, was grinning. He put his hand to his groin and mimed masturbation. Jean-Pierre shook his head and turned forward again. God knows, he wanted the girl too, but *this* one, this one was an animal.

He wondered if they could catch the American unaware. He hoped the couple were fucking. It would make it easier. He slid the .45 automatic from his shoulder holster and tiptoed toward the bedroom door. He hoped the girl would be cooperative. After all this trouble it would not be much fun to have to knock her out before they could start to play.

* * *

Winslow ransacked the armoire in Anouk's bedroom and found a large canvas tote bag. He threw in some slacks, a pair of shoes, some blouses, and a couple of sweaters. He found a bikini in the dresser and some underwear. He should put in some cosmetics, he supposed, but she would just have to use Marianna's. He couldn't begin to choose between the jars and tubes. Then, remembering that they might have to drive through the mountains, he tossed in a down anorak. He stopped, thought for a moment, and went into the bathroom. He picked up the cocaine and a half dozen straws. He didn't like it, not one bit, but if it took that to keep the girl going during the next few days, well . . .

He wished Marianna would get there. He wondered if she'd been able to slip out through the back way as easily as he had. His cigar had gone out. He relighted it and sat down in a deeply cushioned chair to wait. Across the room Anouk slept.

Émile slipped past Jean-Pierre and gripped the doorknob to Marianna's bedroom. He nodded at Jean-Pierre. It was unlocked. He held the knife low in his other hand. Jean-Pierre cocked the .45. Émile bunched his shoulders and then, with a last nod to Jean-Pierre, he threw his weight against the door and it sprung open. The two men charged into the bedroom. It was empty.

"Where the hell have you been?" Winslow asked Marianna. She was staring at Anouk.

"What's the matter with her?"

"Stoned," Winslow said. "What happened? It's nearly an hour since I called."

She shrugged. "It took me time to pack."

Winslow handed her a parking garage ticket.

"We'll take her Lancia. Here's the ticket. And some money. Get it out of the garage. Right down the street. And get the gas tank filled. Take the bags. I'll carry her down and meet you at the front door."

Marianna nodded. She picked up Winslow's bag and Anouk's and then her own and looked at Winslow.

"I . . ."

"Yes?" he asked.

She shook her head. "Nothing. I'll meet you in front." She hurried out of the apartment, carrying the bags. She wondered why she hadn't told him why she'd been so long. She tried to smile about it. "An intellectual striptease," she thought. But she remembered how it had excited her, how she had trembled with pleasure rather than fright, and she knew that was why she hadn't told him.

Winslow waited just inside the front door. Anouk stood upright in his arms. Anyone seeing them from any distance would have assumed they were lovers, that perhaps the girl had had a cognac too many. He heard the car pull up and he picked up Anouk and carried her across the sidewalk. There was no one else on the street. Marianna jumped out and ran around to open the door. Winslow placed Anouk as gently as he could on the back seat while Marianna stowed the luggage. He got into the driver's seat and checked the gauges. Everything looked all right. He turned to Marianna.

"Ready?"

She smiled and nodded. He turned once more to the back seat and then got out of the car and pulled off his suit coat. He tossed it over the girl's sleeping form. She stirred slightly and then mumbled something. Marianna turned to Anouk, and the girl, still asleep, said something else. Quite clearly. Marianna sat up straight and turned to stare through the windshield. What Anouk Fayol had said was directed to Winslow.

What she had said, in that most colloquial of French slang phrases, was that Tony Winslow should fuck her. "Again."

Four hours later they were nearing Lyons. He and Marianna had alternated every hour at the wheel. Marianna was driving again. Her face was still set. He lighted two cigarettes and passed one to her. She took it without a word. The road was clear, the sky starry. The great belly of France raced past on either side. The car performed beautifully. In the back seat Anouk slept. Shit, Winslow told himself, they had to talk sometime.

"Look, I'm sorry. I should have told you. It was a situation in which . . ."

"You don't have to explain," Marianna said coldly. "I quite understand."

"The hell you do. We needed this girl. She, well, I know it sounds corny, but there was nothing I could do but go to bed with her."

Marianna's cool smashed. "Damn you, Tony. Don't give me these phony euphemisms. 'Go to bed with her'! Why can't you say what you mean? You screwed her, you fucked her, you . . . and I'll bet you had a damn good time at it too."

He was angry now too. "You're right. I did. I did enjoy it."

"Was it tonight? Was that when you did it? While she was getting high?"

"What does it matter when I did it?" He sounded unhappy.

"Oh, nothing. It doesn't matter at all." She was thinking of the view into her bedroom, of the watchers across the street, and of how she had taken off her clothes and rubbed her breasts and performed nude for those creepy bastards just to give Winslow the breathing space he'd needed.

Marianna took a drag on the cigarette. Calmer now, thinking of her own exhibitionism, of the pleasure she'd taken in it and her failure to mention it to Winslow, she said, less bitterly:

"But with that teenage junkie! That's what hurts. A goddamn cheap little call girl!"

Winslow sensed an easing in the tension.

"No," he said, "not a *cheap* call girl. She gets a hundred dollars a trick."

When he looked at Marianna she was trying not to smile.

South of Lyons they stayed on route seven. Winslow was driving now. Marianna slept, her head on his shoulder. At six in the morning they stopped at a café and had coffee and cheese and used the bathrooms. Anouk was still asleep. At eight they were in Grasse. They got directions to the church at a gas station. Win-

slow got out and went to what seemed to be the rectory. He was
not yet sure how he was going to explain Anouk's being unconscious. Well, with a priest perhaps the truth would obtain. An
elderly woman came to the door. No, Canon Masson was not
there. He was away for the day. Winslow slumped, tired from the
long drive, from the tensions of the night. Damn, why wasn't the
priest where he should be at eight o'clock in the morning?

"Can you tell me where I might find him?"

The old woman shook her head. Then Winslow turned solemn.

"It is a matter," he said, "of spiritual guidance. The young
woman in my car and I . . . well, we . . ."

The old woman stared through her glasses at Marianna, sitting
in the Lancia. She could not see Anouk.

"Ah, well then, if it's a spiritual matter, of course. Canon
Masson is in Cannes."

"In Cannes?"

She nodded. "He goes to Cannes every year in May."

"Oh?" Winslow said, feeling stupidly that he was missing
something.

"But don't you know?" the old woman said. "He goes to
Cannes every year during the film festival. He goes to demonstrate against obscenity in the cinema."

Eighty miles from Grasse a big Citroën DS barreled south
along route seven. Jean-Pierre slept in the back seat. Émile was
at the wheel. He was still thinking about Marianna and he was
driving fast.

FESTIVAL

Cannes is a pleasant town of fifty thousand inhabitants on the Mediterranean coast in the shadow of Nice. Winslow drove the car through Grasse to route N. 567 and headed south. It was only seventeen kilomètres, according to the signpost. Anouk was still curled up in the back seat of the Lancia, but now she woke.

"Alors," she said. Marianna turned in her seat.

"If you say 'where am I?' I'm going to slug you." She turned back to Winslow. "That okay?"

"Perfect," Winslow said. "You're a credit to *Vogue*."

He decided they should stop for a council of war, lay their plans for finding Masson, and what they should say when they got to him. Pretty vague stuff, trying to find a French priest picketing a film festival. Well, their luck had held so far. They came into Cannes and hit the usual traffic. Winslow bore off to the east, and when they reached the waterfront he pulled into a parking space in front of a café. "Come on," he said, "let's get something to drink." The two girls got out of the car. The waterfront loungers watched them appreciatively. The café was pleasant, sun-filled. They sat down at a white metal table and ordered. The jukebox was playing something by Régine. Winslow looked around. The place had a preseason feel to it, the waiter still

186

attentive, eager, the barman rubbing the bar top and looking pleasant. Later, when the season had really started, you would be fortunate to get them to scowl at you.

"Could someone please tell me . . ." Anouk began.

"You were stoned," Winslow said. "Out. Dead. Crocked. You really dig the stuff, don't you?"

"It passes the time," she said.

"Like solitaire," Marianna said sweetly. Winslow hoped she wasn't going to be too tough on the kid. They still needed her.

"So you kidnapped me. Like common thugs. I could go to the police, you know."

" 'Kidnapping' is a bit strong," Winslow said.

"Oh, Tony," Marianna interrupted, "stop mincing words. Yes, we put on the snatch. You were too stoned to make it on your own. You're damn lucky. If we'd left you in Paris you might be dead by now. Like old . . . what's his name?"

"Grumbach," Winslow offered. Marianna really had quite a gift for this sort of thing. They must be doing marvelous things with the curriculum at Yale these days.

"All to find Canon Masson," Anouk said.

Winslow nodded. "To find him and find out what this 'guidance' was your father talked about."

Anouk was quite awake now. She slid closer to Winslow and her leg bumped against his. Looking at Marianna out of the corner of her eye she said, "Well, of course, if *you* think it's important, Tony."

Marianna made the word "merde" soundlessly with her lips. Then Anouk got up.

"I'll be right back," she said. She started for the toilets.

"Go with her," Winslow hissed. "We can't have her snorting more coke."

"Go with her? I just might drown her."

"Dammit, Marianna, that girl is . . ."

Marianna got up. "I know, I know." She followed Anouk. The barman looked very happy. He wondered if they were cinema stars, the two young women. Already it was starting. And usually the stars kept to the center of town and not out here at the fringe. He smiled at Winslow. What a fortunate man to have two such. He wondered if Winslow slept with them simultaneously or one at a time.

The girls returned. The adaptable Anouk had slid into another of her unpredictable moods, this one of complete cooperation. "I'm curious myself about Masson. And his message. Also, this 'Paris One' nonsense." In order that they not take her completely for granted, Anouk needled Marianna. "Myself, I find fashion magazines superficial. And most fashion editors pathetic social climbers."

Marianna smiled sweetly. "I suppose one comes by such knowledge at Madame Claude's."

While they finished their drinks Winslow laid out the plan. It was very simple. They would find Masson; Anouk would identify herself; they would ask about "spiritual guidance." If that fell flat, they would engage him in conversation about the late Fayol, the old days, those cheerful times in the war, and casually Winslow would slip in a mention of "Paris One." It was very simple. Winslow had an uneasy idea it would turn out to be not simple at all.

The festival was coming into bloom. There were lots of flags. Banners were strung across the streets and on the façades of the hotels and the movie houses where the films would be shown. One of the banners welcomed "Dustin Hauptmann." There were blowups of the stars on billboards and temporary hoardings. Raquel Welch looked splendid with bosoms a meter across. The blowups did very little for Barbra Streisand's nose. In another day or two you wouldn't be able to drive a car along the Croisette. Now it was just passable. Winslow drew up in front of the hotel where the festival was headquartered. "Marianna, go ask. I'll stay with Anouk in the car."

Marianna got out. For the first time she felt silly. Inside the hotel she went up to the concierge.

"Je m'excuse, mais y a-t-il un prêtre qui manifeste contre le . . . ?"

The concierge did not permit her to finish. Was there a priest demonstrating against the festival? Was there not? It was Canon Masson, bien sûr, down from the hills for his annual manifestation. There could not be a festival without the good canon! Why, the governors would not permit it to begin without him.

"Then where is he?"

The concierge shrugged.

"Surely on one of the yachts," he said. "That of MGM or Joe Levine or Roman Polanski or . . ." One could never be sure with Canon Masson. He liked to give generously of himself so that no one would be slighted, not even the Hollywood trash.

Marianna thanked him and went back to the car. Anouk had climbed into the front seat. Her tan looked lovely under the hot sun of the Midi, while Marianna had the uncomfortable suspicion her own nose was beginning to redden. Grumpily she got into the jump seat and told Winslow about the yachts. He shook his head.

"Hell of a way to protest obscenity."

They drove out onto one of the wharves that advertised speedboats. Winslow parked the car. "Bring your suits," he said. "You never know. We might have to swim for it."

The lovely little harbor was full of yachts. While Winslow dickered with the patron of speedboats, the two women asked about the priest.

"He is either on the yacht of Paramount or of Sam Creel," Anouk reported.

"Creel?" Winslow demanded. "That son of a bitch hasn't made anything that wasn't X-rated in years. Maybe never."

Marianna smiled. "What better place to mount his protest?"

The speedboat was one of those wonderfully lacquered old mahogany affairs they don't make anymore. The patron of speedboats had refused to rent them the boat without a driver. The driver wore a beret and a dark-blue suit and tie and looked retarded. He was perhaps seventy years old. Winslow whispered to the patron. "Is he okay?" nodding at the man.

"Our finest speedboat driver," the patron assured him. "In the war he commanded a cruiser. Got sunk at Mers-el-Kebir. Very brave fellow."

The speedboat pulled away from the dock at approximately forty knots. Jesus, Winslow thought, I hope we don't hit something. The old man turned as if to reassure him and grinned his idiot's grin. "Oh, boy," Winslow told himself.

"Tony," Marianna asked, "are there sharks?"

Anouk laughed. This was her kind of scene. Winslow wondered if somehow she'd sneaked a snort.

"Par-a-mount," the old man said, pointing while he spun the wheel with one hand and almost dropped Winslow overboard.

"Bon. Arrêtes ici."

They drifted up to the big white ship with the motor cut, and when a sailor peered down at him Winslow shouted up that they were looking for Canon Masson. The sailor cupped an ear. Then a very pretty blonde with long hair and huge sunglasses leaned over the rail. She was naked from the waist up and possibly below.

"Come aboard," she said in Swedish-accented English.

"We're looking for the priest," Winslow said, staring at the girl's nipples.

"A priest?" the girl said, confused.

"We need him for the last rites," Marianna said, somewhat sourly.

The blonde shook her hair. "Not here. Try Fellini's boat. They say he's very religious."

Winslow signaled the speedboat driver and the old man threw in the clutch. They all sat down abruptly as the boat roared off. The blonde was still waving. Her breasts moved beautifully in the afternoon sun.

"I'm going to get out of my clothes too," Anouk announced.

"Where now?" the old man demanded.

"Le bateau de Samuel Creel," Winslow ordered.

Anouk took off her shirt. She wasn't wearing a bra.

"Jesus," Winslow said. The old man had turned from the

wheel and was gaping. The speedboat headed directly for a yacht showing British colors.

"Well, I will too," said Marianna. She started to unzip her pants. The old man left the wheel entirely.

"Alors," Winslow shouted. The old man smiled wetly and held his hands out, palms upward. Reluctantly he turned back to the wheel and they missed the British boat by several feet. On deck a man in a blazer took his pipe out of his mouth and shouted something. Winslow assumed it was uncomplimentary.

Anouk and Marianna were both down to their panties now. Marianna dug into the tote bag. "Here," she said, tossing a bikini to Anouk. She pulled out a bikini top and put it on. Then the bottom. She looked pale but fine. Anouk looked at the bikini she'd drawn and pulled off her panties. Her tan was startling against the tiny white strip. She tugged on the bikini bottom and tossed the top back toward the bag. "In the Midi *no one* under thirty wears the bra," she said, looking meaningfully at Marianna.

"Bullshit," said Marianna. But she kept her top on.

Sam Creel's yacht was even bigger than Paramount's. Unlike the others in the harbor, it was pale blue. It showed the usual flags and a giant banner with the initials "S. C." There was a landing stage and the old man deftly brought the speedboat up alongside. He smiled at Anouk. Marianna, with her top on, had been forgotten. The old man licked his lips.

The speedboat lost headway and bobbed up and down abeam the landing stage. A uniformed sailor held them off with a long gaff, waiting for instructions. A bald head appeared over the rail.

"Yes?" he said.

Winslow guessed this was Creel.

"Hello, there. I'm Anthony Winslow. From Rousselot & Partners in New York. I heard you were out here and I . . ."

Creel was looking at the two girls. At Marianna. But even more at Anouk. Winslow realized she was still topless.

He resumed. "I believe we have mutual acquaintances who . . ."

"Yes, yes," Creel said, "of course. Do come aboard."

They moored the boat and the old man was told to wait. He looked unhappy to see the women leave. Creel was at the top of the ladder to greet them. Talking to Winslow, but staring at the two young girls, he said:

"It is always pleasant to meet an associate of Henry Rousselot."

Winslow and the girl were not the only travelers from Paris who had come to Cannes. Aboard the yacht of Sepp Gardolfi, the Italian producer, Zader Nafredi was enjoying a siesta. Only he was not alone in the big stateroom bed. With him were Soroya, the Iranian mannequin from the Maison Fayol, and a little blond German actress who was in Gardolfi's party. The German girl, whom Gardolfi thought very promising indeed, was kneeling between Soroya's legs. Nafredi was observing. He tended to agree the girl was promising. She was, after all, only sixteen.

On the same yacht, working on his suntan, was the most famous of Fayol's "little monks," Max, interim director of the great fashion house. Why was Max in Cannes, on the same yacht as the Shah's man, Nafredi? Max would have laughed at the question. He was there because it was much more chic to be tanning oneself in Cannes than to brood in Paris where malicious folk might suggest one had not gotten an invitation, not one, to someone's yacht in Cannes. There was an additional reason: He was there because Nafredi had paid him to be there.

On yet another yacht, her own, was Maggy Moal, flanked by several of her mannequins, swilling beer, chain-smoking, and rasping orders to her captain to keep steam up lest the political crisis force them beyond the three-mile limit into the safety of international waters. Maggy's yacht, which she rarely used, was a converted destroyer painted white, with a crew of ninety. Now she reclined on a chaise in the shade of a striped awning, asking questions and shouting directions to her valet, who dutifully focused a high-powered telescope on the other yachts and reported to his mistress who was clad, who was naked, which famous actress was going to fat, and which movie producer was oiling the back of which young starlet not his wife. At her age, voyeurism was one of the last sports left to Maggy Moal.

Tony Winslow, Anouk Fayol, and Marianna Troy lounged comfortably in the sun on the flying bridge of Mr. Sam Creel's 4,500-ton yacht. Young Italian girls made up in sarongs and leis to portray Polynesian maidens passed around the drinks. Mr. Creel, who suffered from duodenal difficulties, drank milk. The Reverend Canon Masson, a huge man in sandals and a black cassock, fanned himself with a straw hat, puffed on an impressively long cigar, and accepted another drink. Piled neatly by the priest's deck chair was a stack of printed leaflets urging strict censorship of films and television.

"Canon Masson and I have argued the point for years," Creel was saying. "My conscience is clear. I sleep like a babe. Wickedness is undeniably in the eye of the beholder."

The priest laughed. "There is weakness in all of us, Monsieur Creel. It came in the same post as original sin."

A lean young man in a shirt open to the waist, linen trousers, and a number of gold chains twisted his fingers in the long hair of a girl who sat at his feet drinking Coca-Cola. He was the Communist candidate for Grasse in the coming election. He creased his suntanned brow.

"Canon Masson and I are at opposite poles on most questions," he said. "The election, for example. His obsolete regard for the late de Gaulle for another. But on film festivals and dirty movies, he and I are as one. Solidarity forever." He melded his hands together.

Creel scowled. "But why? Movies, images on the wall, shadow play, what are they but an entertainment, a divertissement? Harmless in themselves. Light and shadow. Chiaroscuro. What damage is there?"

Anouk had taken one of the leis and in deference to the priest had arranged it rather attractively over her nipples. Now she leaned close to Winslow and whispered.

"By any chance do you have a joint?"

Winslow shook his head. The girl was beautiful, she was intelligent, and she was clearly unstable. She was also crucial to their chances of recruiting Masson to the cause. Anouk sulkily moved away from Winslow. He could see Creel eyeing her.

"I don't understand," Marianna was saying to the communist, "why you're against the festival. I appreciate Father Masson's objections. But not yours."

The young man smiled. He had nice teeth. It was easy to see why he got votes.

"Mademoiselle," he said, "this may sound bizarre to an American convinced that all Communists are godless and immoral. The truth is, we are godless and disgustingly moral. Where Canon Masson finds dirty films obnoxious to his god, I find them obnoxious to the people. So, for different reasons, we are both enemies of our host, Monsieur Creel."

"Then why," Winslow asked, "do you pass the day on his yacht?"

The Communist laughed. "Because neither of us has a yacht of his own."

"Yachts to the people," Winslow murmured.

Creel was watching Anouk. "My dear," he said, "have you done any film work?"

"A few private movies," she replied obscurely. Winslow could imagine what they were. Creel looked confused, not knowing what to make of her.

Anouk stood up. The lei didn't do her body any harm. None at all.

"I'm sleepy," she said. "Is there somewhere I might . . ."

Creel jumped up.

"There are several unoccupied cabins," he said. "Permit me." They disappeared into one of the corridors. Marianna looked at Winslow, an eyebrow raised. He nodded "Okay," relieved Anouk was at least temporarily offstage. Now was his chance to talk to Masson. He got the priest off into a corner of the deck.

"I wonder if I might speak with you, privately."

The canon waved a big hand. "But of course. I am at your disposal."

Winslow looked around. Marianna and the Communist were talking politics, Creel's other guests appeared occupied. Well, he thought, here goes. Then, just as he began, Masson looked over his shoulder and held up a hand.

Sam Creel had returned, alone. "She really *did* want to sleep," he said, incredulous.

Masson beamed. "The young, they need more sleep than old fellows like us."

Creel was comforted, at least slightly. He slung an arm around the priest's ample shoulder.

"My best friend and source of inspiration," he said expansively.

Marianna wrinkled her nose.

"With due respect to your friendship," she said, "I still don't understand how a priest demonstrating against pornography can spend his afternoon on a pornographer's yacht."

The producer looked hurt. Masson, however, smiled tolerantly.

"Mademoiselle," he said, "in our baptismal vows we pledge to renounce Satan and all his works and pomps. I consider Monsieur Creel's films to fall into the latter category. I renounce them. But not the poor, misguided chap who produces them."

The Communist laughed.

"What sublime casuistry. I am stunned. You should *really* be in politics."

The priest shrugged. "You and I are both in the business of providing conviction to the undecided. You in politics, I in another realm."

The Communist shook his head. "What I don't understand is how such an intelligent man can testify to superstition, to gods he cannot see, address himself to souls he cannot touch, to spirits and dominions invisible to rational men. I simply don't understand it."

Masson thought for a moment. "Monsieur," he said, "it is true I believe in a god I cannot see. Yet I know Him to be." He paused. "Consider yourself. You have never seen your asshole and yet you know it to exist."

Maggy Moal crinkled her nose.

"What species of stink is that? My God, they must be discharging merde into the harbor."

The valet's eyes widened. He stared at Maggy's lap, where blue smoke wreathed up from the burning wool. She had set herself afire once again.

"Madame," he said sharply.

Maggy shrieked at him. "Get back to the telescope, you. Do you deprive me of the simplest of pleasures?" The valet's eyes remained wide, but docilely he turned toward the glass. Maggy Moal waved a hand impatiently in front of her.

"They must be burning garbage," she remarked. "The air is full of smoke."

Cocktails were being served on Sam Creel's yacht. Winslow was at last alone with Canon Masson.

"Canon," he said quickly, "we must see you privately. It concerns Jacques Fayol and his daughter."

"His daughter?"

Winslow nodded. "The girl who is asleep. She is here to see you. It concerns her . . . spiritual guidance."

The priest's face lost its cherubic charm. He looked shrewdly into Winslow's eyes.

Then, making a judgment based on what he saw there, or failed to see there, he said, "Alors, wake the girl."

THE LEGACY

The helicopter taking Maggy Moal to the burn center at Marseilles passed over the speedboat at five o'clock in the afternoon. Nobody looked up. The boatman was in something of a sulk. Anouk, in deference to the hour, or to Canon Masson, had shed her floral arrangement and had tied on her bikini bra. They paid off the boatman and crossed the Croisette. Masson led the procession. "My motorcycle and picketing equipment," he apologized, "I left them at the Splendide."

Since the Hôtel Splendide was the headquarters of the festival, and since Masson was dedicated to its forcible closure, Winslow thought this was chutzpah indeed, if a Catholic priest could be said to possess "chutzpah."

In front of the hotel there was a promising little demonstration. From the hastily lettered signs and angry shouts it was obvious that some species of Czech had won one of the minor awards over an Italian competitor. The Italian claque was manifesting its displeasure. Canon Masson, his great stomach preceding him, waded through the demonstrators, making signs of the cross and giving benediction as he went.

"Bless you, my son," he said to a young man who was spitting at one of the jury.

The young man fell to his knees, blessed himself hastily, and got up to spit again.

Masson turned to Winslow and beamed.

"Isn't it splendid to see such fervor?" he asked.

Winslow nodded.

"I'd feared our young people had become so obsessed with material things," Masson said piously, "that they had abandoned completely the joy of aesthetic polemic."

Just then a rioter, perhaps more than normally inspired by the aesthetics, threw a punch at Masson. The old priest slipped the blow and dug a stiff hand, palm rigid and fingers extended, into the man's ribs. The victim toppled and looked up, stunned. "Qu'est-ce qui arrive?" he asked, gasping for breath.

"Bless you," Masson intoned. "Bless you."

He shoved another demonstrator from his path and they reached the railing where his motorcycle and a number of furled signs were parked.

"Can we get all this in your car?" Masson inquired. "I dislike these roads after dark. My headlamp is a feeble thing."

They shoved the signs in the trunk and lashed the motorcycle on the back bumper. The Mediterranean sun blazed down. The girls got in the back seat and Masson arranged his skirts and sat up front with Winslow. The American started the car and slowly nudged his way through the crowd and up out of the town and toward the road to Grasse. He did not notice the two men in cheap suits who climbed into their Citroën DS and set off behind him.

The sun was low over the hills when Winslow drove into Grasse. They dropped Canon Masson at his church and checked into the Hôtel Muraour. Anouk was being very pleasant, refreshed from her nap and the sun and as enthusiastic about their mission as Winslow. Marianna and Anouk went off chatting like friends to their room. Masson had asked them to dine with him at nine. The American peeled off his clothes and left a call for eight thirty. He was immediately asleep.

Jean-Pierre and Émile parked the Citroën on a side street and went into a café across the Boulevard Jeu du Ballon. They ordered marcs and Jean-Pierre drank off his right away and went off to telephone. Émile sat at a table by the window and watched the entrance to the hotel. The marc warmed his belly. He was tired. He needed a bath and a shave. And he was still angry about Paris, about the empty bedroom, about the slim American girl. Well, he consoled himself, now there were two of them. And the second, if it were possible, as good-looking as the first. He did not yet know her name or who she was. But he wondered how Anouk Fayol would look stripped naked. Jean-Pierre came back to the table. He ordered a second marc.

"Well?" Émile asked.

"We wait," Jean-Pierre said. "There's some sort of document, a deed or letter or something. That's what they're here to find. We wait until they do."

Émile nodded. That was simple enough to understand.

"Then what?" he asked.

Jean-Pierre waited until the waiter had put down the drinks and gone off.

"Then we take the document from them and go back to Paris with it."

"And that's all?" Émile asked, incredulous.

Jean-Pierre nodded. "What else?" he wanted to know.

Émile smiled. It was not a very winning smile. "Oh, I might be able to think of something," he said.

Jean-Pierre sipped the second drink. God knows, they were good-looking girls and he had no love for the tall American. But this Émile, he would have to watch him. A man like this, with his brains in his scrotum, you never knew. When he noticed that Émile was staring out of the window, Jean-Pierre eased the flap of his shoulder holster. He was glad Émile was a knife man, that he didn't carry a gun. In a situation like this you went for the money, the papers, the key, whatever it was the boss sent you after. You got that first. Then, if it was convenient, you fucked a girl or beat the shit out of someone who had given you trouble. But first, you did your work, you carried out the assignment. The amusements came later. Émile was still looking through the window. Jean-Pierre decided against having another marc. With an animal like this one, he wanted a clear head.

Canon Masson poured the wine.

"Of course this isn't first-rate country for decent wine," he was saying. "Too hot, too much clay in the soil. Just right for flowers, naturally. Myself, I'd prefer to have my hectares in grapes. But ..." He spread his hands. "It wouldn't do for the pastor of Grasse to be quoted thus."

Winslow was at the foot of the table from the priest. Anouk and Marianna, wearing cotton dresses against the heat of the southern evening, sat one on each side. The meal, carré d'agneau and fresh asparagus, had been fine. Winslow felt better after the nap, after the meal. He offered a cigar to Masson and the priest took it.

"With all my vices," he said, "it's a good thing God is all-merciful. Simple justice, in my case, would be condemnatory."

Winslow wondered at what point it would be appropriate to get Masson back to the reason they had come. Then, as if sensing the moment, Anouk asked:

"What about this message my father sent through old Grumbach? This business of coming to you for spiritual guidance?"

Masson puffed on the cigar. He gestured around the room. "Please pardon my rudeness, but these are areas of a rather personal nature, and I'm not sure that you wish me to ..."

Anouk smiled. "Monsieur Winslow and Mademoiselle Troy are good friends. They helped me to get here. You may speak freely in front of them."

"Bien," Masson said, and he sat forward in his armchair, his great arms resting on the table.

"I knew your father first in the late thirties, just before the second war. He would come to Grasse on business, the usual trafficking with the attar merchants, the farmers who grow the flowers. We were not close. He was a most cosmopolitan sort, charming, obviously intelligent, vigorous, and already quite successful. He enjoyed his table, his vintage, his ... women. I, on the other hand, a country priest.

"Alors, in the course of things, the war came. At first we were not greatly affected here in Grasse. One mourned the dead, one was more or less bitter about the defeat and the Occupation, one was vaguely aware of this fellow de Gaulle issuing grand statements from London. Grasse was part of the unoccupied zone. Oh, there were Germans about, but almost never in uniform. No jackboots, no 'Deutschland über Alles,' no swastikas, no round-ups of Jews. There was rationing, there were limitations on political activity, there was the occasional troublemaker hauled off to prison for some inconsequential act or other, but it was our own authorities that did it. Frenchmen still governed Frenchmen. And if times were hard, well, we had the sense to realize they were much harder in the north.

"From time to time Jacques Fayol, like a number of other Paris couturiers who chose to keep their doors open, would procure a pass from the Germans and come south to engage in a reasonable facsimile of the normal commerce. The Germans had an interest in maintaining the perfume trade. Like all tourists, they wanted an ounce or two to take home to a lady. Travel in that period was of course very restricted. And occasionally Fayol, or any visitor, would be stuck here for a week or two, waiting for the laissez-passer to return to Paris. It was then he and I got to know one another well. Grasse was a quiet town, he was bored, and I was one of the few educated people in the vicinity. We began dining together, late nights over brandy, political discussions, arguments about . . . well, the nature of things."

Anouk interrupted.

"But you were nothing alike."

"Oh, your father made that very point, mademoiselle. Many times. I can hear him now, sounding very much like you, very definite in his speech:

" 'Ah, Masson, we have such different appetites, you and I. You lust for eternal pleasure and are willing to wait a lifetime to achieve it. I want a lifetime of pleasure and am more than willing to expiate eternally.' "

The priest paused and poured more wine.

"I often told him we were not all that different. That we were both passionate, intemperate men. Only our weaknesses differed."

"It's so difficult," Marianna said, "for someone of my genera-
tion to imagine those days. France occupied by a foreign enemy,
people being sent to concentration camps, men being shot. It's as
if it all happened in another age, another century."

Masson laughed. "I am slightly older than you, mademoiselle,
I lived through it and sometimes I do not believe it happened."
He drew in the cigar smoke and resumed.

"In the north there were already the first stirrings of the Resistance. Men disappeared into the maquis or they sailed small
boats to England or they talked their way out of the occupied
zone and went through here headed for Afrique du Nord and
eventually to de Gaulle. In Grasse, in much of Vichy, there was a
good deal of tut-tutting about all this. I remember one friend of
mine, a good man, a fine lawyer, who said to anyone who would
listen: 'It is *we* who requested the armistice. It is *our* law. A
Frenchman who breaks the armistice, who fights against the Germans, is breaking not a Hitler law but a French one. He is, *res
ipsa loquitur*, a bandit.' There were many who considered de
Gaulle a bandit, an opportunist, an ambitious careerist who saw
in the debacle of 1940 the chance to advance himself out of
obscurity. And even for those who did not take such a harsh
view, what was a man to do who had a wife and children to feed,
bank loans to repay, a farm to work, employees to pay? He had
to work each day, and leave the maquis to the disaffected, the
poseur, the unbalanced, the repressed criminal." He nodded. "I
can tell you there are Frenchmen today who will still tell you, in
all sincerity, that it took greater courage to collaborate, to try to
keep a wounded France functioning, than it took to flee to England or to slip into the maquis and shoot German boys in the
back on dark nights."

" 'They also serve . . .' " Winslow quoted.

"Precisely," Masson said. "Now, I did not feel that way. But I
understood. At least I did until 1942."

"What happened then?" Marianna asked.

"North Africa was invaded by the Americans and the British,
and in retaliation, or for strategic reasons, the Germans occupied

the rest of France. For the first time there were soldiers in Grasse. The town was too small to sustain a Gestapo office, but there was one in Nice; and occasionally there would come the knock on the door and one of our neighbors, some man I knew personally, would be taken away. The Jews were rounded up. The woman who had sold me my vegetables in the market, the man who soled my shoes, a teller at the bank—they were taken away.

"So"—and Canon Masson raised his hands—"the war came to Grasse. Mind you," he said, "it was not as if every day there were bombs being thrown and tanks in the streets. No. The overwhelming impression was one of a sort of forced tranquility, an artificial peace. Farmers went into the fields to work, the construction of a small bridge over the river continued, policemen put on their uniforms and went on duty and gave out traffic tickets or arrested drunks. One saw Germans, but we had always had foreigners here in the tourist season. The flowers were harvested, the oils were extracted, the merchants from Paris came to town and stayed in the same hôtels des commerciants, deals were made, houses were bought and sold, the children attended school, there was music on the radio. In the summer it was hot, in the winter cold and wet. And yet"—Masson flicked his cigar ash and paused dramatically, a practiced sermonizer who knew the value of a pause—"and yet, it was different."

"How was it different?" Winslow asked, as entranced by the telling as he earlier had been by the mystery of Fayol's message to his daughter.

"Well, sir, it was like this," the priest said, very much the good storyteller appreciating the timely question, "there was tension. Tension and always tension. And of course, tu sais, now we also, like our brothers in the rest of France, we also had the Resistance." He rang a little bell and the old woman-servant came into the dining room. "There is still some brandy?" he inquired.

"Oui, Monseigneur, mais . . ."

Masson slammed a big hand down on the table. "My good woman," he said impatiently, "I know very well it is not good for my liver. However . . ."

The servant dove into a cupboard and emerged with a bottle of old brandy, unlabeled. She set out some small ponies and poured.

"Your father," Masson said to Anouk, "frequently informed me that this country brew would be the death of me. I am sure he was correct. I only regret," he said with sincerity, "that he did not remain to witness the event."

Canon Masson mused for several moments. Winslow wondered if indeed the priest was drunk, if his story would now drift off into country none of them could navigate, into the half-remembered reminiscences of the old, the tired, and the drunk. Instead, Masson put down his glass and resumed, if anything, more lucidly and less discursively than before.

"Jacques Fayol was in Grasse when the first Resistance cell was formed. Being a good Frenchman and presumably—since he was Parisian and rich—with some knowledge of the world, he was invited to join us. He seemed quite pleased, flattered even, to be part of it. We were amateurs then, in forty-two, not at all what we would later become, and I am afraid those first clandestine meetings were abysmally childish, as if the local boy scouts had decided to declare war because they had not been allotted sufficient candy. Alors, the thing began. It was agreed that Fayol, for his part, would do nothing operational in Grasse. He was to come and go as before, but he was to be our link to more seasoned, more experienced, more professional people in Paris and the north. Since he possessed a railroad pass, we would use Fayol as liaison. Here, in Grasse, we simple countrymen would do the stabbing and the shooting and the bombing."

Winslow could imagine Masson in the pulpit, spinning out parables. Marianna hung on his words. But it was Anouk who surprised Winslow. She listened, she asked pertinent questions, she communicated quiet dignity. She was a long way from the man-crazy, pill-popping child-woman of the past two nights. Then Winslow remembered the cocaine he'd brought from her apartment. What a rotten thing to do! He resolved to flush it down the toilet back at the hotel. Masson went on:

"We were all amateurs, of course. We made mistakes. Guns misfired, ambushes were set up on the wrong street corner, we misused code, we pestered the English with meaningless information *we* thought perfectly splendid and *they* knew to be useless." He paused for a moment and smiled. "I remember once arguing vociferously that we absolutely *must* send a courier to London with the bus schedule between Grasse and Cannes written in invisible ink on a matchbook. Well"—he smiled—"we were young."

"Even from the first, Jacques Fayol was better than most of us at the game. He was a more sophisticated man, more worldly in the good sense. He seemed to know instinctively what was vital, what was marginal. When a man's life should be risked, when prudence was the right course. Small beginnings, of course, until the Resistance in the north gained confidence in our loyalty, in our resolve, and in our ability. By mid-1943 we were pretty good at what we were doing. Grasse is only a few kilometers from the sea. Information got out, men came in, the occasional German was killed, the odd Vichyite roughed up. It was in the intelligence aspect that Fayol shone.

"His couture house was functioning full out in Paris. Despite the shortage of fabric, of buttons, of needle and thread, the couture prospered throughout the war. The Germans, of course, were excellent customers, buying fine clothes for their wives at home, for their girl friends here. French women of means had little to do with their money. They couldn't travel, they couldn't buy new cars, they could not play the Bourse. So . . . they bought clothes. Anything to brighten that drab time of Occupation. Important people, Germans, Vichyites, the rich and powerful, dropped by Fayol's establishment and the other couture houses, and, as people will do, they gossiped. Fayol ensured that most of that gossip found its way to the appropriate ear. He had valid reason to travel, to the mills, to Grasse for the attar, to various retail stores around the country. He used his rail pass frequently. And he used it well.

"Then," said Canon Masson with the properly dramatic flair, "then he made his mistake." He gestured for the glasses and he refilled them all, including his own. Anouk shook her head.

"I didn't really want any more, thank you," she said. Winslow thought she looked especially alert. He realized this was the first account she'd ever really had of just what her father had done in the war, just what his shame had been, and what his excuse. She leaned toward the priest and her suntanned hands clenched pale.

"Poor Jacques," Masson said, with what seemed real feeling, real affection. "Like all of us, he had his weaknesses. Larger than life as he was, even in those days his flaws were magnified. There was an important piece of intelligence that arrived by boat down the beach from Cannes, a courier brought it into Grasse, and it was left to Fayol to carry it to Paris. Well"—and he raised his hands helplessly—"what can one say? There was a woman, Fayol dined too well, in bed they talked, and . . ." He stopped for a moment, looking at Anouk. "I am sorry, mademoiselle. Six members of the Resistance here in the south and several in Paris, no one ever really knew how many, were brought in. One of them survived his conversations with the Gestapo and implicated your father."

"The others?" Anouk asked in a low voice.

"Oh, dead, of course. By various means."

Anouk shook her head. "They didn't think he, my father, did it on purpose?"

Masson nodded heavily. "Well, there were those who did. I didn't. I knew the man. Some others here in Grasse—farmers, commerciants, jealous perhaps of a Parisian, of a famous man, a rich man—they ascribed motives. 'He is a traitor! He is venal, he sold out! He is a coward, he became frightened and talked!' I argued, but who would listen to me? There was no seal of confession, of course: Fayol never Communicated. But I knew his little lapses, I knew his tongue became loose, I knew the woman involved, I knew how . . . susceptible he was."

"What happened?" Winslow asked.

"What usually happened in those days. Drumhead justice. A star-chamber proceeding. Fayol was sentenced in absentia. I voted to acquit, of course, so did one or two others. But the majority ruled and a request was sent up to Paris to the Resistance there to arrest him and send him back to Grasse. Or, if that was inconvenient, to execute sentence right there."

"Without even a chance to defend himself?" Marianna demanded.

"Mademoiselle," Masson said gently, "our country was conquered, two million of our men were still prisoners of war, thousands of others had been arrested, tortured, shot. They were hard times. What was the life of one Frenchman more or less? Especially a Frenchmen his peers considered had betrayed them. But, as I say, Fayol was intelligent. He knew, of course; *must* have known from the first. He hid out, without ever going to the Germans, mind you, for three months. And when things had quieted down he suddenly appeared again, right here in Grasse, and gave himself up. Quel geste! It was magnificent. He dazzled these local peasants at the hearing. Ridiculed their suspicions, admitted he'd been a fool, that the girl had played with him, and demanded which of *them* had never made a mistake. It was in this very building, in the cellar, where the Resistance leadership customarily met. I can see Fayol now."

Canon Masson pushed back his chair and stood up. He weaved slightly. My god, Winslow thought, he *is* drunk. But the priest steadied. He was *Fayol* now, Fayol in 1943 with his life dangling:

"Which of you has never had a glass too many? Which has never spoken when he should have remained mute? Which . . . which of you has never . . . never, I say . . . *never* made a damnfool of himself over a beautiful woman?"

Masson looked at his guests, his eyes, reddened now, engaging theirs and then sliding away. He breathed deeply, sat down heavily, and for a minute or two said nothing. To Winslow he looked emotionally spent.

Anouk, looking very much her age now, face shining, eyes wide, broke the mood.

"But, Monseigneur, what happened?"

Masson roused himself.

"Alors, of course they voted to give him another chance. He

himself offered to dispatch the woman involved. And from then until the end of the war he performed prodigies. It was only afterward, with the hysteria of the liberation, that foul shaving of heads and rolling of tumbrils, that he had once again to stand before a tribunal. That was in Paris, where they knew Fayol only as a successful businessman during the Occupation. And not as *we* knew him, the best courier in the business."

Marianna looked at Winslow. Her face was serious, her brow knit. "But the woman? You said he 'dispatched' her? Did you mean that he killed her?"

Masson nodded. "It was that more than anything, I believe, that turned him to young men." He stopped abruptly and turned to Anouk. "You will please pardon me, Mademoiselle Fayol, for mentioning this in front of you."

Anouk smiled.

It was late. The old priest had obviously tired himself. Winslow decided now was the time.

"Canon Masson, there was this message from Monsieur Fayol to his daughter. Transmitted by the huissier, Grumbach. The message referred to your providing spiritual guidance if ever she needed it."

"Yes?" Masson answered.

Winslow felt awkward. How did you ask a priest about spiritual guidance for a third party? He determined to press on, regardless of the protocol.

"Spiritual guidance would be, bien sûr, a private matter. But I have the suspicion, and Mademoiselle Fayol agrees with it, that her father was saying something else. That he was not a man who spoke in spiritual terms and that Grumbach's message meant something entirely different. Different, but important."

"Yes," Anouk put in quickly, "it would be hypocritical of my father to suggest ..."

Winslow cut her off. He didn't want this to become a theological debate. "As you may not know, Canon, the huissier Grumbach is dead. Killed by a truck just a day or two after having sent his message."

Masson's eyes were glazed. "Ah," he said, "there were many good men killed. In the war. I remember . . ."

"Father?" Marianna prompted him gently, "did Monsieur Fayol leave something here with you for his daughter? Some paper?"

Winslow thought, bless you, my love, bless you. Masson seemed to pull himself together.

"For his daughter? Oh, yes, yes. Some papers."

Winslow flashed a signal to Anouk with his eyes.

"Monseigneur," she said quietly, "may I please have that which my father left here with you for me?"

Masson considered for a moment. Then, slowly, heavily, he stood. He looked at this beautiful young girl sitting at his table, the only child of his old wartime comrade and lifetime antithesis, and he made a courtly little bow.

"But of course, Mademoiselle Fayol," he said.

Winslow exhaled slowly and drained the pony of its brandy.

Masson stood up. "These papers. He used his code name from the war to label them."

"Paris One?" Winslow asked.

Masson looked blank. "But how did you know?" he asked, and then, without waiting for a response, he smiled.

"Jacques was our man in Paris. He was 'Paris One.' We were, you see, a modest organization. There was no 'Paris Two.' "

He left the room.

GASPARD

It was three o'clock in the morning. Anthony Winslow sat in his shorts in his room at the Muraour. His eyes were tired, his back ached. The fake period escritoire was covered with papers, many of them written by hand. Tossed on the bed, opened and empty, was a dusty brick-red manila folder, the same sort of file folder the dead huissier, Grumbach, had passed to him with trembling hands the first, and only, time they met. But this folder was different. Affixed to the top left was a simple gummed sticker on which were written two words in what Winslow took to be Grumbach's own spidery hand:

"Paris One."

Winslow reached for a cigar butt resting soggily in an ashtray. He relighted the butt and stretched wearily. He would have to authenticate the file, of course, but if it was what it seemed to be, the nagging mystery of why Delaware Corp. valued the House of Fayol at a hundred million was no longer a mystery: Jacques Fayol had quietly, legally, and effectively made a corner of the world production of attar. Fayol literally *owned* the flowers of Grasse!

The thing was incredible. Oh, there'd been corners made before in the strategic commodities. Tungsten, vanadium, certain grades of industrial diamond, upland coffee, that sort of thing. The wood-paneled world of merchant banking was replete with

instances. But always the coup had been pulled off by giant corporations, by consortiums, by shrewd, reckless brigands who
gambled millions, leveraged their assets, and ruthlessly destroyed
competitors. The international bully boys backed by Wall Street,
by the gnomes of Zurich, by the oil sheikhs, by the CIA—those
were the fellows for a sweep like this. But it hadn't been they
who'd pulled it off. It had been a fat fashion designer with a
penchant for young men, and a country priest for confidant,
who'd done it. Winslow shook his head in admiration. He wished
Henry Rousselot were here to savor the moment. Then, after a
moment, he wished even more that he could have known the man
who accomplished it.

Canon Masson had left them at table and had gone off, rolling
slightly as if on the deck of a small boat. The file was wrapped in
oilskin and had been concealed in some hidey-hole in the depths
of the old stone rectory. He returned blowing away the dust.
With another little bow, he handed it to Anouk. She held the
think for a moment and then passed it on to Winslow.

"Monsieur Winslow est mon banquier," she explained. There
was no flirtation about it, just a dignified statement, and not even
Marianna could take offense. Winslow smiled at the girl and
unwrapped the file. There was a letter, from Fayol.

"It's addressed to you," Winslow said.

"Read it," Anouk told him.

Winslow turned toward the light.

"My dearest child," it read. "My instructions are that you shall
read this only if I die. Grumbach is a good fellow and Canon
Masson is my friend. Trust them. I am sorry I have not given you
more reason to trust me, but I shall not bore you with regrets or
apologies.

"As any competent lawyer will be able to tell you, these papers
represent valid claim to ownership of a great many of the farms
of Grasse. They are in various forms: outright deeds of sale,
deeds of transmittal in lieu of loan repayment, collateral, even
one or two gifts to me, for reasons even I find difficult to analyze.

"At the time of this writing I estimate this file conveys ownership of perhaps seventy to eighty percent of the attar-producing land of the region. I will attempt, before I die, and obviously before you read this, to augment these holdings.

"I do not really want the land for myself. Masson will tell you how I came by it. It is not my intention to sell at present, although I have initiated preliminary talks with one of the big American multinational concerns and with someone acting for the Shah. I have begun these talks out of curiosity, to determine just how much greedy men might pay for Grasse. And, oh yes, for another reason. Because the playing of intricate games has always amused me.

"This file of papers now belongs to you. Grumbach notarized each in its time. You now own what I amassed . . . the essential oil fields of Grasse. Do with them what your head, and your heart, tell you is right.

"The flowers, dearest Anne, belong to you.

"With all my love."

Winslow looked up.

"It's signed, 'Papa.' "

The girl was smiling. Winslow was surprised. He had found the last words of Fayol touching, moving. He felt a momentary anger at Anouk. Was she this superficial, was the wealth all she was thinking about?

Anouk looked around the room, at Winslow, at Marianna, at the old priest.

"He *did* love me, you see. He really did. Whatever my mother said."

Winslow felt ashamed. The girl's happiness was this last message from a father she'd thought she'd lost. He reached out and took her hand.

Masson had poured a final brandy.

"It was guilt, of course, guilt and expiation," he said in answer to Winslow's question. "Fayol felt he had a debt to Grasse, to the farmers of the region because of his folly during the war that had killed those six men. He lived with guilt and searched for some way to expiate. And there was guilt on the other side too, chez les fermiers. They'd judged the man, sentenced him to death, and now they were sorry. So, after the war, when times were hard, the farmers went to Fayol for loans. He helped them, gave them money, helped rebuild the trade in essential oils. In return, they signed over their land to him, deeded their farms, made him the repository of their hopes for Grasse, for the trade, for the future. You see," Canon Masson said, "they were being naïve, in the best sense. They were demonstrating to Fayol that they trusted him with what they held most precious, their land. They had mistrusted him once, and he had proved himself a better man than most of them, and now they wanted to pay off their guilt."

"I think," he said, "Fayol would have held this paper forever. I do not think he would ever have called in his notes." Then, hurriedly, as if he'd committed a gaffe, he turned to Anouk. "I do not mean to predispose you, mademoiselle. The deeds, the leases, the farms, they are for you to do with as you wish. I am only stating an opinion that obviously is unprovable. Please forgive me."

Anouk ran to him and kissed him on the cheek.

Now Winslow sat in his hotel room, drained, exhausted, pleased to have put an end to riddles. He wondered what the sleeping farmers would think if they realized some smart young merchant banker from Wall Street was sitting among them, literally holding their futures in his hands. Well, he thought, Rousselot always said bankers couldn't play God.

Winslow inhaled. And that, he supposed, meant Delaware Corp. would end up running Grasse.

He stood up. "To hell with it," he said aloud. He needed sleep. Masson was taking them in the morning to meet with one or two of the farmers involved, just to authenticate signatures. It was a formality. But at Rousselot you observed the formalities. He fell into bed and was quickly asleep. He had forgotten to jettison the cocaine.

Émile and Jean-Pierre had seen Winslow and the girls return from the rectory. They had seen the bulky parcel under Winslow's arm. They had telephoned Paris. It had been a long call, and their instructions were quite precise.

They rendezvoused at Canon Masson's rectory at noon. He was jocular, expansive.

"My housekeeper was wrong," he said. "She told me the country wine will kill me. Not at all. It will be the local brandy."

He had telephoned to one of the farmers to warn of their coming. Winslow and the girls had checked out of the hotel. After seeing this farmer, Gaspar, and perhaps one or two others, they would head north. Driving fast and taking turns at the wheel, they would be in Paris soon after midnight. It was a hot day and Winslow put down the top of the car. Anouk asked him to drive.

"I'm still so happy about my father I shall never be able to concentrate on the road," she said.

Gaspar was a huge red-faced peasant in overalls.

"Ah, well," he said, "of course I signed over to Jacques Fayol. I'd been one of those who gave him the black spot that night in the cellar. You owe a man something after a foul business like that." He had them seat themselves in the main room of the house. "My wife is dead, my son spends all his time listening to discs and chasing girls, and I'm alone. Still," he said, "I'll hate handing over this place to anyone else. It's been in my family since, what? oh, since about the time Napoleon went into Italy over the Petit Saint-Bernard pass up there in the mountains." Then, realizing the girl was there, he turned to Anouk and apologized.

"Naturally, mademoiselle, the deed is valid. I don't mean to suggest it isn't. Just an old fellow's meandering over a wasted life."

"Not wasted, not wasted at all," Masson insisted. "Gaspar, it is sinful to denigrate yourself that way. I won't hear more of it. Tu comprends?"

Gaspar served them cold meats and a chilled white wine. He and Winslow and Masson smoked Winslow's Havanas while

Marianna and Anouk went outside into the sun in front of the farmhouse.

"You should stay the night, you know," Gaspar told the American. "That's the time. The workers going out at two, three o'clock in the morning, their gunnysacks ready to be filled with petals. Ah, that's the time. Then, at sunrise, into the town in the wagons, and after you weigh out at the merchants'—the first glass of the day, a fresh brioche, and some café au lait and a smoke."

Winslow went to stand in the open doorway. He could see Anouk and Marianna walking waist-deep in the fields, the flowers all around them. Even through the cigar smoke he could smell the blossoms. "What are they, Gaspar?" he asked.

"Oh, those are the roses of May," he said. "This is their season. Later, the lavender, the pungent mosses, the lilac . . . ah, you can barely breathe in the fields without becoming drunk on it. I tell you, monsieur, stay awhile, stay and smell the bags tomorrow. We'll have a splendid time and drink some wine and smoke more of these wonderful cigars of yours."

"Gaspar," Masson said sternly, "au fond you are a sensualist."

The farmer laughed. "At bottom and everywhere else, Monseigneur."

Winslow looked across the field, shimmering in the heat of early afternoon, the roses barely moving in the still air. So peaceful, so calm, so unspoiled. Tomorrow he would be in Paris, next week in New York; and this field, these roses, this jovial old farmer, would be here, under the Mediterranean sun. That is, if the Delaware Corp. so dictated. He had a sudden, irrational dislike for his clients. Not very bankerlike, he thought, frowning at himself.

Marianna and Anouk had now reached the limits of Gaspar's land. Winslow saw them slow, stop, and turn. He raised an arm to wave, not sure whether they could see him in the doorway. A bee hovered in the warm air just before his face.

"Pollinate, dammit, pollinate," Winslow told the bee. The bee, unimpressed, buzzed again, and then drifted off on the light breath of the wind.

Behind him Winslow could hear the old priest and the old farmer, both of them large men, expansive, loud—in the old world sense, "men with big bellies." He liked the sound of their talk, their laughter. He wasn't part of it, could not be, but that was not to say he could not hear it with pleasure. The thing that was not pleasant was this sense of inevitability about the land stretching off beyond him, land under flowers, land that had not changed all that much since, in Gaspar's wonderful words, Napoleon had passed by. Delaware Corp. Well, Winslow thought, so it was to be Delaware Corp. He gave a brief, silent laugh. At least that bastard up in Paris in his neo-Mussolini office would be screwed. Screwed too, the Iranian, Nafredi. Well, if bastards had to win, maybe it was well that they were "*our* bastards." He wondered who had said that.

But, shit, it was hard to see a man like this Gaspar sign over. If only Anouk would decide not to exercise her prerogatives, leave the land to the farmers, put the fucking "Paris One" file in a safety deposit box and tell him and the bank and the Delaware Corp. that she was saying "no" to eighty-five million. Would he? Winslow asked himself. And could not answer.

The sun weighed down. The flowers stretched red and pink and yellow to the horizon, first Gaspar's fields and then another and then another, until the land began to roll upward and then became fuzzy in the haze and the afternoon heat. Anouk and Marianna, thigh-deep in roses, seemed to float above the flowers. Then the bee returned, buzzing, buzzing louder, and Winslow's hand moved instinctively to shoo it away again but behind the buzzing there was the wind and then he realized it was not a bee but something larger. The flowers rippled and swayed rhythmically first, then erratically, then chaotically, like the angry chop of a riptide in a technicolored sea. Then Winslow saw the helicopter.

The pilot, like Jean-Pierre, was a technician. The man riding shotgun, like Émile, was a Corsican. He fondled the machine gun the way Émile cared for his knives, with care, with delicacy, with passion even. The copter had refueled at Nice and it came in low over the coastal hills and picked up Jean-Pierre's and Émile's car at the appropriate map coordinates. They exchanged waves, and both car and copter set off for their rendezvous at Gaspar's farm.

It was the Corsican who saw the girls. He poked the pilot and pointed. The pilot, being a technician and experienced in this sort of thing, understood. He dropped the nose of the ship and roared in low over the farmhouse. He did not see Winslow but he saw the two girls. Seeing the yellow ship approach, Anouk tentatively raised a hand, as if to wave; but Marianna, without knowing precisely why, recognized danger. She grabbed Anouk's arm roughly and the two of them began to run, awkwardly in the high flowers, toward Gaspar's house. The little yellow craft got there first.

The helicopter hovered a few feet off the ground and then, nearly obscured by swirling dust and thousands of petals torn from the rose bushes, it settled to earth. The glass hatch swung open, and even before the rotor had stopped turning, the Corsican hit the ground, knees bent, the machine gun held low, pointing toward the farmhouse. As the rotor slowed and stopped, the flower petals drifted softly to earth, a colorful, silent snow. Marianna and Anouk had stopped running. The copter was between them and the house. They stood there, tensed, waiting. They did not realize it, but they were holding hands.

"Merde!" shouted Gaspar as he burst past Winslow into the front yard of the farmhouse. Winslow was looking at the girls, frozen, unsure. Gaspar was looking at his flowers. "The fucking bastards," he cried. "My goddamn flowers." He shook his head in rage and raised two great fists to the sky as if to call down god. Then, he wheeled and ran heavily back to the house. Winslow had started toward the copter. The pilot had climbed out now. He was not showing a weapon but Winslow could see all too clearly the automatic weapon aimed in his general direction by the other man. Winslow kept walking, his hands slightly extended, open, to show he carried nothing. He had no idea what would happen when he reached the two men. Out of the corner of his eye he caught sight of a car bouncing along the dirt road toward Gaspar's house. There was a shout behind him.

"Out of the way, mon vieux!"

It was Gaspar, raising an ancient shotgun to his shoulder. Canon Masson was in the yard now too, still smoking his Havana, still holding a glass. He looked bemused. Winslow slid off to the left, trying to move smoothly so as not to draw a shot, but wanting to clear Gaspar's field of fire. Fifty yards away the machine gunner sank to one knee and casually raised the gun.

"Destroy my flowers . . ." Gaspar was muttering, when his face disappeared and then Winslow heard the *rrrippp* of a burp gun and Gaspar fell.

"Oh," Canon Masson said. He put down his wineglass carefully upright in the dust and knelt over Gaspar to bless him. The gunner stood and began to walk toward the farmhouse. The pilot drifted behind him, watching the girls. The car was there now. It was a Citroën DS. Two men were getting out. Winslow had seen them before. On the sidewalk across the street from Marianna's bedroom window. Well, he thought, here we go. Then there was movement behind him and Masson said, "S'il vous plaît?" Winslow turned and watched as the old priest raised Gaspar's shotgun to his shoulder and fired. The shot rocketed past Winslow, momentarily deafening him, and he flinched. When the smoke had cleared he saw that the pilot had fallen but the other man, the one with the automatic gun, was coming on at a trot. Masson fired again. This time there was only a dull click.

The men from the car had reached them. One of them—it was Jean-Pierre—took the shotgun almost gently from Masson's hands. The other, Émile, patted Winslow's body. Then he turned and waved an arm to the girls.

"Alors, venez ici, hein?"

Winslow, helpless, defeated, nodded, and slowly, almost wearily, Anouk and Marianna walked toward the little group of men standing in the yard of Gaspar's house. They detoured around the body of the pilot. No one said anything, and the gunmen simply gestured toward the house and they all went inside. Masson spoke first.

"It is difficult to imagine why a man would load only one barrel of a gun."

He sounded disappointed in Gaspar.

It was cool in the house. Gaspar's cigar was still burning in the ashtray. The dishes with scraps of cold meat and cheese, the half baguette of bread, the wine bottles, Gaspar's napkin, were there on his table. And his body lay in the sun just outside the door.

"Close that," one of the gunmen said, and the one with the machine gun kicked the door shut. Winslow's eyes, used to the bright sunshine, moved around the dim room.

"Alors," said the one who seemed to be the leader, Jean-Pierre, "now we commence."

Winslow decided it was time to break the spell. He hadn't said a word since the helicopter crashed the tranquility of the afternoon.

"You've got a killing on your hands already," he told Jean-Pierre, "but since the farmer also had a gun, you may be able to get off. I suggest you leave all of us alone here before this goes so far you can't . . ."

"Shut your mouth," the machine gunner said flatly.

Marianna and Anouk were quiet. Thank god for that, Winslow thought. If they were hysterical . . .

"It wasn't like Gaspar, you know," Canon Masson said.

"What?" Winslow asked, concentrating not on what Masson was saying but on their predicament.

"A man of his experience with guns. One shell in a two-barreled shotgun. Unheard of."

"Monseigneur," Jean-Pierre advised, "please be still." He turned to the machine gunner. "Give me that thing and go out and bring in your pilot. Then the farmer. I don't like leaving bodies in the open like that."

Émile laughed. "Not in this heat, in the sun. They swell like sausages, tu sais."

The machine gunner did as he was ordered. "Now," Jean-Pierre said, "their luggage. Bring everything in." Émile nodded and went out. Jean-Pierre, his eyes on Winslow as the potential danger, cradled the gun in his right arm and deftly lighted a cigarette with his left. "I hope, monsieur," he said, looking into Winslow's face, "that the papers you received last night chez le prêtre are right at hand. I am myself a gentle soul, but these companions of mine, well, you know Corsica, how they resent foreigners, how they hate, how they ... damage people."

Émile came in with the bags and slung them atop the table, knocking over one of the wine bottles. "Merde," he said, "I wanted some of that. It's damn hot."

The other Corsican returned with the body of the pilot over his shoulder. Jean-Pierre nodded toward the bedroom. "Put him in there," he said. When the man came out he said, "Can't I just roll the farmer under the bench out there? He's goddamn heavy."

Jean-Pierre nodded. "D'accord, mon vieux."

"Tony," Marianna began, but Jean-Pierre cut her off. "We'll have no talk just now, mademoiselle. Later, if we don't find the papers, you will have ample opportunity."

Anouk let off a string of obscenities but Jean-Pierre just smiled. "Oui, oui, I know. But later."

The Corsican came in and picked up a bottle and drank from it. "Must weigh a hundred kilos, that fellow," he grunted.

Jean-Pierre handed him the gun. His own .45 was stuck into the waistband of his trousers. He looked to Émile. "Open the bags," he said. Émile smiled and pulled out a knife, not the Swiss army knife this time but a long-bladed, delicate affair. It slid through the fabric of the bags like a razor. Only Winslow's Vuitton attaché case resisted.

"Look, I'll open the damn thing," Winslow said. He went to the table and unlocked the bag. How silly, he thought. Two men dead, helpless prisoners, and I'm worrying about a ten-year-old piece of luggage. Jean-Pierre smiled. The same thing may have occurred to him. He dug out the cocaine; smelled it; put it aside.

They found the "Paris One" file right away, of course. Winslow hadn't even tried to conceal it. Jean-Pierre started to riffle through the pages. Then he stopped.

"Tie them up," he ordered, "each to a separate chair."

He turned away and sat down in a corner of the room where there was window light. This seemed to be what he'd been told to expect. But he wanted to make sure. His lips moving slightly as he read, he scanned the pages. Émile and the other grabbed Winslow and shoved him into a chair. He started to resist, saw Marianna mouth "no," and he relaxed. They bound Masson next. The old priest still seemed to be cogitating on Gaspar's half-loaded gun. Émile turned to Jean-Pierre.

"Do we have to tie the girls? More fun if they can move their legs a bit, you know."

Jean-Pierre appeared distracted. "Yes, no, do what you wish, I'm trying to read this shit."

Émile pushed Anouk and Marianna against the wall of the farmhouse. "Now just stand there like good girls," he said. "Unless this heat is discomforting and you want to take off some clothes?" He grinned. His ugly face looked better when he was snarling, Marianna decided. The other Corsican picked up his machine gun again and sprawled in a chair facing the four prisoners. Jean-Pierre stood up.

"Ça va," he said. "It goes. It's the thing we were sent for." He looked into Winslow's eyes. "What good fortune for you, monsieur."

He jammed the "Paris One" file back into the Vuitton case. "Permit me," he said. Crisply, he dropped the charm. "Allez-y," he told the Corsicans. "Tie up the women and we march." He went out the door, to reconnoiter.

For the first time since he'd heard the copter, Winslow brightened. To get out of this without anyone else being hurt, without Marianna or Anouk being frightened worse than they had been already, was an incredible bit of luck. "Paris One" was a small price to pay. He looked at Marianna and smiled. She answered. Then Jean-Pierre returned.

"What the hell is this?" he exploded. "Tie up the women, cretins!"

Émile rubbed his mustache with the back of his hand.

"Écoutes, Jean-Pierre. What's the hurry? We have the papers. Paris is a long drive. Can't we relax a little?"

"You can relax in Paris."

Émile grinned. "But in Paris we don't have such drôle companions."

Jean-Pierre looked grim. "Tie them up and we leave. There is no profit to remaining here."

Émile shrugged. "I think there is, mon ami. Great profit." His voice was husky now. He tossed his cigarette aside.

"I don't like it," Jean-Pierre said, less forceful. Émile sensed it. Eagerly he grasped Jean-Pierre's arm.

"You remember, Jean-Pierre, how she looked? How she looked in Paris?"

Jean-Pierre stared at Marianna. Her face flushed. Goddammit, Winslow thought . . .

"Remember?" Émile said, licking his lips. "How she looked when she did that little striptease for us in the rue de Boulainvilliers? Remember?"

Marianna's shoulders slumped. Oh, God, she thought, they're the two on the sidewalk. Suddenly, without rationalizing it, she remembered the sting of the perfume on her bare nipples. Émile was staring at her breasts under the thin shirt. He seemed to be remembering as well.

ÉMILE

Anthony Winslow flexed his arms behind the back of the chair. There was no slack in the rope. He was miserable. The leadership of the gunmen was slipping inexorably from the businesslike Jean-Pierre to the animal, Émile. And what was shifting the balance was the availability, the vulnerability, and the sheer desirability of the two girls. Jean-Pierre made one more feeble gesture toward discipline.

"The boss doesn't like fucking around on the job," he said unhappily.

Émile laughed. He turned to the other Corsican.

"What about you, Coco? You like fucking around on the job?" He gestured meaningfully toward Anouk and Marianna.

The man shrugged. "Ça va, I don't care. Sure."

Émile looked back at Jean-Pierre as if to say, "You've been outvoted."

Jean-Pierre considered. Coco appeared too stupid to care one way or the other about the women. But he was a stinking Corsican and would side with Émile. Jean-Pierre looked around the room. The American, Winslow, was angry, frustrated, alternately hunching his shoulders against the ropes and going slack. Jean-Pierre was pleased to see the exercise was having no effect. He hadn't realized how big Winslow was, not during all those hours they'd tracked him, from the Stade Colombes to Grasse. He was

223

glad they'd gotten Winslow bound before Émile began this shit about the women. He looked at the priest. The old man was mumbling, perhaps praying, with a silly look on his face. Was he senile? Jean-Pierre wondered, or in shock, or perhaps, with all the wine bottles about, simply drunk? The priest could be disregarded.

The women, now, that was another matter. There was simply no way to disregard them. The American, the one of the bedroom window, rue de Boulainvilliers, was frightened. Well, you couldn't blame her. She'd played with Émile and now the Corsican was going to play with her. Jean-Pierre wondered if he wanted to hurt her or just satisfy himself. Probably both. He'd heard things about Émile. Nasty things. Even in their profession there were codes. The codes didn't seem to concern the Corsican. Jean-Pierre watched Émile watch the girl. In those white pants and the Lacoste shirt, you didn't miss much. It looked good.

His eyes moved to Anouk. A kid, he thought, yet with tired eyes. Drugs, probably. She didn't appear frightened at all, just slightly excited, as if she were looking forward to it. To Émile. Jean-Pierre thought perhaps she was on drugs. It was possible with these young girls. He found it rather disgusting.

"Well?" Émile asked. He was grinning.

Jean-Pierre looked at him. "All right, but let's not make a night of it. We've got a long drive."

"Damn you," Winslow shouted. "You've got the file. Leave them alone. I swear, if you . . ."

Émile walked over to him and back-handed Winslow across the face.

"Alors," he said, "are you a pansy who would deprive a man of his pleasures?"

Winslow started to snarl something but Émile hit him again. Winslow could taste blood in his mouth, and his lip was swelling.

"Tony," Marianna said quietly, "don't."

She tried to smile.

Canon Masson mumbled a bit louder now.

"Coco," Émile ordered, "shove his Reverence in the bedroom. He can pray in there without disturbing anyone."

The Corsican turned Masson's chair and slid it across the polished wooden floor and out of the room.

"The American too," Jean-Pierre suggested.

Émile grimaced. "Pourquoi? Let him watch. It will help him pass the time." He turned now to the two women.

"Alors, and which one wishes to be amused first?"

Anouk had a half-smile on her lovely face. Winslow thought she might be in shock still from the killings, and now, from fear. Marianna looked grim. But no longer frightened. Coco came back into the room. "He's praying," he said. "I told him, maybe, after, you might want to confess to him."

Émile laughed. "Pas mal, having your own priest handy. Convenient, tu sais?"

Jean-Pierre picked up the machine gun. "I'll be outside. Don't be too long at it." He started to leave. Émile shouted after him.

"Jean-Pierre, I worry about you!" He turned to Coco. "Mon vieux, how a man could see this beautiful young woman nude and not want to fuck her, well, it baffles me." Jean-Pierre went out and closed the farmhouse door. Émile now turned back to Marianna. He had made his little jokes. He had stopped. Still he grinned, but it was not an amused grin.

"Take off your shirt," he ordered. Marianna hesitated. Émile reached into a back pocket and pulled out the switchblade knife. He flipped it open.

"You can resist and be hurt a lot," he said, "or you can try to get some fun out of it and maybe get hurt only a little," he said matter-of-factly. "It's all the same to me. Either way, you get fucked." He turned to the other Corsican. "Keep an eye on the other girl," he said. "It will be her turn next."

Marianna breathed deeply. Her hands were at her sides, the fists tight. Émile walked to her and stood facing the girl, just a foot away. He was not as tall, but much broader, muscular, the neck set on powerful shoulders. "Non?" he said softly, and when Marianna didn't move he reached out with his left hand to grab the front of her shirt. Then, the knife blade flashed. Marianna instinctively flinched, and Winslow shut his eyes and began to curse, slowly and steadily. He was hoping one of the gunmen would hit him again, hard this time. He didn't want to see what was going to happen. When he opened his eyes Marianna's blue shirt lay open all the way down the front, neatly halved by Émile's knife. Her breasts were bare.

"Regarde, Coco," Émile said. "Not large, but nice. Très jolie, en effet." He reached out his left hand and began to fondle her right breast. Marianna stood there, stiffly, her hands still at her sides. But now a tear ran down her cheek. Émile's hand ran lightly over both breasts and then down to her flat stomach. He undid the snap of her waistband. Then Marianna did a foolish thing. She spit into his face.

"Putain!" he cursed. His left hand darted to her right nipple and began to squeeze. Marianna's knees buckled and she started to slump. The knife came up, and without even seeming to touch her, raked her torso just under both breasts. She did not seem hurt, steadied herself in fact, but a thin line of crimson showed on her pale skin. Blood trickled slowly down her body toward her waist.

"You see," Émile said reasonably, "we can do it your way. Or we can do it mine." He paused. "Get out of those pants," he barked.

Winslow was bellowing now, not really shouting words, just making animal cries of rage. His great shoulders wrenched against the ropes. Émile turned, distracted.

"You keep that up," he warned, "and I'll slice off her nipples before we start. You want that?"

Winslow gasped and fell silent. Jesus, he thought, he'll do it, too!

Then Anouk Fayol laughed.

Even Marianna turned to look at her. Hysterical, Winslow thought. Well, who could blame her?

"Hein?" Coco asked.

Anouk laughed again. It was not a hysterical laugh, not at all. It was throaty, controlled, knowing.

"I don't understand men," she said. "Look at you."

Émile looked down at himself.

"Comment?" he asked.

Anouk stared at him.

"You waste your time arguing and threatening and being spit at by that frigid nun with her legs pressed together instead of taking your pleasure with a real woman."

"Tu?"

"Of course me." She unbuttoned her silk shirt swiftly and tossed it aside. Then she opened her belt and, balancing on one leg, slipped off the denim pants. She was naked now except for bikini pants with little flowers. Even in his anguish, Winslow could not resist staring at her body. Anouk smiled.

"Well?" she said, turning around slowly.

Émile rubbed a big hand over his sweating face. Marianna was forgotten.

"You want?" he asked, amazed.

Anouk looked steadily into his face. "Yes, I want. But then, I always want." She shrugged. "In Paris, chez Madame Claude, sometimes I get two thousand francs for one night. But you know, really, I'd do it for nothing."

"You're one of Madame Claude's girls?" Émile asked. He seemed impressed.

"Bien sûr," Anouk said.

Émile looked back at Marianna. He still wanted her; still remembered the look of her in the bedroom window; was still excited by the look of her now with the shirt hanging from her shoulders, her breasts bare, the trickle of blood glistening on her body. Then there was Anouk.

He turned back to the French girl. She had her hands on her hips. She smiled.

"She can watch," Anouk said. "She can watch and maybe she'll warm up."

Émile licked his lips. Even the sluggish Coco was thinking. Winslow had nearly forgotten the danger, the threat to Marianna. Had she gone nuts? he was thinking. Or is she just a whore at heart? Or . . . ?

"Well?" Anouk said. She moved toward Émile, her long legs, the upturned breasts, the small waist, all as openly offered as that night with Winslow. Émile nodded.

"Oui," he said. His voice was throaty.

Anouk stood facing him. She put her hands on his upper arms and looked into his face.

"You know," she said, "when I make love I enjoy . . . being hurt a little."

"Anouk!" Winslow yelled.

She frowned. "Can't you put him with the priest?"

"Coco!" Émile said. The Corsican nodded and started to shove Winslow's chair across the room.

"There's a trick I know," Anouk told Émile. "With the cocaine. It's very exciting."

"D'accord," Émile said. "I want to try anything you say." He turned to Marianna. "What about her?"

"Let her watch," Anouk said. "Then, if you like, I can play with her a little. Maybe she'll like that." She waited, and then she said, "Maybe you'll like it too." Émile's face shone with sweat.

As Winslow was pushed from the room, toward the bedroom, he turned to look at Anouk.

"Get the cocaine," she said. And she slipped off the bikini pants.

Winslow sagged against the straight-backed chair. Gaspar's bedroom was dim, the one small window heavily curtained. Canon Masson's chair had been shoved into the corner. The old priest sat there, slumped and silent. Coco closed the door behind him and Winslow and Masson were left alone.

"Well?" the priest asked.

Winslow shook his head. He couldn't bring himself to tell the old man. He was torn between wanting to hear what was happening in the other room and dreading what he knew he would hear. "Oh, god," he muttered in despair, and again threw his weight against the ropes. They held.

And then Canon Masson stood up, tossed aside his ropes, and made the sign of the cross.

"For our blessings," he said piously, "let us be duly grateful."

* * *

"Turn her so she has to watch," Émile told Coco. The Corsican was holding Marianna's arms behind her back. He wrestled her halfway around so she could see Émile and Anouk. Except for his cheap pointed shoes and purple sox, Émile was naked now too, the powerful, squat body matted with hair, a heavy paunch set on muscular legs. His penis rode stiffly in front of him. Anouk was on her knees.

"Allons-y, vite," Émile ordered.

"Oui, darling," Anouk replied, using the English word. She had the container of cocaine and was powdering the head of Émile's penis with the white dust.

"It *is* harder," Émile said enthusiastically.

"Naturellement," Anouk told him. "Now just let me put some on my tongue."

Émile leered. He glanced again toward Marianna. "Listen, you," he barked, "watch carefully. You'll be doing this yourself tout de suite. You want her to do this, Coco?"

Coco grinned and nodded his head quickly. He slid his right hand around Marianna to cup her breasts.

"You'll do us both," Émile told her.

"Come on," Anouk said, "I'm ready now. Don't keep me waiting."

Émile turned to the girl kneeling in front of him and took hold of her long hair with both fists and pulled her mouth toward him. Anouk's beautiful eyes were wide and she was smiling.

Marianna Troy tried to turn away but Coco forced her to remain where she was. She closed her eyes and prayed the nightmare would end.

In their stocking feet Anthony Winslow and Canon Masson moved along the hallway connecting the bedroom with the rest of Gaspar's house. The priest carried an old sword, a relic of the Franco-Prussian war from some ancestor of the dead farmer. Winslow had a liter bottle of foul-smelling toilet water of Gaspar's in his fist.

"My rosary beads have sharp edges," Masson had explained with childlike simplicity when the astounded Winslow asked how he had freed himself. "Deus ex machina," the old priest added, lifting his eyes toward the beamed ceiling.

They reached the end of the hallway.

Anouk Fayol looked up at Émile and opened her mouth. The gunman thrust himself into her. One of Madame Claude's thousand-franc-a-trick beauties and he was in her mouth. He could feel her tongue sliding over him. He was thinking only of Anouk now, not of Marianna or the job or of that idiot Coco gaping at him. Only of this beautiful young girl who . . .

Then Anouk's teeth clamped down!

Émile's strangled scream was still echoing as Winslow and the old priest sprinted into the room. Coco's eyes bulged and Marianna let herself go limp in his grip. He started to reach for a gun but instinctively tightened his hold on the girl instead. He was still holding her when Winslow smashed the toilet water bottle over his head. Canon Masson stood over Émile, writhing on the floor, both hands digging into his groin, his mouth making little whimpering sobs, his body shaking. Masson put the old sword to his throat. Anouk sat cross-legged on the floor, naked, wiping the back of her hand across her mouth.

"That was good luck," she said calmly. "I had no idea what I was going to do next." She spat on the hardwood floor.

Marianna ran to Winslow. He kissed her, but when she put her arms around him he pulled away.

"Wait a minute. I want to see where Jean-Pierre is." He went to the window. The Frenchman was sitting on the hood of the Citroën, smoking a cigarette with one hand and industriously picking his nose with the other.

"He must have thought it was one of us screaming," Marianna said. She stood close to Winslow. She looked under control, but he could feel her body tremble.

"He's got the machine gun. And he's got the cars," Winslow said. "Any ideas?"

Masson looked thoughtful. "Could you hit him from here with the shotgun?" he asked in his mildest manner.

Winslow shook his head. "Too far. He could just sit out there and riddle this place. He's got the range on us."

He tried to remember things he'd done as a marine. If he could circle Jean-Pierre, come up on the blind side, get within shotgun range . . . But it was risky as hell. If he failed, if Jean-Pierre came out of it alive, Marianna and Anouk, and the old priest, would be at his mercy. And after what Anouk had done to Émile, what went before would be child's play. He looked back into the room. Coco was still unconscious. Émile was no longer moving but his hands were cupping his penis, and Winslow could see a little blood trickling through the fingers. He was moaning now, but not as loudly. Masson continued to stand over him with the sword.

"I'm going to brush my teeth," Anouk announced. She'd pulled on her jeans and had slipped into the shirt but left it unbuttoned. What an extraordinary girl, Winslow thought, to have conceived a way to protect Marianna and damage Émile. And if he and Masson had not gotten free? He shuddered to think of what Émile would have done. Winslow looked out of the window again. Jean-Pierre was pacing now, back and forth between the two cars, and glancing at his watch. He'll give them only a few more minutes, Winslow thought, and then he'll come in. Shit, if only he had a rifle. He looked at Émile and Coco once more. Then, before even framing the thought, he rejected it. You don't kill men who are helpless. You just don't do it, he thought, and wished that he thought otherwise.

"There's another way out," Canon Masson said. "A root cellar and some steps. They bring you out behind the house. Away from the side that fellow controls."

"Then we don't have a car," Winslow said.

Masson shrugged.

"It's only a few kilomètres into Grasse. You can find a car there, surely."

Winslow nodded. It made sense. Once they got away from the isolated farm, among people again, their chances would be better.

"Okay," he said. "Marianna? You ready?"

She nodded. Her torn shirt flapped open. He looked at her and smiled.

"I think maybe you better change."

She looked down at herself.

"I'd forgotten all about it," she said. Then, more soberly, "about the shirt, not about the rest."

Winslow nodded. He went to her and kissed her on the forehead. She had stopped trembling. Anouk came back into the room. She was fully dressed now and her hair was wet.

"I didn't want the smell of his hands on me," she explained. With the long hair pulled back into a ponytail she looked more the teenager than ever. Winslow found it difficult to imagine the whore who'd stripped herself bare in front of Émile and urged him to try the cocaine trick.

"Leave the luggage," Winslow ordered. "Just take a sweater and the anoraks. We may need them later, after the sun goes down. Tie them around your waists. Keep your hands free."

He pulled out a sweater and a down jacket for himself and tied them on.

"Canon?" he said, "have you got everything?"

"Non, Monsieur Winslow," the priest replied. "I will need that shotgun."

Winslow said he didn't understand.

The priest smiled benignly. "To keep that fellow off," he said. "I should be able to permit you a decent start, given a bit of good fortune."

They argued. Winslow insisted they could all get away, together. As they went into this mess, together, so would they escape. No, the priest insisted, the machine gun was too potent. If Jean-Pierre had only a handgun, yes, they would stand a chance in the rose fields. "I no longer do the hundred-meter dash very swiftly," he said apologetically. Marianna insisted if he would not go, none of them would. Masson quietly told her she was wrong, that she and Mlle. Fayol and this young man deserved their chance, and that he meant to give it to them. Winslow agonized, casting a look through the window to where Jean-Pierre had stopped pacing and now stood staring toward the house. He imagined he could see impatience cloud his face. The debate went on and then Anouk said:

"He's right, you know. It is the best plan." She looked at Masson.

Marianna said angrily, "You have no right . . ." but Masson mildly interrupted her.

"No, my child, you are wrong. Mademoiselle Fayol has every right. It was her resource, her courage, her self-negation that enabled us to overcome these two . . . gentlemen." He looked at Anouk.

"There is much of your father in you, mademoiselle. The same ability to think clearly, to reach conclusions, to make difficult choices. Remember that, if you will excuse a brief sermon. Remember that his weaknesses concealed great strengths. They did not stifle those strengths. But only made them difficult to find."

Anouk smiled and went to the priest and kissed him lightly on the cheek.

"I will always think of you," she said, "for giving my father back to me."

Winslow picked up the old Vuitton case with the "Paris One" file. He and Masson exchanged weapons, the old priest taking the shotgun and Winslow Coco's Smith & Wesson. He stuck it in his belt.

"Well?" he said. Marianna kissed the priest and Winslow shook his hand, and then Masson led them into the kitchen and lifted up the trapdoor to the root cellar.

"How many happy hours I spent down there," he mused. The girls had started down the ladder.

"In the war," Winslow said.

Masson smiled beatifically. "Oh, yes, in the war, of course. Plotting all variety of beastly things against our German visitors."

Winslow started down the ladder and then he stopped. Masson was looking down at him, his broad, aged face wrinkled in smiles.

"Father," Winslow said, "you're sure you want to do this? Alone?"

Canon Masson made a little gesture with his hand.

"Alors, mon vieux, when you were still in the École Maternelle I was doing this sort of thing. Hiding in cellars and firing shotguns through windows at men mistaken in their beliefs. And now, well, now I shall do it once more. To some effect, one would hope."

"Okay, then," Winslow said. He reached back his hand, once again to touch the gallant old priest. "Merci bien pour tous."

"Cela ne fait rien," Masson said. "It's nothing. And besides" —and he looked behind him and reached back—"there is always this, if it comes to it."

He had Gaspar's old sword in his other hand.

Winslow turned away and went down the ladder, and then the trapdoor closed over them. In a moment they were through the cellar and out of the house and headed at a purposeful trot into the rose fields. Behind them, the farmhouse, old Gaspar's farmhouse, was silent.

They were halfway across the field, staying low, moving quickly now despite the thorns that tore at their clothing, at their bare arms and hands, when the firing began. The shotgun's blast, then the *rrripppp* of the automatic weapon, then Masson's second barrel, and then . . . the machine gun once again. After that, it was quiet, and Winslow told them they had better get all the way down now and crawl. Because Jean-Pierre would be coming after them.

They crawled. As the late afternoon sun came down they smelled the roses through their own sweat.

THE ROSES OF MAY

Émile lay on top of the heavy wooden table. Jean-Pierre examined the bite marks on his penis.

"You'll live," he said.

Émile groaned. "Am I damaged permanently?" he asked.

"Take a look for yourself," Jean-Pierre advised.

Émile shook his head.

"I can't," he said. "I can't look at it."

Coco came back into the room, his head wet from the sink.

"A bottle," he said, "he hit me with a bottle. Some variety of cologne."

"You smell like a Marseilles whore who works the tramp steamers," Jean-Pierre said. He was fed up with these two. The papers gone, the American gone, the girls gone. And the old priest dead. All because these two had to get laid. And they didn't even accomplish that. He thought about what the boss would say. He probably wouldn't say anything. He'd simply finish the job Anouk began. But it would be all their balls this time.

"Come on," he said. "I suppose you can fly that thing," he asked Coco.

The Corsican nodded. "Sure," he said. "That other guy was no better than me, just maybe a little smarter."

"What about you?" Jean-Pierre asked Émile. "Can you move?"

Émile shook his head. "I don't know. Am I still bleeding?"

"It's stopped." Then Jean-Pierre had a thought. "But they say human bites are very dangerous. Rabies, gangrene, that sort of thing."

Émile groaned anew.

"Yes," Jean-Pierre said, half to himself, "I guess that would be the best thing."

"What?" Émile demanded.

"Prevent infection, save your worthless life. Cauterize the wound, kill the germs that whore had on her teeth."

"You have medicine?" Émile asked hopefully.

"Better than medicine," Jean-Pierre said cheerfully. "Coco, bring me that bottle of brandy from the counter."

"Brandy? To drink?" Émile asked. "Will that do it?"

"You aren't going to drink it, idiot. I'm going to get you up on your feet so your Corsican copain here can fly us over the fields until we find our friends." He stared at Émile, hating him for his stupidity, his lust, his ugliness. Bastard, he thought, fucking me up with the boss this way.

"Lie down," he ordered the injured gunman. He opened the bottle of brandy and poised it over Émile's groin.

"I don't think this will hurt," Jean-Pierre said. "Not too much, tant pis."

He poured.

Winslow did not hear Émile's scream. He and the girls were a quarter mile away by now. He had signaled a break and they lay exhausted, panting, scratched, and sore in the dry dirt between two rows of May roses. Winslow looked around. Marianna had a scratch across her cheek and her hands and forearms were spotted with blood. She was thinking about Canon Masson and did not look back to Winslow. Anouk had torn her shirt and now she ripped it off in anger.

"I don't know whether it's better to let the thorns get me and move fast or let them get my clothes and go slow. Damn," she said, "I'm going to smash every bottle of perfume I own when I get home."

Winslow breathed deeply. He tried to calculate what Jean-Pierre would do. Was there another pilot among them? That would make it really hairy. These rose bushes were hell to move through but they wouldn't give much cover from the air. If the gunmen had to follow on foot, or follow the farm roads in a car, they had a chance, a damn good chance. But with a copter? He pulled out the Smith & Wesson and sighted along the barrel. He wondered if he could hit a low-flying helicopter. The Vietcong had done it with small-arms fire every so often. He might get lucky.

"Tony," Marianna said, "when we get to Grasse, we'll go right to the police, won't we?"

"I don't know," he said.

"Why not the police?" Anouk demanded. "Those men are murderers."

"I know," Winslow said somberly. "And they may also *be* the police."

He told them about the Minister's guarded threats over the Maison Fayol. "I don't know *who* the bastards are working for," he admitted, "but if there's any chance at all they're government agents, I'm not about to turn myself in at the nearest police station. Not with the election coming up Sunday and Monsieur le ministre making ugly noises at the back of his throat about looting France's national treasures."

Anouk swore. "The House of Fayol. The House of Fayol. I wish I'd never heard of it. I wish my name were . . . du Pont, something common like that."

Winslow laughed despite himself. "Common," he said. "Like du Pont."

Anouk missed the American joke. "I'm serious," she said. "I want no part of it. I did nothing to earn it. It was my father's, not mine."

"It could be worth a hundred million dollars," Winslow reminded her.

"Money, money." She spat out the words. "That's all everyone thinks about. No wonder the communists are going to win on

Sunday. I don't want the fucking money." She thought for a moment. "I'll get a job."

"Chez Madame Claude?" Marianna asked sweetly.

Anouk frowned. "No," she said thoughtfully, "I'm through with all that now. I don't need it anymore. Perhaps I'll . . . teach English."

Winslow laughed. Anouk was just what every teenage boy should have as a teacher, sitting there in the rose field wearing jeans and a serious look on her lovely face, and nothing more.

Then they heard the helicopter.

It was nearly seven o'clock at night and still the goddamn sun hung in the western sky. The copter had just made another pass. Winslow was drained. He looked at the girls. Even Anouk had stopped babbling. She lay on her back in the dust, her bosom and belly caked with dirt and streaked with angry red scratches. Marianna lay on her stomach, the slash of Émile's knife forgotten, her slim body rising and falling as her lungs sought air. Winslow badly wanted a cigar. He wondered if they could see smoke from the air. Better not, he thought. He pulled out his grimy handkerchief and once again cleaned the revolver. The last, best hope they had, he thought, giddy with fatigue. Thank you, Mr. Smith. Thank you, Mr. Wesson. Jesus, he hoped the copter would run out of fuel. How long could it stay up there?

He used the filthy handkerchief now to wipe the sweat from his face. He was staring at Marianna's back, without really focusing on it. Then something moved. His eyes clicked. It was a scorpion, one of those small scorpions so common in the dry heat of the south of France. It scuttled across Marianna's sweater. The girl just lay there, unknowing. Winslow hated things that crawled. But he reached over and with a snap of his middle finger, flipped the scorpion into a nearby bush.

"What was that?" Marianna asked, dreamily.

"Nothing," Winslow said. "Not a thing." He was bone-grinding tired and the sun was still up there.

* * *

Jean-Pierre tapped Coco's arm.

"All right," he said, "just one more sweep and we go in."

Coco squinted at the gauges. "Says empty now," he reported.

Jean-Pierre nodded. "I know. Now make the sweep."

Émile was propped on the duffle behind the two seats. He was dressed now, but his trousers were opened at the waist and his fly unzipped. He still did not like to look down there. But it was too painful to close his pants over the wound. He no longer had any desire at all to fuck Anouk or the other one, the tall American girl.

He wanted only to hurt them very badly with his knives. To hurt them and then to kill them.

At nine fifteen it was dark, and Winslow and the two girls came out of the rose fields, crossed through a patch of woods, and found one of the roads leading into Grasse. The question now was not finding a car or getting to Paris or calling for help. It was simply finding a place where they could sleep, a place where Jean-Pierre could not find them.

At ten o'clock they found a warped door in one of the smaller oil refineries on the edge of the old town and Winslow put his shoulder against it and shoved. The door swung open on rusted hinges and they went inside. The scent of the flowers was overpowering. Winslow felt giddy for a moment, much the way he'd felt during the chanting at Hélène Fayol's house, and he was afraid he was going to black out. Then Marianna took him by the hand and they stumbled deeper into the darkened building, half factory, half storehouse, until they came to a small mountain of gunnysacks full of rose petals.

"Here, Tony," Marianna said gently, "we're safe now. You can sleep."

Exhausted, Winslow threw himself on the sacks without saying a word. Four hours later he woke. Anouk and Marianna lay on either side of him, sleeping quietly. He inhaled. The roses of May, he thought. Would he ever forget the smell, get it out of his clothes, his hair, his nostrils, his very skin, the inside of his mouth and the back of his throat? He was sure, right then, that if he urinated, had a bowel movement, the waste would smell . . . like flowers.

The gunmen had landed and gone to the hotel. Winslow had checked out, the clerk said. Well, they knew that. He hadn't returned? He or either of the women? No. Émile painfully put himself to bed. Coco went to the station restaurant for dinner. He liked the food they served at station restaurants. It was good, it was plentiful, it was cheap. He was saving his money. He would not always be in this foul business. Then, over the potage de jour, he considered that he had never had a girl who looked like either Anouk or the American. He inhaled the soup, and for several seconds at least, thought about scx. Jean-Pierre, who settled for a sandwich and some wine, spent a deal of time on the long-distance telephone. It was not a pleasant conversation.

Later, when Émile resumed complaining about his wounds, Jean-Pierre sent for a doctor. He didn't at all mind that his colleague was in pain; the son of a bitch deserved everything he got. But Jean-Pierre had a low tolerance to whining. To spare himself, he called. The physician, a rustic sort, examined Émile thoughtfully.

"Ah," he said, half in admiration, half in regret, "to encounter a woman of such passion. Monsieur, I felicitate you. Such pain is merely transient. But your memory of the climactic moment . . . it should linger always."

When he had done his patchwork and left, Émile stared angrily at Jean-Pierre. "The bitch bit my cock halfway through and he felicitates me. I'm marking that one down in my book as well, for when I'm on my feet."

Jean-Pierre nodded. "Well, you won't have long to wait then. You'll be on your feet in the morning. The boss says we get Fayol's papers or we don't come back to Paris."

A few miles to the south Zader Nafredi was also passing an unpleasant evening. Teheran *had* sent a message; it was forceful;

certain options were declared open to Nafredi. He could nail down the Shah's agreement to purchase the Maison Fayol; he could return home in disgrace; or he could commit suicide. On balance, Nafredi reflected, the first alternative was the most attractive. Well, Nafredi told himself, the affair is easier wished than consummated. His last bit of intelligence about the American had come from Maggy Moal, bandaged and lubricated in the burn center at Marseilles. Nafredi had phoned to console her over the accident and had a recitation of all the second-rate people she'd seen parading themselves at Cannes: "Americans even, and not simply the Hollywood trash. There was that young banker, Winslow, and Fayol's daughter, the little tart. How one permits folk of that sort entrée to society, I fail to imagine. France started to rot when the monarchy went out. Your Shah, now, there's a fellow who understands one doesn't rule with ballots; one rules with whips."

Nafredi agreed profusely, and finally, clicking the receiver to mime a fault in the connection, hung up on the old woman. So they were *here*! In Cannes. Or, and he began to become excited, perhaps in Grasse. Why not? The Fayol interests extended to Grasse. He picked up the phone and ordered his driver to prepare the car. It was a shame to abandon the festival. But he had no choice. It was an even greater shame to abandon that charming little German blonde. She had a way about her. He loved seeing her together with Soroya. He must talk to one of his producer friends in Paris. Surely they could do something to push along the child's career.

In Greenwich, Connecticut, Henry Rousselot looked at his digital clock and then picked up the telephone. He asked for the transatlantic operator. He'd tried for hours the day before but without success. Winslow's Paris hotel simply had no idea where he was. He had retained the room; left some things behind. Surely he would be back. No, there was no forwarding address, no additional information. The operator picked up.

"Yes?"

"Keep trying," Henry Rousselot said. It was important. Very important.

Because now Henry Rousselot knew why Delaware Corp. was willing to pay a hundred million for a Paris fashion house.

Winslow was awake. He could feel the old Vuitton case under the gunnysack on which his head had rested. On either side of him, the girls slept. Had something wakened him? He sat up, slowly, and listened. The perfume factory was still. The scent rolled over him in waves, making him woozy, but there was no sound in the building. The sounds came from outside. He looked at his watch. Three o'clock in the morning. Who the hell would be . . . ?

What woke Winslow was the sound of the people of Grasse going out into the fields to pick the flowers. It was three in the morning and their day had begun. On motorbikes, in dented 2 CVs, in pickup trucks, jammed into a superannuated bus that once serviced the Levallois–Paris commuter route, they headed for the fields and a day of casual labor that could earn a diligent picker as much as 150 francs. Winslow got up carefully, without disturbing the women, and went to the door of the old factory. The long, slow parade of vehicles was headed out into the country from the Old Town, passing the perfume factories on the outskirts of Grasse.

Winslow knelt down quickly between Anouk and Marianna and gently shook them awake.

Anouk's eyes were frightened. Marianna simply looked sleepy.

"It's okay," he said, "but get up. I think we can get the Lancia back and get out of here."

They hurried outside behind him, rubbing their eyes, pulling back their hair, and waited alongside the building until Winslow stepped into the road and flagged down an ancient flatbed truck.

"Alors," the driver cried.

"We missed our ride," Winslow told him in slangy French.

"My wife and her sister." He gestured vaguely toward the

women. The driver peered out, all peasant-suspicion. He saw the two young women.

"Ça va," he said, "climb in. Don't keep me waiting."

They pulled themselves in over the tailboard. Winslow had brought along a couple of gunnysacks. In one of them was the Vuitton case containing the Fayol papers. Three men and a woman sat in the truck, trying to sleep as it jolted over the rough road on broken springs. Overhead the stars spattered the Mediterranean sky, but the night was cold. Marianna and Anouk wore sweaters and anoraks and cuddled close to Winslow. Two of the flower pickers dropped off as the truck passed farms close to town. At one of the stops the driver shouted back asking where Winslow was heading.

"Gaspar's place," he said, hoping the driver knew who Gaspar was.

"Gaspar?" the man shouted. "You've got the devil of a chance to make a day's wage out of that fellow. He's so tight he'd rather pick his own and damn the arthritis."

Winslow shouted back agreement. "His arthritis is worse. He can't do it this year."

"Oh," the driver said cheerfully, "that's good," and turned back to the wheel.

It was still dark when they got there. Winslow dropped lightly to the ground and helped the women down. He waved thanks to the truck driver. They walked down the dirt lane from the main road. The farmhouse was silent, dark. The DS was gone. The Lancia sat there. Winslow silenced the girls with a gesture and looked the car over. He wondered if it could be booby-trapped. Not likely, he thought. Getting the other car away and leaving theirs was probably part of a scheme to have the police start chasing them once the various bodies were found.

"Get in," he whispered. "I'm going to look for the priest."

He stowed the gunnysack containing the "Paris One" papers in the back seat and pulled out the Smith & Wesson. The dead Gaspar still lay under the bench, just outside the front door. The heavy front door was splintered, the windows smashed. Inside,

Canon Masson lay on the floor. He stared up at the ceiling, the shotgun, emptied, a few feet away. Off to the right, where it would have been conveniently at hand, the old Franco-Prussian War sword, stuck, handle up, in the hardwood floor. Winslow knelt down next to the old man. He had been shot in the chest. Winslow looked down into the old face. He closed the lids over Masson's eyes. He remained there for a moment, thinking about Henry Rousselot's briefing that had sent him to France, that had brought terror to two young women, death to this marvelous man, to an old rose grower, to an unknown helicopter pilot, and almost surely, to the huissier Grumbach.

"All for a few bottles of lousy perfume," Winslow growled, angry at Rousselot, angry at the dead Fayol, angry at whoever had sent Jean-Pierre and Émile to hunt them down. Angry at himself for having come to France to light the fuse. He heard a sound behind him and wheeled, leveling the revolver.

"It's me," Marianna said. She was looking at Canon Masson. She came to Winslow and put her hand on his shoulder. "You all right?" she asked.

He nodded.

"You?"

"I don't know. Until yesterday I never saw a dead person. Not even at a wake. Now . . ."

If they kept this up they'd be sharing a Kleenex. Winslow slipped into a tough-guy role. "Well, you have now," he said.

"Have what?" Marianna asked. Her mind had moved on.

"Never mind. Get those bags in the car. I don't want to hang around here."

Marianna started to gather the luggage, staring at the upright sword. She tried not to look at the dead priest.

"Where are we going?" Anouk asked as the little car sped away from the farmhouse, skidding in the dirt and then jolting onto the paved road.

"Away from here," Winslow replied.

"Oh?"

Neither of the women spoke. Winslow knew what they were

thinking. That he had no plan other than to put miles between themselves and the slaughterhouse of Grasse. As he had the day before when Jean-Pierre had the range on them with the machine gun, Winslow tried to scour up long-forgotten lessons: What would the enemy expect him to do? What tactic would the enemy employ? How could he be fooled? How to overcome a numerically-stronger, better-armed, faster-moving opponent? He glanced at the road map on the seat beside him. There was a junction ahead, their first critical decision. National route 7, the road they had taken south, was the better road, more direct, it would get them to Paris hours faster. But it was too obvious a route for fugitives, and anyway, did he want to go to Paris? Better to follow route 202 winding up through the mountains, keeping Italy on their right hand and Switzerland due north. That way, if they were cornered, they could made a run for the border. Anouk broke in on him.

"You know," she said, "I'm not sure this is such a great idea, using my car. They *do* know what it looks like."

Since the same uneasy notion had occurred to Winslow just moments earlier, he cursed himself for stupidity. But not wanting to frighten the two women, he blustered. "Stop playing the bloody fool," he snarled at Anouk. "Just shut up. I know what I'm doing."

Anouk and Marianna sulked in silence. Winslow pulled a cigar from the glove compartment and chewed on it, unlit. He was convinced he was an idiot, that he had no workable plan, that this mindless, aimless flight would end in disaster. Ten years ago, danger, tactical decisions, violence, and weapons had been his trade. They were no longer. Now his trade was balance sheets, acquisitions, certificates of deposit, interest rates, three-piece suits, and wood-paneled boardrooms. He was out of his accustomed place. Now knowing what else to do, aware of the bundle of papers he was carrying, the two vulnerable women who were his responsibility, he bit into the cigar, tightened his strong hands on the wheel of the little car, and drove north.

* * *

At six that same morning, Jean-Pierre was up, drinking black coffee and poring over road maps. At seven he woke the others. At eight a yellow helicopter lifted off from a field just outside the town, dipped low over the farm of a man called Gaspar, ascertained that a certain Lancia abandoned there yesterday had gone, and swung north.

PURSUIT

The road climbed. In the beginning they were still among the rose farms, and off to either side in the fields they could see day laborers harvesting the petals, using flashlights and butane lamps against the dark. In the east, dawn was breaking, the sun still well below the curve, but the night sky streaking and mottling purple and navy and drab gray. It was cold. But Winslow had insisted on driving with the top folded down. The women, dulled by lack of sleep, annoyed with him for his anger and mulishness, curled up in corners of the car, bundled against the cold, sullen and silent. There was very little traffic. A few trucks, a cyclist, a tractor. Winslow swiveled his head, trying to cover the flanks and the road behind him, the road from Grasse. He was thinking of the Citroën. And he was thinking of the helicopter. You could see a copter coming a long way off with the top down, you might even hear it. He didn't like those blind spots the Lancia had with the bonnet up. With the "Paris One" file next to him, with the two girls his charge, Winslow wanted any edge he could get.

"Hey," Anouk called from the back seat.

Winslow swiveled to look at her.

"Yes?"

"Il faut faire pipi," she said, with a pleased smile.

Barcelonette was the next town. Forty kilometers, maybe 25 minutes. He told her to wait. She threw him a sour look and sank

back into the corner of the back seat. In the other corner Marianna slept. Her hair blew in the wind, her face was scratched, the
one hand he could see was grimy and bruised. And she looked
beautiful to Winslow. By seven they were at Barcelonette. Winslow pulled the car into the courtyard of a local inn lacking stars
or other Michelin symbols. A scrofulous chicken fluttered out of
their way, and Winslow went inside and took two rooms. "We
won't be staying," Winslow informed the proprietor. "We're just
looking over the neighborhood for a possible film location."

The proprietor, who loved the films, and suspected Winslow of
all sorts of erotic behavior with the two young women, assigned
them the best rooms in the inn. One of them even had a sink.

The Shah's man in France was also driving north. But Zader
Nafredi did not believe in traveling rough. He left Cannes at
seven in the navy-blue Bentley, a wicker basket put up by the
chef of the Carlton on the seat next to the chauffeur. Alongside
Nafredi, the little German starlet. The Iranian had fully intended
to set off on the chase the night before. He had given Soroya
some money and ordered her to enjoy herself for two more days
at the festival and then meet him in Paris. The mannequin took
the money and the two days and promptly went off to join le beau
Max and the American cowboy actor who'd promised to teach
them both such naughty things. But when Nafredi summoned the
starlet to his stateroom to break their date, she had responded by
pouting and removing her clothes. Nafredi was anxious to catch
up with Winslow, still intent on nailing down the Fayol deal,
more than a little terrified by the prospect of returning in disgrace
to Teheran. He had begun biting his nails, drinking too much,
sweating through his Turnbull & Asser shirt, turning the alligator
strap of his Cartier watch soggy. Yet, when the girl widened those
blue eyes and undid her long blond pigtails and poised herself on
all fours in the middle of his bed, Zader Nafredi's zeal for the
chase diminished remarkably.

He too had taken route 202, not because he suspected Winslow would be on it, for he had only the vaguest hope of catching

the American this side of Paris, but because the German girl, whose name was, inevitably, Heidi, wanted to see the Alps.

Heidi, like Anouk and Marianna, had curled up in a corner of the big car and had gone to sleep. It was cozy in the Bentley, with the heat on and soft music playing. Nafredi watched her for a while and then, having issued instructions, drank a glass of Dom Pérignon to clear his sinuses, and fell asleep.

He did not see the helicopter pass overhead.

The instructions given Jean-Pierre by phone the night before, and then in a final call this morning, were quite precise. There were only two roads the American could take. The helicopter could easily swing back and forth covering both the major route 7 and the secondary route 202. Further north, as a backstop, there would be road watchers along the way. Jean-Pierre was to keep his radio tuned to a certain frequency. When the fugitives were overtaken (the word "if" was not used), the papers were to be recovered. It did not matter what happened to Winslow or the women. If they proved an obstacle, they were to be eliminated. But there was to be no more of yesterday's time-consuming foolishness. If Émile insisted on sport, he was to be left behind to enjoy it. Jean-Pierre and the papers were to be flown to Paris with Coco taking the most direct route. A final alert was issued: there were indications other parties might have the same objective. They were to be ignored unless they impeded the mission. In which case, Jean-Pierre was told, "tant pis pour eux."

His trousers fastened at last, Émile reclined on the blankets and assorted gear behind the copter's two seats. He had been assigned the machine gun and it lay across his thighs. But Émile, still in pain, still angry, had no intention of using the gun. He thought of his precious knives, he thought of Anouk's body, and he passed the time by conjuring up interesting permutations of steel and flesh. Marianna and Winslow barely entered his mind. He would do them quickly. It was Anouk over whom he would labor unceasingly.

* * *

The inn had no real dining room, only an ambitious bar. A plump girl with goiter served breakfast. They were the only guests. Marianna had changed into a turtleneck over pants and Anouk wore one of those pink buttoned-down Brooks Brothers shirts French girls so love.

"You both look marvelous," Winslow told them. He had had a shave and a bath and a change of clothes and was feeling better about things, concerned only that the women would be nervous, anxious, full of advice of no practicality at all. He had decided to put on a show of confidence, a confidence he was actually beginning to feel. They had gotten this far without incident; surely the further they were from Grasse, the safer they were. He smiled with satisfaction and lighted a cigar. And then Anouk and Marianna descended on him, shattering the mood he had worked so hard to create.

"Tony," Marianna began, "it *isn't* that your judgment is in question. But Anouk and I wonder whether our tactics are precisely what's called for. We, Anouk and I . . ."

"Merde," Anouk declared. "What Mademoiselle Troy is attempting to say in her stilted fashion-magazine style, is that we are three innocents among the wild beasts and that we are likely to be chewed up. Three children playing with grown-up toys, like that large revolver you . . ."

"Not so loud, Anouk, for God's sake," Winslow cautioned. Only the waitress seemed close enough to hear, but he was jumpy.

". . . that you wave about so dramatically. It's as useful as that sword poor Masson was going to wield. Tony, be sensible. These are hard men. Either get someone to help you or give it up. If you don't trust the French government . . ."

"Goddammit, Anouk, you weren't there. You didn't hear your Minister tell me they aren't going to let any little issue like these flower gardens of your father's even threaten this election."

Marianna put a hand on his arm.

"All right, all right," he said. "I'll calm down. But as a banker I've got a fiduciary responsibility to you, Anouk. When Canon Masson turned over those damned papers, they became your property. And you handed them on to me. We're supposed to be stuffy in my business. And I guess we are. So I'm stuffy and I'm stubborn and my tactics aren't out of the Marine Corps manual and we *are* innocents in the fucking forest. And, yes," he said, smiling, "I wave that gun around a lot more dramatically than I can shoot the damn thing."

The two women were silent. The waitress shoved plates onto the table. The otherwise empty room echoed with the sound of crockery. Nothing else.

They ate breakfast. Or rather, the girls did. Winslow pushed the food around his plate. The competence he had begun to assert, the confidence he tried to communicate, had shattered. He *was* in over his head. Charlie Casey had made it clear he could expect no great help from the American Embassy. The bad guys were somewhere back there and tracking him. The women and the goddamn "Paris One" papers were in his charge and he really had no idea how to safeguard any of them. Boy, he thought, if my father could see me now. He drained the cup of gritty coffee and stood up, rather dramatically, he realized, but maybe it was time for dramatics.

"Okay," he said. "You're right, I don't have a plan. I've gotten innocent people hurt already. I've fucked up splendidly."

Marianna looked up at him, as if she didn't believe any of that, as if she loved him.

"Tony," she said, "you aren't *really* stuffy, you know."

He exhaled, and then ran a big hand awkwardly through his hair.

"Non, Antoine," Anouk said brightly. "peut-être juste un tout petit peu . . . maybe just a little bit."

Winslow grinned. "Okay then, maybe you have some ideas."

"What about Italy?" Anouk said. "Turin must be only a hundred miles. We could . . ."

Winslow sat down again, once more dejected. "Anouk, we didn't bring your passport."

Marianna said "Shit" and then they talked; argued some more. Anouk was all for trying the border anyway.

"If these guys are working for the government," Winslow demanded, "do you think we've got a chance of getting through?"

Then Anouk said she'd crossed borders before, without passports. "There are always young guards. One can reason with them, you know, smile a little."

Marianna laughed. She could just imagine turning Anouk loose on some young border guard and letting her "smile a little." The kid wouldn't stand a chance. Then she jumped up. "Hey," she said, "we could phone Delane. He could get Anouk's passport. He could meet us somewhere."

Now even Winslow brightened. Reinforcements! Paul Delane. Anouk's passport and a run for the border and to hell out of France until the damned elections were over. Italy, where they'd be safe, where Anouk could consider calmly the sale of the house, where Jean-Pierre and Émile could not easily get at them.

"I'll phone Delane," he said.

Nafredi woke. It was nine in the morning. He pushed back the window separating the passenger compartment from the chauffeur.

"Where are we?" he asked.

"That town we just passed through was Barcelonette," the driver said.

"Good," Nafredi said, never having heard of it. "Pass me some of that chicken and a clean glass."

He sat back and nibbled at his breakfast, watching Heidi sleep. She snores! he realized with a start. My God, how fortunate I realized it before making a more permanent arrangement.

He did not realize, of course, that he was now ahead of Winslow. And the heiress, Anne Fayol. The Bentley raced on northward as Nafredi listened, in irritation, to the sounds that emerged from Heidi's slightly parted cupid's-bow lips. Quel dommage, Nafredi told himself, that those young lips which have given me so much pleasure, could produce such a vulgar noise.

Anouk wanted to drive. "It is my car, tu sais."

"Oh, shit," Winslow said. He tossed her the keys. Then he

turned to Marianna. "You sit up front. Maybe I can get some sleep in back." He folded his long legs into the back seat of the little car. But he had no intention of sleeping. The top was still down and he would be watching the sky.

The proprietor of the inn stood on the front doorstep and watched them pull away.

Formidable, he thought. What a wonderful thing to travel about the country in such a splendid automobile seeking out film locations and sleeping with such attractive young women. Only, he wondered, why had the tall young man been in such a rush? Had he himself had such an opportunity, he would surely have invested more time in the project. Well, he concluded, what did one expect of Americans? What did they know of the subtleties. The scrawny chicken reappeared in the courtyard and began to scratch up the dust. The innkeeper sighed and went inside where he came face to face with the serving girl.

"Qu'est-ce que tu fais, mademoiselle?" he demanded. The girl, terrified, scurried away.

"Alors," she thought, "so I won't tell him about the gun the tall one spoke of. Why should I, the way he snarls at me?" She went into the ambitious barroom and began to clear the table.

The helicopter came down at Briançon. Jean-Pierre was irritated. The pilot, Coco, saw to the refueling while Jean-Pierre went to the telephone. Émile stayed in the cargo space. It was too painful to get out. If he had to piss, that would be one thing. Otherwise, there was no reason to move. Not until he had found his prey. The helicopter had not yet been completely fueled when Jean-Pierre came back, hurrying across the tarmac.

"Allez vite," he ordered.

The mechanics finished their work and put their thumbs up. Coco hit the ignition and they lifted off.

"Où?" he asked.

"Highway 202," Jean-Pierre told him. "That blue Bentley we passed. It's the competition."

Coco swung the little helicopter to the right and then right again. The Bentley must be south of them, he reckoned. He wondered why they were now chasing a Bentley instead of the little Lancia. Behind them Émile slumbered, dreams of Anouk's ripe body dancing in his head.

The terrain began to change. With Anouk at the wheel Winslow had more of an opportunity to look around. The road climbed before them. The blazing ball of the sun had paled to a thin, heatless disc. Off to the east, above the mountains they could not yet see, a gray film descended, not so much cloud as mist. In the valleys daylight became gloom, and men working in the fields put up their collars against the chill. Winslow pulled a sweater and an anorak out of his bag. Marianna smiled at him, but her face was red and looked cold.

Winslow shivered. But he took more comfort from this bleak lunar landscape they were entering than from the soft, damp orchid softness of that floral jungle around Grasse. They had reached a temperate climate; they were out of the tropics. Behind them were the yachts of Cannes, the farm of Gaspar, the roses of May. Ahead, far to the north, would be Paul Delane. Delane and the passport and safety.

The sun dimmed, the temperature dropped, and the road climbed into the foothills of the Alps. Off to the east, unseen, rose the needles of Chamonix. Mont Blanc, also unseen, loomed gigantically to their right. Beyond, the Matterhorn, Val d'Isère, and the snows. In the south of France, it was full summer. Here, in the month of May, it was still winter.

Anouk drove on, handling the Lancia beautifully. But soon the road became wet, and a light rain—more fog than rain, really— began to dampen the windshield and the concrete of route 202. And still the road climbed.

Ahead of them, Nafredi's Bentley slowed. Heidi was awake.
"Hey," she said, "I were asleep."
"Yes," Nafredi said. He was more intent on the road ahead, a road that was fast dissolving into mist and rain. The chauffeur

had looked back, checking with his employer, and Nafredi had made a casual gesture, "Push on, push on."

Now, with the visibility closing in, Nafredi was not so sure. A truck roared by, passing them on the left. That was comforting, Nafredi thought, those fellows know these roads. He opened the glass and tapped the driver.

"Faster," he said, "we can go faster."

The chauffeur nodded and pushed his right foot down against the accelerator. Nafredi slid the glass shut. He looked around. Heidi sat in the opposite corner, her legs pulled up under her, looking vulnerable, looking hungry. Nafredi smiled at her. The little German girl smiled back. Then Nafredi, who found long drives boring and had lost all patience with the multilingual baby talk of this sexy but retarded child, decided to divert himself. He reached into one of the smaller travel bags and fetched out a tin of white powder and a packet of straws.

"Here," he ordered, "take a sniff of this. I wish to be distracted."

Heidi licked her lips and pulled the sweater off over her blond head. The chauffeur made a conscious effort to keep his eyes on the road and in the cab of a tractor-trailer truck that rushed past, the driver goggled and wondered if he had seen what he had seen.

The helicopter swung back into the stiff wind from the east, searching for the blue Bentley. Jean-Pierre looked around in irritation.

"You don't look with your prick," he told Émile. "Sit up and use your eyes."

The Corsican propped himself up and halfheartedly stared through the port. He wasn't interested in any damned Bentley. He was interested in a Lancia.

Coco put his hand on Jean-Pierre's arm. "This visibility," he said, "it gets much worse, I have to put down."

"Merde," Jean-Pierre said. "You put down when I tell you to put down."

Damn all Corsicans, Jean-Pierre thought. They give you an assignment and then they give you shoddy tools to accomplish it.

It was getting dark. It was now afternoon, the sun had long gone, and they were over the mountains. The little copter bounced up and down in the wind and the drafts. Then the radio crackled. Jean-Pierre spoke into the mouthpiece. It was Paris.

"Your American," Paris told him, "made contact with friends here. A rendezvous is planned. They're to meet at Bourg Saint-Maurice. Repeat, Bourg Saint-Maurice. Tonight. Did you get that?"

"Oui," Jean-Pierre said. His spirits lifted. He signed off and turned to Coco. The pilot looked expectant.

"Can I put her down?" he asked.

Jean-Pierre shook his head.

"No," he said, "I have a new course for you," and he pushed his finger at the map. Coco nodded.

"Okay," he said, "but we'll be flying into the storm."

"I know," Jean-Pierre said. He turned to Émile. "You can forget about that Bentley now."

The injured man grinned. "Bon," he said. But what he was thinking was, "I didn't give a shit for the Bentley. I was looking for something else."

The helicopter flew north into the storm.

Marianna reached forward and tapped Winslow on the shoulder.

"Can't we put up the top now? It's cold as hell back here."

Winslow glanced at the lowering sky. He knew what she meant. While Anouk drove he'd huddled in the back seat in the wind. By now he doubted he could see the helicopter even if it flew right over them.

"Okay," he said. He slowed the car and pulled off the road. They were in the hills now, gray water rushing alongside the road headed for some distant valley and the sea. The foliage was gone, the trees were conifers, Winslow could see his breath when he exhaled. He and Anouk struggled with the top. When it was fastened he pulled back onto the road.

Knowing that Delane was coming south to convoy them to safety, that they would no longer be alone, that they would have a guide through the slough of despond, cheered him. He threw the little car into gear and sped north through the gray afternoon. How clever of Delane to have chosen such an out-of-the-way meeting place. The gateway to Val d'Isère and to the pass over the Alps into Italy. A town so obscure even Frenchmen got its name wrong. Winslow turned to grin at his passengers and then, to himself, he said:

"Bourg Saint-Maurice, here we come."

They drove north.

By three o'clock it was raining heavily. The windshield wipers clicked efficiently back and forth, back and forth, and Marianna, taking her turn at the wheel, found no difficulty staying on the road. Winslow was in the back seat, studying the map. They were only fifty kilometers south of Bourg now, high on the western flanks of the alps of the Haute Savoie. Even with the rain they would be there easily before dark. And Delane would arrive on the train from Paris sometime that night. Then Marianna braked! The rain, slashing against the windshield, had turned to sleet. Pellets of ice, driven by the wind, lashed at the car, bounced up from the mountain road, and in a matter of seconds had turned the hillsides white.

"Maybe I'll drive for a while," Winslow said. Marianna pulled over and they all changed seats. Winslow started up again. The wind was stronger now, coming down off the high mountains. It was much colder. They drove through intermittent rainsqualls and sleet, and all the time the wind whipped at the canvas roof of the little car.

And behind the wind was the snow.

STORM

The great storm swept across western Europe as sulky winter reluctantly gave way to spring. Damp gloom and heavy rain in Paris cleared the streets of young toughs of both persuasions who had turned this last week before the election into a series of nasty, murderous little brawls. The Cabinet, meeting perhaps for the last time under this regime, bickered nervously. Any little thing now—some petty scandal, an innocent gaffe—could tilt the vote. Ministers briefed the Premier and were questioned in turn. One minister, whose responsibilities included foreign commerce and the export trade, studiously avoided mention of the bizarre possibility that a celebrated Paris fashion establishment might pass into the hands of foreign speculators and create a rash of damaging headlines on the very eve of the vote. His Premier had a volcanic temper and the minister prudently decided against bringing up this annoying business of the House of Fayol. Besides, he consoled himself, he had taken steps to ensure the sale would never occur.

Three hundred miles to the south, in the Alps, the storm had a character of its own. Heavy snow fell on the peaks and in the high valleys; and avalanches of sodden, unseasonally moist snow hurtled down the flanks of the great hills to bury secondary roads and sweep away signposts and telephone poles.

Zader Nafredi's blue Bentley was already in trouble. The driver was worried. This late in the year he had no snow tires in the trunk, the big car had already skidded badly on several of the curves, and he didn't like the way the badly cambered road skewed off toward nasty little ditches and sudden gorges. The visibility was bad and getting worse, it was colder now, and the wind was up. Snow had begun to drift across the road at the exposed places.

"I'd like to find a side road and pull off, sir," the chauffeur told his employer.

"Nonsense," Nafredi blustered. "This is an urgent matter. We simply must press on."

"There may be danger, sir."

"Oh, well then," Nafredi said reasonably, "in that case I suggest we find a side road and pull off."

He climbed back into the seat next to the little German girl.

"Ja?" she said.

Nafredi laughed. "The chauffeur is nervous about the road," he said. "I've given the fellow permission to find shelter."

Heidi smiled. Perhaps they could stay at a farmhouse overnight. It would be a splendid adventure.

Nafredi put his arm around the girl's bare shoulder.

"Yes," he said, conjuring up pleasant visions of old-fashioned double beds, down comforters, and Heidi's blond pigtails while the storm blew outside snugly fastened double windows. How *gemütlich* it would be.

The little yellow helicopter, laboring through the storm, set down at Briançon to deice and then, just before dusk, landed in a field outside Bourg Saint-Maurice. Jean-Pierre and Coco helped Émile from the craft. Wet, cold, and sullen, they took rooms in the station hotel to wait for the arrival of the evening train from Paris. Coco stripped down the machine gun and oiled the moving parts while Jean-Pierre bickered with a long-distance telephone operator of monumental stupidity. Émile changed the dressing on his wound, sat in bed against a couple of plumped-up pillows, and got out his whetstone.

Anouk's little car didn't seem capable of taking them much farther. Twice Winslow and Marianna had to get out into the cold and the blowing snow to push while Anouk rocked the car back and forth, back and forth, alternately gunning and reversing the engine, competently slipping from forward low to reverse gear. They were moving now, but barely. Winslow glanced at the map. There was no chance they could get to Bourg tonight. Route 202 would climb another four hundred meters before it fell off again into the valley. There were six inches of new snow on the ground and it was drifting badly. The car was all right, the Michelin X tires were doing a reasonable job, but it was growing colder, darker, windier. They skirted a small avalanche and then, just as he was becoming *really* worried, the road widened and they were in the single street of an old stone village.

The farmer who took them in was named Viot. He and his family lived in a three-hundred-year-old stone house with their animals stabled on the ground floor and the family living above, so that the body heat rose from the stable to help warm the house through the long winter. Once they got used to the smell, it was pleasant, and Winslow and the girls talked half the night away with the old farmer and his sons while Mme. Viot knitted and cooked and passed around strong country brew. Anouk had been uncharacteristically still, breaking in only once when Viot spoke of his love for this hard land and the satisfaction he got from knowing his sons and their sons would work the plot, and their little flock and the land would remain always in the family.

Anouk nodded. "I knew a man who felt like you," she said. "He had the same feel for the land. His name was Gaspar."

In the morning the snow had stopped. Pride assured, winter had once again relaxed its hold on the high mountains and on those who lived there, and spring was permitted to come. The sun was up and the wind backed away to the south and the world sparkled under a foot of fresh wet snow that had already begun to melt, thawing from the stone houses and the branches of trees. Just a few miles from one another the chasers and the chased had slept, each unaware of precisely where the other was, but destined to meet in the town of Bourg Saint-Maurice. And another player had been dealt in. During the night, on the train from Paris, Paul Delane, couturier and Harvard man, had come to Bourg.

BOURG

Delane was in the dining room of the hotel, munching on croissants and sipping scalding coffee that was half cream when he saw them standing in the doorway.

"Alors," he said, "the prodigals return."

He and Winslow made pleased noises and shook hands. Anouk flirted and Marianna kissed Delane as the waiter brought up more chairs.

"If this is what the fashion business is all about," Winslow said, "it's not my line of work. Not at all."

Delane laughed. "I assure you the couture is rarely so diverting. Months go by without a single designer assassinating another."

It was a wonderful breakfast. Having the Frenchman there, with Anouk's passport ("safe in the room, my dear"), reinforced by Delane with his muscle, his quick wit, his élan, meant the hard, lonely, dangerous part of the job was virtually accomplished. Once, when Anouk and Marianna were in the ladies' room, Delane looked narrowly at Winslow and wrinkled his nose.

"Do you smell something? Something foul?"

Winslow told him about sheltering the night at Viot's house. Delane shook his head. "What an extraordinary time you've had. Sleeping among the flowers one night, in the manure and chicken droppings the next. I hope the bank appreciates what you've done."

262

Winslow sobered. "Yeah, what I've done." He was remembering Gaspar and the other flinty old men of Grasse whose rose gardens were now to become the property of the Delaware Corp., and would if he did his job. The women came back and he drew his chair in closer to the table and lowered his voice. "Okay," he said, "what's the scheme? Do we duck into Italy or what?"

Delane lighted a cigarette and looked around. There was no one eavesdropping.

"I thought it out yesterday, in the train. I called your boss, Henry Rousselot, before I went to bed. He thinks it's the thing to do. As far as the French are concerned, Tony, you're the threat. They don't want you to ply Mademoiselle Fayol with your charms and talk her into selling. Neither does your own embassy, correct?"

Winslow nodded. Anouk made a face. "The audacity of bureaucrats trying to tell me what to do with my inheritance. If I want to sell, I shall!"

Delane smiled. "Precisely. Now what I suggest is this. Tony writes up a simple contract, an agreement to buy the Maison Fayol, and Anouk signs it. Marianna and I can witness. Today's date. In that way we beat the election deadline and if the Left gets in, there's no threat they can nationalize a company that's already been sold.

"Then the three of you slip over the border into Italy until after the voting on Sunday. I'll simply take the train back to Paris with the contract and the papers and put them in a safety deposit box. No one's looking for me. There'll be no problem."

They talked. Winslow had to admit it sounded plausible. Exasperatingly, perversely, Anouk was now all for selling, now that Delane had reminded her both Paris and Washington were opposed. She seemed to have forgotten Gaspar, forgotten her brave little speech to farmer Viot. Well, Winslow told himself, Rousselot sent me here to buy and this seems like the time.

"Okay," he said, "I'll draw up some sort of contract. I hope the damn thing holds up in court."

Delane had arranged rooms and they all went upstairs to bathe and for Winslow to write up the bill of sale. As the women went ahead in the tiny elevator, Winslow asked, "Rousselot have any other messages for me?"

Delane shrugged. "Just to wish you well. And . . . oh, yes. Once you're safely across the border you're to call him. Give him an interim report."

Winslow was in the shower and did not hear the insistent rapping on his door, nor see the knob turned and rattled to no avail. Thirty minutes later he was sitting on the toilet, thinking about the bill of sale he would draw up, and paging listlessly through the local paper, a Grenoble daily. The story was buried on an inside page:

> ### "NOTED RESISTANCE HERO AND RELIGIOUS LEADER FOUND DEAD."

The story said the well-celebrated Canon Masson and a farmer called Gaspar had been found shot to death at the latter's farm. There was no mention of the dead helicopter pilot. The possibility of a double suicide was being investigated. Also, the story said, the police were interested in questioning a man, a foreigner, and two women seen with Canon Masson in Cannes two days earlier.

Suicide! Since when did aging Catholic priests commit suicide with machine guns? And if they knew Masson had been with them in Cannes, they damn well knew who he was, who the girls were. It looked as if the fix were in, Winslow decided. He folded the paper, determined not to let Marianna and Anouk see the story. Then another item on the back page caught his eye:

> ### "FAMED COUTURIER RECOVERING FROM BURNS; SAYS SHE'LL VOTE COMMUNIST."

Maggy Moal, claiming an attempt had been made on her life, an attempt that involved arson aboard her yacht, had announced in Marseilles that she could no longer support a government that permitted such beastliness. Winslow whistled softly. If the old bag were feathering her nest, Sunday's election was going to be damn close. Then, thinking of Maggy, he thought inevitably of Paul Delane. He was grateful to Paul, really grateful, for having hurried south when Winslow cried for help, for offering himself as courier, for having proposed the obvious step of consummating the sale right here and now.

Only there was something Delane had said at breakfast, something that, like Jacques Fayol's "spiritual guidance," did not ring true. He was trying to recall what it was when the telephone rang.

It was Jean-Pierre. He recognized the voice immediately and his shoulders sagged.

"The two young ladies and Monsieur Delane have joined us. You can have them back, undamaged, if you wish."

"Yes?" Winslow said. His voice was choking, strangled, not his own.

"A simple barter, Monsieur Winslow. That little bundle of papers for your friends."

"Yes?" Winslow said again, stupid, dazed.

"Remain in your room. I shall call you within the hour."

There was a click. Winslow, naked, still holding the Grenoble newspaper, sat down on the side of the bed, the phone in his hand. He thought for a moment he would vomit. He put down the paper and replaced the phone. He rubbed his hands together, not knowing what to do. Hopelessly, because he believed Jean-Pierre, he picked up the phone and asked first for the room Marianna and Anouk were sharing, then for Delane. No answer. He realized he was being overly polite to the hotel's switchboard girl, that he was thanking her profusely for her help. His reaction had gone beyond anger, beyond frustration. He was physically sick. He got up and went back into the bathroom and leaned over the bowl. Nothing happened, and after a few moments he dampened a towel and sponged off his face.

Just as it seemed this improbable roller-coaster ride of horror and violence was over, there was this. Nothing that had happened previously had hit him as hard: not the huissier's death; not the red herring of Marrakesh; not the gunfight in Gaspar's rose gardens; not Émile's sadism or the lung-bursting, thorn-ripped flight from Gaspar's charnel house; nor even the death of Canon Masson. All those things had been manageable, sustainable, reduceable to some sort of action, however despairing. This—this was a vacuum of horror, devoid of hope, gelding him into impotence. He sat on the side of the bed, thinking of Marianna, of Paul, of Anouk, and of his inability to do a thing to help them. Except surrender.

He looked at the Vuitton case. There was no question of what he had to do. There was no choice. Only to wait now for the second call and to hope the psychopath Émile was under some sort of control.

Without the "Paris One" papers, the deal was off. No one, and certainly not Delaware, was going to pay eighty-five million dollars for the fashion house alone. Shit, he thought, they can have the fucking file. He pulled on a pair of shorts and began to dress. His fingers trembled.

A few miles away, Zader Nafredi alternately consulted his road map and watched the naked Heidi scamper about the bedroom of an old farmhouse, brushing her hair and chattering about the sun on the fresh snow. There was a sizable town just a short drive away. Nafredi folded the map. They would go into town for breakfast and he would consider his next step in what seemed to have become a hopeless quest. The town he chose was Bourg Saint-Maurice.

While the Iranian dithered and Winslow agonized, Jean-Pierre and the Corsicans, reinforced by a local who knew the ground, had driven to the fellow's farm, a poorly-tended place with a scatter of dun buildings badly in need of paint and carpentry. It was now late morning and under the hot spring sun the snow was melting even more swiftly than it had fallen. The local had a van, and when he pulled into his property Jean-Pierre asked which building was which. The largest, a barn, was empty, the fellow said.

"Bon," said Jean-Pierre, "we put them there."

He and Coco pushed their three prisoners out into the slush. Émile, looking pleased, painfully let himself down from the back of the van. He kept his eyes on Anouk. Delane's hands were tied behind his back but the women were unbound. Jean-Pierre noticed Émile.

"Coco, put them in the barn. Fasten the door and stay there. Émile, you stay with me."

Émile's smile faded.

"I'll watch them," he said. "I'll be happy to watch them."

"Certainly," Jean-Pierre said sarcastically. "I know how happy you would be."

The two women, who knew what kind of men these were, said nothing. Delane, who seemed confused, tried to speak, but Coco shoved him so that he fell to his knees in the snow. With his hands tied, he struggled to get up. Marianna helped him to his feet. She shook her head, urging silence. Coco prodded them into the barn and slammed the big door. Jean-Pierre, Émile, and the farmer went into the house.

"Now," said Jean-Pierre, "where's your phone?"

They went into the kitchen. Émile caught Jean-Pierre's arm as he reached for the telephone.

"Jean-Pierre, you aren't just going to hand them over to him? For the papers?"

"Shut up," Jean-Pierre snapped.

"No, listen, mon vieux. The American comes out here with the papers, what chance does he have? We grab the papers, we shoot him, we have some fun with the girls, and we're in Paris tonight. Let the Frenchman live, if it amuses you," he concluded, tossing Delane's life to Jean-Pierre as a bone to a dog.

"Is there to be killing?" the local asked. "No one mentioned killing. Simply the temporary utilization of the farm."

Jean-Pierre stared at the man, who shuffled his feet nervously and was quiet.

* * *

In the barn, Anouk took hold of Marianna's hand.

"Look, this time, I don't know. There'll be no tricks this time. That one with the knife, the one I bit . . ."

Marianna nodded. She talked, calmly, comfortingly, not so much to make sense but simply to soothe the other girl.

"Don't worry. Tony will think of something. Paul is here. You think they're going to do anything serious with so many witnesses? Of course not." She looked at Delane. "Isn't that right, Paul?"

Delane nodded. He hadn't been listening. Something had gone terribly wrong.

"The way he stared at me in the van," Anouk said. "I know what he was thinking. I hurt him, I humiliated him, and now . . ." She sobbed and Marianna put an arm around her, holding Anouk's slim young body and feeling the sobs that racked her.

Delane didn't even try to free his bound hands. He felt betrayed, helpless.

Anthony Winslow shoved the Smith & Wesson into his belt and pulled on the down jacket. He wished he had sturdier shoes. But he had stopped regretting everything else. The second telephone call from Jean-Pierre had purged him. He knew now where he had to go. He knew what he had to do. He picked up the Vuitton case, glanced around the room, and went out. He went down the stairs two at a time and crossed the lobby. The desk clerk said something and Winslow went on without answering, without slowing. His long legs carried him through the front door and out onto the sidewalk. The snow had already melted in the town and the midday sun momentarily blinded him, bouncing off the wet streets and the windshields of parked cars. Winslow held up a hand to shade his eyes. He had a plan, a plan of action, but he hadn't worked out the details. He needed a car. The little Lancia was there. He felt in his pockets. Anouk must have the keys. There had to be a taxi in this fucking town. He looked up and down the main street. Cursing, he started back toward the hotel. He would have them call a cab. He . . .

"Winslow," a man called, "Winslow, isn't that you?"

He wheeled toward the curb. An impressively large navy Bentley stood there, motor running, uniformed chauffeur at the wheel, and a blond child with pigtails and a dark, older man who looked vaguely familiar were smiling up at him.

There was nothing to do now but wait, Jean-Pierre told himself. How would he place the men, what precautions must he take? The assumption was that Winslow would come alone, come unarmed, and peacefully hand over the papers and go his way with the hostages: a good bargain made, a good bargain kept. That, Jean-Pierre reminded himself, was the assumption. All through this filthy operation assumptions had turned out false. He intended to be ready for the unexpected. The local man, the one who owned the farm, sat on one of the kitchen chairs, eating cheese and wiping his mouth on his sleeve. Émile paced up and down the room, stiffly, favoring the wound. He was sullen. He had again made his pitch to Jean-Pierre; had again been silenced. Rudely. Now he paced the worn linoleum of the farmer's kitchen and wondered whether he could eventually convince Jean-Pierre of the rightness of his cause. Or whether he would have to kill him. For Émile, still in pain, still unable to copulate, could feel the knives in various pockets and sheaths, and fully intended to have his revenge on Anouk Fayol. He hardly wasted thought on the other girl, the one he had seen through the window nearly a week before in Paris, in the rue de Boulainvilliers.

Winslow sat between Nafredi and Heidi. He leaned forward and rapped on the glass. The driver turned.

"Go straight out this street. Then turn left at the highway."

"Winslow," Nafredi said cordially, "I won't even ask where we are going. I won't ask. My car is at your disposal. My man. Myself, even." He glanced sideways at the girl who was curled up on the seat, showing a good bit of leg and smiling vapidly at the American. "*Whatever* I have is at your disposal. But we must talk. Talk seriously. My superiors in Teheran . . ."

"Right here," Winslow shouted at the chauffeur. "Make the turn."

The big car paused and then shot ahead onto the highway. Winslow leaned back.

"I'm sorry," he said. "I wasn't listening."

"It's nothing," Nafredi assured him. "But for weeks now I've been assuring Teheran I had the purchase of the Maison Fayol locked up. And had poor Jacques not died, who knows? But he did die. And you came to Paris. And suddenly I am in an exceedingly precarious situation. You see, when His Imperial Majesty, my Shah, determines that he wants something, there is no other response except to say yes. And to procure it. A woman, a jewel, a squadron of your excellent jet fighters . . . whatever it is, there is no saying 'no' to the Shah. Now, in this instance, I . . ."

His voice droned on. Winslow was no longer listening. He was trying to imagine what the layout would be at the farm, where Marianna and Anouk would be, whether Paul Delane would be of any help, what weapons Jean-Pierre had, how badly Émile had been hurt, what others there were, whether he could use Nafredi to create a diversion. He was thinking now, thinking clearly, no longer numbed or confused or sick. The Smith & Wesson felt good against his belly. They sped along the highway, past the fields of melting snow. To the east the sun shone off the white flanks of the great hills.

"Four kilomètres," he told the chauffeur. "Four kilomètres and then we turn right. A dirt road."

". . . and so you see," Nafredi was concluding, "why I absolutely must be permitted to close the sale. I can tell you, dear Winslow, your commission can be whatever you wish, if you help me convince the girl to sell. A million? *Two* million. It can be arranged. It *will* be arranged." He paused. "Of course, you understand, I am not talking in rials or francs. I speak of dollars."

Winslow ignored him. The chauffeur turned.

"Four kilomètres, monsieur."

There was a break in the rail fence that paralleled the road.

That must be it! The car slowed and Winslow nodded urgently. The driver swung the car between the posts and it began to bump along what felt like a dirt surface under the wet snow. There were several sets of tire tracks stretching ahead of them, brown against the white. Winslow knocked on the window and the driver slowed to a halt. Winslow jumped out, knelt down to examine the tracks. Good, he thought, the same marks, coming and going. That might cut the odds a bit. He got back in and the Bentley rolled forward. A couple of hundred yards ahead Winslow could see a small group of buildings. It looked like a farm.

Winslow sat forward in the seat, trying to catch movement. From the corner of the car came the young girl's voice.

"Zader, schatzi, he are cinema leader also?"

"No, my dear. He is not a 'cinema leader.' But he is even *more* important. He is a banker. And it is the banks that make movies these days."

Heidi clapped her pudgy little hands together.

"Sie gut," she said, "me will fuck he also."

The farm was just ahead now. Winslow tapped the window and motioned the driver to slow. He slipped the revolver out of his belt. He thought he saw someone moving near one of the buildings, the one that resembled a barn. He wondered if it was Jean-Pierre. He was worried about Jean-Pierre and the machine gun.

It was not Jean-Pierre. It was Émile. Jean-Pierre lay unconscious on the worn linoleum of the farmhouse kitchen. The farmer, the local who was supplying the amenities but who drew the line at killing, knelt over his body, trying to revive him. He did not understand at all what was happening, why the man who limped had hit the one with the gun. "Wake up, wake up," he said. But he said it softly, not wanting the other one to hear, and not quite sure he wanted this one awake either.

Émile nodded at Coco.

"Open it up," he said.

Coco pulled the bolt on the barn door. "Where is Jean-Pierre?" he asked.

Émile laughed. "He is resting. He has named me chef."

They went into the barn.

Anouk heard the bolt and then she saw them come in. She reached out to touch Marianna. They both drew back. Delane sat on the ground, in the straw and the filth, his back against the wall, his hands behind him. He did not react. Émile meant nothing to him. Only his bound hands and the realization these people did not understand why he was in Bourg, that something had gone wrong, terribly wrong.

"Well," Émile said, "so it is Grasse all over again, eh? Only this time not quite the same, non?"

Coco stood a few paces behind him. Émile turned and barked out an order.

"Watch for the American," he said. "Let me know if you see anything. I don't want to be interrupted."

Coco returned to the door and stood just inside, peering out into the bright sunshine. Somewhere, not far away, a church steeple chimed the hour. It was eleven o'clock in the morning. Anouk counted the chimes. She wondered if she would hear them when they marked twelve.

Émile had one of his knives out, the long, thin one. He waved it at Anouk.

"You," he barked, "take this. Tie her against this post." He tossed a length of rope to Anouk, who dropped it and then quickly retrieved it. She looked at Marianna, miserable, her hands trembling. Marianna nodded and tried to smile.

"It's all right, Anouk, just do whatever he tells you." The French girl awkwardly wrapped the rope around Marianna and made some sort of knot. Good, Marianna thought, she's left it slack. She stood against the post, trying to make the ropes seem tight. But Émile couldn't care less; he wasn't looking at the ropes, or at her. His eyes were on Anouk.

"Now," he said, "come over here."

Anouk moved toward him, shuffling her feet, moving as slowly as she could.

"Dépêches-toi," Émile said. "I haven't all day. Your American friend is en route."

Marianna inhaled. Surely Tony would not come alone. He'd have the police, someone.

Now Anouk was standing just in front of the Corsican, facing him. Tears coursed down her lovely face.

Émile spoke to Coco without taking his eyes from Anouk. "Anyone?" he asked.

"Pas encore."

"Good. Keep watching, Coco. I'll save the other one for you. But this one, this one is reserved for me." He reached out and grabbed Anouk's shirt and pulled her toward him. "Now," he said, "kneel down. Just as you did that other time, just as you did at Grasse." He jerked her forward and down and Anouk fell to her knees. She was sobbing. Émile grabbed her hair and jerked her head back.

"Oh, please don't cry yet, chérie. I haven't begun yet. You'll have much reason to cry in a moment. I promise you."

His knife hand whipped past her face. As if miraculously, for he had not seemed to touch her, a thin red line appeared across her cheek, and then, very slowly, drops of blood began to form along the line and to run down toward her chin. Anouk's hand went up to touch her face. She did not yet realize she had been cut. Then she saw the blood on her fingers and she screamed. Delane shouted something in French and Marianna closed her eyes and began to pray.

Émile smiled.

"Now," he said, very quietly, "we have begun to communicate. I bled, now you bleed. It's fair, isn't it? You hurt me, I hurt you?"

Anouk was blubbering now, half crying, half begging. Émile loosed his grip on her long hair and stepped back a pace.

"Such a beautiful face. Those lips. Later we do something

about those lips. Considering what happened in Grasse, it would be appropriate."

The knife hand whipped out again, and blood spouted from Anouk's other cheek. Again the blood ran down her chin and began to drip onto her pink shirt.

Émile wiped his hands, one after another, on his thighs. His palms were sweating. He was very excited. He had begun to experience erection and it hurt. He would have to be careful. He didn't want all that pain again. Feeling his own wound and frustrated by what Anouk had done to him, unmanning him, if only temporarily, made him even more furious with the girl. Enough of this child's play, he told himself. Get her stripped and begin to work on the body. The face? The face was nothing, an amusement. It was the body that would give satisfaction, that would pay the debt.

"Take off your clothes," he said, trying to keep his voice calm. He debated with himself whether to start with the nipples or down below. The girl, quiet now, numb perhaps, started to unbutton her shirt. Émile stared.

"Écoutes, Émile, c'est l'Américain."

The Corsican turned away and limped to the barn door. Coco made room for him.

"That car," Coco said. "Three or four people, I can't quite see."

"Merde," Émile said. He'd been afraid of this. Jean-Pierre had been *so* sure the American would come alone, with the papers. He turned back. Anouk, shocked and in pain, was still fumbling with her buttons. Marianna sagged against the ropes. Delane, cursing to himself, slumped helplessly in the filth.

Émile turned to look out across the farmyard. There were three people standing at the car—no, four. One of them a woman. Then one man, the tallest, detached himself from the group and started to walk toward the barn. He had a gun in his hand.

Émile cursed himself for a cretin for not having taken Jean-Pierre's machine gun. He disliked guns, was no good at them, but at this range even he would have been able to do damage. His mind was working now. Behind him he heard Anouk sob. She had her shirt off and sat squatting on her heels, crying. Her face was a mask of blood, and it was running down onto her upper body and breasts. Despite Winslow, despite his irritation at not having the gun, Émile focused on the girl. Her blood had excited him, the way it began to trickle slowly down between her breasts. He knew now how he would do it, how he would do it and what he would do. Take care of the American, somehow, get those fucking precious papers, and get out of here with the girl. He'd hole up somewhere until he was healed. And then, when he was all right again, once again able to copulate, he would cut her again—lots of little cuts, all over—and take her while her blood lubricated their bodies, while she screamed, while she bled away and died. Only, he told himself, he would make sure they were very tiny cuts. He did not want the girl to die that quickly.

"Émile," Coco whispered. "Regardes!"

Winslow was a dozen meters from the barn door, moving slowly, the gun in his right hand, his knees slightly bent. Émile threw open the door.

"Okay," he shouted. "Just put up the cannon. Your girls are inside. And your pal. My partner has a gun on them. Stand right there and we'll talk."

Winslow nodded.

"Talk," he said coldly.

"Okay, don't be in such a rush. Those papers you have, the ones the old priest gave you, hand them over and you can have the American girl and the monsieur."

"What about the other girl?"

Émile grinned, showing his bad teeth. "Non, she decided to stick with me. She and I, we have the same ideas."

"I don't believe that," Winslow said. He tried to gauge whether he could edge closer to Émile, whether he could risk a shot from here.

"I don't give a shit what you believe," Émile shouted. Flecks of foam formed in the corners of his mouth. "You want the

American girl cut up, or your want her in one piece? Get the papers."

Winslow could see Coco in the doorway. He could shoot Émile easily at this range. There was no way he could hit them both.

"Okay," he said. He turned and waved an arm at Nafredi. "Send the driver with my case," he said. Nafredi nodded and the chauffeur picked up the Vuitton bag and slogged toward the barn.

Émile waited. When Winslow had the case, he waved the chauffeur back.

"Très bien," he said. "Now toss it here."

Winslow shook his head. "Not until I see the girl and Delane."

"Damn you," Émile said. "You don't trust a man. All right. Coco, open the door wide."

Winslow peered into the gloom of the barn. He could see Marianna but not Delane.

"Marianna?" he called.

"All right," she said. "Paul too. But he's hurt Anouk."

Anger surged through Winslow. He fought it down. At least the French girl was alive. But of course this sadistic bastard would have seen to that. It would have eliminated his fun to have killed the girl.

"Well?" Émile asked.

"D'accord," Winslow said. He tossed the case underhanded. It landed in the slop at Émile's feet, splashing his trousers with slush.

"Merci bien," the Corsican said politely. He half turned, "Coco, écoutes, mon vieux, get the French girl on her feet and walk all three of them out here when I tell you. Comprends?"

"Oui, Émile."

As ordered, Winslow had backed up a dozen paces. He held the revolver low, not wanting to trigger a reaction by lifting the muzzle. Now Coco came out of the barn, pushing Anouk before him. Winslow saw her face and took a step forward, the gun seeming to lift itself. Émile's voice stopped him.

"Just a little blood, mon ami. Just behave like a gentleman and no one else will be hurt. See, she walks perfectly well. Just a scratch, I assure you."

It was true, Anouk walked freely. She was bare from the waist up. There was a little blood on her jeans but she was moving all right, if a bit unsteadily. Marianna and Delane looked fine, except that the Frenchman's arms were tied behind his back. Coco moved all three captives off to the left, prodding Delane, with Émile walking backward, knife in hand, watching Winslow's eyes. Now Winslow saw the helicopter for the first time. It was parked just behind the barn. He wondered where Jean-Pierre was. He had a feeling the machine gun was trained on his back. It was not a comfortable sensation.

The Corsicans were nearly at the copter now. Winslow circled the barn, not moving toward them, but keeping them in view. He was still trying to calculate where Jean-Pierre might be, with the gun.

"That's far enough, American," Émile shouted. "You can watch us fly away in our little bird with your wonderful valise."

Coco jumped in and did things to the controls and the ignition whined and the main rotor caught and began to turn, slowly.

"Thirty seconds," he shouted, "to warm up." Émile nodded, knife low and moving ominously this way and that in the direction of the prisoners. He motioned Anouk toward the craft, and when, dazed, she did not react, he grabbed her long hair and pulled her toward the cabin door. Coco gunned the engine and the rotor turned faster. The helicopter began to tremble.

Winslow knew he could not stall much longer. There'd be a chance for that one lucky shot, now or just as they lifted off. The rotor was turning full now and it sent up a gust of snow. Winslow had to turn half away to clear his eyes. The fingers of his right hand tightened on the revolver. Jesus, he thought. Suppose I hit Anouk. He steadied his feet in the slush and began slowly to bring up the gun.

It was then that Paul Delane yelled. It was not so much a word as a roar. One moment he was standing there, slumped, eyes dulled in impotent confusion; the next, hands still tied behind him, he was all raging energy. Émile, shoving Anouk bodily into the helicopter, wheeled to see Delane bearing down on him, head low, knees churning, a rugby forward in full charge. The Corsican let the girl collapse into the snow and he swung his knife hand to meet the oncoming Delane. Winslow lifted the revolver, but before he could fire, Delane had crashed into Émile and the two men fell, skidding, in the snow. Émile was first to his feet. Coco, his frightened face staring through the Plexiglas, began to lift the copter. Émile scrambled to get aboard as Delane tried awkwardly to get up. Winslow swung the gun toward the helicopter.

The *rrrripppp* of the machine gun, from somewhere just behind him, deafened Winslow. He spun, dropping to one knee. He could hear the copter's motor roar as the craft struggled to rise, and then he saw Jean-Pierre, feet apart, the gun at his shoulder, pointing upward. The gun chattered again and Winslow shot, all in the same instant. Jean-Pierre dropped the gun and sat down slowly in the snow. The helicopter was making a different sound now, as, wounded, the little yellow craft reached for the sky; and then, like some grotesque moth, it twisted, turned, twisted again, and began to fall.

Paul Delane was finally on his feet. He looked up; saw the copter stagger and start to fall. He was still standing there when the rotor blade caught him and the copter crashed to earth a few yards from where he fell.

PARIS ONE

"Alors, mon vieux, we have come a long way from Harvard, have we not?"

Winslow told Delane not to talk. "We'll get a doctor. There must be a phone. Just lie still and . . ."

"No, my dear," Delane said. "A physician would be decidedly redundant at this point."

Winslow knew he was right. The rotor blade had caught him a glancing blow, not cutting so much as clubbing him down. From the angle at which he lay, Delane's back seemed to be broken. Marianna knelt in the snow beside him.

Beyond them the helicopter was a jumble of twisted metal. Jean-Pierre's bullets had killed Coco. Émile, his knife still in his right hand, was alive, but only academically—a lance of splintered steel through his chest, a foam of blood coming from his mouth. Jean-Pierre was dead, in a sitting position, Winslow's single shot through his throat. Anouk was on her feet, dazed, still not functioning.

Marianna smoothed Delane's hair and wiped his face with a handkerchief.

"Would it feel better if we tried to turn you and cut the ropes?"

"There is no pain," Paul said. "Numb. Quite numb. Please do not move me. It is quite all right."

Winslow looked around. "Marianna," he said, "Anouk can use help."

279

When she had gone, Winslow saw Nafredi and the girl edging toward Delane.

"Get back," he shouted, bitter over what had happened and the emptiness of it, and not wanting these outsiders to listen to what he was going to ask and what he expected Delane would answer.

"Do you mind talking or should I shut up?" Winslow asked.

Delane laughed, briefly, and then the laugh became a cough.

"I think, Antoine, we should talk. And quickly."

"Okay," Winslow said, sitting down in the slush so he'd be closer and Delane would not have to exert himself to be heard.

"These two weren't working with you, I take it," Winslow said.

"Animals like that? Really, one retains some taste."

"Okay, then, why did you do it?"

"Tony," Delane said, "you remember, at Harvard, that crucial edge we were always striving for, that advantage . . ."

"Leverage."

Delane nodded. "Leverage. A splendid word I have never been able to master. Or to achieve. Until now." He paused as a shadow of pain worked its way across his eyes and then cleared. "The day you had your interview with the minister. It happened then. Until that time I was on your side, not very efficiently if truth be told, but cheerfully, and with all my heart. And then, well, an offer was made, an offer of leverage, of advantage. Something I had wanted all my life."

Winslow waited. Delane looked up.

"Do you think, my dear, you might light one of those foul little cigars of yours and permit me to enjoy a puff or two?" Winslow pulled out a cigar, lighted it, and stuck it in Delane's mouth. The Frenchman resumed.

"You may not remember him," Paul said, "but there was a man at Harvard in our year. His name was Caster. That same day you were at the ministry, Caster called. We met. He represented important financial interests. They were seeking to purchase the Maison Fayol. If I helped them, if I were instrumental in getting hold of some papers, if I could convince the unpredictable though undeniably tasty Mademoiselle Fayol to sell, they would install me as designer. I would wear the mantle of the great Fayol."

"But why, Paul? You had your own house. You were doing well."

Delane smiled. "If you could remove this cigar, please? Yes, I had a nice little business. But compared to Fayol, the last of the 'grands couturiers,' ah, my dear, *nothing*. To become the head of the Maison Fayol is a thing for which a fashion designer would do many things. He would even betray a friend."

"And Caster? Who was he working for? Nafredi?"

"Mais non, Tony. Even villains such as Caster and I draw the line at Persians."

"Then who?"

"Your own client, the Delaware Corp."

Winslow recoiled, stunned.

"The Delaware Corp.? Bribe *you* when I was already working for them?"

Delane's eyes rolled expressively.

"But this is the really delicious part," he said. "They no longer trusted you. Nor your splendid employer, Monsieur Rousselot. Rousselot had learned of their plans for the flower gardens of Grasse. In New York he had been making sounds of disapproval. They believed he might have communicated these reservations to you. They knew you were on the trail of Fayol's leases, that you were . . . close . . . to Anouk. That in the end you would influence her decision. That decision, Delaware Corp. feared, would not be in their favor. Delaware was no longer sure of you, Tony. It was then they decided to double their chances by enrolling me in the plot. I was to do no harm, only to watch over you and to do their bidding. Only"—he paused—"neither Delaware nor I had anticipated the ruthlessness of these animals with their little helicopter.

"In the end," Delane said, "I forgot about wanting to be Jacques Fayol and reverted to Paul Delane."

Winslow nodded and reached out his hand to Delane's shoulder, touching it gently. "Were Émile and Jean-Pierre working for the French government?"

"Tony, with governments and great corporations, *nothing* is impossible. May I have a final puff, please?"

Winslow put the cigar to his lips. Delane inhaled. Then he asked, "How did you guess, Tony, about me?"

Winslow looked down at his old friend. "After breakfast. You said Henry Rousselot wanted an interim report. Henry never asked for an interim report in his life."

Delane smiled.

"My dear," he said, "I never really was very good at leverage, was I?"

He died minutes later.

Marianna had Anouk functioning again. The man who owned the farm was still in a state of shock. Nafredi and the girl, frightened off by Winslow, huddled by the car. Winslow went into the farmhouse and tore out the phone wire. Then he reached into the helicopter, a wrecked toy, and pulled the old Vuitton case from between Émile's legs. The Corsican was barely breathing a bloody froth. Winslow still had the Smith & Wesson in his belt, and now, as he passed Jean-Pierre's body, he picked up the machine gun and cradled it in his arm. He glanced toward Nafredi. The Iranian recoiled as if fearful he himself might be the next victim.

Well, Winslow told himself, trying to think ahead, we're not hanging around here until the cops show or any more Corsicans arrive. He looked again at Anouk. Marianna had rinsed her face. The French girl seemed okay. When he looked at Marianna she nodded and tried to smile. Winslow smiled back. This was *quite* a woman. He examined the machine gun, muddy and wet with slush. Probably it wouldn't work now anyway, but he didn't want to leave it when he made his move. He kicked out the magazine and worked the bolt until the chamber was empty. He threw the cartridges halfway across the yard.

Nafredi had recovered. He came toward Winslow.

"My God," the Iranian said, "they are all dead?"

Winslow nodded. As far as Émile was concerned, he was exercising poetic license. But he didn't think anyone would care.

"Who were they?"

Winslow knew what he was going to do to Nafredi so he turned cold, his eyes flat and menacing.

"I thought they belonged to you."

Nafredi's reaction seemed honest enough.

"Mine? Mine? Thugs like that?"

He was outraged.

Winslow held up the case.

"Well, you wanted this thing. So did they. I figured it might be a squeeze play."

"I assure you, Winslow, I . . ."

Tony cut him off.

'Okay. Now, get your chauffeur over here. With the keys."

"The keys? To my car?"

Winslow put his hand on the handle of the Smith & Wesson in his belt.

Nafredi turned and called to the chauffeur.

"The girl too," Winslow ordered.

The chauffeur, Heidi, and Nafredi stood in front of him. He had the manic notion that if he called them to attention they would salute. Thank you, Mr. Smith, he thought. Thank you, Mr. Wesson.

"You," he shouted. The farmer smiled and trotted across the farmyard, splashing up the slush.

"Oui, monsieur?"

Winslow looked at his watch.

"It is now nearly noon," he said. "In six hours at eighteen hours this evening, you will notify the local authorities there has been a plane crash. Not until then. Do you understand?"

"Oui, monsieur." Then he paused. "But the other man . . . ?" He gestured toward Jean-Pierre.

Winslow looked at the body.

"He was thrown free. Somehow his gun went off. Who knows? In an accident of this magnitude, anything can happen. Tu comprends?"

The farmer again said yes.

"I pulled out your telephone wires and I'm going to disable your van. This is understood?"

"Oui, monsieur."

"Ah, Winslow," Nafredi said, "you are indeed a man of action. A decisive fellow. I so admire a man who . . ."

"Shut up, Nafredi. I'm taking your car. And the driver as well." He looked at the chauffeur. "You agree?"

The driver nodded his head vigorously. Anything to get out of this charnel pit.

"My car? But how shall I . . . ? How shall Fräulein . . . ?"

Winslow gave him a sour look.

"Nafredi, I don't care how you and the Fräulein work it. I need a car. You have one. Now I have it and you don't."

"But, listen," Nafredi said, "let me speak with Anouk. Let me make a bid for the Maison Fayol. Whatever the amount. I must buy it."

Winslow regarded him bleakly. Nafredi continued to plead.

"As I said, Winslow, a million, two million. *Five*, even! What is it to you but a bank transaction? To me, it is life. *Life!* I implore you, let me close this deal for the Maison Fayol and I will . . ."

Winslow turned and went to the farmer's van. Marianna and Anouk followed after him. He lifted the bonnet and pulled some wires. He did not understand very much about automobile engines, but he figured if he pulled enough wires the damn thing would not go.

"Come on," he said to Marianna, "let's move."

The chauffeur fell in behind them. He seemed quite happy to be going along. Nafredi, moving unsteadily in the slush and the mud, and still babbling, came after them.

Winslow turned and gestured for the driver to get into the Bentley. He and Marianna and Anouk climbed into the back seat. It was then Heidi spoke for the first time.

"Herr banquier, me are go mit you also, nein?"

Winslow looked at her. She smiled. Seductively.

"Fuck off," he said, and slammed the car door.

As the big blue car backed, turned, and then pulled away, Zader Nafredi ran after it, shouting as he went, waving his arms, until the car had left the farmyard and was picking up speed. Then Nafredi halted, breathing hard, spattered with mud and melting snow, watching his car recede. Behind him the German girl pointed a pudgy finger and laughed. It was not a kind sound. Nafredi turned to stare at her and with a semblance of control, he hissed:

"Nazi!"

The Bentley bounced along the dirt road and then turned neatly into the highway and headed west.

Italy was out now. The passports were still back at the hotel, and he wasn't going near there. Delane knew about Italy. God knew who else did. Now it was Paris. Out here in the boondocks they were as obvious as Jean-Pierre's blood on the farmyard snow. In Paris they could lose themselves; hide out until the election; contact Rousselot.

While Anouk slept, exhausted, Winslow told Marianna about Delane. Even before he suggested it, she agreed that in whatever story they were forced to tell, Paul Delane would come out of it all right, a friend, a loyal ally, a casualty to be mourned. The chauffeur, a Frenchman delighted to be away from Nafredi, the crazy German girl, and the death house of Bourg, drove competently, following Winslow's instructions. The Bentley was too easily identified, Winslow knew, but it could get them to Lyons, where there was a good direct train service to Paris. The thing was to contact Henry Rousselot and hopefully to stay out of the hands of the police, or of whoever else was tracking them, until Sunday, until the elections. Once the votes were cast, the 'Paris One' file became moot, just another set of papers in a commercial deal with no political ramifications.

They halted at Aix-les-Bains for a meal and to wash up. The girls went into the Restaurant Lille and Winslow took the driver aside. He still had three thousand francs, maybe six hundred dollars. He told the driver that if he got them to Lyons, the car and a thousand francs were his. He could report to Nafredi that Winslow had forced him at gunpoint to go with them. The driver looked into Winslow's face and nodded. Prudently, Winslow held onto the car keys.

Anouk said she couldn't eat. She went back to the car to curl up and sleep again. Marianna's face was scrubbed, her hair tied back in a ponytail. She looked younger than twenty-three, she looked rested, she looked marvelous. "You are a goddamn phenomenon," he informed her, and went into the men's room while she ordered drinks. Over the meal they talked about what they would do when all this was over, the chase ended, and normality returned. Winslow would go back to New York, Marianna to *Vogue*, begging forgiveness for her absence, pleading poverty, and resuming the fetching of coffee and the taking of notes. Carefully they skirted the nightmare, Delane, and what Anouk would now do with her inheritance.

In Lyons they paid off the driver and mingled among the tourists, the silk buyers, the traffic congestion of Friday afternoon in a big provincial town. Winslow vetoed checking into a hotel with the necessity of showing one's papers. Anouk, speaking and reacting normally now, had her cuts washed and dressed again by Marianna in the ladies' room of a cinema while Winslow slumped in the back row watching a Jerry Lewis retrospective. Lewis, he concluded, was funnier in French. He stayed in the theater while the two women, less readily identifiable than a tall American with a Louis Vuitton case, went to the depot to reserve a compartment on the eleven o'clock train to Paris. Then they went to Prisunic to buy a change of clothes and makeup for Anouk. He kept making transatlantic calls to Henry Rousselot, but the office kept insisting he was out of town. Each time Winslow refused to leave his name. It was stupid, he knew, paranoid, but by now he wasn't trusting anyone.

The station, a big echoing shed, full of the noise of idling steam engines and forklift trucks and hawkers' cries, was as clamorous and chaotic as Winslow had hoped. Lines of school-children going up to Paris for the weekend, foreign workers, commercial travelers, soldiers on leave, French men and women headed to their own cities and towns to vote in Sunday's election. There were cops, of course, but they were busy with the crowds and the pickpockets and the occasional drunk. Peddlers sold oranges and bottles of good cheap wine, sandwiches and slabs of cheese, newspapers and dirty books. Marianna bought a bottle of Évian water and another of wine, and just before eleven they climbed aboard; and after Winslow handed his tickets to the conductor, they locked themselves inside the compartment and drew the shades. At eleven precisely, the big engine shifted into gear, the wheels spun once or twice on the rails, the horn blasted, and they rolled out of the station and into the darkness.

They drank some wine and talked of Paris and pleasant things, and around midnight Winslow went out and stood in the corridor while Marianna and Anouk undressed. When he went back inside they were both wearing cotton T-shirts that said "OUI," and both of them had their hair pulled back. Anouk's cuts now appeared little worse than the scrapes all of them had from the rose bushes. Winslow marveled at their recuperative powers. "You look like a couple of coeds in the dorm after lights out," he said. He climbed into the upper berth and the two girls shared the lower.

At three o'clock, with the train rocking along that fast stretch of level track north of Dijon, Winslow woke to see Anouk sitting cross-legged on the foot of the berth, staring out of the big picture window as the trees and the lights of an occasional village or an isolated farm sped by, looking out over the trees into the black colander of the sky, riddled with stars.

"Beautiful, isn't it?" he said softly, trying not to wake Marianna.

"Oh, yes," Anouk said, without looking at him. "Beautiful and speeding past us in confusion."

He lighted a cigarette for her and they sat there quietly for a time and then the French girl said, her voice different now, "Could I have my papers now? I'd like to have them."

Winslow reached behind his pillow and brought out the Vuitton case. "My papers!" Well, they were, weren't they? Still, he resented the possessive tone. Anouk opened the attaché case and emptied the "Paris One" file into her lap. She sat there with the papers spread across her long, suntanned thighs and then she flipped on the little reading light of the berth.

Well, Winslow thought, now she'll want me to draw up that paper Delane proposed. A simple little bill of sale. Well, how the hell could he blame her? Eighty-five million dollars was a lot of bread.

Then Anouk began to read aloud, but in a low, throaty voice:

"I, Pierre Ducrot, hereby cede my farm and buildings in the town of Grasse, measuring thirteen hectares, free and clear, to Monsieur Jacques Fayol, in full payment of loans extended to me during the period . . ."

Winslow looked up.

"Ducrot. Another poor son of a bitch like Gaspar who put down roots." He looked into Anouk's face. "Like old Viot in the Alps."

"I know," Anouk said, "Like them and like so many others who loved the land. My father's wartime comrades. Men who trusted him and put themselves in his hands."

She fell silent then, and Winslow, sensing the forces at work on this young woman, and respecting her, said nothing, did nothing, barely breathed.

Then, quite neatly, Anouk lifted perhaps the top dozen sheets of paper in the "Paris One" file and began to tear them in half.

"I can't do this to such men," she said.

He exhaled. Then, responsibility heavy upon him, he said quietly, "You know they're worth millions. That legally you're entitled to them."

She nodded. "But of course." She looked up at Winslow then and held out a batch of leases. "Don't you want to help me?"

Winslow grinned. Henry Rousselot would have his balls. His strong hands tore through the layers of paper.

When the deeds were thoroughly shredded, Winslow rolled

down the big window and Anouk began slowly to feed the scraps of paper into the night wind rushing by. The "Paris One" file fluttered and dove and sailed across the night and across the miles.

Marianna was awake with the sound of rushing air and she sat up at the head of the berth, the blanket tucked up to her chin, watching. He looked down at her and smiled. She understood.

The train hurtled north toward Paris and the dawn.

YOUR OWN GOVERNMENT

They were arrested at the Gare de Lyon before they ever got off the train. It was all very polite, no handcuffs, no rough stuff. Two men, not the same ones who'd come to his hotel room, suggested they come by the ministry. There were a few questions. Some sort of red tape, surely, and of no great importance, but it would be appreciated if . . .

"These ladies know nothing of this matter," Winslow told them.

There were nods, a smile even, but it would be necessary for the two women as well to present themselves. They might perhaps cast some light on certain matters which . . .

There was a car waiting. No markings, just another anonymous black Citroën. They drove easily through the early morning streets of Paris, still quiet and cool at this hour. It was Saturday, the day promised sunshine and later some heat, and it was the last day before the national elections. The wall posters and scrawled slogans were everywhere, more strident now, the type-faces larger, the colors more dramatic, the dire warnings and prophecies more terrifying, the soothing promises and pledges of the good life more winning in their prose. There were a lot of cops. There were riot troops. And, especially around the train station, there were soldiers dozing in army trucks.

290

They were kept in an anteroom at the Ministry. One of the goons brought them bad coffee in paper cups. Yes, they could smoke. But another of the goons sat there at a cheap desk watching them, and listening. They said nothing. At his feet Winslow had the empty Vuitton case. No one tried to look into it. At a quarter to nine Winslow was called.

"Marianna," he started to say, "if you . . ."

She nodded. Anouk smiled.

"It's okay," The American girl said. "Don't be afraid for us."

He went through a door and was led to another floor, up a bureaucratic green stairwell. There was a knock and he was let into an office. The minister sat at a bare desk. It was not his own office, not the Mussolini suite. He was not trying to impress anybody this time. The guard indicated a straight-backed chair and Winslow sat down, the attaché case on his lap.

"Leave us," the minister said, and the man went out. Winslow could hear the door close behind him. The minister hitched forward on his chair.

"We won't fence, you and I," he said. "Some time ago I informed you it was not in the interests of the French government to permit a sale of the Maison Fayol to foreign buyers. You represent one of those buyers. What can you tell me of the state of the negotiation?"

"There is nothing to tell, Minister."

The Frenchman got up, angrily.

"Look, you, don't provoke me. I am in a position to make life very hard for you. For you, and for the young women with you. Do you seriously think I am going to fret about your sensibilities, about the niceties of protocol, while this election hangs in the balance?"

"No," Winslow said quite sincerely, "I don't think you will."

The minister sat down again, calmer.

"For example," he said, "sometime yesterday there was the crash of a small plane—a helicopter, I believe—in the Haute Savoie, near the town of Bourg Saint-Maurice. Several people are deceased as a result. Unfortunately there can be no identification of the bodies until forensic experts can arrive from Paris. I am told those experts have not yet arrived at Bourg."

"And there will be no story about the crash in the press," Winslow said.

The minister spread his hands. "How can one tell? France has a free press. No one can tell an editor what to print, what not to print. It is simply that with all the news of the elections a report of a small plane crash in an obscure mountain hamlet can hardly attract the attention of great newspapers at such a busy time."

"And the disappearance of two American citizens?" Winslow asked.

The Frenchman shrugged. "Once the voting is finished I am sure proper representations will be made. I understand (he pushed a sheet of paper in front of him), I understand your own government is also not anxious that this sale be made in these parlous times." He looked up, as if having scored a point.

Winslow stood up.

"Bullshit, Minister. Now listen to me. I didn't ask to come to France. I was sent here by a reputable merchant bank on a purely commercial and entirely legitimate assignment. I have no interest in the outcome of your elections. I am not paid by anyone except Rousselot & Partners in New York. But because someone—you, perhaps—didn't want me to close a straightforward business deal between two companies, people have been tortured, people have been kidnapped, people have died. You want to know what I think of you, *and* your country right now?"

"Yes?"

"I think the House of Fayol was a small issue in a small election in a small country. And I don't think the whole fucking country was worth the death of Canon Masson or Paul Delane or of a rose grower called Gaspar."

The minister did not say anything for a moment. Then, very quietly:

"You are half French yourself."

"No," Winslow said. "My mother was French. There's a difference."

"We're splitting hairs. The question is, will the deal be made?"

"Suppose I let you sweat that one out for a day or so?"

"Winslow, you're being childish."

For the first time, Winslow recognized the Frenchman was making sense. He *was* being childish, tormenting the cabinet minister, wanting to drag it out, not wanting to give him the satisfaction that the deal had not been made, would never be made.

"No," Winslow said, tired, finished with the game. "No, there will be no deal. Mademoiselle Fayol has decided not to sell."

Anouk was brought in. She said the same thing. The minister hunched over the desk. After a few moments he sat back, satisfied. Anouk was let out again.

"All right," he said, "you may go."

Winslow stood up. He towered over the minister.

"One thing," the minister said. "You referred to the election as a small affair in a small country. Perhaps you are correct. I would like to remind you, this small country is *our* country."

Winslow had turned and started for the door, carrying the empty case. Now he stopped, and turned back.

"Some country," he said, "using psychopaths like that."

"The fellows who caught up to you at Bourg?"

"Yes."

"Monsieur Winslow," the cabinet minister said, speaking very calmly and precisely, "I sent men after you. Unfortunately they turned out to be incompetent. This ministry cannot afford the caliber of man Interior can call upon. I am afraid," he said in a low tone that smacked of sincerity, "I am afraid the men I sent lost track of you very early on."

"Then Jean-Pierre and Émile and the helicopter men . . . ?"

". . . were working for someone else," the minister said.

"Nafredi!"

The minister laughed. "As inept as my poor department can sometimes be, we are equal to the challenge of the Persians, I assure you."

"Then who . . . ?"

The minister resumed his seat. "Your interview is terminated,

Monsieur Winslow. Perhaps when you have the leisure to cogitate and inquire of your excellent sources at the American Embassy, you may be enlightened. It may occur to you that your own government had its reasons for ensuring this negotiation of yours was aborted."

Badly shaken, not wanting to believe, Winslow left the room. Behind him the cabinet minister picked up a phone, and after a short delay informed the Prime Minister of France that one more small problem had been eliminated that might possibly have influenced the shift of a handful of votes in the next day's elections. The Premier thanked him and hung up. If only *every* nagging little irritation could be cured as easily, the Premier sighed.

There was one more ugly chore for Winslow. He dropped Marianna and Anouk at their apartments, and returned to his hotel. They were delighted to see him. Yes, the room had been held for him, bien sûr. Was he not a good customer? Winslow peeled off his clothes and ran a bath. He felt grimy, drained, frustrated. He placed a call to Henry Rousselot at his home in Connecticut. He hoped to hell Rousselot was out playing golf, so he wouldn't have to give him the bad news. The call came through when he was in the tub. He picked up.

"Winslow," Henry Rousselot barked, as if resuming a conversation broken off only a few hours earlier, "before you tell me where you've been or what's happening, just answer this: Have you acquired those papers you were after?"

"No, sir."

"Good," Rousselot said.

Winslow was not sure he was hearing correctly.

"Good?" he repeated dumbly.

"That's right. I've been trying to reach you for days. I'll brief you fully when you get back. Which should be Monday at the latest, mind. But in short, our friends down south (Delaware Corp., Winslow understood) have been playing fast and loose with us in what I consider to be the *most* unethical manner. Nothing illegal, you understand, but highly questionable."

"Yes?"

"It turns out they wanted those flower gardens, you know what I mean, Winslow, simply to shut them down! Turn off production. They've developed some sort of synthetic, a petroleum-based ester—don't ask me what that means—that can do everything the natural oils can do. They're investing millions in it. They're out to corner the world market and they wanted those farms, they wanted your Paris fashion house, just to stop growing flowers. That way, they figured, they could grab the world market, and once they were ready, could raise the price to whatever the traffic would bear."

Winslow slumped in the tub, holding the phone. Perspiration ran down his tanned face.

"Winslow, you still there?"

"Yes, Mr. Rousselot."

"Well, needless to say, I told them the whole thing smacked of a combination in restraint of trade, and Rousselot and Partners would resign the account, that there'd be one hell of a stink, and that questions would be asked at Antitrust, at the S.E.C., and on the Big Board."

"Yes, sir," Winslow repeated.

"Well, I think they'll back away. Their board is split on it. But I just wanted to make sure you didn't negotiate the sale before I got to you. You're *sure* it's a closed door, are you?"

Winslow nodded, to himself more than to his employer.

"Don't worry, Mr. Rousselot. The whole thing smelled bad from the start. There *are* no papers. There is no valid claim. Our friends down south got some faulty intelligence, is all."

"Good man, Winslow, good man. Now get yourself home here before that damn country goes red or something else happens. There's a utility in New England I want you to take a look at. It could be a very tidy bit of business for the firm."

Winslow promised to fly home as soon as he could.

"Oh, Anthony," Rousselot said, "one more item."

"Yes, sir?" Winslow replied, wondering about the uncharacteristically friendly use of his Christian name.

"My spies tell me Delaware was hedging its bets, that they had some of their own men in the field. You didn't run into any trouble, did you?"

Winslow thought of Gaspar, of Masson, of Émile's knives, of Paul Delane. What was the use of going into it now?

"No, sir," he said after a moment. "No trouble."

"Good," Rousselot enthused. "There was even some suggestion our own government people might get into the act. Delighted you had no trouble. Trouble means publicity and publicity means more trouble. Merchant banks don't want either."

Winslow agreed and hung up. Morosely he thought about what Rousselot had just said, what the French minister had suggested. "Your *own* government . . ."

Outside the window a loudspeaker truck blared some sort of partisan election oratory.

"Bullshit," Winslow said, as he turned on both faucets full so he did not have to listen as he lay back in the tub, hot, soapy water up to his chin.

THE HOUSE OF FAYOL

It was Saturday evening. The voting would begin in just twelve hours. And in a beige and gray room on the rue Cambon in the first arrondissement of Paris, Anthony Winslow and Marianna Troy, curiously sunburned so early in May, sat side by side on straight-backed little gold chairs watching a fashion show. Winslow had never seen one before. And he alternated watching the clothes, which he found mystifying, and Marianna, who scribbled notes nonstop and whom he found even more mystifying, but totally admirable: a twenty-three-year-old girl from Connecticut who that very morning had been arrested by a minister of France, who the night before had watched millions in real estate shredded and tossed into the night from a speeding train, who thirty hours earlier had seen four men die, and who could now turn to him and hiss, "Tony, at least *try* to look at the clothes. This is goddamned serious."

Like banking, the fashion business seemed to have priorities all its own. On the next day France would hold its first general elections in seven years. The polls said it would be very close indeed, and beyond France, from Moscow to Washington, powerful men awaited the results. Within the country aging officers of the French army whispered "coup d'état" and in the workers' districts Communists and Socialists bickered over who was to lead the Front Populaire. Millions of Frenchmen would watch Giscard

297

issue his final televised appeal that evening. But on the rue Cambon, in the couture house of Jacques Fayol that Saturday at dusk, the talk was not of politics. But of fashion.

As had become the tradition, the ready-to-wear showings would end on the second Saturday in May with a champagne reception following the final collection, that of Jacques Fayol. There were clothes to see, deals to be made, reputations to be hashed over, feuds to be fueled, lovers' quarrels patched, and always, delicious gossip to be exchanged. And this time, the gossips scarcely knew where to begin, the pickings were so choice.

There was, of course, this extraordinary defection of that arch-Royalist Maggy Moal to the Communist party. Had Maggy received certain "assurances" from the Left? Or was it simply that the old bitch had become so senile a single favorable review in a Communist newspaper had turned her head? The tragic death of Paul Delane had come over the radio late that afternoon. The dashing Delane, tragically killed in a helicopter during a ski trip to one of the high glaciers! There was talk of Paul, of his work, not yet matured but so promising, of the man himself—"sportif, tu sais, jusqu'au fin!"—and of his loss following so closely on the death of the Master, Jacques Fayol. The whole fashion apparat was here: the press, the retail buyers, the Seventh Avenue cutters, the actresses and discotheque owners and the other rich and fashionable women; for none of them would have considered *not attending* a "last" collection. Later, when emotions had cooled and more objective judgments been made, critics would say that, while this was a "representative" effort, it was by no means Fayol's greatest collection ever. But such calm judgments were for tomorrow. Tonight, as the last model went off to applause, to weeping, to cheers, and to thrown kisses; as the waiters bounded into the beige and gray room with the traditional trays of brimming champagne glasses; as fashion editors clucked and buyers wrangled for exclusivities, the collection was unanimously declared a masterpiece. And how could it not be? With a beautiful young woman, a stranger to most of them, sitting in their midst throughout the collection, the flesh-and-blood inheritor of the

House of Fayol, there in the place of her great father, dead these
few weeks and hardly forgotten. Quel drame! Quel théâtre! Quel
triomphe!

Now they clustered about Anouk, congratulating her, gushing,
pressing her hands, jostling for a closer look at this young beauty
with the curiously scratched face and arms, the green eyes deep-
set, and the arrogant and mocking air of her extraordinary father.
Anouk had begun by looking bored and then, gradually, as the applause built, and more and more it seemed directed toward her,
smiling proudly, possessively, as if she, and not the dead Fayol,
had designed this last production. Winslow wondered what the
reaction would be if they had seen her at Gaspar's farm, stripped
and kneeling before Émile, cocaine dusting her lips.

A waiter passed, and Winslow snatched two glasses and
pressed his way through a knot of women to Marianna.

"Winslow," she warned, "don't get me drunk. I promise you,
Vogue isn't in the mood." Her nose was peeling and her bare
arms sunburned and scratched and she looked perfectly splendid.

Marianna was picking the brains of one of the more articulate
buyers, and Winslow stood there, half listening; and then, behind
him, he heard a cultured and familiar voice. He turned. It was
Maggy Moal's "king"-turned-PR-man.

"It wasn't easy, of course," the "king" was telling some people, "but once she announced she was voting the Communist line
I simply had to make the break. I could no longer in good conscience work on behalf of someone who had allied herself to the
regicides of the Romanovs."

Maggy's sudden espousal of the Left, the "king" was explain-
ing, had come about when bedridden in Marseilles, she had read
a flattering review of her new line in *L'Humanité*. The "king's"
friends congratulated him on his declaration of independence
from the House of Moal. Winslow silently hoped some of them
might also put him on retainer.

The celebration continued. Anouk seemed in no mood to have
it end. In one corner of the great salon Max held court, a loyal
handful of "little monks" around him. Winslow did not think

either Max or his fans seemed terribly happy. But Max was making the most of things, in a subdued way, when from the middle of the room Anouk's voice crackled.

"Max," she ordered, "dismiss your little friends and see that there's more champagne. Some of my guests have run dry."

Max blushed and then, obviously struggling for control, he said, "Mais oui, Mademoiselle Fayol," and disappeared in the direction of the pantry.

Winslow stared. "What the hell was *that* all about?"

Marianna laughed. "Anouk reduced him in rank. She found out somehow he was being paid off by Nafredi. Apparently he'd been promised he could run the house permanently if the Iranians took over. Anouk was going to fire him. Then she realized revenge would be even sweeter keeping him on as a flunky."

Women, Winslow thought. Then he asked, "Who *will* run the house for her?"

"I dunno. Let's hang around and find out."

By eight o'clock the crowd had drifted off, one of the last to leave, a mournful-looking Nafredi. He paused in front of Winslow.

"This is, I believe, my last hurrah," the Iranian said.

"Oh?"

"Hadn't you heard? I thought my fate was known to all. I return to Teheran tomorrow. For 'reassignment.' Dreadful word, isn't it?"

Why not ask him? Winslow thought, and he said:

"Nafredi, now that it's all over, just how high would you have gone to buy up Fayol? How serious were you about taking control of Grasse?"

The Iranian looked puzzled.

"Grasse? Grasse? But my dear fellow, I had no interest in Grasse. None at all. My task was to purchase the couture house of Jacques Fayol. Any real estate holdings would have been dealt off. We wanted the fashion house."

Winslow shook his head. "I don't understand. Without the farms at Grasse, Fayol just wasn't worth . . ."

Nafredi smiled.

"But it was, Winslow. His Imperial Majesty the Shahenshah wished to purchase the greatest maison de couture in the world, the House of Fayol. And with this new round of oil price increases, the cost was immaterial."

"But why the hell does the Shah want a fashion house?"

Nafredi tried to be patient. "To give to the Empress Farah Diba, of course. Her birthday is next month."

Winslow shook his head. "Well," he said, "I wish you well."

"And you, Winslow. But tell me, haven't you also failed? Won't you also be 'reassigned'?"

"In my business, Nafredi, you're always being reassigned. To Cleveland, even. But somehow, I don't think I failed."

He stuck out his hand and Nafredi took it, and left. As he went, Soroya, the Iranian mannequin, whispered mockingly to another girl. Poor Nafredi, Winslow thought. He wondered whether in the salt mines of Teheran there would be a little German blonde to console him.

By nine o'clock most of the guests had drifted off and Winslow and Marianna relaxed in one of the private offices where they had been asked to await "Mademoiselle Fayol, elle-même."

Anouk swept in, triumphant.

"My God! It's like opening night. It's tremendous. The way people carry on. The applause, the kisses, the congratulations." She flopped down on a couch, her long legs sprawled. "And my two best friends in the world here to share it."

She reached out and pushed a buzzer. A waiter came and she ordered more champagne. "I really should have Max serve it," she said. "He deserves it, the con!"

They exchanged toasts. "There was even a wire of congratulations from Madame Claude," Anouk declared. "I never knew it could be like this. It's even better than getting stoned!"

"Speaking of Max," Marianna said, "who will you get to run the place?"

Anouk sat up. "Marianna, idiot, cretin! That's what I'm talking about. I'll not hire anyone. Am I not my father's child? Isn't it in the blood?" She looked from one to the other, enjoying their startled expressions.

"I shall," Anouk said with the right touch of the dramatic, "run it myself. Once again a Fayol will head the Maison Fayol!"

It was perhaps an hour later. Marianna and Tony Winslow were walking along the rue de Rivoli. He had his arm around her waist.

"Oh, shit," she said. "It makes me so sore."

Winslow laughed.

"You have to admit it's funny," he said.

Angrily, Marianna shook her head. "I do not."

"Oh, come off it. Just a couple of days ago we saved her from kidnappers, from rape, from a knife-crazy nut-case, tonight she announces you and I are her best friends . . ."

". . . in all the world. . . ."

"Right. 'In all the world'! And then, when you ask her to let V*ogue* shoot some pictures of the new clothes, she goes all uptight and professional on you and says, no, she's sorry, but she's promised the first exclusive shots to a magazine with a bigger circulation, to *Time*! I think it's funny as hell."

Marianna stopped. She turned and looked into his face and the annoyance oozed out of her.

"How can I be sore when I have you?" she said.

He shook his head.

"You can't."

They kissed. Then they turned and walked, much more slowly, across the great square toward the Champs Élysées. Above, the night sky blinked with stars, shone with a sliver of moon. Off in the distance, the Tour Eiffel and the Arc de Triomphe were still alight, in deference to the next day's elections. It was very quiet, very beautiful, but under the great trees sat the armored cars, the olive-drab trucks, the dark-blue buses with mesh over the windows, all of them full of troops, dozing and smoking cigarettes and grousing the night away. A couple of CRS riot cops on motorcycles drove past slowly, throwing a glimpse at them before pulling away.

The two Americans strolled along the broad pathways of the Champs, under the trees, under the stars, through the lovely Paris night, past the troops and the tanks and the submachine guns. Winslow knew that he was ready to go home, that in an odd way he yearned for the heat and dirt and crime and bankruptcy of New York. He hailed a cab and they went to Marianna's place and they made love, very slowly and gently, through the night, their last night together; and just before dawn Winslow got up while she still slept, and he dressed and returned to his hotel. In the east a new day began, a sun rose, on the street corners the cops and soldiers lounged, bored and ready, France still trembling on the brink of the political unknown. Winslow threw himself into bed and slept.

Across the street a beautiful woman who did not know his name, rose early, went out into the sunlight of her balcony in a very pretty nightgown, and leaned against the iron railing, staring across at the hotel and wondering why that tall young man in the top-floor room had not so much as thrown a look at her for so many nights. Perhaps, she thought romantically, he had fallen in love.

ADIEU

Marianna drove with him to the airport. The Concorde would take off at one, it would be in New York two hours earlier, at eleven in the morning. He would have lunch in Manhattan. But Marianna would not be there.

"You can still come, you know."

She shook her head. "I've got to work. I'm cheating as it is, but I'll claim you were a very important fashion designer, a setter of trends, and you insisted on a very long lunch. Besides, I'm broke."

"I could . . ."

She put her hand on his arm.

"No," she said, "no, you couldn't."

They checked his luggage, all except for the old Vuitton case. There was nothing in it now except some magazines, a pair of shorts, and a dirty shirt he'd found balled up in the bathroom after he'd closed the valpack. But he carried it, a habit, a talisman, a memory.

They went up into the vast atrium of Charles de Gaulle airport, along the inclined moving belts, through the plastic Space Age tubes that rose level after level to the departure gates. At the last newsstand before the gate she wanted to buy him some newspapers.

He glanced at the headlines. They were all about the election. "No," he said, "I'll pass on today's papers, thank you."

Marianna picked up the Paris *Herald-Tribune* and carefully tore off the front page. She handed him the rest of it.

"There," she said, "now you can read Red Smith and the comics and the classifieds and you can ignore the election."

He grinned. "I'll do the crossword."

"Oh, you. You *don't* forget, do you?"

"No."

They walked to the gate. The passengers were going through now, showing their tickets and their passports. There were plenty of cops, the usuals and the CRS too. There had been soldiers around the building, soldiers all the way out the autoroute. No one looked terribly happy. Winslow turned to the girl again.

"Look, we don't know what's going to happen here. After this past week, don't you think you deserve a break? Get away from France, from the politics, from . . . ?"

She interrupted.

"I didn't run away at Grasse. Or at Bourg. I stayed with you. You don't expect me to run away now? To abandon *Vogue*? Do you?"

Winslow was miserable. "It isn't a matter of . . ."

Marianna stopped him by reaching up to kiss him on the mouth. He dropped the Vuitton bag and the paper and put his arms around her. He could feel the whole, lean, slender strength of her. When they were kissing, a few passengers had stopped to look, and to smile. Marianna and Tony Winslow did not notice them.

"Final call for TWA flight 101 to New York."

He kissed her again, quickly this time, and turned to show his papers at the gate. When he was through he looked back. She raised a hand, just slightly.

"I'll get some vacation time," she called out.

She was smiling. Winslow tried to smile and then he strode through the passageway.

"I'll save up," she called. He turned and waved again.

"I'll fly Ice-land-ic."

Then he was through the departure gate and could hear her no longer and she was gone.

The Concorde was only half full. Winslow took a window seat and tossed the attaché case and the paper on the next seat. He loosened his tie and stretched his long legs out ahead of him. He felt drained, tired, and at the same time as happy as he could ever remember. The girl was still very much with him.

Thirty minutes later they were high above the lovely green countryside with its winding yellow roads, its patches of blue lake, its dark forests. Winslow picked up the *Herald-Trib*. The stewardess brought him the vodka martini he wanted and he took the first cold, wonderful, stunning sip. Then he turned to the sports page. The Knicks were still in the playoffs, still winning. Bradley had scored sixteen in the last game. Shit, Winslow thought, doesn't *anyone* in that league know how to play him? He finished the drink and waved the empty glass at the girl. She smiled and went off for the refill. Winslow slumped further down in the seat. He would get very drunk and go straight to bed when he got to New York. The office could go to hell until tomorrow. The office and France and elections and politicians, American *and* French! They could all go to hell. The second drink was there and he sipped at it and closed his eyes, not wanting to see France anymore, not wanting to see anything but Marianna Troy. He had finished the drink and was nearly asleep when the pilot's nice Midwestern voice came over the speaker.

"Because of the closeness of the French election results," the pilot announced, "and because of its importance to the United States, we'll bring you from time to time during our voyage, the latest reports on the voting."

Winslow groaned.

The great plane slid smoothly through the sound barrier and headed west out over the Atlantic as France, dark and brooding from this altitude, fell away behind and was soon out of sight.